TORCHED HEART

TRINITY OF MIND

BOOK 3

WRITTEN BY

J. ABRAM BARNECK

Quality
2022
Publishing

This book has met the rigorous quality standards needed to earn the Certificate of Quality Publishing in 2022.

These Quality Publishing Standards are intended to raise the quality of small press and independent works.

For more information, see this site:
http://scififantasyreaders.com/services/certificate-of-quality

DEDICATION

For my brother Jacob, who suffered just like my character Charles O'Brien,

loves life more than most, and has always been my best friend.

OTHER WRITING

By J. Abram Barneck

TRINITY OF MIND

Fire Light   Book 1
Breaking Glass   Book 2
Torched Heart   Book 3
† *Untitled*   Book 4

OTHER

† *Technically Magic*

SHORT STORIES & NOVELLAS

Drindél the Winged One
Winged Ones
* Future 7, Inc
* Mud in the Gutter

POETRY

* Post-millennial Sonnets
* Fantasy Poems
* Free-verse Poems

† Release forthcoming
* Available at: https://jabrambarneck.com/writing

CHAPTERS

CHAPTER 1
SCARLETT RESCUE

I don't know who I am. Eldra's memories are dominating my mind. Add in Kendra's, Lexy's, and Caradoc's memories, and I think I'm losing myself. —Jake

"**W**hen I pull this door open, all hell is going to break loose," I spoke verbally instead of mentally through the Trinity of Mind because Luiz and Ariel had refused to be left behind.

I panted quietly as I hung on the rusty metal handle of the heavy warehouse door. We had parked a half-mile away at a church and ran through alleys halfway here before changing to a stealthy walk. My ankle, partially crushed before sunrise this morning by a voodoo witch's magic-preventing rope, throbbed in agony despite my near overdose on ibuprofen. Why was I the only one out of breath? I ignored the obvious answer.

Lexy stood just left of the doorway, red eyes locked onto a thick-but-short Polynesian man who stood guard at the door. She wore a black leather top and pants that, as usual, stuck to her like another layer of skin. Over her top, she wore a leather vest that acted as body armor. She had a blade strapped to each thigh—her runed dagger on her right and a skull-hilted blade on her left that had once belonged to a tall voodoo witch. Wearing thick-soled, knee-high combat boots, she stood much taller than the Polynesian. He wore a button-up Hawaiian shirt, damp at the armpits, gray shorts, and black river sandals. To Alexis, he smelled like he'd been sweating in the heat all day. Lexy's pumpkin spice allure hid his smell from the rest of us. Her allure—an enticing scent that could short-circuit almost anyone who smells it—had taken control of him and prevented him from sounding the alarm.

1

Lexy forced the Polynesian's black eyes to meet hers and read his mind, which proved fruitless as he hadn't been allowed inside the warehouse. She put a hand on his cheek—the skin contact increasing her allure's controlling power—and ordered, "Sit down." Mesmerized by Lexy's allure, he sat down on the weed-ridden asphalt and leaned back against the brick building.

Ogden used to be the armpit of Utah. Recently, both the city government and the Church of Jesus Christ of Latter-day Saints had put deodorant on that armpit by updating certain areas. The abandoned warehouse was not in one of the areas where deodorant had been applied. Rust splotched the doors. The asphalt had crumbled, and tall, dried weeds had popped up in random patches. Weathered-gray plywood boarded over the few windows. The August sky, orange from the setting sun, illuminated the graffiti on the dilapidated brick building.

My legs wavered and almost gave out. My thick denim pants rubbed my road-rashed legs. My new Kevlar armor under my black hoodie weighed me down. Of course, Luiz didn't even notice the extra weight of his Kevlar. Using both the door and Eldra's staff to hold myself up, I hoped to hide my physical weakness like I hoped to hide my hideous face. The Trinity of Mind—a permanent mental connection between Kendra, Lexy, and me—prevented me from hiding either. Kendra and Lexy shared my thoughts, so despite my efforts, they knew that I'd grabbed the door not to open it but to stay on my feet.

He is not OK, Lexy thought to Kendra, nodding at me.

He's tough, Kendra answered, tossing her head as if she still had long hair instead of the boy-cut she'd managed to grow the past week. *At least he used to be,* she added.

It didn't matter that I could hear Kendra's and Lexy's thoughts. They mentally talked about me as if I weren't there.

"Why are you wobbling?" Luiz teased under his breath. "Too lazy to work out?" He grinned.

I yanked the door, hoping that opening it would shut all three of them up. Except it didn't open. Locked.

"If the door is too heavy," Luiz continued his quiet mocking, "I can help you out."

Alexis and Kendra each stifled their laughs. I usually enjoyed it when Luiz lightened the mood, but at my expense? Not helping.

I reached out with magic to unlock the deadbolt, but it needed a key on both sides. Eldra's favorite spell to magically twist the thumb turn on the other side wasn't an option. That trick had never failed me—er Eldra—before, so she'd never learned to pick a lock with magic. I could magically slide the pins in the lock, but that didn't mean I knew which key pattern to use when doing so. I made a mental note to research lock picking later.

I'd already filled both my body and Eldra's staff with magic, and now was the time to use it.

"Can *you* do this?" I whispered my comeback to Luiz. "*Hætan!*" *Heat.* Eldra knew this spell well. Kendra and I gulped, thinking of her sacrifice. She should be with us. Our hearts hadn't stopped aching since early this morning. None of us were OK enough to be here. But Scarlett—er, Jody—needed us. No, she wasn't *just* a stripper. She was Carl's mom and a good mom, too. Carl needed her. If we had to give our lives for her, she was worth it.

I used the pain of our loss to augment the heat, focusing inside the deadbolt. The red glow of melting metal illuminated the door jamb. The heat radiated outward, warming my hand, but I redirected it back to the deadbolt, not letting it burn me. Alexis had taught me how to control heat with magic. She could touch anything hot without getting burned. The smell of burnt metal, plastic, and paint permeated the air, causing Alexis to wrinkle her nose.

The protector magic had provided me a vision of this moment. In it, local gang members with handguns stood on the other side of the door. I nodded to Luiz and Kendra to step to the right side. I poured magic into my new Kevlar armor, making me double bulletproof. We'd checked all the trunks of the various vehicles in the mansion garage and had found two men's Kevlar vests. Some of the druids killed on the Day of a Thousand Deaths had worn Kevlar, and it had failed to protect them. Kendra and Lexy pulled at my magic to make their leather body armor bulletproof as well. They weren't double bulletproof. Earlier, Luiz and I had tried to chivalrously give the vests to the girls, but they didn't fit well, so the girls refused. Alexis made a call and special ordered Kevlar vests to custom fit their feminine figures, but their order wouldn't arrive for weeks.

Kendra stepped next to Luiz. Lexy, however, left the Tongan in a daze on the left side of the door and tiptoed to stand directly in front of the door as if to offer an easy target, testing if they dared shoot at the Princess of the New World. Ariel stepped in front of me, dressed in a coral camisole, gray shorts, and Converse shoes that matched her hair. Yes, a seven-year-old girl with lavender hair planned to use herself as a human shield to protect me, which is not something I would normally allow. In fairness, she was thousands—maybe millions—of years old, but doesn't remember much of it, which is probably good since she used to be evil. We'd only met Ariel earlier this morning. She was Coyote's hybrid granddaughter, half water baby—a freshwater mermaid thought to be a Native American myth—and half ancient alien shapeshifter. She swore an oath to Coyote to protect me, then fought with us against her own kind—all of whom seemed to have kept their memories. After we survived that battle, she transformed her sea-lion-like mermaid tail into the legs of a seven-year-old girl. She joined our operation, code-named Scarlett Rescue, to fulfill her promise to Coyote. I wasn't sure if I could trust her, but her willingness to stand in front of me as a human shield was a good start.

We've got this, Kendra added, posing motivationally in a half-T position by standing with her shoulders back and pressing her fists together above her chest so that her forearms formed a straight line. She always posed like that and spoke that phrase before her drill-team performances at half-time. Luiz teasingly copied Kendra, first cupping his pecs with his hands as if he were a girl adjusting her breasts, and then mimicking Kendra's fists-together stance.

I grinned, grateful Luiz could ease my stress, this time at Kendra's expense. I yanked the door a second time. This time, the red-hot deadbolt collapsed, and the door swung open.

Only darkness presented itself on the other side of the entry. Lexy could see inside fine, which gave me the quarter-second I needed to dive—more of a fall with my weak legs—to the right side before the machine gun spit bullets that would have ripped me apart. Three bullets hit my pants. I'd tested the bulletproof spell with the expectation that it would stop a few shots, not thirteen massive rounds per second.

Why hadn't the protector magic showed me a machine gun in my vision?

After taking a couple bullets yesterday, Lexy had dressed more prepared today. But like me, she hadn't expected an AR-15 illegally modified to be fully automatic. She side-stepped out of the way, but not before a line of five bullets hit her leather body armor, right above her heart. Without magical assistance, the first bullet would have torn through her chest, but the bulletproof spell stopped all five before she'd shifted out of the doorway—actually, four and a half. One of the rounds hit near her right hip. It had stopped, sort of. A half inch of the bullet stuck out of her leather armor. She could already smell her own blood. She pulled the projectile out and looked at it. Her blood dripped down from a very sharp point. Armor-piercing rounds. The scent of honey—Lexy's hunger—mixed with her pumpkin spice.

"We got 'em!" a young man's nasally voice shouted with nervous glee after the machine gun stopped. Then he swore. "We killed a little girl!" his young, nasally voice changing from glee to panic.

I found myself on the asphalt to the right of the door at Luiz and Kendra's feet. My palms bled, scuffed, again, from diving to the asphalt. Eldra's staff rolled to a stop a few feet away. I reached for my lower right hip to see why it hurt worse than my ankle and found nothing wrong. Lexy's hip hurt, not mine. The Trinity of Mind had its flaws, such as the difficulty distinguishing her injuries from mine—both hurt.

Ariel had taken the worst of the bullets. Her seven-year-old body lay mangled on the aged asphalt. Blood oozed from a hole in her forehead. A dozen more holes splotched her chest, coloring her coral camisole in crimson. One of her legs had almost been severed. It bent awkwardly, held together by the outside flap of skin, the separated bone visible. She lay motionless—corpselike—her lavender-brown eyes just empty glass, staring directly at me. I couldn't believe she'd died the very same day that she promised to protect me. Her eyes looked so lifeless. A pang of regret that I would never really know Ariel pinched at my heart.

Until she winked at me.

Footsteps padded inside the darkness.

Luiz reached around and stuck the muzzle of the shotgun just inside the doorway and fired, shouting, "You got *nada!*"

He must have hit someone because a scream of pain wailed from the darkness inside the doorway.

Lexy darted inside with inhuman speed. Through her eyes, I saw one body on the ground and another holding a pistol sideways. They looked like teenagers—neither old enough, Ivy League enough, nor elite ex-military enough to be a Skull Shadow. A tan, Caucasian young man lay bleeding on the dirty, once-white tile floor. He had blond hair and was dressed in black shorts and a black T-shirt sporting a half-naked image of Harley Quinn. The wet blood on Harley Quinn's bare legs and abdomen almost looked like it belonged. Next to him stood a Latino, maybe a year older than me. He had black hair and dark eyes over wide cheekbones and was dressed in dark gray cargo shorts and a black shirt with a skull next to a whiskey bottle. Both had tattoos of three letters in a decorative font on their upper left arms—I could only make out the "W"—branding them as members of some local gang. The pair could have been Luiz and me. Well, I wasn't tan anymore. I was road-rashed and almost albino, and neither Luiz nor I had tattoos or their poor taste in clothes. Still, the similarity hit me.

The Latino teen pulled the trigger. Lexy stepped to the side to avoid the teenager's erratic shot. The bullet whizzed through the air. He fired again. Lexy angled closer as she dodged each shot, then ripped the gun from his hand before his fourth trigger pull. The first two bullets traveled out the doorway; the last hit the doorjamb with a loud, echoing crack. Lexy put her hand on the Latino's cheek, and using her allure, short-circuited his self-control. The artery in his neck called to her. Despite being a gang member recruited to be a pawn for the Skull Shadows, his youth still convinced her to push aside her own honey-scented hunger.

As I started getting up, I focused on Lexy's senses, not just visual, but her heightened hearing and sense of smell, too. The doorway didn't lead to the open warehouse floor. Instead, it opened into a short, ceilingless hallway that turned left after a dozen feet. The right wall consisted of concrete bricks. New gray-green sheetrock covered the left wall, suggesting the Skull Shadows had recently installed it. The thin sheetrock failed to hide the noise and smell of additional men and the oily, metallic scent of their guns.

Kendra stepped inside the doorway, followed by Luiz, before I could even get to my knees. My mental warning reached Kendra, who stopped and turned to go back, causing Luiz to bump into her.

"Get down!" I shouted, diving into the doorway in a pushup position, my head tilted left, just outside the door while my right shoulder pressed against the doorjamb. I spread my bleeding left palm over the asphalt that went right up to the doorsill, using the blacktop like I used pebbles. I stretched my right arm out and placed my palm flat onto the gray-materialled sheetrock, pouring bulletproof magic into it. A half-second later, the sound of a dozen AR-15s thundered from the warehouse.

If one AR-15 shot thirteen bullets per second, then for a dozen, my magic needed to stop one hundred and fifty-six bullets a second. I didn't think. I couldn't. I just converted the asphalt into magic as fast as I could and shoved that magic into the gray-green sheetrock walls.

Not every bullet deflected. A few rounds blew through the wall. One hit Kendra's leather armor at her right shoulder, the

6

bulletproof magic deflecting it away. Another deflected off the back of my Kevlar vest.

Luiz grabbed Kendra and twisted to put himself between her and the bullets like a best friend should. With a direct hit, the armor-piercing rounds would go right through Luiz's Kevlar. They needed time to take a few steps to get out—time they didn't have unless I gave it to them. Lexy dropped to the tile floor, unconcerned about getting the gang member's blood on her leather armor, instead more enticed by the blood's coppery scent. She grabbed the young man's body and twisted, using it as a shield.

The bullets pounded against the sheetrock and my magic like a debilitating migraine throbbing behind my eyes. Every projectile that hit the sheetrock hit me—not literally, but metaphysically— through my magic. The pounding continued along my spine and around my ribs. It spread through my shoulders into my arms and through my hips into my legs. When the pounding reached the tips of my fingers and toes, every part of me shook. Time slowed, and the seconds, like the bullets, dragged on. I should have passed out. No, I should have died. My mind blanked. I couldn't focus. I'd lost connection to the Trinity of Mind. Only inertia kept my magic flowing. Luiz needed two more steps to exit, his arm extended, shoving Kendra in the lower back to get her out the door. Lexy lay in that hallway. The bullets fired all over, many directly at Luiz and Lexy. Was it possible to save them? Not with that many bullets. I tried anyway.

Why had we not considered that they would have ARs? We'd made what could be the ultimate mistake. We'd placed too much trust in my vision. Well, what good was I as a *protector* if my visions weren't accurate? If I couldn't protect Lexy and my best friend?

My right cheek touched the rough asphalt just as the bullets stopped flying—which didn't make sense because my left arm still burned with the effort to keep it extended straight below me. How could the asphalt be touching my face? My straight left arm should have kept me two feet off the ground.

"*¡Diantre!* Jake!" Luiz exclaimed, looking down at me. His long nose looked twice as long as usual as I looked up at him. He grabbed my torso and pulled me up. My left arm slipped out of a two-foot deep, hand-shaped hole. I'd burned through the multiple asphalt layers into the rocky earth beneath to stop bullets.

Without the vibration of bullets pounding against me through my magic, I sought out Lexy's mind, latching back onto her senses. She quickly stood up in the hallway, holding the AR-15 from the previously downed gang member in her arms, reloading. The bullets should have riddled the gray-materialled walls with holes, leaving it ready to collapse. Instead, less than twenty bullet holes dotted the sheetrock, most above six feet high. Pungent gun smoke rose into the darkness above the ceilingless wall. The audible clicks of reloading weapons urged Alexis to hurry.

Lexy took three steps toward the wall and jumped up, lithely landing in a sitting position on the exposed two-by-four at the top of the wall, the AR-15 whipping around to point into the darkness of the warehouse. As a dhampir, she could see quite well in the dark. She fired three quick bursts, then dropped back down just before the enemy returned fire. The bullets shot toward the top of the wall where Lexy had briefly sat, but she'd already dropped down. She ran to another part of the wall, jumped up, and fired again.

The bullets now exploded through the sheetrock, but the shooters had lost their form. Instead of spreading out, they all shot at Lexy, but she danced just fast enough to stay ahead of their aim. She leaped to the top of another part of the wall and fired two more quick bursts.

Luiz took one step inside the doorway, put his shotgun into a fresh bullet hole in the wall, and fired, then darted back outside. The ARs turned toward him, which gave Lexy the chance to find a fourth point on the wall to land and fire. Only four ARs returned fire.

I picked up Eldra's staff and used it to help stay on my feet. Despite the pain, and with most of my weight on the staff, I stumbled weakly into the hallway. The running had left my legs burning. They still felt like Jell-O. Worse, bulletproofing the sheetrock wall had drained me further. Ariel dragged her bleeding form forward after me. I struggled to use magic, too worn out to draw much. I managed four smaller-than-a-marble orbs and used Lexy's eyes to choose my targets as I tossed them over the wall. I felt them hit the remaining four ARs, not the people wielding them. The micro-magic missiles erased the remaining machine guns. No ecstasy came with erasing the lifeless metal weapons. Every element was sentient in some way, but erasing a living soul provided more pleasure than erasing an inanimate object. I craved erasing a person, but if Lexy could shake off her hunger, I could shake off my own temptation, right? Still, I glanced at possible options. The teenage gang members were no longer options. Both lay on the dirty tile in pools of blood, as glassy-eyed as Ariel had been. Only they weren't going to wink.

Lexy beckoned the Polynesian security guard to come inside. He lowered his shoulder and plowed through the bullet-shredded wall, taking a pair of two-by-fours with him. The hallway now opened into a large, mostly empty warehouse. The tile ended at the wall, and beyond that, a cement floor receded into the darkness. The shadows of rafters hung viewable through what used to be a high drop ceiling that now had no panels.

Luiz and Kendra went to the door down the hallway, but I followed Lexy through the opening the Polynesian had bulldozed for us.

Four men stood, wearing all-black military armor, surrounded by eight bodies dressed similarly. Lexy could see the far cement wall and the emptiness in between, but I couldn't. She could even see the detail of their weapons. They didn't have modified AR-15's, but full military machine guns. Thanks to hours playing first-person shooter video games, I recognized the AK-47.

Princess Alexis released the full force of her allure, filling the room with the scent of pumpkin spice, but the remaining four men standing in the warehouse appeared unaffected. Military-grade gas masks covered their faces. I had known pheromones made up much of her allure, but I hadn't guessed that modern technology could prevent its effects.

Lexy wasted no time. She sent the Polynesian after one of the mercenaries and charged the closest one, the tallest, herself. Both pulled out handguns and fired. The Polynesian went down. My bulletproof vest took two bullets, which knocked me down. The bulletproof spell on Kendra's leather deflected at least one round. Lexy dodged any bullets directed her way, then kicked her target in the stomach, and ripped off his gas mask, revealing a middle-aged man with white hair—white-blond, not white-old.

"Stop!" a guttural voice shouted to our right, far in the back of the warehouse.

I followed the voice using Alexis's eyes because I couldn't see what Alexis could until a flashlight clicked to life on top of a handgun, blinding my eyes. The light turned from pointing to us to illuminate a woman tied to a chair. The dark-haired woman flinched. Her slightly overweight body trembled despite being tied to a metal folding chair. She was not Jody. Before I could ask where Scarlett was, Lexy spotted her silhouette tied to a chair just a few feet to the right of the dark-haired woman. I now recognized the woman as Jody's roommate. She helped raise

Carl, who waited back at Lexy's mansion, hoping for both of them to return. Both the dark-haired woman and Jody shivered in fear.

The light reflected enough to show the man's face. Unlike the mercenaries, he didn't wear body armor. Instead, he wore a white, button up dress shirt with rolled-up sleeves. The light illuminated the skull tattoo on his wrist. I also noticed his ring and the way it gave off a faint glow of magic. His white shirt matched the color of his short hair. Where was vertical-scar guy? I'd seen him in my vision, not this old guy. I'd also seen dozens of men with handguns and not gang members with ARs. The scene in my vision didn't match this scene at all.

At his command, everyone but Lexy stopped. Lexy only glanced his way but dashed to the next closest mercenary, breaking the glass in the right eye of his gas mask.

If we stop, we die! Lexy urged us to move.

Luiz fired his shotgun at the mercenary farthest from Lexy. He hit his target, but the pellets didn't penetrate the body armor. Luiz retreated to the hallway to reload his shotgun.

Kendra, I called mentally. She entered from the hallway to our right. Too tired to use more magic myself, I tossed her my staff. She caught it, shouted, "*Ligetu!*" and blasted two of the remaining four mercenaries with lightning before they could fire their handguns at us.

The Skull Shadow fired. Jody screamed. The woman she had relied on to take care of her son while she worked slumped forward. The well-dressed Skull Shadow stepped around the dead woman and pressed his handgun into Jody's red hair.

"I said, stop!" he shouted. "Stop, or you lose the redhead, too!"

Jody's scream turned into a whimper. I couldn't help but think that just meeting me had ruined Jody's life. She'd dealt with Keagan, seen voodoo zombies, been kidnapped by Skull Shadows, witnessed her close friend and roommate get shot in the head right next to her, and now sat covered in her friend's blood and gore. She would never be the same, and it was all my fault.

This time, everyone obeyed the man, even Lexy. Emotional sadness plowed into me. Kendra froze in fear. He'd just killed Jody's roommate. We'd failed to stop him. Being a protector meant I'd foreseen Jody getting shot, but I didn't know how to stop it. With his handgun pressing against Jody's skull, if he pulled the trigger, how would I save her? Jody whimpered, inches from death. I could blast him with lightning, but that might not save Jody. I didn't know what to do. I couldn't think.

While Lexy had stopped, the other woman's death didn't faze her at all. She'd only stopped because Kendra's and my sadness rolled into her through the Trinity of Mind. Our plan had been to come as prepared as we could and use our magic to overcome. That strategy had failed. It had cost Jody her roommate—basically, Carl's second mother.

Alexis used her calm, emotion-free state to help Kendra and me focus. *Cry later.*

Our only option now was to hope for him to point the gun at us, giving us a window to save Jody. I felt drained, both physically and magically. Had I even recovered from the Lost Rhoades Mine Melee? I had nothing left. My magic wasn't stopping another bullet.

The two remaining mercenaries raised their pistols. The white-haired one pointed at Lexy while the other, a Middle Easterner with short salt-and-pepper hair, pointed at Kendra.

"Luiz," Lexy called and shook her head at him. He stood in the doorway to the makeshift hallway, his shotgun pointed at the blond Skull Shadow. He lowered the barrel.

I looked upward. Whether looking toward God or looking at the ceiling for some possible option, I wasn't sure. Perhaps since we'd parked at a church, I had God on my mind. Well, I—we—needed help. I didn't know where help could come from. So, yes, I mentally prayed. Kendra approved with her own mental amen.

"We underestimated you," the man spoke, filling the quiet air. "We came up with six different plans and changed them randomly every hour, but still, you were ready for us."

Is he monologuing? I questioned. *Incredibly stupid, right?* How could I joke after seeing the Skull Shadow shoot a woman? Perhaps I'd learned from Luiz to use joking as a tool to hold off emotional pain. I needed that tool now.

"You all need to be put down," he spat. "We put down so many of you last year." He grimaced, clearly referring to the Day of a Thousand Deaths. A day that now lived in infamy with Pearl Harbor and Nine-Eleven. "It is unfortunate that we missed you. We'll remedy that for most of you." His eyes landed on me. "You," he started, then stopped speaking. His eyes blinked, confused, looking at something on the floor behind me, where I heard a dragging sound.

That *dragging sound* came from Ariel. What did he think of a bullet-ridden, seven-year-old girl who used her flat palms to worm her mangled body toward him? Drips of blood marked her face. Black blood oozed from multiple bullet wounds and from her almost-severed leg. Kendra and I shivered at the sight of her. Alexis didn't shiver, but her breath caught. Coyote's granddaughter scared the living crap out of Lexy, Kendra, and me—and she was on *our* side.

"I said stop," his voice wavered.

"Why?" Ariel asked, her childlike voice soft and high like a piano note. Another drop of blood dripped down the left side of her face. She towed her leg as she slid with her hands toward the man.

"If you don't stop, I'll shoot her." He pressed the gun harder against Jody's head.

"OK," her sweet voice replied as she continued dragging herself toward him. "Can't I eat you either way?" The meaning of her words conflicted with her sweet melodic sound.

The Skull Shadow gulped. I could see his face much better now that my eyes were fully adjusted to the dark, but Lexy could see him quite clearly. White eyebrows pulled down toward the corners of his eyes. His wrinkles and skin spots placed him in his sixties. His blue eyes pinched in fear. A wireless communication device stuck out slightly from his left ear.

The scrape of our mythic mermaid dragging her dangling leg continued.

"Shoot that thing," the man ordered the two mercenaries.

They hesitated, not obeying him, but then both fired a single shot each. The bullets went right through Ariel's chest, so quickly she barely flinched. The two new holes oozed as she looked down at them with her lavender eyes.

"Owie!" Ariel frowned and pouted her lip. "That makes me more hungry."

"The word is 'hungrier,' not 'more hungry,'" Lexy verbally chided the girl with an exaggerated motherly tone. Lexy's outward appearance gave nothing away, yet inside, her fear had subsided, and she replaced it with mental laughter.

"Shoot her again!" the aged Skull Shadow ordered.

"It didn't work," the white-blond mercenary shouted back in a Russian accent.

"Take the freak," he nodded toward me, "and kill the rest," he commanded.

I froze. They wanted me. Only me. I couldn't help but wonder why? All this time, I thought they were looking for potentials and druids, but they didn't care about Kendra. Why was it about me? I'd done everything I could to stay out of the limelight. Even avoiding being quarterback in high school. I'd switched to running back even though I could throw much better than Mike. O'Brien had faked my death with the very purpose of making me invisible. Yet it hadn't worked. I remained the primary target. Lexy's grandfather had sent vampires after me before coming after me himself. The caplatas had come after me on orders of my Darth dad. Yes, I had an evil, magic-wielding father—only without the burned body, robot parts, and labored breath. Now the Skull Shadows had captured Jody to lure me to them, to find me. Did my Darth dad send the Skull Shadows, too?

"The boy, sir?" the Russian mercenary responded.

The aged Skull Shadow nodded, barely moving his head once.

The mercenary proceeded toward me, stepping around a black, armor-clad body and then around the fallen Polynesian.

I shook my head at the absurdity of the situation.

"I like Jake. He gives me beef jerky." Ariel glanced at me. "Jerky is nummy. If you try to take him, I'll eat you, too," our mythic mermaid monster spoke every word with her sweet seven-year-old voice. "I bet you taste better than jerky."

The mercenary stopped a step from me. Behind him, the white-haired Skull Shadow's eyes shifted rapidly from his prisoner to Ariel to his mercenaries and back.

"I said take the boy and kill the rest," the aged Skull Shadow repeated his order. The mercenaries didn't respond. Finally, his eyes settled in a wrinkled squint on the nightmarish little girl who still slid herself toward him incessantly.

"Damn you, Donaldson," he muttered between clenched teeth, quiet enough we weren't supposed to hear. But Lexy heard.

"Kill them all," he shouted, and he quickly swung his gun arm in Ariel's direction and fired. Jody flinched, expecting the bullet to go into her skull.

Too weak to use magic, I pulled my last resort backup plan from behind my back. Yes, I brought a gun—a forty-caliber Smith and Wesson. No more running out of magic and being helpless for me. Both mercenaries switched from Lexy and Kendra and put two rounds each into their fellow Skull Shadow's white shirt. He should have noticed Alexis had removed one gas mask and broken the glass to disable the other. By the time I fired my shot, he'd already spun from the impact and started dropping. My bullet missed just above his left shoulder. It would have hit him had the mercenaries not shot him sooner and if he weren't already collapsing.

Alexis had urged Kendra to fire a magic missile, but Kendra remained frozen, almost catatonic. So Alexis cast a small, ping-pong ball-sized magic missile herself. Not a soul-erasing one. Her magic missile—glowing red where mine was blue—hit last. The Skull Shadow fired one last erratic shot as he hit the floor. The bullet deflected off a metal crossbar high near the ceiling, redirecting to the cement floor between Kendra's legs, breaking her out of her fear-caused catatonia and sending her into a drill-team jump. She landed, legs spread, and staff ready.

If the Skull Shadow had survived the two bullets, the magic missile would finish him off. Except its red light warped. The ring pulled the magic into it as if it were a vacuum sucking the light in. Still, he was dead.

I breathed a sigh of relief. Jody had survived. We'd saved her. Kendra, Alexis, and Luiz made it through this battle unharmed. Ariel's bullet-ridden and gore-covered body still creeped me out, but she would transform herself back to perfect about an hour after a good meal. She just needed food.

I hadn't forgotten my prayer. Was our little mythic monster girl the answer to my prayer? As I stared at her, I wondered whether God could answer a prayer with such a horror show.

"Can I eat him now?" Ariel asked me. "I won't eat anyone unless you say I can."

CHAPTER 2
AFTERMATH

I've let others down, Jake and Alexis especially, nearly getting them killed because I let fear control me. Why can't I just dance on drill team? I know, because there are nightwalkers, vampires, and voodoo witches that can make zombies, both living and dead. Not to mention shapeshifting water babies descended from ancient deities from another world. Now, a secret society is involved, which might sound tame in comparison, but regular humans may be the worst monsters of them all. Is my ability to use magic enough to protect me from all of this? I keep freezing up in fear. How can I learn to be brave? —Kendra

Except for Ariel, we all rushed as one to Jody. Only, my rushing involved asking Kendra for Eldra's staff and limping over. Lexy pulled out her runed blade and cut through Jody's bindings. Once free, Jody fell forward out of the chair and into Kendra's arms, sobbing. Jody wore the same clothes she'd been kidnapped in; light blue jeans and a fitted white blouse with no sleeves that tied at the shoulders. Blood and gore ruined the white blouse, some of which transferred to Kendra's black leather shirt as she held Jody in a hug.

That smell will never come out of your leather shirt, Alexis thought to Kendra. The coppery smell of blood enticed Alexis, but the smell of gore repulsed her. *We will have to dispose of it.*

Luiz unfolded a curved karambit knife that doubled as brass knuckles—a recent purchase—and used it to cut the ropes that tied Jody's dark-haired friend to her chair. I tried not to look at the gory bullet hole in her head. My failure weighed down on me every bit as much as my exhaustion.

"Carl?" Jody questioned through her sobs, her tears dripping down her face, streaking the blood and gore.

"He is safe at our house," Kendra answered.

15

Our house? Was Lexy's mansion *our* house now? That was a debate for a later time.

"Everything is going to be all right," Kendra assured, looking for something to wipe Jody's face with. The white-haired Skull Shadow had worn a black suit jacket which now rested on another chair a dozen feet behind Jody. Alexis grabbed it and tossed it to Kendra, who caught it with one hand while still hugging Jody.

Good acting back there, I commended Lexy. *He had no idea the mercenaries were yours.*

And good puppeteering while acting, Kendra mentally added while stroking Jody's red hair.

Ariel did most of the work. Despite deflecting the praise, Lexy enjoyed the compliments. She bent over the dead Skull Shadow and pulled the communication device from his ear. It had a tiny microphone in it.

"Are you coming, Donaldson?" Lexy asked into the earpiece. She wondered the same thing I did. Was Donaldson vertical-scar guy's name? "We dismantled your team in minutes." She pulled out her phone, took a picture of the white-haired old man, and texted it to her grandfather. "I have spoken with the Vampire King. He is displeased that the Skull Shadows attacked the Princess of the New World in her territory. You fired without warning. That is a declaration of war."

Nice bluff, I thought to her. Her grandfather wanted her dead and would likely thank them for trying. Unless they broke his laws, he wouldn't care.

Perhaps they will not attack us again until they have spoken to my grandfather. It may buy us a few hours. We should leave quickly in case this ruse fails.

Lexy tapped her separation stone. Kendra did, too, and just like that, the two girls left me alone in my own mind, mostly. Their emotions still came through. Kendra comforted Jody. Lexy looked at Ariel with mirth—mirth that contrasted with my powerful regret. I tried not to look at the dark-haired woman again, but I did anyway. I didn't even know her name.

Luiz gently laid the dead woman on the floor and looked up.

"Should I get the car?" he asked.

Lexy nodded.

"*Me voy,*" Luiz commented and sprinted out the door.

"We need to go," Kendra urged Jody, but she didn't move.

Lexy pulled at the ring on the Skull Shadow's lifeless finger, but it wouldn't come off. I knelt and gave it a try myself, but the ring wouldn't budge.

16

"One finger," Lexy offered Ariel.

"I need his permission," she turned her blood-covered face to me.

"Fine," I answered.

"You have to say the words."

I didn't want to say the words. I hesitated, but Lexy eyed me like only a moron would hesitate. We couldn't leave a magic ring. It wasn't about to reveal secret words when immersed in flame, nor would it rule the minds of men, but it was still a magic ring. It had absorbed Lexy's magic missile. What was the ring's purpose?

"We need that ring," I swallowed. "Eat the finger."

Lexy's eyes flickered to me, and a melting pot of unpleasant emotions trickled from her. I had no idea why. Did she *not* want me to give Ariel permission? Why did she have to tap off our mental connection?

Ariel dragged herself closer to the Skull Shadow's corpse. I turned away, preferring not to watch her bite off the finger. A few seconds later, while our little mythic monster girl chewed, we eyed the ring in Lexy's palm. It had a similar glow to the protection stone that we each wore. Lexy's leather armor stretched tightly around her figure, so I doubted the ring could fit in any of her pockets, which is probably why she handed it to me. I tried to investigate it by sensing it with magic, but the magic I pushed into it simply disappeared. Still unsure of the ring's purpose, I pocketed it.

Jody asked Kendra a question, but I'd missed it. She held a soiled handkerchief from the suit coat, her face wiped clean. Her splattered white shirt now lay in a clump on the floor, and she now wore the suit coat, which did little to hide her lacy, white bra.

"Jake brought us here," Kendra answered Jody, pointing to me.

"Oh," she sobbed and turned away from Kendra to me. I was still kneeling and didn't have time to stand, so she leaned down to hug me. The suit coat opened, and my face awkwardly ended up pressed against her chest—covered only by her bra. She wrapped around me and squeezed me into her body with an unexpected and very tight hug. She held the hug for long seconds, which deepened the awkwardness. Finally, Jody pulled away.

Alexis tapped into my mind for a half-second. *After that hug, you need to slip twenty bucks into the top of her jeans.*

That's your jealousy talking. Jody, not Scarlett, hugged me, I assured. My retort was either too late or ignored.

Alexis pulled out her cellphone again. She texted someone and then called.

"I'd like to buy a rug," she said, then paused listening. I could hear the voice speaking, but I couldn't make out the words. Lexy glanced around the warehouse, first at the ten dead mercenaries in black body armor and then at Jody's friend and the Skull Shadow. Two more bodies, the teen gang members, lay in the hallway. "Fourteen feet long," she answered, then glanced at the Tongan who appeared to still be alive, "and only one foot wide. This thin size is critical." She listened for a second, then added, "No, not hidden under the table in the dining room, in the entry hall for everyone to see. And save as much of the existing rug as you can."

Again, I wanted her to tap off her separation stone so I could know who she was talking to. I like to count things, so I noticed that we had left fourteen dead bodies and one live one, and Lexy had said fourteen feet long by one foot wide. Was that a coincidence? Or was she speaking in code?

A cry of pain echoed in the warehouse. The short-but-thick Polynesian twisted on the floor in between a pair of black-armored bodies.

"I'll tend to the wounded," Lexy assured me. She moved to the Polynesian, bit her own finger, and let a couple drops of her blood drip into his bullet wounds. Vampire blood had a virus—well, actually a multicellular, symbiotic protist incorrectly termed a virus—that enhanced healing. Unless their immune system completely collapsed, the protist couldn't live long in a human.

A few minutes later, Luiz honked from the blue BMW 335i. It still had the dents from a few days ago when a Skull Shadow in an SUV had clipped the front corner. Despite the dents, Alexis didn't want to ruin the inside with blood, so she looked at the white-blond mercenary and pointed at Ariel and said, "Put her hideous corpse in a bag." He walked to a rusty metal barrel farther back in the warehouse. A stack of oversized, black plastic bags hung over its open rim—the size to put bodies in. The other mercenary gathered the ARs and other weapons.

"A bag?" Ariel whined as if she really were only seven years old. "After you ordered these two men to shoot me? You're a meanie!" she stuck her tongue out at Alexis.

"I could have had them shoot you many more times," Lexy smiled mischievously. "I should have. For you, nothing is mean enough."

"I don't like you," Ariel tried to pout, but behind the blood-soaked face, her eyes were smiling.

The Russian mercenary grabbed our mythic monster girl's shirt with both hands, lifted her up by it, which stretched her shirt into two peaks, and dropped her into the bag.

"And I would prefer that your corpse not make a mess in my BMW. If we are lucky, you will suffocate," Alexis bantered, also smiling with her eyes.

Great. The two monsters were hitting it off.

Outside, the sky had faded to purple. Three light poles jutted up from cement cylinders evenly placed in the parking lot. Without lightbulbs, the tops of the poles merged invisibly into the dark sky. Only stars and the partial moon lit the night.

The two mercenaries went out first, the Middle Easterner with a body bag of weapons and an AR-15, and the Russian with Ariel in a bag. The first mercenary set the bag of weapons down and put his right eye against the night vision scope of his AR-15. With his machine gun tight to his shoulder, he looked through the scope to all the possible hiding spots, one at a time. The other mercenary hurried to the BMW and put the bagged Ariel in the trunk.

I leaned against the staff with one hand, and with the other, I fiddled with the ring in my pocket. It had protected the Skull Shadow from Lexy's allure. It had absorbed the red power of Lexy's magic missile. My attempts to sense its purpose were also absorbed. It wasn't only a protection stone as I'd first expected. It was more, but what? I couldn't tell yet.

Kendra escorted Jody to the back of the BMW. The Russian mercenary returned from the trunk to put his arm under my shoulder and help me to the front passenger door. Lexy followed me. Luiz curiously gazed down his long nose at us from the driver's seat.

Great, was Lexy going to ask me to sit in back?

"I will ride with these boys," Alexis pointed at the mercenaries. "I need new bodyguards," her eyes wouldn't meet mine.

And you're short on servants, I added for her, not needing our Trinity of Mind to read her. Just two nights ago, the caplatas had killed most of the maidservants at the mansion and animated them into voodoo zombies that attacked us when we'd arrived home. She'd just chosen two men to replace her maids. I didn't expect the wave of jealousy that rose through my chest. I'd have plenty of time to think about that on the way home.

A very muffled child's voice shouted something from the trunk.

"She's hungry," Kendra interpreted, speaking with a soft voice while holding Jody, who wiped tears from her eyes with a clean corner of the soiled handkerchief. Jody was clearly in shock.

"I have hunger, too," Luiz agreed, the idea of food distracting him from Jody's pain.

The clock on the BMW's dash read 9:57 P.M. My stomach growled at the thought of food. We'd eaten dinner at six, four hours ago. It was late Saturday night, so a second dinner sounded good. We couldn't just stop at a drive-in and expect Jody to be OK if we didn't address the situation. I removed my seatbelt and twisted as best as I could in my seat to look back at Jody.

"Jody, you are safe," I spoke slowly. "We are going to do what safe people do and get dinner. Do you want to feel safe with us?"

Jody wiped her eyes but nodded.

Kendra blinked wide-eyed at me and tapped her separation stone.

You've changed. That was surprisingly sensitive. Was that you or Eldra?

I shrugged. I didn't want to think about Eldra, but I thought of her anyway. I couldn't help it. I'd lived Eldra's entire two-hundred-year-life as an instant one-second download to my brain. Like in the Matrix, only without an input port in the back of my skull. Kendra had already perused hundreds of Eldra's memories—mostly key life moments, both happy and terrible.

"Burger Bar?" I offered.

"*Aye, sí.* Who can argue with Diner's, Drive-ins, and Dives?" Luiz looked at me in the rearview mirror.

"I could use a few Triple Cheese Bens. With bacon."

"And me," Ariel's melodic child's voice muffled its way from the trunk.

"Will Lexy pay?" Luiz asked.

I pulled out my phone and texted Alexis our second-dinner destination: Let's eat at Burger Bar.

She texted back: Delayed. Go without me.

I pushed at Lexy's separation stone, curious about why she'd be delayed. I caught a glimpse of a man—no, a vampire—walking down a bright street with lots of lights—the Las Vegas strip.

Another text followed: You pay. Check your balance on the CryptoCurrency app.

I checked my phone and found on my home screen a new icon of a credit card with the words CryptoCurrency. I clicked into it and read the first few introductory screens. The app worked with any of the current pay-by-phone methods. I swiped the introduction away and clicked to check my balance: $5,000.

My jaw dropped. I'd never seen that much money in my life. I forgot everything else and just stared at my account balance.

Another text: As my general, that is 10% of your bi-monthly salary. Will discuss later.

What did she mean by only ten percent?

I texted again: Disable your separation stone.

Lexy responded with: Not now.

Ugh!

Thirty minutes later, including waiting in line at the drive-through, sauce from the first of three burgers dripped from my mouth. Earlier, I'd removed the Kevlar body armor, placing it on my lap. So I kinda used it as a table. I hoped the sauce didn't stain it through the wrappers.

"*¡Cuídate!*" Luiz laughed, glancing at me as I shoved the rest of my first burger into my mouth. He drove with one hand and ate chicken fingers and fries with the other—a wise meal choice for a driver. "You want to put on fifty pounds, sure, but maybe not in one meal." He pushed his belly out and patted it.

By the time we pulled into the garage in Alexis's mansion, I'd pounded down my three oversized burgers, three sets of fries, and an extra-large, cookies-and-cream shake.

Eyeball spotlights in the garage ceiling illuminated each of a dozen expensive cars. Some were ordinary sports cars, like the maroon Audi, the black Lincoln Navigator, and the two silver convertibles—a BMW and a Porsche. Others were less common, such as the Lamborghini and a couple of concept cars. As impressive as the vehicles were, I'd almost started getting desensitized to seeing them.

Jody held a fry in her hand with one bite out of it but otherwise hadn't touched her fish and fries basket.

It seemed like déjà vu when Carl opened the garage door wearing Incredible Hulk jammies and ran toward us. This time, I didn't leave him disappointed.

Jody leaped from the BMW, still wearing the Skull Shadow's oversized suit jacket, and met her son in an embrace that encompassed motherly love, reunion, and relief. Both cried. I slowly made my injured way out of the car, using Eldra's staff to stay off my ankle. The flaky white skin on my own cheeks dampened. I looked down, hoping no one noticed my damp cheeks. Kendra put her arm around me, crying and looking at the mother-son reunion.

"Where's Maggie?" Carl asked his mother.

Jody gulped, and her chin quivered. A strand of her red hair stuck to her wet cheek. She pulled it from her face and tucked it behind her ear before answering her son.

Nope. I'd still failed. I'd brought Carl's mother back, but I had still managed to leave Carl disappointed. I hadn't even known the name of Jody's dark-haired roommate until this very moment.

CHAPTER 3
DREAMS

Jake and Kendra are naïve. They only think in right and wrong, in monsters versus non-monsters. They are just learning that the world is not that simple. There is no black and white. Everyone can be a monster or not. My world's political landscape is full of challenges for power, most of which are surrounded with secret plots. To many, there is no right and wrong, only strength and weakness, winners and losers. As Princess of the New World, I will become a target. We must be ready. Losing means death. —Alexis

"We are going to church tomorrow," Kendra stated flatly as she walked me to my room. Kendra didn't expect an argument, and I didn't provide one. Church was part of who she was. We stopped at my bedroom door, my arm over Kendra's shoulder. Kendra shed my arm to let me go in alone.

"You're quite chivalrous for a lady," I said, grabbing both sides of the doorjamb with my hands to bow, mocking myself because I should have walked her to her room, but with my ankle and my weakness, she'd chosen to be the chivalrous one tonight. Unlike Luiz, I had to make conscious efforts at humor. My attempt at humor made Kendra smile, so I considered it a success.

I took one step without Kendra and nearly collapsed. She lurched forward and grabbed my left shoulder to stabilize me. She ducked back under my arm.

"Looks like my chivalry isn't finished, sir knight." Kendra smiled, her eyes inches from mine.

"I thank thee, fair maiden," I bantered back, enjoying our knight-maiden chivalry game.

She walked me the rest of the way into my room and then helped me sit on the edge of my bed. I sank into the soft mattress, wrinkling the black comforter.

Like all the mansion's rooms, mine was large. My king-sized bed pushed up against the back wall. Three large windows took up most of the space on the left wall, and a black burn marked the wall on the right where, a few days ago, I'd accidentally erased an intricately carved mahogany desk and the druid manual—the only one I had—with a magic missile. On the floor, a silver Star of David symbol wrapped in a perfect circle had been cut into the hardwood with precision. Bolt holes marked the floor where my bed had once been bolted inside the inner hexagon of the silver symbol and where two chains had connected. New, decorative carpets lined each side of my bed. Aged paintings as big as the windows and surrounded by gilded frames hung on each side of the door.

I shifted to get a better seat on the bed.

"Now, as a chivalrous maiden, I shall undress you. Do not fear," she winked. "I shan't take advantage of you in your weakened state."

She lifted each of my legs and pulled off my boots. Next, I lifted myself up with my hands so she could remove my denim pants. Ordinarily, having a hot, drill team girl undressing me would have been a dream. I should have bantered back, but I didn't. I considered telling her that she had my consent and so she could never take advantage of me, but I said nothing. As a hideous and skin-disfigured weakling, I didn't want her to see me without clothes. With my pants off, she helped me out of my hoodie. Underneath, I wore a T-shirt to keep the Kevlar from rubbing. Kendra tried to ignore her revulsion, and outwardly, she succeeded, but it was the only emotion that sifted into me through her separation stone.

The road-rash-like skin looked worse on my legs. At the warehouse where the Skull Shadows had kept Jody and her roommate, I'd split and scraped my knees on the asphalt. Dried drips of blood ran down my right shin and dyed my sock brownish-red. My left knee only had two scrapes, each with a drip of blood that ended halfway down my shin. The color of these two socks would never match again.

Carolyn—the young servant just a few years older than us—entered my room carrying a small bucket with a sponge. Carolyn dressed like a servant, with a light blue servant's dress and white pinafore over it. I liked the usefulness of servants but not the idea of enslaving anyone. Lexy had purchased regular clothes for them, but so far, they had refused to wear them. However, at Lexy's request, they had stopped wearing bonnets, which left Carolyn's healthy auburn hair hanging free. Her hair looked nothing like Jody's. Although both were redheads, Jody's hair was curly and dyed a darker red, while Carolyn's natural auburn hair hung straight.

"I'll wash him," Carolyn offered, sponge in hand.

Oh, no! I dreaded the sponge bath. Eldra had given many sponge baths. She had been a nurse during more than a dozen wars, including World War I and II. She'd also been a midwife until the mid-nineteenth century, when midwifery had been rendered obsolete by modern medicine, so a sponge bath should have felt normal. Except that earlier this summer, I'd twice helped Luiz clean up at Taco Time so he could get off earlier. I'd cleaned the tables with a sponge. So, to me, it felt like Carolyn was treating me like a dirty restaurant table. Why couldn't it have been Lillian and not Carolyn?

"I can shower myself," I grumbled.

"You will not deny another fair, flaxen maiden her opportunity to show chivalry," Kendra interrupted.

"Flaxen is yellow-blonde. Carolyn is a redhead," I shook my head. "And I'm serious, Kendra. I'll shower myself!" I growled, no longer interested in this game. The revulsion rolling off Kendra had taken the fun out of it for me.

"You showered this morning, good knight. Your wounds prevent you from soaking your skin twice in a day." Kendra remained in character, even though I hadn't.

She was right. Until my skin healed, I wasn't supposed to soak it often. Dr. Stewart's orders. That annoyed me more. I was barely more than an invalid, and tonight, there wasn't a thing I could do about it. I swore under my breath and slapped my bed.

"I'll take my leave, sir knight," Kendra curtsied, still refusing to end the game. She started to leave then looked back like she wanted to ask me something. Instead, her revulsion remained, and shame joined it. She left without another word.

"The boxers stay on!" I looked at Carolyn, who tried not to smirk.

Carolyn's hands moved the damp sponge softly over my bare skin. I counted by prime numbers to distract myself. I cringed as she scrubbed right to my boxer's waistband.

"You have blood underneath," Carolyn no longer stifled her smirk.

At some point at the warehouse, I must have scraped my left hip near my back. Blood had dried all over my left butt cheek, so to my ever-increasing embarrassment, Carolyn grabbed my waistband and slid the boxers off. She failed to muffle her laughter. My counting faltered as she scrubbed my bare cheek vigorously. I didn't find anything about the sponge bath chivalrous. Especially not the way she ended by slapping my now clean backside and giggling as she informed me she'd finished. The slap was light enough that it didn't break my damaged skin.

Once Carolyn left, I crawled under my covers. My thoughts turned to my sister and then to Charles O'Brien. I couldn't imagine being paraplegic. I dwelt briefly on my plan to help him until I fell asleep a bit past eleven. For hours, I didn't dream. As I felt sunrise approaching—or perhaps Alexis felt it, not me—the dreams began.

I stood in front of my biological father, who sat at the table in the same dining hall I'd visited before with the caplatas. A dark wood table, a slightly lighter shade of wood than the dining table at our mansion, stood between my biological father and me. Matching wood chairs surrounded the long table. Three silver chandeliers hung evenly over the table, lighting the room. For half a second, I expected Voodoo Whoopie and Stick Witch to be there. But I'd erased Voodoo Whoopie, and Manouchka, now free, had returned to Haiti.

My evil dad scowled at me. I didn't want to be alone with him. Lexy had followed me into my dream at the Lost Rhoades Mine Melee. I reached for Lexy, wishing she were here now. A second later, as if in answer to my wish, Lexy's mind flooded into me, and I found her standing next to me.

Clothes? I asked.

You know I wear nothing to bed. Alexis glanced down at herself unapologetically. *You're only in boxers,* she countered. However, an instant later, regal black leather armor appeared, stitched together with red thread, covering her body. A flowing, red cape hung at her back.

"You look just like your mother," my biological father interrupted before I could think to dress myself. At first, his statement confused me. Was he talking to me? I didn't look anything like my mother. I looked very much like him—at least, I did before magically flaying myself. But no, his eyes looked Lexy up and down as he spoke.

I raised an eyebrow at Alexis. *Aren't you curious how he knows your mother?*

I already know, she answered. With great mental effort, she hid that information by thinking of one of her mental lockboxes that Eldra had helped her create. Having lived Eldra's two-hundred-year life, I now understood how Alexis hid thoughts and memories from Kendra and me. Inside the mental lockboxes were scenes from her past, intense and surprising memories, but not ones she wanted to keep from us. The lockboxes contained only distractions. Lexy hadn't told Eldra which memories she planned to hide. The more we had tried to pry into her boxed-up memories, the easier it had been for Lexy to conceal her secrets *outside* of the boxes. I now knew to ignore the boxes. I'd have better success prying outside them.

Please, do not pry, Jake, Lexy pleaded.

"The Unforgiven!" Eldra shouted. Dead or not, Eldra joined us in our dream.

One of the AR-15s from earlier in the day appeared in Lexy's hands, and she unloaded it at my evil biological father, who disappeared before the first bullet hit him. Alexis didn't care that he left. She didn't want that man near me. She continued firing for what, in the dream world, felt like five minutes—no reloading necessary. Her red cape flapped behind as if the machine exhaled wind from its stock. The bullets eroded the long dining table and chairs until they disappeared—video game-like—replaced by shrapnel and empty shells.

Alexis dropped the AR-15.

"What did he tell you?" Lexy demanded. As quickly as my mind could answer, she changed her question. "Are you OK?" She put her hands on my strong shoulders and leaned against my dream-provided muscular body.

"He didn't have time to say anything, and I'm fine."

Her attention to my muscles reminded me that I didn't have them anymore. I found myself back in my room at the mansion, lying in my bed, my thin body and hideous skin restored. Alexis slipped under the black comforter, joining me in my bed. She put her arms around me to comfort me.

"I will stay here until you fall asleep."

"I am asleep," I reminded her. "This is already a dream." Besides, we weren't being fair to Kendra. She should be here.

"Until the dream changes then?"

Kendra interrupted us. "You're naked in his bed, Lexy! What kind of change are you expecting in this dream?" she scolded.

Kendra stood at the edge of my bed in last year's West Jordan drill-team outfit, with sequins and everything. Despite her glaring, thin eyes and her pursed lips, her emotions were mixed. She either wanted to slap both of us or jump in next to me, opposite Alexis.

"Clothes in a dream are optional, are they not?" Lexy teased. "You are welcome to slap me or join us. I would find both quite fun," she winked.

Eldra interrupted before Kendra could respond. "Both girls' separation stones are turned on. How are you sharing their minds?" Eldra questioned, then flattened her lips at me, making her mouth look like just another one of her wrinkles.

"That is not all that is turned on," Lexy teased, causing Eldra to chortle loudly as if Luiz had made a joke.

Kendra ignored Lexy's comment and Eldra's laughter as she wondered how she could possibly be sharing my dream.

"Wait, Jake?" Kendra's eyes widened. "Are you pushing through our separation stones like you push through a containment?"

I shrugged. "Am I?"

"Try to stop," Kendra suggested.

No longer in my bed, Alexis stood next to Kendra, her red sheet wrapped around her. "Kendra is no fun," she pouted.

I tried to stop whatever magic I was performing to push past their protection stones. Alexis and Kendra blinked away.

Interesting. Could I do this when I was awake? Awake, it had taken all my mental strength to push past Lexy's separation stone and get one word. Maybe I'd remember how I did this in the morning, but I doubted it.

I looked at Eldra. "You can go away, too," I told her, and she did.

Without the girls in my head, my dreams became nightmares. Atabei stood above an altar. Both Kendra and Alexis lay strapped to it. Both girls screamed as Atebei inserted a hand into each of their chests, *Temple of Doom* style, and ripped out their hearts. She handed the hearts to a pair of water babies.

The horrific, bullet-ridden mythic monster version of Ariel dragged herself toward the altar.

"Coyote," Ariel called. He appeared in front of her and she asked, "Can I eat the protector now?"

"You only protected him for one setting of the sun," he grimaced. "Perhaps a single, mooned night is long enough."

Ariel's face turned toward mine. She heaved her body and its broken leg towards me. I tried to move, but I was chained to the cavern wall. Alexis stood over me.

"Jake," Alexis frowned. "I need to replace my heart." A large hole in her chest showed a vacant spot where her heart should have been. As she bit my neck, Ariel bit into my shin.

I screamed.

I sat up in my bed, awake yet still screaming.

I looked around my room, embarrassed and expecting Alexis to appear out of nowhere and laugh at me. But I was alone. The clock read 8:43 A.M. It was Sunday morning. I'd slept for close to ten hours. Wow! I usually slept only four hours and woke up more rested than an average person who slept eight. I hadn't slept this long since I'd magically flayed myself and slept for days.

Lexy's healing stone hung around my neck. I slid out of bed and tested my ankle. It ached less than it had yesterday. I could put my full weight on it this morning. Not that I weighed much anymore.

My stomach didn't feel right. It felt bloated and uncomfortable. But as I focused on my stomach, the feeling faded away. It wasn't *my* stomach that had felt that way after all. Perhaps Kendra or Alexis ate something that didn't agree with them?

I stared at my grotesque complexion in the bathroom mirror, trying to see if my skin looked any better today than yesterday. I couldn't see a difference. Why wasn't my skin healing faster? My eyebrows and eyelashes used to be missing, which had creeped me out. Now, they stuck out a quarter inch, like I'd just had them trimmed too short. Still, no hair grew on my arms, legs, armpits, or pubic area. I may have burned away all the follicles below my chin.

I was far more hideous now than I had been as a wrinkly old hag for the past fifty years. Wait. Eldra had been the wrinkly hag for the past fifty years, not me.

The warm shower felt magical running over my body. Literally, magical. Strangely, I couldn't do magic in the rain the other night, but in the shower, the water augmented my power. Rain is uncontrollable, so perhaps magic is uncontrollable in the rain. However, a shower is controlled water, so perhaps magic is controllable in a shower? Eldra had studied magic for almost two hundred years. According to her, magic was never controllable in water. In fact, she was showering with Robin when Dane caught them indisposed.

Did I just call Eldra's husband Robin? That had been Eldra's pet name for her husband. She chose it because his last name was Locksley and his first name, Robier, sounded so close to Robin. My mind spun dizzily for a second. And I thought having Caradoc's memories was disorienting.

I didn't just have a Trinity of Mind with Kendra and Lexy. I also had another form of a Trinity of Mind with Caradoc and Eldra. Was I even the same person I used to be?

After letting both my thoughts and the warm shower flow for far too long—with my skin, the doc wanted me to keep my showers short—I finally turned off the water and carefully patted my tender skin dry with a towel.

Back in my room, the servants had made my bed. A black suit, white shirt, and a crimson necktie lay on the bedspread. Church clothes. The suit didn't surprise me. A card table had been set up with a brunch for a king—or at least a Princess's general. Still in my towel, I sat and ate breakfast. I washed my hands when I finished, then donned the new suit. I checked my spiffy duds out in the mirror bathroom. I liked that the suit mostly hid my skin. I'd have preferred a way to hide my face, too, but there wasn't an outfit that both covered a person's face and was acceptable to wear to church.

I felt Kendra's presence at the bedroom door before she knocked.

"Come in."

The door opened, and Kendra entered. She wore a cream-colored dress with a floral pattern of large gerbera daisies. The princess-cut dress hugged her chest and waist. The boatneck stayed modestly above her breasts, and the cap sleeves covered only the tops of her shoulders while leaving her arms bare.

"Church is at noon."

"OK."

"Everyone is coming with us."

"Who is everyone?"

"Alexis, Jody and Carl, and Ariel."

"Luiz?"

"He has Catholic church with his mom today. She's still grieving."

"Yeah, that's weird. What about Carolyn and Lillian?"

"Well, the servants aren't coming."

"And Mr. Espinoza's thralls?"

"Not them either."

"Lexy's new mercenaries?" I grinned at Kendra's expense.

"OK, not everyone is coming. Just who I've said," Kendra smiled back, able to laugh, too.

"Are we going to send our mythic mermaid monster to primary with the other seven-year-olds?"

Kendra's eyes widened. We'd only been acquainted with Ariel for barely more than a day. Taking a monster to a children's gospel class didn't sound like the best idea.

"Maybe we'll only stay for the first hour," she suggested.

Kendra didn't say anything for a good minute, but I could tell she wanted to ask me something. Our minds were forever joined, and yet she felt too nervous to ask me a question. Why? It was silliness.

I put my hand on her shoulder and smiled at her, then I quickly tapped off her separation stone.

"Hey," she complained and slapped my hand away.

The back of my hand turned bright red from the slap, and the edge of a scab on my middle knuckle started bleeding. Kendra's mind simultaneously apologized and told me I'd just gotten what I deserved. Our unfiltered thoughts made mental communication a lot harder. Sometimes people wish they could know what another person thinks as if that would help them understand the person better. It wouldn't. Hearing all of a person's thoughts is so much more confusing than only hearing the thoughts they choose to share.

I discovered Kendra's unasked question.

Eldra knew how. So, you know how, too, right?

I reached up and touched Kendra's boy-cut hair. *New shampoo?* I asked, inhaling a hint of citrus. Kendra nodded. Eldra's memories came back to me. I spoke the words: "*Locc lengan.*" Magic poured through me and into Kendra's hair. I could feel the hair molecules energize. Her hair would grow a quarter inch today. Eldra couldn't tell when the magic faded, so she'd only used her magic once a day. I could see the magic in Kendra's hair. I'd know when it faded. I doubted the spell would last till lunch.

I have things to do in Eldra's room, I explained, then grabbed my phone and excused myself. I had a text from Luiz that he would be with his mom all day, and then he had a date with Andrea, but he would come to the mansion tonight for Eldra's memorial.

Kendra found the tasks I planned to do interesting, but she tapped her separation stone to leave me to them. We walked out of my room together. She went one way, and I went the other. I felt just as interested in what Eldra had been doing—and hiding from us.

CHAPTER 4
ELDRA'S TASKS

I'm not sure why my skin has stopped healing. But I don't hate myself anymore. Something changed in me when the girls staged a micro-intervention after we survived the battle in the Lost Rhoades Mine. I've resolved to accept my hideousness. My looks don't horrify Kendra and Alexis as much. Maybe constant exposure has numbed their senses? I can rebuild my muscles over time. Maybe I'll always be ugly, but even so, life is worth living. —Jake

I walked into Eldra's room and the strangeness gave me the chills. I'd only lived there for over a week. I mean, Eldra, not me, had lived there a week. I'd only been in her room once. The circle she'd drawn to protect herself, Lillian, and Carolyn from detection by the caplatas still marked the wood floor. She saved them from being killed and turned into undead voodoo puppets.

The room looked lovely. I compared it to mine. First, this room's desk still existed. My room had three windows on the wall opposite the desk, while Eldra's had one large window over the bed. With the curtains tied to the side, the window let the morning light flood the room.

In the corner of Eldra's room, Robin's—Robier Locksley's—staff, *Raijin,* stood as a hidden reservoir of power. Robin always named his staffs. He'd gone through many staffs over his long life, naming each of them after gods of lightning. *Raijin* from Japanese lore followed *Xolotl* from Aztec lore, which shattered fighting a mystic in Taiwan. He'd named Eldra's staff Astrapí, after one of the Greek twin goddesses of lightning. Robier had named Eldra's previous staff after the other twin, *Bronte.* Eldra found the names silly and rarely used them. However, I liked the names.

31

I slipped my suit jacket off, hung it on the wooden chair at Eldra's desk, and then sat down. Alexis had scheduled a woodworker to come a week from Monday to build a new desk for me. Until then, I could use Eldra's.

A slim laptop sat on the mahogany surface. Eldra had purchased it after the Cabin Battle of Bear Lake and still hadn't removed the screen's clear plastic cover. Next to the laptop sat a new leather book—her magic journal. A thin, leather-strap bookmark connected to the spine and looped into its pages. I used the strap to open the book. Dark horizontal lines marked the soft brown pages. She'd written a dozen pages of notes in handwriting almost as beautiful as Lexy's. She'd titled the last page as *The Leaky Soul*. She described Kendra's soul being captured by the caplatas, Eldra's failed attempt to find her, and the possibility that they could hide a person from being tracked. I flipped the page to the previous entry, which Eldra had titled *Real Life Undead Voodoo Zombies*. She discussed the caplatas' attack on the mansion and their voodoo puppeteering of the murdered servants—a type of necromancy.

As I flipped the pages backward, I noticed Eldra had titled each entry. I reached the page titled *Cabin Battle of Bear Lake* and read the entry. Eldra described how Kendra and I hit them with magic missiles, killing her husband and knocking her unconscious; a tear dropped from my cheek onto the page. I'd expected that to be the first entry, but it wasn't. I flipped back two more pages to the first entry called *The Embarrassing Capture of the Locksley Druids*. I laughed. In this first story, she warned of the importance of druids using protection when having sex, only instead of writing about condoms and birth control pills, she wrote about spells to prevent capture. A vampire's allure has a greater effect on individuals who are already in the midst of intimacy. It also mentioned that while water made magic impossible, it did nothing to prevent a vampire's allure. Eldra wrote, "I'm certain a vampire's allure is inherently magical."

I marveled at her handwriting. Perhaps my handwriting would be as beautiful as Eldra's now? A plastic pen holder sat on the desk. I'd expected a fancy fountain pen, but instead, I found a translucent, blue plastic ballpoint with a missing lid. Eldra liked the way they rolled, and to someone who grew up in the eighteen-hundreds, she appreciated them and never took them for granted as cheap. I wouldn't have to worry about getting ink on the sleeves of my new white shirt.

I turned to the next clean page and wrote a new title: *The Lost Rhoades Mine Melee.*

My square palm and thick fingers prevented me from matching Eldra's beautiful script—even writing with her natural movements. Still, my new handwriting did decorate the page, though not as nicely as Eldra's.

I handwrote the story of the battle with the caplatas and the half-water-baby, half-ancient-alien shapeshifters. I described their doppelganger abilities in detail. I spent more than a page on Coyote and another page on Ariel. I didn't know much about either, but what I knew, I wrote. Ariel and I still needed to have a talk, protector-to-pardoned, to figure out if I'd made the right choice in letting her live. I dipped into Eldra's memories, using them to include her thoughts and feelings in the story. I spent two pages on Eldra's sacrifice and another page wrapping up the story.

Robin would often rub my—er, Eldra's shoulders while I—er, Eldra wrote. I took a deep breath. Eldra's life and memories pushed against me in a way that concerned me, trying to take over my mind. I shoved back against her memories as best as I could.

I looked around the room for a clock but didn't find one. I flipped open Eldra's thin laptop, and the screen came to life. The facial recognition login failed. My hideously healing face wouldn't match Eldra's less hideously wrinkled face. I found the password amongst Eldra's memories, so I typed it and logged in.

I opened the email application. I recognized Encrypted Contact as a mail program written by Kevin's dad. Problem: I needed to touch the screen with Eldra's fingerprint to open any emails. I could see who the emails were from and the first line, but nothing more. I read the first line of the twenty-seven unread emails. I felt the sense of desperation just from the first lines. I hadn't understood how many people needed Eldra. When she gave up her life for us, she risked other people's lives, as well as the continued existence of large corporations that employed thousands. Many people were counting on Eldra's responses, and she expected me to fill that role now.

I installed notepad++ on her laptop and made a task list.
- Get new druid manuals for Kendra, Lexy, myself, and the Nuchu (Ute) boy.
- Figure out how to reset the fingerprint in *Encrypted Contact.*
- Answer Eldra's emails

I did an internet search on the second one. The information I found explained that if your fingerprint was ever damaged, cut, or burned, the company could help you for a small fee of five thousand dollars. Extreme security came with a high price tag. No wonder Kevin's dad was loaded.

I added Kevin's name with a question mark to the second task on my list. Maybe Kendra could talk to him on the sly like she did to get us secure phones. I missed Kevin. I missed hanging out with the jeeks—my part jock, part geek friends. I had Luiz, of course. Maybe that was enough. Maybe I'd never hang out with Kevin or Ethan again.

Sitting at the desk in a white shirt and tie, my suit coat hanging on the chair, I felt very professional, as if I were the businessman that Eldra would need me to be to replace her. Eldra was not good at delegating.

Again, Eldra's mind pushed at mine, this time with more force, and again, I had to fight to keep in control of myself. I took a calming breath. I needed to make sure I didn't lose who I was—my very identity.

I couldn't get into Eldra's computer, but I had more to write, so I moved back to the pen and journal and wrote some more notes.

After about two hours and a constant battle to keep Eldra's memories from taking over my mind, a knock came at the door. Without waiting for me to answer, the door opened. Kendra stood there in her cream-colored dress. One of the large gerbera daisies in the dress's pattern had been cut in half at the collar seam— clearly a flaw. Even the best clothing designer could never guarantee perfect dress patterns once their design reached mass production.

"Time to go."

I stood up, quickly grabbed my suit coat, and flung it on. I felt the dizzy, lightheaded sensation in time to try to sit back down before I blacked out. Seconds later, when my eyes reopened, I was sitting safely in the chair. Physically, I'd avoided falling to the floor, and with my skin, who knows how much damage the fall would have caused. Mentally, the blackout put my mind further into a haze. Eldra's two-hundred-year life pushed my mind aside. The part of me that was Jacob began slipping away.

Kendra now leaned over me, her face just a foot away from mine. The bangs of her boy-cut golden-brown hair hung almost to her blue eyes that focused on mine. I breathed in her new citrus-scented shampoo. She grabbed my right hand with her left and put her right palm softly against my cheek as if checking if I had a fever.

"Stand up too fast?" Kendra outwardly smiled, but inwardly, I felt concern roll past her separation stone. The boatneck collar of her dress hung down, giving me a view of her lacy white bra. I could see all the way down to her navel. Eldra wouldn't have noticed. However, I—Jacob Stevens—noticed. In fact, the view rescued me. I lurched back into control of my mind, pushing Eldra's two-hundred-year-life back into the depths of my brain.

I could only imagine the rescued-by-boobs joke Luiz would have made. If he only knew.

Kendra pulled her hand from my cheek and adjusted the top of her dress as she stood up, reprimanding my straying eyes by thinning her own. Her smile flattened to pursed lips.

"I just need to eat again." Not wanting to add to her concern or admit to ogling, I explained only the fainting. She could wait until she disabled the separation stone to find out about Eldra's near-domination of my mind.

I touched the healing stone, a teardrop, black diamond that bumped out behind my tie and under my white shirt. "The healing stone requires a lot of food." I could already eat more than the next two teenagers I knew, and healing *did* add to my hunger.

Eldra hadn't felt hunger like this since her last pregnancy more than a century and a half ago; Beth was the only child I— she bore outside of the United States, in London. When those cravings came on, Robin and I—er, Eldra would head to a pub for fish and chips. I remembered getting drunk while pregnant— taboo now but not back then. That memory, even though, with my religion, I'd never drank alcohol in my life, jarred my thoughts. Eldra's lifetime of memories still pushed to take over, but I managed to hold it back.

"Where is Lexy?" I changed the subject. I hadn't seen her all morning. Usually, she swapped her healing and protection stone with me at night, then traded back in the morning. Why hadn't she traded back this morning? Whatever she was doing, she wanted to hide it from us.

Kendra shrugged. "She said she'd meet us at church."

CHAPTER 5
CHURCH

I hurt for Jake. His mom is in prison. His stepdad is dead, and his real dad is evil. He's cut off from Justine. What more can go wrong with his family? Hopefully, Lexy's lawyer will clear his mom of all charges, then everything will get better. At least it can't get worse! ——Kendra

In most of the world, the *Church* meant the Catholic Church, but in Utah, it meant *The Church of Jesus Christ of Latter-day Saints.* That name was a mouthful, which is probably why the Church had multiple nicknames. I could tell from the red brick, roof, and windows that this church building was newer than the one I attended in West Jordan. Some buildings were older, some newer, some had different colored brick, and the landscape varied. Still, they all had a similar layout involving a large chapel connected to a basketball gym with a surrounding hallway and smaller rooms. Out of every three church buildings, one had a larger chapel, a full NBA-sized basketball gym, and a large stage with additional surrounding rooms. These larger buildings were called Stake Centers and were designed for multiple congregations, called wards, to meet together in larger conferences called Stake Conferences. This building was a Stake Center.

Red, yellow, and purple flowers decorated the flower beds between the building and the grass and sidewalks. Rock landscaping took advantage of the rising mountain terrain. In the background, increasingly large homes rose partway up the Bountiful mountains before the slope steepened and rose like a wall, providing a perfect background for the church building's steeple, which cut into the mountain view like a dagger.

Kendra parked the Lincoln Navigator—the roomiest vehicle in the mansion's garages—in the second row. My ankle had me limping a bit as the five of us, Kendra, me, Jody, Carl, and Ariel, filed across the church building parking lot.

Gina sat waiting for us by the entrance in her red Ford Mustang. The cartop was down so the wind blew her hair. None of us had known she was coming. She jumped out wearing a white and black checkered dress that ended at her mid thigh and left her shoulders bare.

"Hey, all y'all," Gina greeted us before giving Jody a huge hug. Gina had come to mourn with Jody and comfort her.

The warm summer wind picked up, lifting and fluttering the bottom fringe of Kendra's dress. Jody's dress clung too tightly for the wind to move it, but it blew up Ariel's long, lavender dress, revealing her legs, reminding me that when I had first met her, she had a sea-lion-like mermaid tail. She'd changed that tail into legs yesterday morning. Last night, she had looked monstrous with a bloody, bullet-ridden body—but she had still looked seven years old. Now, she stood four inches taller, her lavender hair hung further down her body, and her face stretched to a more oval than round shape. Had she aged herself two years overnight?

As we approached the entrance to the church building, she noticed me analyzing her and must have read my mind because she answered my look by saying, "I'm nine, now. The same age as CJ."

CJ is Carl's nickname, Kendra tapped into my mind to explain. *Carl Jacob Prouse. His middle name is the same as your first name.*

He has a nickname? I hadn't known Jody's and Carl's last name either. Of course, I hadn't known that O'Brien's first name was Charles until the nightwalker had spoken it. *Names are important,* I reminded myself. I'd promised to do better. So far, I'd failed.

Ariel just gave him the nickname this morning. You missed it. And I agree, names are important.

CJ's a better name than Carl anyway, I explained as I pulled open the entrance door and held it open. *I mean, what if we needed to save him? I'd have to yell: "We have to save Carl!" And it just wouldn't sound right without Rick Grime's gruff fatherly angst.*

Kendra responded to my joke with a single syllable giggle as she walked inside. Her dress immediately stopped fluttering.

I thought you'd laugh harder than that.

She shrugged. *Now that I've been one, zombie jokes aren't as funny to me.*

The rest of us filed into the church's double door entrance— well, there were two sets of double doors with a space between, so was it a double-double door entrance? Or a quadruple door entrance? *Maybe a breezeway,* Kendra offered, unsure herself. The word *vestibule* popped into my mind. That word didn't come from Kendra or me, which left me wondering whose memory provided it: Lexy's, Eldra's, or Caradoc's. Once through the vestibule, a drinking fountain greeted us on the far wall. Brown brick lined the interior walls, which helped soundproof the various rooms. Thin, gray carpet covered the floor. We knew where to go because, as usual, the hallway wrapped around the gym to the chapel.

While the building was similar to the one that I had attended in West Jordan, the people were vastly different. I don't mean *just* different people than those in West Jordan. They were a separate *class* of people. Think there isn't a class system in the United States? Wrong. Just drive to a poor area of town, then to an affluent area, and compare. The difference in class becomes obvious. We didn't belong. Or maybe we did. We each wore expensive clothes, purchased and funded by a princess. Still, the difference extended beyond the clothes. Each woman we passed sported expensive salon-style hairdos. High-priced jewelry decorated their necks, earlobes, and wrists. The women's faces boasted flawlessly applied makeup. Their dresses, sewn from the best materials, all fit their figures. Some could have easily walked runways. There wasn't a single run in a nylon to be found and . . .

I yanked my thoughts to a stop. Why was I analyzing every article of clothing the women wore?

Because your almost eighteen years pales in comparison to Eldra's two-hundred, Kendra suggested. *Add in the Trinity of Mind with Alexis and me, and you're thinking like a woman.*

I imagined Luiz teasing me in childlike song, singing, "Jake is a girl! Jake is a girl!"

What's wrong with being a girl? Kendra challenged.

We reached the foyer. Wooden double doors led into the chapel on the right, while on the left, a glass, double doorway led outside. A tween boy held the glass doorway open as three families walked in. Next time, we'd park near this entrance.

Eldra sits on the board of a fashion conglomerate owned by a private equity that used to be run by the druids, I added.

Wow. You sounded like a thirty-something businessman just then.

Ugh! That isn't how I wanted to sound. I was just a guy—only seventeen. I didn't care about business yet. I didn't care what someone wore. Unless the slight mountain breeze from the open door pressed her floral dress against the shape of her beautiful body underneath. *There is nothing wrong with being a girl!* I agreed, unable to take my eyes off Kendra.

Kendra blushed at my thoughts. *Too bad you're ugly and too thin to fill out a suit.* Her unfiltered thought ruined the moment.

She couldn't stop her unfiltered thoughts, so she tapped off our connection with her separation stone. She pressed her lips to my cheek apologetically, then took my hand, leading me through the wooden double doors to the chapel. I forgave her. One thing we'd learned about the Trinity of Mind is that we can't judge each other by our unfiltered thoughts. We each threw away hundreds of thoughts a minute. Kendra had thrown that thought away. She'd sensed more throwaway thoughts coming and cut her mind off to protect me from them, proving with her actions that she cared for me. It still hurt, though.

Many people we passed stared with pity-filled eyes while others tossed us furtive glances. The hum of the congregation talking in low voices quieted as we walked in. I tried to lie to myself and chalk it up to Kendra's attractive beauty, but I caught myself in the lie.

We should have arrived one minute late instead of ten minutes early. We could have slipped into the overflow section at the back of the chapel by the gym without becoming a circus attraction. Fewer people would have noticed and stared at me.

I breathed in the clean chapel air. A dozen white lights hung like giant-sized upside-down wine glasses from the tall ceiling. Two dozen soft, white lights illuminated the room. I counted sixteen rows of center pews, then a walkway on each side before additional pews angled toward the white-brick wall. At the front of the chapel, three stairs led to five rows of cushioned stadium seating that faced the congregation, and behind them, organ pipes climbed the high, peaked wall.

Kendra thoughtlessly chose a pew in the center of the chapel. Seriously? So much for my hopes of discretion. I glanced longingly at the overflow section in the very back.

The Church divided its congregations geographically, grouping one or more neighborhoods together into a *ward*. Usually, one to three wards attended the same chapel, just at different times. Because they were all in the same neighborhood, everyone knew everyone. As new attendees, we stood out. The people gave us extra glances. After seeing my repulsive face, the onlookers' emotions changed to either pity or horror.

Kendra fit in, Gina almost fit in, but Jody clearly didn't. She also received two kinds of looks: judgmental and missionary. Which meant she either didn't belong or she needed to be converted to belong. Her stripper-red hair dye seemed to shout, "Look at me!" Her tight dress's cap sleeves and cleavage-revealing scoop neck attracted the wrong kind of attention. Some men ogled her then looked at their wives as if worried they'd get caught. Some wives caught their husbands and glared at Jody, blaming her for their husband's gawking.

Jody swallowed and shifted uncomfortably, glancing around. She pulled at the front of her dress in a failed attempt to cover her cleavage. As if aware, Gina took her hand comfortingly.

How did Jody even motivate herself to come after yesterday's tragedy?

It must be tough to live in Utah and *not* be part of the church. I wondered if Luiz and Andrea ever felt similarly ostracized. I didn't remember ever excluding Luiz. I'd invited him to plenty of church-sponsored activities. But how would I know whether he felt included? I'd ask him about it later.

"Church is two hours—a separate meeting each hour." Kendra leaned and whispered quietly to Jody. "This first meeting is called Sacrament. It starts with a prayer and then some announcements." She pointed to three men sitting behind the pulpit, elevated above the seats in the congregation. "There is a Bishop and a First and Second Counselor called the Bishopric. The speakers sit on the left side."

Her explanations were common knowledge to me, but Jody and Gina struggled to take it all in.

Kendra leaned forward and put her hand on the shoulder of a thin blonde woman with two kids who sat in front of us. When the woman turned around, Kendra asked, "Which one is the bishop?"

"He's the smiler with silver hair," she pointed to the middle of the three men sitting behind the pulpit. "Bishop Wassel."

The tall, bald man to the bishop's right, so bald the light reflected from his head, stood up and stepped to the pulpit.

"That's the First Counselor," the woman in front of us whispered to Kendra before turning back around.

The Second Counselor remained in his seat next to the bishop. Two patches of white hair above his ears ruined his otherwise full head of black hair. I probably wouldn't have even noticed him, except he stared at me hard with his nervous, dark eyes. *Yes, my skin's ugly; get over it!* I tried to push my thoughts at him but to no avail. He kept staring.

The First Counselor discussed the names of people who were changing their volunteer positions in the church. During the announcements, I sensed Alexis. I looked left to the double doors that already stood open, certain of her pending arrival. A few seconds later, she appeared, stopping in the center of the double doors, her eyes scanning to find us and considering when to interrupt.

The man at the pulpit stopped speaking. I glanced his way. His jaw fell open as he stared speechless at Alexis. My protection stone warmed against my skin under my white shirt and tie. The scent of pumpkin spice filled the chapel.

Alexis wore a long, red dress with black pinstriping. The dress covered her from her neck to toe and fit tight against her body. A black ribbon belted over her hips, tied in a bow on one side. Almost anywhere in the world, it would have been considered relatively modest and elegant. Just not according to Utah modesty. The Grecian neckline left her bare from shoulders to fingertips, and the dress's tight fit down her legs required a slit that rose high on her thigh.

Her allure affected everyone in the chapel—children excluded, as kids were always oblivious—causing all the adults and teens to stare at her. Alexis tapped her separation stone, which hung in front of her dress, to ask for our help.

Is there a reason you unleashed the full force of your allure into the chapel? Kendra reprimanded her.

I did not intend to, Alexis explained. She had tried to turn off her allure, but stepping into the chapel, the less-than-welcoming threshold surprised her, and her allure had released instinctually.

You're invited, Kendra assured her. *Just come sit down. There is no way to avoid the awkwardness now.* Having each been baptized at age eight, Kendra and I technically belonged to the church, but we weren't officially members of this ward, so did we have the right to fully invite her?

My allure should not be effective inside a threshold.

Well, it's effective, Kendra confirmed.

Perhaps Alexis was half-invited? Thresholds took on the nature of those inside them, and half the congregation welcomed her while the other half wished she'd turn around and leave.

Maybe I should leave.

Before Alexis could turn away from the door, a tall woman in her sixties stood. Her long, gray hair hung over each shoulder, and wide-brimmed glasses framed her happy eyes. A gray dress provided a neutral background for her gold necklace with a heart pendant—the literal jewel of her outfit. The woman stepped toward Lexy, her smile completely free of anything but concern and caring as she asked, "Can I help you find a seat?"

I'd never seen Lexy speechless before, but she stood there silently. Her mouth hung in the same half-open position as the First Counselor, who stared stupidly from the pulpit. Alexis pointed toward us, and Kendra waved.

The kind woman smiled. "Thank you for coming. Guests are always welcome."

With those words, the half of the threshold that fought against Lexy's visit conceded, and her tense shoulders noticeably relaxed. The lady put her hand gently on Lexy's elbow and ushered her to our pew. We all slid over a spot, allowing Alexis to sit on the end.

"It seems we have some visitors," the First Counselor announced from the pulpit, having recovered from his stunned silence.

I glanced at the Second Counselor. He'd stopped staring and now held his phone in front of his face, clearly texting, which I found odd. Bishopric members didn't usually text during Sacrament.

Ariel and CJ whispered to each other as CJ folded a half-sheet of paper into an airplane, oblivious to the whole incident.

Sacrament lasted only an hour, but it felt longer. Probably because so many eyes gazed curiously at the six of us the entire time. Kendra kept whispering to Jody, explaining what was happening, with Alexis carefully listening in.

The meeting ended with a prayer. Alexis stood and quickly made her way through the double doors to the foyer. I tried to follow but couldn't move as fast. Kendra and Gina hung back to help Jody get Carl moving. Carl thought that since the meeting had ended, he could fly his airplane. It traveled up past the pulpit. Gina said she'd handle it for Jody.

I shrugged at Kendra and walked out of the chapel.

Alexis stood near the foyer exit, waiting for us. I walked over to her.

"That wasn't so bad," I lied.

It was not the worst hour of my life, Lexy tapped her separation stone to reply, *nor the most awkward.*

"Excuse me," a short, aging woman behind me interrupted. She stepped up to Alexis with a smile as fake as her acrylic nails. A flowery blouse wrapped her stocky frame, and her maroon skirt extended below her knees. Her dyed-blonde hair curled on top of her head like she had visited a salon this morning. The jewel on her necklace rivaled Lexy's expensive, pear-shaped, black diamond. "You may not know this," the woman continued, "but we don't go flashing our bare shoulders at church," the woman frowned at Alexis. "It sets a bad example for the youth."

"I prefer to dress as I please, thank you," Alexis responded cordially. She wore blue contacts, which, with red eyes underneath, looked lavender and almost matched Ariel's. I noticed them change from lavender to dark blue. I didn't need her darkened eyes to feel the rage growing inside her.

"You should have checked with someone before coming here dressed like that. Anybody could have told you—."

"Excuse me," Jody stepped next to Alexis. "Are ya harass'n Alexis?" Jody asked in her southern, rural accent. She had Carl in tow but dropped his hand to come to Lexy's aid.

Was Jody even mentally or emotionally stable? She'd just experienced extreme trauma, being held captive by the Skull Shadows and seeing their leader shoot her friend in the head right next to her. This could go downhill fast.

The disagreeable woman took Jody in with a sweep of her eyes that ended with a disapproving look at her cleavage.

"Well, I suppose you need to know, too," the woman began, "you can't go around with bare shoulders or showing cleavage at church."

"Who the—"

"Whoa," I elevated my voice to drown out her swear word.

"—are you to tell us how to dress," Jody stepped into the woman's face.

"Excuse me," the woman took a step back. "What's your name?"

"Jody Prouse. And we'd thank ya ta let us all dress as we damn well please," her rural accent thickened.

"Prouse?" the disagreeable woman spoke the last name like a question. "Well, between the dress and that language, it's more like *Prouse-titute*."

"Yep, three times," Jody confessed, stepping into the woman's space again, leaning her face within six inches of the woman's. The aged woman blinked in surprise, taken aback that Jody had volunteered such information. Her jaw opened like she wanted to say something more but didn't.

I'd been to church my whole life, and not once had I ever had an experience like this or met a woman so disagreeable. Who was this woman? She needed to be careful. Maybe it seemed impossible that Lexy had four knives hidden under her tightly fitted dress, but she did. She seriously contemplated the pros and cons of embedding one of them into this woman's throat.

"Sister Gaul," a lady's firm voice called from behind me, belonging to the kind woman who had welcomed Alexis to the chapel and walked her to our pew. The kind woman grabbed Sister Gaul's arm and turned her around, and not in the kind and gentle way she had taken Alexis's arm. "You are out of line. You need to go to Sunday School. Now, *please*."

We had become a scene. People piled at the double doors to the chapel and stopped in the foyer to watch our interaction with Sister Gaul.

"But," Sister Gaul started.

"No buts! You're acting like your last name's alternate spelling!" the nice woman shook her head.

Sister Gaul gasped. Her lips pursed together, and she shook in anger.

"Oh, yell at me tomorrow night at our widows' dinner," the nice lady chided. "Just leave, please." She swung Sister Gaul around, facing her away from us, and gently pushed her down the hallway. She kindly turned back to Jody and Alexis. Her genuine smile and happy excitement reached her aging eyes.

"My apologies for Sister Gaul." She reached her hand out to Jody, "I am Larae." Jody took the woman's hand hesitantly. "Can I help show your two children the way to primary?" Jody started to speak, probably to say we were going to leave, but Larae preempted her by adding, "I hope I can convince you that Sister Gaul is the most disagreeable woman in the state of Utah. Please don't leave on her account."

Jody closed her mouth and shrugged her semi-bare shoulders.

With the scene over, the congregation migrated down the hall, and only a few gawkers remained.

Larae turned to Carl and Ariel, who Gina had just ushered toward us, and asked, "What are your names?"

Neither wanted to answer at first.

"Tell them your names," Alexis prompted.

"I'm CJ," Carl answered, immediately obeying Alexis. He seemed overly eager to go by his new nickname. Coyote's granddaughter ignored the command. She didn't want to share any information with a stranger—even one as nice as Larae. "She's Ariel," Carl answered for her.

"CJ and Ariel. Those are great names. How old are you?"

"We're both nine," Ariel finally spoke.

"How would you two like to meet the other nine-year-olds?"

Carl hesitated. So far, he hadn't shown any sign of being anything other than a normal kid. He hadn't acted autistic at all while around Ariel.

"I'm not sure if Carl—CJ—will be ready for other kids," Jody answered.

"I'll take care of CJ," Ariel promised in her melodic child's voice. She grabbed CJ's hand. "Do we just follow the other kids our age?" Not waiting for an answer, Ariel dragged CJ off toward some young kids she had spotted.

I thought we weren't going to let the monster go to Sunday School class with the other kids, Kendra questioned.

44

OK. Then, you tell her she can't go to Primary with Carl, I challenged. *She promised not to eat anyone unless I gave her permission, right?*

Fine, Kendra let it go.

"Surely, you are much too young," Larae spoke to Jody yet gestured with her left hand toward Alexis, "for this lovely young woman to be your daughter."

Jody turned to Alexis and deferred to her.

"No. We are not related. I am Alexis."

"Pleased to meet you, Alexis," Larae offered her hand.

Should I have worn gloves? Alexis asked me.

Try to turn off your allure and just shake her hand, Kendra answered.

Alexis shook her hand. If her allure affected Larae, the widow didn't show it.

"And who are you?" Larae looked at Gina, who moved next to Jody and took her arm in comfort.

"I'm Gina," she answered.

"Well, if you all wouldn't mind following me, I'll lead the way," Larae offered.

We followed Larae to the Sunday School classroom that held about fifty people. This time, we sat down in the back. Except for a few babies with one of their parents, everyone was an adult. Kids, like CJ and Ariel, had their own Sunday School classes, separated by age.

"Sunday School is literally like school," Kendra whispered to Jody and Gina. "Just instead of history, algebra, or English, we learn about Jesus."

Jody nodded.

"Is it anything at all like any church you have attended before?" Kendra whispered the question.

"I ain't never attended church before."

"Never?"

Jody shook her head.

"Daddy took me all the time," Gina also answered. "Evangelist. Very different. He'd wring my neck if he knew I attended the heathen Utah church. Maybe I'll come more often," she grinned naughtily.

Larae put a finger to her smiling lips, and then with her eyes, she drew my attention to the two teachers who stood at the front of the class. Larae hadn't given me a pity look. Just a smile, as if my macabre face didn't affect me at all. I'd never met an angel before—though I had recently heard one whisper in my ear—but Larae acted as close to an angel as I could imagine.

The teachers, a middle-aged man in a suit and his wife in a simple blue sailor dress, looked directly at us. The wife asked, "Would you introduce yourselves?"

I sighed. I hated visiting or being new. It guaranteed we'd be singled out for introductions. I stood and said, "I'm Jake. I'm ugly. Don't ask," and I sat back down.

Kendra stood next. "I'm Kendra. Jake, Alexis, and I will be attending this year at Woods Cross High School."

"We are all seniors," I added.

I'm a junior, Kendra reminded.

Eldra pulled some strings, I replied. *You're a senior now.*

Kendra wasn't sure how she felt about that.

Alexis stood, said, "I am Alexis," then immediately sat back down. Everyone in the room stared at Alexis.

"Gina Godard." Gina quickly half-stood as she spoke.

Jody stood last. Her eyes found Sister Gaul on the other side of the room, and she glared at the mean woman. Until Jody spoke, most eyes remained on Alexis. "I'm Jody Prouse. I'm a stripper at Club Exposed." She smiled mischievously at Sister Gaul's horrified expression, then sat down, enjoying the dropped jaws and wide eyes from everyone else in the room, too.

The judgmental hum of whispers rose immediately, but with introductions over, the teachers took over, and except for the constant glances our way, the Sunday School class resumed as usual.

"Welcome, all of you," the pair of teachers said simultaneously.

"Quiet down," the husband calmed the class.

"We are always happy to have visitors," the wife added as if speaking for everyone.

Ten minutes into Sunday School, Jody started crying into her hands. Gina held her.

You were right. She isn't emotionally stable, Kendra thought.

Alexis jumped into our minds to ask questions a few times throughout the Sunday School class. She couldn't hide her reasons to attend church from the Trinity of Mind. Her reasons had nothing to do with an interest in Jesus and his gospel and everything to do with defending herself as Princess of the New World. The plan was fine. It was the motivation behind the plan that we disagreed with.

I got up to use the restroom. I walked through the halls for a minute before I found the men's room near the far exit where we'd entered. After using the facilities, I noticed a couch near the entrance. I considered sitting there until church ended. I never used to go to Sunday School. The familiar comfort of the foyer couch called to me. But Kendra and Alexis would notice. I sighed.

I took one step when I thought I heard someone say "D.S.S." I recognized that acronym from the letter Alexis had received from some guy with a death wish named Trenton. Danite Secret Seventy. A secret society in the Church. Maybe I misheard? I took a step around the corner near the bathroom that led to the exit. A man with black hair stood in the space between the two sets of glass double dors—the vestibule. He turned, not enough that I could see his face, but he held a phone to his ear, above which a white patch ruined his otherwise perfect black hair—the Second Counselor.

"She offended them so badly that the older redhead dropped the f-bomb." He laughed. Then he listened for about thirty seconds, saying, "Uh, huh," every few seconds. I wished Alexis were here. She could have heard the other side of the conversation. "I know it might not be enough," he said. "I'll take care of it."

Had he really said D.S.S.? Maybe I'd misheard. Perhaps he was simply telling someone about the strange people—us—he'd encountered today. I was getting used to being mocked.

He hung up. I didn't want him to see me, so I stepped back around the corner before he could turn around. I passed Gina on the way back to Sunday School. She had to leave to dance the Sunday afternoon shift. I'd been a little negative toward Gina after she spent the night with Luiz, but after seeing her come to support Jody, I couldn't help but like her despite that.

After church ended, Alexis wouldn't leave before scheduling an appointment to meet with the Bishop. She booked Tuesday evening at seven. While setting up the meeting, the Bishop asked Alexis to let the missionaries visit sometime Wednesday morning. She agreed. I wasn't sure who would be more shocked to meet the other: Alexis or the missionaries.

As we walked out, I asked Alexis, "What do you call this space between the two sets of double doors?"

"A vestibule," Alexis answered without hesitation.

Kendra and I looked at each other and shrugged.

Alexis raised an eyebrow at us.

Church hadn't been so bad. Nobody—monster or secret society—tried to kill us. We'd met a widow whose actions embarrassed the entire church and a Second Counselor who liked to make fun of us. But we'd also met another widow whose actions shined an angelic light on the church. Still, I think we all thanked God when we finally arrived home.

CHAPTER 6
VISITING MOM

Kendra and I made a pact that neither of us would make a move on Jake, at least not behind the other's back. If the three of us are together, the competition is too fun to pass up. We decided that we are teenagers, likely to live two hundred years or more. We have time to let the next few years play out. Besides, with the opportunity to attend a senior year at a high school, well, what girl does not want to be free to have fun their senior year? —Alexis

The drive home was short. Kendra was having a crisis of faith. It wasn't just that church had been weird; it was everything. Finding out vampires were real, that she was a druid, fighting witches and zombies, and all of it. Where did her faith fit in all of that?

Christ's atonement—his sacrifice on the cross, paying for our sins, and resurrecting—was central to our religion. Did his atonement extend to a dhampir, like Alexis? To Ariel? How could it not? If Alexis and Ariel weren't included, would Christ's great act even be worth believing in? But if it did extend to them, where did God draw the line?

If God created mankind, both men and women, did he also create vampires? Nightwalkers? Witches? Zombies? Transients? Why did God allow such monsters to exist? How do such creatures fit into the plan? Or was God's plan just something made up by religion? Monsters weren't like mosquitos, created to torment God's children after Adam and Eve partook of the forbidden fruit; no, many monsters began human. They were either part of humanity, God's children, or an anathema to us. We believed that God created worlds without number, so Ariel seemed the least worrisome. It wasn't like the bible didn't mention magic and

48

monsters. Demons, Giants, asps, spirits, leviathans, etc. Magic also plays a role in the most famous bible story. Moses performed some crazy magical acts. While he wasn't given the title of druid or wizard, pharaoh's wise men were called magicians. That thought process made religion seem farfetched. What if it was all a lie? Was religion just created to comfort us in trying times?

I wasn't much help, though Kendra left her separation stone disabled hoping I could give it. Did I believe or just participate because I'd been raised in this religion? I mostly managed to keep my mind clear and let Kendra think, but still, she eventually tapped on her separation stone.

"We have an appointment at 3:30 P.M. to visit your mom," Kendra informed me as we entered the mansion from the garage. The mansion's cool air conditioning fought off the summer heat, allowing me to drop the barrier of magic around my skin that I used to stay cool. "Justine will be there. On our way home, we'll swing by and visit O'Brien again."

"I can't visit my mom," I argued. "I know we aren't close like a normal mother and son, but she's still my mom. She'll see right past my disfigured skin. Can't we just go straight to visiting O'Brien?"

"She won't recognize you if you use one of the disguise potions that you pocketed from the druid cache."

I couldn't hide anything from the Trinity of Mind. Only Alexis tried. With Eldra's memories, I now knew how to try, but I also knew the risks. The *myndtiegan* would eventually drive any who fought against it insane.

"OK. Fine." What else could I say? I looked around. We were right next to the receiving room with the secret entrance to Lexy's underground bedchamber, where Mr. Espinoza slept with his thralls. Everyone stood in the hallway from the garage, eavesdropping on our conversation. We could have communicated through the Trinity of Mind and avoided the eavesdropping if only Kendra hadn't tapped on her separation stone. But Alexis had hers off, and Kendra didn't want her crisis of faith on display in front of her.

"It'll just be me, you, and Sis," Kendra continued.

"I'm coming," Ariel added in her melodic child's voice.

"No," Kendra started.

"My future existence is contingent upon keeping the protector alive," Ariel answered, her voice still melodic but no longer sounding anything like a child's. In fact, a hint of magic accompanied her voice, much like the magic that had accompanied Coyote's. "If you leave me, I will follow."

"OK. You, me, and Ariel will meet Sis there."

"I shall arrive with the lawyer later," Alexis added.

"I'm supposed to work tonight," Jody commented.

"Gina took care of that," Alexis assured Jody. "I also contacted your day job." Alexis hadn't forgotten that Jody also worked days as an office assistant. "You have two weeks off from both jobs."

Jody's face pinched together in concern.

"Try not to worry about lost wages. We," Alexis glanced at me, "take full responsibility for involving you. Tomorrow, I will pay the rest of Carl's tuition for the year."

I expected a huge show of gratitude, but instead, Jody simply blinked away her concern and nodded.

"You can also stay here as long as you want. You never have to go back to either job again. With Eldra gone, we need a full-time mother in this house. Please do not be confused. As Princess of the New World, I shall remain in charge. However, on paper, for school and to prevent social services visits, we need a mother. Would you consider the job?"

Jody didn't answer.

"You must not answer now. Let me know when you are ready."

Couldn't we just use Lillian? I asked.

Lillian is a last resort. Remember, the servants are not mine. I do not know to whom they belong. They may not be loyal.

With that, everyone left the hallway and went our separate ways.

I hadn't used a vial of disguise since attending my own funeral. I stood in front of the mirror and drank the magically glowing liquid. I stared at myself, mesmerized as my face and skin changed. I could feel movement under my skin, but it felt very different than when sensing evil. A couple minutes after I drank, I looked normal. Well, not normal like I used to look; normal like an almost eighteen-year-old. I looked nothing like the muscular, athletic Jacob Stevens I used to be. Nobody would recognize me. Even better, nobody would stare at me. This new look was a bit handsome. My skin changed to one color, a nice pale complexion with a hint of red. My hair turned almost blond and grew out a quarter inch, maybe even a bit more on top, giving me a military-cut look. My eyebrows and lashes also grew out and lightened as well. My eyes changed from brown to green. The skin still hung too thin on my face, but I'd take thin and handsome over thin and monstrously repelling any day. Maybe I didn't need a hoodie.

We rolled into the West Jordan City Penitentiary at 3:27 P.M., which was right on time. The city jail was new but small, built onto the West Jordan Police Station shortly after the large prison moved from the Point of the Mountain to out west of the Great Salt Lake. A prison had no business having quality brickwork and a new roof, did it? Well, my mom was in this prison, so maybe the fact that it was new and nice was something I could get on board with.

I hadn't seen my mom since my funeral. Most everyone, my mom included, thought I was dead. While attending my own funeral, I'd compared myself to Tom Sawyer, but that hadn't been accurate. Tom Sawyer had the pleasure of letting everyone know he was alive. Would my mom ever know?

The inside of the prison started with an airport-like body scanner that blocked our path into the main foyer to reach a check-in booth. A tall Polynesian security guard stood just left of the scanner, and a short, thick woman operated a computer to the scanner's right. The foyer's two-story-tall ceiling had more windows than I expected, letting in a lot of light. It smelled clean, which is not something one would expect to say about a prison. Of course, it wouldn't be new for long. And maybe it only smelled clean because Alexis wasn't here to tell me what it really smelled like.

I wore tan cargo shorts and a blue-gray T-shirt with a V-neck. It felt good to see my own skin not looking repulsive; though I still favored my aching ankle—almost healed now—as we made our way toward the body scanner.

I'd recently started carrying a forty-caliber Smith and Wesson handgun. I'd left it under the BMW's driver's seat. I wasn't about to leave it home, but I wasn't about to bring it into the prison either. I shouldn't need to shoot anyone here. I also didn't dare wear my bulletproof vest. But I'd brought some rocks to power my bulletproof spell.

I stepped into the scanner, and it beeped.

"Why do you have rocks in your pockets?" the middle-aged woman next to the scanner questioned.

I answered the woman with a shrug.

The woman's brown hair was pulled back into a ponytail, and she was dressed in her blues, which were too small, so the material played tug-of-war with the buttons to stretch around her figure. We women get a sitting job, and soon all our clothes no longer fit. I'd seen it hundreds of times in my long life . . . Wait. I wasn't a woman, and I hadn't lived a long life. I tried to push Eldra out of my head.

The policewoman grabbed a small round plastic container and held it out to me. I pulled the rocks from the pockets of my shorts and put them in the container. Instead of running them through the scanner, the woman simply dumped them in the trash. An ominous sense of vulnerability washed over me. Hopefully, I wouldn't need a spell to stop bullets here. In the future, I'd consider using something else besides pebbles for the spell. I'd have to find a list of metals that would be allowed through a prison scanner.

I stepped through the scanner again and stepped out on the other side. I turned around to see Kendra walking back to Ariel, who hadn't followed us.

"What's wrong?" Kendra whispered to Ariel.

"That," she pointed at the scanner. Ariel didn't look scared. She just looked thoughtful, as if she were trying to solve a problem. Sure, except for her purple hair, she looked like a normal human girl from the outside. She had tan skin and wore a black blouse and gray shorts that almost took on the lavender color of her hair. But what would the body scan show inside of a mythic mermaid monster's body?

Maybe you don't get to see your mom after all, Kendra informed me.

My chest lurched in unexpected pain. Ariel couldn't come inside, and she wouldn't let me go inside without her. I hadn't realized how emotionally important it was for me to see my mom.

As I stood looking back, the security guard took notice of Ariel's hesitation. He didn't look anything like the Polynesian gang member who had guarded Jody's warehouse prison. This man stood about six-foot-six. He had biceps like Dwayne Johnson, but with his full head of black hair and darker skin, the comparison ended there. The guard's long nose would have reminded me of Luiz's, except it was also wide, and his big, comforting smile widened it further.

"She doesn't have to go through that thing," the tall guard gestured toward the body scanner. "If she's scared, I can scan her." He grabbed a wand behind a security stand.

Kendra heard him and looked back.

"Bring her over here," the security guard waved with a large hand.

Kendra turned and whispered into Ariel's ear, "Maybe act scared."

"I wouldn't know how," Ariel answered, but she took Kendra's hand and pretended to hide behind her as they walked to the security guard. She peeked around Kendra and then ducked back behind her. For not knowing how, she was doing an excellent job of looking scared. She was a trickster's granddaughter, after all.

Kendra turned and stooped low to make eye contact with Ariel. "It will be OK." Kendra wore peach shorts that extended to a few inches above the knee. Her phone stuck out from the right of the two unusably small back pockets. Her cream, short-sleeved blouse had ruffles over the shoulder seam and pleats between her breasts. The shirt ended at the top of her pants, and in a stooped position, she flashed a few inches of her lower back.

Kendra lifted Ariel's arms into a T position and covered her lavender eyes with her hand. The security guard started scanning her with the wand. Once the security guard completed scanning Ariel, Kendra removed her hand. "See, that wasn't so bad." She gave Ariel a nudge toward me, then turned and walked through the body scanner. Kendra's acting may have just stolen the show from Coyote's granddaughter.

I felt the pain in my chest dissipate as my tense shoulders lowered.

A second later, both girls stood next to me. Kendra offered a hand to both Ariel and me, and we each took one. We walked to the check-in, where a chubby blonde woman in her fifties looked way too happy to be working at a prison and way too happy for her crazy hair. It looked like a bomb went off, and she called it a hairdo. Her uniform also stretched too much at the chest. Another sitting job causing a woman to need a size bigger—Ugh! I was judging the way a woman dressed again. *Eldra, I am not you!*

"We are here to see Annie Stevens," Kendra told her.

"IDs, please," the blonde woman asked.

I froze. I didn't have an ID. My stepdad had refused to let me get a driver's license, and even if I did have one, I was disguised. My face wouldn't have matched it.

"Uh," I responded.

Kendra pulled out her learner's permit. She'd completed all the hours she needed for a full driver's license, but she'd been busy since turning sixteen.

"No driver's license?" The crazy-haired woman asked me.

"My stepdad didn't want his insurance bill to go up," I explained.

"You're not eighteen yet?"

"Not till September third."

"Minors aren't required to have ID." She gestured with both her hands to the two electronic tablets mounted on the counter. "Each of you fill out a form."

The form had basic questions. First name? Last name? What does a person who is supposed to be dead put in those fields? I couldn't put Jacob Stevens. I didn't dare put Jake Estevan, either, which was the name I would attend Woods Cross High School with, because it was too close to my real name.

Steve Trevory, I made up the name on the spot and typed it into the digital keyboard. For my date of birth and the other fields, I answered correctly.

"Kendra," a voice called. I recognized the voice and turned to see Sis stepping out of the scanner. She'd curled her long blonde hair, which she only did rarely, as it was naturally straight. Sis obviously hadn't changed out of her dress after church. She wore a solid, cream-colored gown with button-up pleats cut straight below her bust and a mauve, yoke-waist accordion skirt. Her cream-colored peep-toe slingbacks matched her blouse—and I'd just analyzed every inch of my sister's outfit. *Eldra!*

Justine walked over and hugged Kendra.

"Who are you with?" Sis asked.

"Hi, I'm Steve. Steve Trevory," I offered my hand, and then I mouthed, "It's me, Jake."

Her eyes widened and blinked, indicating that she read my lips just fine.

"Magic," I mouthed while gesturing an explosion with my fingers.

"This is Ariel," Kendra added.

"Nice hair," Justine smiled at our mythic monster, who smiled back but said nothing.

After we finished filling out our forms, a policeman escorted us down a hall. I started watching my feet and counting my steps, nervous to see Mom. I had just counted step thirteen when I glanced up and saw *him* down a hall to the right. Officer Connelly or Donaldson—whatever vertical-scar guy's real name was. He saw me, too. He touched his index finger to his good eye and then pointed at me and silently mouthed, "I know what you are, druid."

My disguise didn't fool him. How did he know? A part of me wanted to pause right there and erase this Skull Shadow from existence. But we were in a prison. Cameras lined every hall. I couldn't do anything but continue to walk. By step sixteen, he was out of sight, and I'd done nothing.

The policeman leading us opened a door, and we followed him inside. He left us in a visiting room devoid of any décor. The only furniture consisted of a table with one chair on the far side and two chairs on our side. Ariel and I stood back against the wall. Justine and Kendra sat at the table. Mom would sit on the other side. I wanted to be at the table, to be right across from her, but I couldn't, so instead, I stood by the exit.

I regretted not erasing Donaldson. His presence in this jail could not be good. Kendra didn't like it either. We already knew that he was parading as a policeman, and I'd wondered if he was interfering with my mom's arrest. Of course, he was. The only question now was, how deep was that interference?

Sis lifted a pair of chains that were bolted to the center of the table. She looked back at me, then dropped the chains, which rattled loudly. "I hope she isn't chained," Sis sighed.

"Hope is a good thing, maybe the best of things," I replied.

"What's that from?" Sis asked. She could always tell when I quoted a movie.

"Andy Dufresne says it in *Shawshank Redemption*."

"I didn't watch that one with you," Sis shrugged. "But I like it."

The far door opened, interrupting us. Two policemen escorted Mom, handcuffed and wearing an orange jumpsuit, to the table. They didn't remove her handcuffs but instead hooked the chain around them. Justine glanced at me, gulping and fighting the dampness from her eyes. Her fears that mom would be chained up during our visit were confirmed. The two policemen left, but the second one stopped and put his head back in the door just long enough to say he'd be right outside if we needed him. As if Mom were a danger to us.

Mom's light brown hair had been pulled back into a ponytail, which emphasized her strained face. Dark circles surrounded her eyes. Her sunken cheeks and thinning figure worried me. She still looked a bit overweight, especially for only five-foot-four, but she had to have lost at least twenty pounds since my funeral. I wasn't sure if it was Eldra or me that noticed her thinner figure. I hoped it was me.

"Justine," Mom breathed Sis's name with a sigh of relief.

Sis reached over the table and hugged our mother. Our mother tugged at the chains but couldn't hug back, so it was a one-sided hug. Still, it lasted a good ten seconds before Justine pulled away.

"Thanks for visiting," Mom cried. Tears already streamed down her raw, red cheeks. Her tears were clear, as she wore no mascara or makeup.

Kendra reached over and hugged my mom, too.

Mom glanced at each of us, and something inside me broke when she didn't recognize me. I would have taken a flinch over a complete lack of recognition. I had underestimated how bad it was going to hurt to not be able to hug my mother. Sure, we weren't close. She'd let Grandma, whom I missed to this day, raise me until I was eleven. Losing Grandma had cut deep, and Eldra's loss had reopened that wound. Until Eldra gave her life for us, I hadn't realized how I'd attached my feelings for my grandmother to her. Because Grandma raised me, I didn't have near the relationship with Mom that Sis had. Still, I loved my mom. Unfortunately, I was a constant reminder of something terrible that had happened in her past. I couldn't change that. The best thing I could do for her was to keep pretending I was dead so I would never have to remind her again.

"I just," Mom wasn't full-on crying anymore, but her chin still quivered some, "don't know what happened. I left him. I moved out. Why would I . . ." she trailed off.

"Let's not talk about that," Justine forced a smile. "I went to Disneyland," she tried to change the subject but paused as if waiting for enough courage to continue. "With a boy," she added, her embarrassment dimple fully exposed.

"Did you have fun?" Mom asked.

"It was amazing. We were there for three days."

"Did you stay in a hotel?"

Justine's mouth opened but then closed. She looked down and nodded.

"Did you have sex?"

"No, mom," Sis shook her head.

"You spent multiple nights in a hotel room with a boy," Mom accused. "And you expect me to believe—"

"We didn't," she looked back up and met our mother's eyes.

"A boy in a hotel? Surely he tried—"

"We stopped it."

Mom pursed her lips. "You stopped it? What's that supposed to mean?"

Justine glanced at Kendra, then back at us. Then turned back to Mom with a pleading look.

"Justine," Mom sounded stern. "We've talked about this, and—"

"I know, Mom," Justine cut her off. "But we didn't. And Disneyland was so fun. We saw Mickey and Minnie and a bunch of the princesses: Rapunzel, Elsa and Anna, Snow White, Ariel twice, once with her mermaid tail and once with legs, and a bunch of others."

Hearing her name in the list of Disney princesses, Ariel gave me a quizzical look, asking me if I had really named her after a mermaid Disney Princess.

I nodded with a hint of a smile.

Ariel returned a scowl, which looked a lot more threatening than one would expect from a nine-year-old girl.

"Dylan loved Star Wars land," Sis continued.

"Is that Dylan?" With a rattle of chains, Mom pointed with her handcuffed hands at me.

"No, Mom. That's," Sis hesitated. She wasn't going to tell Mom who I was, was she?

Kendra tapped her separation stone and jumped into my mind. *What name did you make up?*

"Steve Trevory," Kendra answered for Justine. "He's just a friend who gave me a ride," she lied.

"Why didn't you ride with Justine?" Mom's eyes returned to Justine and thinned with suspicion. "Aren't you staying at Kendra's?"

"Yes," Sis nodded, only answering the second question.

"Kathleen and Kenneth are good people," Mom added. Then she took Sis's hand. "I better let you tell me all about Disneyland."

I listened to Justine and my mom for a half-hour. Kendra jumped into the conversation now and then, and I wanted to interject so many times, but I couldn't. I had plenty to say, too. I wanted to shout, "It's me, Jake! O'Brien faked my death." Then I could be part of the conversation. But revealing that I was her son and alive wouldn't help her. Worse, it could put her in danger. I could only help her by staying silent. And maybe I could take vengeance on my evil biological father for what he did to my mom. He wanted to find me, and perhaps I would let him. Or maybe I would find him first, capture him, and hang him from his ankles. I would watch him writhe in agony as I sliced him with my runed blade and licked the blood dripping from his body as he screamed.

OK, that thought was dark.

What better way to let you know I arrived, Lexy thought, *than to help you think of fun ways to torture and kill your evil dad. I still cannot believe The Unforgiven is your father.*

Through Lexy's eyes, I could see that she and Mr. Brandt, her expensive lawyer, were just walking into the foyer. *The foyer does smell new,* Alexis confirmed.

We are early. Mr. Brandt wanted to talk to you and Justine.

The door had a window to the hallway, and even though I knew I couldn't see to the foyer, I looked through it. The hallway led to the doorway to the check-in desk, and vertical-scar guy stood halfway down it, his eyes focused on mine. He nodded and then disappeared down a different hall.

Lexy swore with her unfiltered thoughts.

CHAPTER 7
LAWYER

Today the lawyer will free Mom. That will relieve a ton of stress. Justine needs her. Sis has had it hard lately, so getting Mom back should help. I know I can't tell Mom that I'm alive, but maybe someday, if everything settles down, I'll be able to. Hopefully, nothing else will go wrong for a long while. —Jake

As Alexis struggled to get through the security scanner, Kendra and I mentally discussed with her the possibility of killing Donaldson right here in the prison. Unfortunately, we decided we couldn't get away with it.

I turned my focus back to Mom and Justine for the next few minutes until the door opened and a policeman escorted Alexis and Mr. Brandt in. Alexis stepped next to me and took my hand. Her chin-length hair hung perfectly straight. She still wore the blue contacts that left her eyes slightly purple, and the two freckles—burned into her from my blood—still decorated her left cheek. She dressed in a new leather outfit, though it was more of the same. A line of open-holed rivets ran from hip to ankle down the leather seam, and another line of them circled the top of her waist. The same rivets ran down the shoulders of her matching black leather shirt, also at the seam, forming a line from her collar to her wrist. On the front of her shirt, a decorative set of rivets formed a diamond shape, the top point starting an inch below the crewneck collar and the bottom point plunging between her bosoms. Let's just say her leather outfit was riveting!

"Forgive us the early intrusion," Mr. Brandt interrupted in his nasal voice, speaking directly to my mother. Mr. Brandt stood four inches shorter than me, which put him at five foot nine. He looked to be in his late thirties, maybe early forties. His wavy chestnut hair fringed up, and the first hints of gray caught the light. His bangs formed a wave that crashed pointedly downward atop his forehead. His light-blue dress shirt brought out the matching pinstripes decorating his dark-blue suit. His red power tie matched his red-jeweled cufflinks, and black Berluti dress shoes completed the outfit. This man knew how to dress.

Alexis breathed in. *It smells like fear in here.* She shared an unfiltered thought, *Your mom is scared.* She instantly regretted making me feel worse.

"It would be helpful for your case," Mr. Brandt continued, "if I could speak to you and your daughter together. Just you two, if you don't mind." He exaggerated his body movements as he turned to the rest of us in the room, his look clearly a dismissal.

"We'll wait in the foyer," Kendra suggested. She hugged my mom one more time, thinking, *This hug's for you, Jake.*

I wanted to astral project into Kendra's body to experience the hug, but it ended before I could try. Sharing the hug through Kendra's mind would have to suffice. My eyes dampened, so I dropped Lexy's hand and hurried out before Mom saw me crying. Obviously, I couldn't hide the first tear that dropped down my cheek from Kendra and Alexis, but my mom didn't need to see it. With my disguise, to her, I was a stranger—just some boy who gave Kendra a ride. Why would a stranger cry? She'd either be confused or suspicious.

Mr. Brandt is a fantastic lawyer, Alexis assured me as she walked out with Kendra.

We waited in the foyer for almost an hour. Kendra sat on my right while Alexis sat on my left. Each held one of my hands, and both kept their minds open. They just sat with me, feeling my emotions. They even managed to avoid catfighting, which left silence replacing the usual background noise in our minds. It was peaceful. It helped that I didn't pry at their memories.

My sadness calmed after ten minutes. I started to get bored, so I pulled out my phone and launched Madden to pass the time. Alexis and Kendra watched as I played against the Madden all-star team. My interest in football rubbed off on them, and they found themselves riveted to my phone—not riveted like Lexy's outfit, the other riveted. I won thirty-four to thirty-one on a last-second field goal. The three of us high-fived afterward.

Wow! Football is so complicated, Kendra gazed at me with amazement.

This is the first American football I have ever watched, Alexis admitted. *It is like chess with athletes.*

That is why I love it! I declared.

Before I could start a second game, Justine and Mr. Brandt walked into the foyer, so I switched off my phone and slid it into my left pocket. Sis came directly over to me, which felt good. Alexis dropped my hand and moved over, giving her space to sit.

Unlike a typical nine-year-old, Ariel had sat still the entire time. Without a view of my phone, or a screen in her face, she sat still better than we did. In fact, she continued to sit, knowing the lawyer would talk to us for a while as well. Her stillness reminded me that, as the granddaughter of an ancient being, she was far older and far more patient than any of us.

"Did the deposition go well?" Alexis asked.

"I can't discuss the details here," Mr. Brandt answered, "but I believe we have the beginnings of a defense."

"The beginnings?" I asked. "You can't free my mom today?"

Mr. Brandt gave me a flat smile. "A murder defense takes a long time. I'll need to analyze what I've learned today and come back with more questions. I'll also need to have discussions with other individuals, like you. Expect the process to take months."

"Months?" I'd gotten my hopes up stupidly. I should have been smarter than that.

Mr. Brandt leaned in and whispered, "You should avoid calling her Mom." He knew about me. Alexis had given him all the details. As the son of a druid woman and a wealthy businessman, he was privy to the existence of druids, vampires, and other beings, though he hadn't inherited his mother's magic. His mother was killed on the Day of a Thousand Deaths. He was unaware that the vampires had played a significant part, or he might change his opinion of Alexis. Then again, she was only half-dhampir.

Did you play a part in the Day of a Thousand Deaths? I asked Alexis.

No. Grandfather sent me to assassinate a disobedient vampire. Viktor. Grandfather was disappointed that I survived. He thinks I fought Viktor and won. Kendra and I watched her memory. Viktor had looked young but had been approaching four hundred years old. Alexis had simply told Viktor that she was a gift. The Vampire King had gifted Alexis to Viktor before, so he didn't hesitate to accept her into his bed. Alexis removed his head with his own machete while he slept naked. She'd chosen noon, when the sun was highest, and Viktor was in his deepest sleep. He'd never woken.

You have the basic instincts of Catherine Tramell, I mused.

Kendra frowned. *You shouldn't watch racy movies.*

Grandfather had me kill Viktor because he refused to assassinate a druid, Alexis lamented. Viktor had once been a vicious killing machine, so she hadn't hesitated, but she'd heard rumors since his death that suggested he'd changed. He hadn't killed in decades—proof that even the most vile killers can change.

We tried not to dwell on Lexy's murderous memories. Kendra and I couldn't imagine being "gifted" or being ordered to kill people—especially at our age. I still regretted not erasing Lexy's grandfather when I had the chance. In her grandfather's distorted mind, age was not a determination of adulthood. He considered a girl an adult at her first period. Kendra's first period started at eleven. No way an eleven-year-old is ready to be an adult. With that thought, Kendra couldn't hide that she started this morning, and her embarrassment trickled alongside our conversation. That explained the bloated stomach—not mine—that I'd felt when I woke up. Alexis had noticed earlier this morning and could smell her blood. I still exuded awkwardness at that thought.

In Albania, adulthood is fourteen. In other countries like Scotland, it is sixteen, Alexis noted, quickly changing the subject.

Fourteen? No way. Kendra replied. *But I'm sixteen, so . . .*

Maybe fourteen to sixteen is too young for some, Alexis conceded, *but eighteen is too old for most. Seventeen is a good year to come of age.*

I'm seventeen, so I can agree with that, I added.

Lexy's thoughts drifted to her thirteenth birthday. *Life can make anyone an adult at any age.*

Mr. Brandt had asked us a question twice, but we hadn't heard him either time.

"Sometimes they ignore us," Ariel's melodic voice answered the lawyer as she nudged Alexis. We *had* lost ourselves in the Trinity of Mind.

Justine sat next to me, my arm around her waist. I used to zone out thinking, a personality trait of mine. From Sis's point of view, the Trinity of Mind hadn't changed me much.

"Your patience is appreciated, Mr. Brandt," Alexis noticeably did not apologize. She started to say more but her eyes locked on two men walking into the foyer. Officer Connelly and Officer Weekes. Mr. Brandt caught the intensity of Alexis's stare and looked over as well. His brows pulled together.

Officer Weekes focused his eyes on Justine while Officer Connelly directed his at me, his face rigid and emotionless. Despite my disguise, he looked at me as if he could see through it. Did he know who I was? How?

A palpable pause hung amongst us as the two men crossed the foyer. None of us spoke. Whatever was about to happen couldn't be good, so I breathed in magic.

Officer Weekes stopped in front of my sister.

"Justine," he swallowed and held up a warrant with his right hand. "I have a warrant for your arrest." He hadn't swallowed the last time he'd tried to arrest my sister.

"I'm sure you remember me," Mr. Brandt stepped between Justine and Officer Weekes. Officer Connelly reached forward to grab Mr. Brandt, but Officer Weekes put his hand between them.

"Let him read it," Officer Weekes handed the warrant to Mr. Brandt.

Mr. Brandt took the warrant in hand and started reading, then pushed up his upper lip with his lower lip, clearly thinking. He took a deep breath and nodded. He glanced at Alexis, then back to Officer Weekes.

"All seems in order," he nodded.

He has been caught off-guard, Alexis worried.

"You better hope that this evidence stands up," Mr. Brandt added. "I am going to come at this hard. I see that you used the same judge. I doubt he will still be a judge when I get through with him." Mr. Brandt verbally took the offensive.

"You can try," Donaldson mocked as he pulled out a pair of handcuffs.

"Turn around, please," Officer Weekes told Justine. She shied away from Officer Connelly, eyeing the scar that sliced vertically down his right eye.

Sis looked at Alexis and Kendra, who nodded, then to me. I shook my head, refusing to accept that this Skull Shadow was going to arrest my little sister.

I stepped forward, ready to breathe out my magic into a soul erasing magic missile. My arms moved, and my hands prepared to form the magical orb, but Kendra grabbed my right arm while Alexis grabbed my left.

Stay calm! He is trying to bait you into action, Alexis warned me. *Look just below his neck.*

The faint glow of a magic crystal hung from a silver chain under his uniform. I shouldn't have known what that magic item might do for him, but my instincts—or perhaps Eldra's—told me it detected druids. The silver chain also had two other crystals, but maybe since they were not in use, I couldn't detect their purposes.

"Take a breath, son," Mr. Brandt put a hand on my shoulder, then he shifted to Justine and helped her turn around.

Donaldson grabbed Sis's arms and roughly put on the cuffs, causing her to cry out.

"Justine Bennett," Officer Weekes spoke, taking my sister away from his rough partner, "you are charged with aiding your mother, Annie Stevens, in the murder of John Braen, your stepfather, and Jacob Stevens, your half-brother."

I took a step forward. "I am Ja—" I started, but Alexis put her left hand over my mouth.

Justine teared up and started to collapse to the floor, but Officer Connelly grabbed her by the handcuffs and yanked her up, growling, "Stay on your feet, bitch."

I broke out of Kendra's and Lexy's grip and lurched forward threateningly, magic forming a missile in front of me. "I am Ja—" I started again, but again, Alexis put one hand over my mouth while Kendra grabbed my hands to stop my magic missile from forming.

The Skull Shadow reacted to my threatening move almost as quickly as Alexis and Kendra. He pulled the .45 from his hip and fired. Officer Weekes slapped Donaldson's gun arm down, causing the second shot to hit the floor. Mr. Brandt grabbed Justine and shielded her with his body.

Lexy's fangs extended as pain screamed through her forearm. I didn't have any pebbles to magically bulletproof either Alexis's clothes or mine. The bullet crashed into her forearm just below her elbow. The loud crack of the bullet breaking a bone—her radius—followed the gunshot. The bullet stopped inside her arm, but it should have passed through it and killed me. Why didn't it? Ariel stood between Donaldson and Alexis. A giant exit hole in the back of her head led to a small entry hole in her forehead. I could see all the way through it. By the time the bullet had hit Alexis's radius, Ariel's skull had slowed it and mushroomed it.

The giant Polynesian security guard wrapped his thick arms around Officer Connelly, lifting him off the ground and setting him down away from Officer Weekes. The female security guard ran to Ariel, squatting down in front of her, offering first aid. Now wounded, Alexis unleashed the scent of honey, filling the room with its fragrance. My protection stone warmed. Alexis became more interested in the blood pulsing up through the security guard's carotid and down his jugular. She closed her mouth and fought off the instant hunger that her bloody and broken forearm caused.

Officer Weekes swore. "What did you do, Connelly?"

"He lunged at us!" Connelly shouted in his own defense as he thrashed, trying to free himself, but the Polynesian held him wrapped tight.

A door cracked open, and the first of what was likely going to be a storm of officers peaked in.

Lexy focused on Connelly. For a second, he stopped thrashing and met her eyes. He'd dropped his mental wall. The stress and the emotion of being tackled and held down prevented the concentration he needed. Lexy pulled out his real name. Mark Donaldson, but he went by Slash.

Attack Jake or any of us again, and we will kill you, Alexis forced the thought into his head.

Donaldson's eyes widened. He had known *what* I was, not *who* I was. He had identified me as a druid, but until Alexis gave me away, he hadn't known that I was Jacob Stevens. Alexis pulled another valuable piece of information. Slash Donaldson and the other Skull Shadows had yet to be paid for their role in the Day of a Thousand Deaths. Caradoc's head had been the last requirement for their thirty-million-dollar payday. With his digital scope, Donaldson had recorded a video of sniping Caradoc. In the video, his bullet hit Caradoc in the heart. Then a crystal that hung from Caradoc's neck lit up, and the druid disappeared. Unable to deliver Caradoc's head, my father had refused payment of the thirty million.

Alexis could feel Donaldson's will fighting to get her out of his head, but blocking her was far easier than removing her once she was in. Alexis increased her mental will, pitting it against the Skull Shadow's. She pulled another related but separate memory from Slash Donaldson, a memory from just a few days ago in which he negotiated with my Darth dad.

"Where is my son?" my biological father demanded.

"Hiding. You sent the vampires and those witches after him and spooked him. Had you trusted me, this would all be over."

"I need him to come to me willingly. I need him eager to do anything I ask of him."

"He will need strong motivation for that."

"Do you know how to motivate him?"

"I'm quite motivating," Slash answered. "But your debts are not paid."

"What debt? You didn't deliver," my biological father scoffed.

"I sent you a video of a bullet hitting Caradoc's heart."

"The requirement was for his head!"

Slash shrugged. "If you want the boy, pay your debts first?"

"If you bring my son to me willing to obey my every command, I will consider the entire venture complete and pay all frozen wages."

"I'll bring him willingly," Slash offered, "but you'll pay up whether he obeys your every command or not. And set your expectations because motivating him to come willingly will take months."

"I'll wait," the Unforgiven assured. His words feigned patience, but his eyes raged with the lack of it.

Before Alexis could get more out of him, Slash Donaldson increased his concentration and pushed up his mental wall. "Get out of my head, bitch," he yelled at Alexis. She fought to stay inside his head, but this time his will won.

"Get him out of here," Officer Weekes told the Polynesian security guard. He watched and waited for the Polynesian to forcibly escort Officer Connelly, who still shook in anger, out of the foyer.

Alexis's honey-scented allure filled the room, and when she was injured, her allure was always overwhelming.

Officer Weekes took a step toward Ariel to check on her, but Alexis met his eyes and told him to stay away. He shook his head as if to gather himself, disoriented by her allure, and turned to Justine. "Please bear with me. Some things can't be overlooked. You have the right to remain silent . . ." he continued reading Sis the Miranda Rights.

Doors were opening all around, and at least twenty different officers stormed into the foyer to investigate the two gunshots.

Everyone stared at Ariel. A nine-year-old with a bullet hole in the head shouldn't act calm and uninjured. When we'd shot the water babies in the Lost Rhoades Mine, they had collapsed and stayed down for a few minutes. Our mythic mermaid monster looked unaffected, and the hole in her head didn't reveal brain matter as I would have expected. Hadn't Coyote hinted at her superior abilities?

"The bullet missed," Alexis spoke. The female security guard stopped trying to administer first aid to Ariel for a second but then continued. More people came into the foyer. Alexis repeated, "The bullet missed." Her influence struggled against the visual proof that her words were a lie, so she covered the bullet hole in her left upper forearm with her right hand. Ariel followed Lexy's example and put a hand over both her entry and exit wounds. Alexis repeated the phrase a third time, "The bullet missed." The third time, with all evidence hidden, everyone in the room believed her.

"Good thing that bullet missed you, honey," the female security guard smiled. She gave Ariel a comforting squeeze on the shoulder. "You'll be fine, girl."

"Erase the security camera," Alexis ordered. "Protect your own," she gave them personal motivation, which added power to

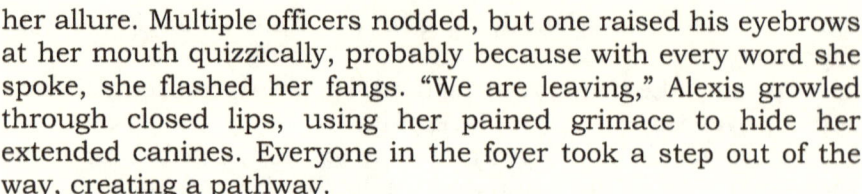

her allure. Multiple officers nodded, but one raised his eyebrows at her mouth quizzically, probably because with every word she spoke, she flashed her fangs. "We are leaving," Alexis growled through closed lips, using her pained grimace to hide her extended canines. Everyone in the foyer took a step out of the way, creating a pathway.

Alexis and Ariel started toward the door. Kendra and I hesitated, our focus still on Sis, who stood panicked in handcuffs.

"Go," Mr. Brandt urged me and physically moved me toward the door. "This is my territory. I'll take care of her."

Alexis urged me to follow, but I blocked her out as best as I could. Kendra started walking backward toward the door. I still hesitated.

"I do this every day," Mr. Brandt assured me. "Go."

I went. But I hated myself for leaving my sister.

CHAPTER 8
UNEXPECTED CALL

I'm feeling a bit overwhelmed. Jake and I are druids, hanging out with Alexis, a half-dhampir, which is basically a vampire in denial. Both Jake's mom and sister have been arrested. We've nearly been killed several times by vampires, voodoo witches, shapeshifting water babies, and a secret society. Did I mention I was temporarily a zombie? The craziness doesn't end there, and I need a distraction from all of it. What's my favorite distraction? Drill team. It is hard to believe, but practice starts tomorrow morning. Drill team is really going to happen. I squealed just writing this! I'm trying not to think about the fact that I'll be dancing for Woods Cross instead of West Jordan. It's still drill team, right? I'll miss Justine at practices. I've never been to drill team without her. Instead, I must tolerate Lexy. I'm not sure how I feel about her dancing on drill with me. At five-foot-six, I'm considered almost too tall, and Lexy is four inches taller than me. Most girls that tall look awkward. Will Lexy have that problem? Probably not. She better not be a better dancer than me! —Kendra

T he sun still hung high in the blue sky, reflecting off the many car windows in the West Jordan Penitentiary's parking lot. The warm, blue sky and slight breeze suggested that everything was all right with the world. The weather lied. Or perhaps it was unaware of the events that took place hidden from its view under the roof behind us. The heat rising from the black asphalt refracted the light, blurring the various car tires. Unlike the sun and sky, the blacktop blur told the truth. I lived in a distorted world.

When we reached the BMW in the parking lot, Lexy grabbed at my right sleeve, and I knew through the Trinity of Mind that she wanted to borrow my shirt. I lifted it over my head and found

Alexis also removing hers because a mass of Ariel's gooey skull matter covered and dripped from the back of it. I worried she'd be topless, as she didn't always wear bras with her leather shirts, but fortunately, this time she had. She shook off the leather as best she could, then rolled it so the goop wouldn't get all over.

The sun's hot rays warmed my scalp, shoulders, and bare back for the first time in weeks. I handed my shirt to Lexy, but instead of putting it on, she wrapped it around her bloody forearm, staunching the blood before getting into the passenger's seat.

I was shirtless—and not hideous. Lexy was shirtless but bra-covered. Kendra eyed Ariel's oozing bullet wound, which was small and circular in front but a massive exit wound in back.

Just do it, Lexy snapped.

"Fine!" Kendra sighed. She slipped out of her shirt, too, and wrapped it around Ariel's head before helping the ancient little girl into the back seat. Kendra wore a cream-colored bra that matched her blouse. It covered more skin than her white bikini top covered. "But we're adding first aid kits to the cars after this."

The three of us sat in the BMW without shirts. Luiz was missing out.

Lexy suggested we not sit around the police station shirtless. She could deal with the pain as we drove.

With Kendra sitting in the back with Ariel, I drove. Alexis swore in pain. She knew some creative curses. She didn't have two hundred years' worth of cursing practice like Eldra had, but she might have just locked down rookie of the year. Her honey-scented desire for blood filled the car and warmed our protection stones. Through the Trinity of Mind, Kendra and I helped her control her pained hunger.

I had thought that visiting my mom would be stressful and not go well, but I hadn't expected it to go like it had. My mom and I weren't tight. She'd never wanted me as her child, which wasn't her fault. Now, she didn't even know I was alive, and I was in disguise, so Mom had ignored me the whole visit. I'd expected all of that. However, I did not expect Justine's arrest, or the Skull Shadow to be there and shoot at me, hitting Ariel and Alexis. Not to mention the memories Lexy pulled from his head.

Ariel sat in the back seat, eating a bag of jerky. She had put herself in front of a bullet for me. She had moved quickly to shield me—at least as fast as Alexis. The bullet might have still hit my heart if Alexis's arm hadn't been there. While arresting my sister, the Skull Shadow had stared me down. He wanted me to know that he could get to me and had been trying to rile me up, to get me to react so he could justify killing me. Alexis had warned that he was trying to bait me into action. Despite her warning, I had let him do just that. I'd lost control of my emotions.

Why shouldn't I come forward now and let everyone know I was alive? Would revealing who I was get my mother and my sister released? Which would be worse for Mom? Going to jail for life for a crime she didn't commit, or bad people, and maybe monsters, kidnapping her to get to me?

My thoughts continued as I raced north on I-15. Alexis, in pain, didn't interrupt my thoughts, and Kendra kept her mind in listen mode, hearing my thoughts instead of sharing her own. Both ignored my constant glances at their state of dress.

The leather seat drew sweat from my shirtless back, making it sticky. I glanced at Alexis grimacing in the passenger seat. She glanced at Kendra, hungrily. Two days ago—which seemed like weeks ago—other Skull Shadows shot Alexis in the stomach and the shoulder. She'd completely lost control, and I had to intervene to keep her from draining a first responder. Now, Donaldson had shot her again in the forearm. Her prior two bullet wounds had fully healed. A water baby had bitten a chunk of flesh from her shoulder, and that had healed within a day. She just needed fresh blood, and she would heal, but she needed it before she lost control and fed off Kendra.

The bullet is preventing my bones from fusing back together, Alexis realized.

With my magical senses, I reached into her body. I followed her skeletal structure down her neck and into the shoulder. From there, I followed it to just below her elbow. I settled on the break and wrapped my magic around the misshapen bullet.

Pay attention, Kendra warned. I looked up and swerved back into my lane, but not before a large blue F-250 honked at me.

I lost my concentration on the bullet.

Try again, Alexis urged.

I followed the same process, flowing my magical senses into her until I once again focused on the bullet. Kendra reached from the back seat and grabbed the steering wheel to keep us in our lane. Kendra leaned between the seats, and her bra ended up three inches to the right of my face, which caused my attention to falter again. Kendra's position put the right side of her neck dangerously close to Alexis. If she latched onto her neck, would she let go?

I let Kendra steer, and for the third time, I focused on the bullet.

69

I pulled at the elements of the bullet, intending to convert them to magic. However, using my magical mind, I delved deeper into the bullet's elements. The symbiotes that made Alexis who she was—protists often misclassified as a virus—swarmed around the wound, already working to dismantle the bullet. Each protist pulled a copper atom from the outside of the bullet and fused it to Alexis's bone, strengthening it. They didn't want the bullet erased. They wanted it disassembled so they could make use of its elements. Could I do that?

I focused on the bullet, just as if I were converting it to magic. I communicated to the copper elements, treating each atom as sentient, asking them to separate individually. Most of the bullet's outer layers were copper, but inside, I found nickel then mild steel. At my magic-infused request, the molecules in the bullet separated into individual atoms. The bullet lost its mushroom shape as the atoms spread out. With the bullet dispersed, the bone closed considerably, causing Alexis to wince. The protists went crazy, like a hive of ants. In a few seconds, they pulled the split bones together and gathered the shattered bone fragments, putting them back into place. Then, they began to harvest the metal atoms, fusing them around the break, like a permanent metal cast. Once healed, the metal would leave her bone stronger. Healing her flesh would take longer. The protists had done what they could but now waited for fresh blood to finish.

Thank you, Alexis offered, her chest moving in and out as she breathed deeply through her pain.

I dropped my magical focus on her bones and the protists. Feeling me take control, Kendra let go of the steering wheel. She turned her head slowly to face Alexis, then eased back to her seat, not tempting the half-dhampir's predator side with sudden movement.

Almost subconsciously, I had headed toward Club Exposed. Alexis wanted to feed, and she'd fed there last time. Luiz had been with us then, and he'd eagerly accompanied her inside. I wished Luiz were here today. If he knew where we were headed, he'd probably wish he were here, too.

When we arrived, I turned into the rear parking lot. The back of the building remained unchanged. The parking lines were barely visible over the deteriorating asphalt. Above the back door of the building, the shattered porch light, not yet repaired, reminded me of the caplatas and zombies we'd battled here. Remembering their shadow blades increased my breathing. Just a couple of days ago, we'd met with Keagan assuming he was our enemy, but he wasn't. In fact, he was on Alexis's side. He'd even asked Alexis to marry him and suggested that she replace me with him as one of her generals. She didn't say yes, but neither did she say no. Then the caplatas and zombies attacked. Kendra was bitten by a voodoo zombie, and her spirit had started leaking out until she, too, had become a mindless zombie under the Voodoo Whoopi's control. I blamed that Haitian witch for Eldra's death. I glanced back at Ariel. It took a second for me to get my breathing under control.

I parked, and to both my and Kendra's surprise, Kendra followed Alexis across the parking lot toward the strip club. Was Kendra warming up to the strip club? It wasn't that she accepted the career choice of the women who worked there. It was more that she now accepted those women as real people. It wasn't like strippers were damned souls. This wasn't the Titty Twister, and I wasn't a Gecko brother—though Alexis could likely pass for Santánico Pandemonium—and these strippers weren't going to turn into evil vampire demons. No, like Jody and Gina, these women lived complex lives. They had friends and loved ones, and they struggled through many of the same problems as anyone else. They were more than their choice in career and deserved the respect that any person deserved. In my religion, we believe that everyone is a child of God and that the worth of every soul is great, even a stripper's soul—no, especially a stripper's soul.

That was deep, Jake. Kendra answered my thought. *But I just wanted to borrow a shirt.*

I stayed in the car. If the strip club had a shirt I could borrow, would I *want* to borrow it?

Inside the strip club, Kendra and Alexis entered the dressing room where clothes were optional, so they tapped on their separation stones, cutting me off from their minds. They had used the separation stones far less today. Was that because I wasn't trying to pry into their memories? Instead, I let them share the memories they wanted to share when they wanted to share them. Another benefit I obtained from reliving Eldra's two-hundred-year life in a one-second download.

I looked down and saw my splotchy white skin. My disguise had worn off. Had I subconsciously ended the magic myself? I should have brought a backup shirt. Now I sat, bare-chested and cringeworthy, in the car with Ariel. I found her staring at me through the rear-view mirror. Awkward!

"Thanks for jumping in front of the bullet."

Ariel nodded but said nothing. Despite looking like a nine-year-old girl, she was not young. She was born thousands of years ago, the granddaughter of Coyote, an ancient alien shapeshifter. The small hole in her forehead had closed. She now held Kendra's cream shirt against the back of her head with one hand and ate jerky with the other. She'd started on a second bag. Had she stocked snacks under the seat? Probably.

Not for the first time, I wondered about her past. Coyote had said she was the first of his granddaughters to turn evil, the one that had corrupted the others. Yet, here she was, working with me, a *protector*. Not once had my protector magic suggested that I needed to protect anyone from her. How had she changed so thoroughly? Sure, she was a changeling, but that was mostly physical. How had she changed her soul and turned away from evil? Or had she? Perhaps she was simply on her best behavior because Coyote made a pact with her that required her to keep me alive.

I didn't dwell on Ariel for long. My sister's arrest was too distracting of a worry, and I kept coming back to it. Alexis would feed slowly, and I didn't want to sit at the strip club parking lot. Not because it was a strip club, but because of the memories of the caplatas, their shadow blades, and the voodoo zombies. So I decided to take a drive. I started down Beck Street toward the capitol and let loose all my worries for Sis.

The Utah State Capitol Building stood on top of a hill just north of downtown Salt Lake City. It was a massive, white rectangle of a building with a tall dome rising from the center. Behind it, the blue sky above the towering Wasatch Mountains gave it a beautiful background.

I would have continued to worry about Sis, but my phone rang. I pulled it out of my pocket to look at the number, but there wasn't one. I hesitated. Who could be calling me? Who would have this number? Could someone I didn't know call me directly on my secure phone? Had vertical-scar-guy and the Skull Shadows figured out my phone number?

I let the phone ring once more, then I answered with the usual, "Hello."

"Jake?" an excited voice asked.

I recognized the voice, so I hung up. I pulled over and parked on a side street. The phone rang again. I sent it to voicemail. It rang again. And again. Then a text came through. It read: I can call a thousand times until you answer.

A few seconds after I read the text, the phone rang yet again.

"Hi Kevin," I answered, and I took in a deep breath.

"Oh, wow. It is true." Kevin's next word came out as a loud shout, "Yes!"

"Don't tell anyone else, Kevin." Of my three jeek friends, now only Ethan didn't know I was alive. While Luiz was my best friend, Ethan was Kevin's.

"Come on," Kevin complained, "Luiz and Kendra already know. We can't leave out Ethan."

I imagined the jeeks' faces, pale and drained of blood by a vampire, or more simply, shot dead. Of course, death isn't the worst outcome. What if a nightwalker's scream shattered their minds? Would I visit them in the psych ward? I also glanced at my skin and imagined O'Brien in a wheelchair.

"Yes, we can. It is safer for him. You shouldn't have called. It's safer if you hang up and forget about me."

"Jake, is everything OK?"

"Sure, Kevin. I faked my death because everything is OK!" I answered sarcastically. I didn't explain that it had been O'Brien, not me, who had faked my death.

"Sorry, Jake. I just," he paused, "I just don't know what is going on."

"Me either," I answered with a partial truth. "How'd you figure out I was alive? Was it the phone?"

"It started with your body supposedly disappearing from the morgue," Kevin answered. "Then Kendra refused to believe that you died. Next thing I know, she isn't living at home anymore. Luiz isn't ever available to hang out, and Andrea asked me to help her track Luiz's phone. I refused until she told me that she thought you were alive and Luiz was secretly meeting with you. The moment Kendra asked about a secure phone, I knew it was all true."

"Why did it take you this long to call?"

"I didn't know how to call you. These are secure phones designed to be untraceable. Over the next few days after my conversation with Kendra, I added the companies that ordered phones to a list. We sell the phone, but the phone company provides a bank of numbers, which for security reasons, aren't directly linked to your phone. I also downloaded the full list of phone numbers given out by the phone company during those days. Then I logged which of those numbers hit cell towers in the Salt Lake Valley and were routed to our secure system. A second bank of numbers—owned by us—links the secure phones to our system. But the assigned number changes after every phone call or daily. Tracing a phone call from outside always ends at our data center. But I had inside access. Still, we have a lot of customers. I cross-referenced all the ESNs manufactured by our company with our bank of numbers the past few days."

"ESNs?" I interrupted.

"Electronic Serial Numbers for cellphones," he answered. "I narrowed it down to twenty-three phone numbers. Luiz's cell phone was in the same vicinity as three of those ESNs far too often for it to be a coincidence."

"You did all that?"

"Well, my dad's dev team had already written a lot of the tools. We are always trying to hack our secure phones so we can make them more secure. I did customize some of our tools to find you," an air of pride filled his voice.

"How long have you been tracking us?"

"Triangulating the location of the three cell phones," he corrected me. "The three of you visited the prison where your mom is being held, then you stopped in North Salt Lake at Club, uh," he paused, "well, that can't be right?"

He was about to say Club Exposed, but he couldn't believe it. He probably assumed his triangulation was slightly off.

"You didn't finish explaining how you found my number," I distracted him.

"I added myself to the list of numbers allowed to call these three numbers. When this cell phone went off alone, I called to see who would answer. I know you only said, 'Hello,' but you have a distinct voice, Jake."

What was I going to do? Should I drag Kevin into this dark world with me? My mom and sister were in jail because of me. Should I lie and tell him this was all a hoax? Not that he would believe me. Maybe I could convince him not to get involved. He didn't know about druids, nightwalkers, transients, or water babies. Of course, he would have heard of vampires, voodoo witches, and zombies, but he probably didn't know they were real. More creatures existed, too. Many creatures were rare, like Ariel. Eldra knew of dozens of monsters that could pass for human and many more that couldn't.

Eight billion people populated our world. Before the Day of a Thousand Deaths, there were just over a thousand known druids, which is only 0.0000125 percent (1 in 10 million) of the world's population. That number was so small, they could hide in plain sight. Lexy's grandfather had a vampire registry, and there were just under ten thousand vampires in it—ten times the number of druids. Still, they only made up one per million of everyone. Her grandfather believed that vampires were more numerous than all other monsters combined. So, doubled, only two per million were monsters. A person would have to meet a half-million other people before, statistically, they would have met a single druid, vampire, or other monster-like creature. Even then, most looked and acted human. Statistically, a regular person like Kevin just wouldn't know that druids and monsters exist unless someone told them. Even then, most people wouldn't believe it without proof of their existence. Letting Kevin know I was alive was one thing. Telling him I was a druid and introducing him to other human subspecies—some monsters— and letting him know they were real was quite another.

"You still there, Jake?"

I hadn't said anything to Kevin for some time, lost in thought and indecision. Ariel watched my reflection in the rearview mirror. "I'm still here."

"Can I meet you?"

"I don't know."

"Well, I'm triangulating your position, Jake. You're parked on a side street by the capitol building. Your phone and two others spend most of their time at a house in Bountiful. If you don't agree to meet me, I can just show up there."

"When do you want to meet?"

"Now."

"I have to pick up Kendra and Alexis in a bit, then we are going to the University of Utah Hospital to see," I almost said O'Brien's name, but I stopped and just said, "a friend."

"What building? Is there a room number?" Kevin asked eagerly.

"The new building for spinal injuries. Wait for us in the gift shop."

"I'll be there as soon as I can."

"No rush. I still have to pick up the girls."

"About that," Kevin asked. "Is my triangulation off, or are the girls at, uh," Kevin hesitated again. His inability to say either Club Exposed or strip club seemed so naïve and childish to me. Had my experiences over the past two weeks matured me in such a way that Kevin and I were at different levels?

"Club Exposed. Yep."

"Kendra's at a strip club," Kevin chuckled. "That I would like to see."

"Is that so, Kevin?" I questioned with a suggestive, sarcastic voice.

"No. That, uh, I mean, not, uh, stripping, but, uh, just there," Kevin stammered almost unintelligibly.

Imagining Kendra stripping probably hadn't been on his mind. Of course, he meant seeing her as a patron, not as a stripper. Kevin was far more religious than I was. He went to church every Sunday and liked it. He was always talking about going on a two-year service mission to some foreign country. Kendra shared his firm convictions. Yet, she'd recently stripped off her shirt in front of me. She'd also run into the strip club in only her bra. Her faith had wavered early this morning. I decided against telling Kevin all that.

"See you in a half-hour, Kevin," I hung up while he was still floundering out an apology.

What would Kevin think when he saw my thin figure and hideous skin? What would Alexis and Kendra think when they turned off their separation stones? I could be in trouble.

I also needed a shirt. I couldn't meet Kevin, let alone visit O'Brien, bare-chested. I circled around the capitol building, then drove back toward Club Exposed to pick up Kendra and Lexy.

CHAPTER 9
VISITING O'BRIEN

We shall visit Charles O'Brien today. I am providing him the best care money can buy. Even paralyzed, he could be an asset. He can both still shoot and share his wisdom from a wheelchair. Jake needs him. Will he join us willingly, or will he force me to use my allure to keep him from leaving? —Alexis

As I drove west, the tall Wasatch Mountains hid above the reflection in my rearview mirror. In front of me, the blue sky met the blue of the Great Salt Lake. Two suns glared from the west, one in the sky and one reflecting off the water. As I drove, both suns moved with me, reminding me that some forces in this world are inescapable.

I pulled into Club Exposed and found Lexy and Kendra waiting. Lexy was on the phone. Both wore matching black, long-sleeved, button-up cowgirl blouses with pink thread, clones of the shirt Alexis had borrowed the other day. The place had once had a dozen of them from a matching costume set, but now only had two left—size medium. Lexy had borrowed the remaining large the other day, so at five-foot-ten—way above average height for a girl—the medium stretched around her figure. She'd left two buttons—actually they were snaps—undone at the top, exposing her cleavage, and one snap undone at the bottom, exposing her navel. On Kendra, while the blouse hugged her shape, it fit with the expected snaps fastened. Lexy also wore the matching pink cowgirl hat, but Kendra didn't. Alexis had taken the last one.

Was I analyzing their outfits because of Eldra or because they were stripper shirts?

Kendra walked to my door and offered me a black hoodie sweater. I guess the strip club did have a top I could borrow. Of course, the front of it had two silhouette pinup girls on each side of the Club Exposed logo.

Lexy walked to the passenger seat, still on the phone. "Thank you for the call, Bishop."

"Is that the bishop from church, or someone who happens to be named Bishop?" I asked Kendra.

"Bishop from church," she sighed, glancing back at the building she'd just walked out of. She tapped off her separation stone, sharing her crisis of faith with me.

Why didn't I feel dirty after visiting the strip club? She wondered. *Sure, we hadn't gone into the front, where the exotic dancing happened, but we'd been in dressing rooms as they prepped.*

So? You're on the drill team. You're in and out of the girls locker room all the time, I defended her.

Their dance outfits are designed to come off piece by piece, and they did a lot more prepping naked than in an average locker room. They had a warm-up pole in the dressing room.

Lexy had consumed three pints, one each from three dancers. Neither Jody nor Gina had been there, so Kendra had felt awkward at first; not awkward for being in a strip club, awkward because she didn't know the other dancers well. Kendra had talked with them about life as if they weren't about to dance naked on a stage. She'd forgotten that what she was doing as against her religion's values until the bishop called.

Yes, Kendra had tried out the pole. Her mental images, which she had been indifferent to moments ago, now embarrassed her; especially her interaction with a girl who had golden-brown hair in a pixie cut and could have passed as Kendra's sister. Alice— dancer name, Malice.

I gave her tips on dance moves! She now imagined her using those dance moves in the front of the strip club.

I'm not sure what I even believe anymore. Who am I? Kendra begged for my help, but I had no help to give.

"Sorry, but a visit tonight will not work. We . . ." Lexy paused and glanced back at Club Exposed. Was she going to tell him where she was?

Please no! Kendra pleaded.

"We are not home," Lexy finished, then sat in the passenger seat and closed the door.

Kendra and I sighed with relief as she hung up.

Lexy's wound had closed, but inside, the tissue and radial bone were still healing. Kendra kicked me out of the driver's seat, which I didn't mind. I didn't have a driver's license, despite being a month from turning eighteen, while Kendra, just barely sixteen, already had her learner's permit. I moved to the back seat by Ariel.

Lexy disabled her separation stone, and with both their separation stones disabled, it didn't take the girls long to learn that Lexy wasn't the only one to receive an unexpected phone call. They perused my memory of Kevin's call.

"I told you so," Alexis verbally tossed the words at Kendra, who took the brunt of responsibility for Kevin's sleuthing. "'I asked Kevin on the sly,'" Alexis imitated Kendra's voice, mocking her. She continued to regale her mentally, asking, *Do you even know what sly means?*

I did my best to stay out of it, letting Alexis blame Kendra and letting Kendra defend herself. They were big girls. They didn't need me involved in every little mental spat between them. Besides, I was busy stressing out about Sis's arrest.

Lexy's phone buzzed—a text.

Who's it from?

Her mind flashed an image of a man walking down the Vegas strip with a dozen women behind him.

Who is the guy on the Vegas strip? I asked.

The top vampire in the United States, Lexy answered before she could tap off her separation stone.

"Please do not pry, Jake," Alexis requested from the passenger seat, glancing back at me with the mirror in the visor.

Through Lexy's reflection, I met her eyes. I hadn't been prying. She had simply let that thought slip.

"I am not trying to keep secrets. I am trying to protect you." She broke our eye contact to glance at Kendra. "Both of you."

"As your generals, isn't it our job to protect you?"

"Can we not protect each other?"

"Fine," Kendra and I answered in unison.

Once we arrived at the University of Utah Hospital, we pulled into a stall on the parking garage's first floor. The dark asphalt, gray cement pillars, and low, concrete ceilings darkened the garage's interior, making the outside sunlight seem too bright.

"Should I have worn my bulletproof vest?" I wondered aloud. My question went unanswered.

"How does the back of my head look?" Ariel asked, unwrapping Kendra's soiled blouse—which no longer looked cream-colored—and turning to show Alexis the back of her head.

"Your hair covers the wound," Alexis answered.

Ariel nodded, satisfied, and she followed as we made our way out of the parking garage. We passed a trash bin, and the ancient little girl threw Kendra's shirt into it.

"Ah. I liked that shirt," Kendra pouted her lips.

Alexis stopped and pulled up her phone, a mischievous smile on her face. "I can order you a new one from Aeropostale online. I shall order it on the sly," she winked and giggled at Kendra as she finished, "so you will never guess."

"Let's just keep walking." Kendra continued past Alexis, moving more quickly than my tender ankle wanted her to.

We nodded at the security guard at the front desk. My excitement mixed with dread as we neared the gift shop where we were to meet Kevin. Even wearing a hoodie, I couldn't hide my physical state from him. How would he react? Would I be prepared to see pity in his eyes? Did I have it in me to explain what happened again? We saw Kevin before he saw us. He stood with his back to us, looking at knickknacks. *Knickknacks?* Another word I'd never used before. Surely, that word came from Eldra. Kevin wore a short-sleeved, white, button-up shirt with blue squares. Untucked, the shirt covered the top of his khaki shorts, which hung too loose on his long but thin legs. He'd pushed his long socks down so that they bunched up at the top of his low Nikes. He should have worn ankle socks. My critique of his outfit also came from Eldra.

"Kevin," Alexis called his name.

He turned and smiled. Sweat glistened off his forehead, proving he was nervous. Lexy's pumpkin-spice allure flared to life, restoring her control over Kevin. I'd forgotten she'd taken control of my family and friends—jeeks included.

"We are visiting a friend. Come with us. Stay silent," Alexis ordered.

Kevin nodded and obeyed.

"You didn't even let him say hi to me." I scowled at Alexis.

We took the elevator to the seventh floor. As soon as I exited the elevator, the hospital smell hit my nose. I wanted to hold my breath. The whiteness of the tile floor and walls felt unnatural. A painted line marked the path for visitors to follow.

O'Brien had changed rooms. A gunshot had shattered the window in the room he was in previously, so changing rooms made sense. He was now in room 713. Interesting room number. Did the lucky number seven counteract the unlucky number thirteen? I wasn't superstitious, but Eldra was. To both ancient Egyptians and tarot card readers, thirteen meant death. To this day, Eldra refused to schedule a salon appointment on the thirteenth.

80

The tall police officer with a dark, bald head, the one whom Alexis had ordered to watch over O'Brien, leaned against the wall just outside O'Brien's door. He hadn't shirked his duty but sat watchfully, already wary of our approach. He gave me an apprehensive look, his gaze traveling from my hideous face under my hoodie to the provocative decor of my sweater. His eyes thinned, suggesting he assumed me a threat.

"He is awake," the officer told Alexis.

"Let Jake go in alone," Alexis suggested. "O'Brien doesn't trust strangers."

Alexis took in the surrounding room. She glanced to the nurse's station and around at all the exits, checking the place out. She remembered the Skull Shadows' attempt on O'Brien's life, and she planned to be ready this time.

"He still thinks you are an *it*," I reminded her.

"Am I an *it*, too?" Ariel asked, her face tilted questioningly.

"Without a doubt." I smiled at her as if she really were just a nine-year-old girl. She smiled back.

If Alexis hadn't said for me to go in, the officer wouldn't have let me near the door. He still eyed me warily, and his hand moved to rest on the firearm at his hip.

I went inside O'Brien's room alone.

I'd seen a dozen hospital rooms like this one. To the right, O'Brien lay on a hospital bed with white linens and medical equipment in place of a headboard. A door to a bathroom hung half-open on the left. Just past it, a thirty-inch flatscreen TV hung directly across from the hospital bed for easy viewing—except it was off. On the far wall, a couch sat under a large window that let in the daylight and provided a view of the mountain's face north of the building.

"Jake?" O'Brien lay back in his bed, not moving but awake. "What happened to you?"

"A spell. You're looking at the side effects."

He nodded.

"How are you?" I asked.

"Better," he lied.

He wasn't better. Do paraplegics ever get better? "Glad to hear it," I didn't call him out on his lie.

"I thought you were dead."

"You're the one who faked my death. Did you forget?"

He grinned. "After that, I thought . . ." he swallowed. A single vein stood out on his left temple. He was straining to speak to me. "I thought the nightwalker killed you."

81

He should remember more than he did, shouldn't he? He'd been under Alexis's control at the Cabin Battle of Bear Lake, almost too soon after the nightwalker's attack. Had he ever been fully lucid?

"You don't remember anything after that?" I asked.

O'Brien blinked in thought. "I'm not sure."

"What is the last thing you remember?"

"The nightwalker."

"Do you remember anything after that? Alexis's mansion?"

"The dhampir?" O'Brien questioned. "It wasn't a dream?"

"Nope. She's real but only half-dhampir."

"You yelled at me for calling her an *it*."

I sighed in relief. O'Brien *did* remember some of it.

"What about the cabin at Bear Lake?" I prodded further. "Alexis's grandfather and his generals attacked us."

He blinked. "It—she—the dhampir can't be trusted. She took control of my mind and . . ." he had to swallow.

"O'Brien," I didn't let him continue, "she saved my life."

His eyes thinned.

"She saved your life, too. She brought you here and is covering your medical bills."

"You can't trust her," he shook his head.

"She stood up to her grandfather," I added. "He tried to kill her. To kill us. We survived. Don't you remember?"

He shook his head.

"You don't know how a creature like that thinks," he countered. "You can't trust it."

"I do trust her," I answered. "I know exactly what she thinks."

His eyes closed for a long second, and the vein on his left temple swelled. "Take my hand."

I took it, and magic flowed from his hand into me, so faint I almost didn't detect it. The magic eased all my concerns, assuring me that O'Brien was trustworthy and urging me to listen to him. He'd told me that his only magic was sniper accuracy. Did he know he could use emotional magic?

"If it—she—has taken control of your mind, you can fight it."

I shook my head, but he gripped my hand more firmly.

"You have the power to fight off her control. If you hear her thoughts—"

"I'm not under Alexis's control. That isn't how I know what she thinks."

"Then, how?"

"*Myndtíegan*," I pronounced the Old English word clearly.

Both his eyebrows raised in disbelief.

"With both Alexis and Kendra. We call it the Trinity of Mind."

"Jake," O'Brien shook his head. "It's a trick. It's—she's controlling your thoughts."

"What makes you think that?"

"Because you can't join three minds," his eyes fixed on me with certainty. "If you join three minds, you will all go insane."

Eldra had said something similar. Still, we hadn't gone insane. Yet.

"Is that true if we joined it under a life and death situation? That forced us to work together to survive?"

"That wouldn't . . ." he trailed off.

"Is that true if I'm a protector?"

He didn't have an answer.

"Is that true if I was in a coma for days and before I woke, Eldra had given Alexis and Kendra separation stones?"

He looked away. He didn't know how to answer me because none of that had ever happened before.

"I am not hers," I assured him. I looked into his eyes. I leaned my hideous face close to him. "Look in my eyes. You will know. Use the sight."

O'Brien couldn't cast sight on himself, but it had been cast on him before by Caradoc. I held the memory in my mind as I gave him the enhanced ability to see all types of light.

Kendra, Alexis, come here, please. Alexis followed Kendra into the room. They came and stood next to me, Kendra on my right and Alexis on my left.

"Now, look at Kendra. Look at Alexis."

Even though I didn't push sight into my own eyes, I knew from prior experience that a hazy connection existed between Kendra and Alexis and myself. O'Brien saw all three of us up close. Seeing the Trinity of Mind caused him to blink rapidly. He knew.

I removed the sight.

"Who is that?" O'Brien pointed at Ariel, who was peeking in the doorway.

"Her?" I winked at our mythic monster, and she came into the room, followed by Kevin. "She is definitely an *it*. Just ask her." Ariel smiled at us. We'd had this conversation just outside the door. Disturbingly, Coyote's granddaughter found being called an *it* a compliment. "She can be trusted to try to keep me alive, but only because her life depends on it." As I looked into Ariel's eyes, I realized I trusted her. Was whatever evil she once had gone? Either ripped from her or trapped so deep in her subconscious it would never escape? Hopefully.

"We must speak of more important matters," Alexis interjected. "O'Brien. They want to operate again. It is risky, but Jake has a plan that might work."

I hadn't consciously discussed this plan with either Kendra or Alexis, but I hadn't had to. I thought about it often. O'Brien's eyes, filled with distrust, settled on Lexy.

"With the sight, I can see when a backbone works and when it doesn't," I answered. "I have a vial of Bones of Steel. If the doctor gets your vertebrae aligned, and you drink it, your spine will lock in the correct place for however long it lasts, and with the healing stone, it should fuse enough to stay there."

"It is completely your decision," Alexis assured O'Brien, "but you should know the risks. With the surgery, the doctors believe there is a chance that you may recover some movement. If they operate, you have more than a one-in-ten chance of not waking up."

"Operate," O'Brien didn't hesitate. The distrust left his eyes, replaced by emotions that I recognized in myself. Giving up my quality of life was proving more difficult than giving up my life. A part of me still wished that I had died at the Cabin Battle of Bear Lake. Instead, I became this scarred thing. O'Brien would rather die than live his life as a paraplegic. I wasn't sure he would feel that way forever. Even ugly, I still felt happiness, and an ounce of happiness validates even a lesser quality of life. Paraplegic or not, O'Brien could have happiness. Not to mention we needed him. His life held value to me.

Alexis stood and said, "I will inform the doctor," then left the room.

I pulled out Eldra's leather book. "How would you like to hear about the Cabin Battle at Bear Lake?" I asked.

O'Brien nodded.

Kevin stepped closer to listen with interest as well.

I read, pausing only when a nurse came to visit. O'Brien stayed awake until after the part where we subdued the Vampire King with Carina's help. He fell asleep without hearing that Mr. Espinoza had woken a vampire or that Eldra woke up free of Dane's control. Perhaps on the next visit, I would finish reading it to him.

The story also served to bring Kevin partially up to speed. He didn't have the details of the occurrences before or after the Cabin Battle of Bear Lake, but it would probably take him a bit to digest what he had heard.

We said our goodbyes and promised to come again soon. As we walked out of O'Brien's room, Alexis's phone rang.

"Alexis, come home," Jody urged on the other end of the phone, her voice shaking. "We need you now."

CHAPTER 10
MR. ESPINOZA

Football practice starts tomorrow morning. I'm so excited. I love football. I do have concerns. I can barely run. My looks will turn heads at the school, and not in a good way. How will the football team treat me? High school is very unfriendly to those who are different. What senior would want to start a new high school looking like I do? —Jake

"Meet us at the mansion," Alexis told Kevin before dashing toward the elevators. Kendra sprinted after her. I started to run, but my ankle ached and I lost my breath, forcing me to stop after only a dozen yards. As I caught my breath, Ariel waited with me. Kendra and Lexy were long gone by the time we reached the elevators. When Ariel and I finally exited the building, Alexis sat in the driver's seat of the BMW 335i next to the curb right outside the entry doors, so we hurried and jumped in the back.

Alexis tried to set a land speed record on the way home. She also tried to run as many red lights as possible. Fears flooded into all three of us as we remembered the prior trouble at the mansion when the caplatas had killed and turned some of the servants into voodoo zombie puppets. Alexis had removed their heads. We hoped to avoid a similar experience, especially with Jody and Carl there. Could we bear it if something tragic happened to either of them?

The bottom of the setting sun nearly touched the mountains to the west. That didn't bode well. Sunset is when dark things wake. Did the approaching sunset have something to do with Jody's call? Alexis screeched the tires as she sped around the curves on Eaglewood Drive. The curves tossed us left and right, but our seat belts kept us from flying into each other. I gripped the handle above the car window so tightly that my blue-green veins popped out on my splotchy white wrist. What would we find at the mansion? Even Ariel seemed worried. She'd begun to bond with Carl—er, CJ. Did she have the ability to care for the boy? I wasn't sure yet.

A few minutes later, Alexis pulled into the garage, hitting the brakes to keep from crashing into the inside wall. In a movie, the tires would have screeched like a banshee, but this was real life, where a BMW had antilock brakes, and uh, were banshees real or not? Eldra didn't believe banshees were real, but her husband did. The jolt threw me forward so hard that my palms slapped the back of the front seat. The seat belt stopped my forward momentum, and my head whiplashed.

With graceful speed and before I had even opened the rear door, Alexis lithely slipped out the car door and darted into the house. Kendra and Ariel both made it inside before me. Alexis sprinted so far ahead of us that we wouldn't have been able to follow her if not for the Trinity of Mind. The garage jutted out on the southeast of the house on the second floor. Alexis headed to the northwest side on the first floor—the other side of the mansion—to a room I knew well: the in-home gym.

Eerie quiet hung thick in the air. As we moved from one end of the mansion to the other, nobody crossed our path. There should have been a number of people at the house, but we found no one. Not a servant. Not Jody. Not Carl. Not the two former Skull Shadows turned into Lexy's thralls. Nobody. Where were they?

Alexis arrived, and she mentally shared the source of trouble with us. We saw the man-creature's fanged-face turned from a wooden door it scratched at to Lexy, who stood a hallway's length away, the sight—even through the Trinity of Mind—bit fear into us. It just took us a bit longer to get there—twenty-seven seconds. Yes, I counted. Ariel and Kendra could have left me behind, but they stayed with me, matching the "blazing speed" of my hurried walk. I used to be the fastest football player on my team. Now, I'd be lucky to be the fastest in an assisted living facility for the elderly.

Alexis took slow, cautious steps toward the man-creature, but not cautious enough. It—he attacked. As we turned down the final hallway, it—he attacked. Alexis ducked and spun away from a bare arm that swung so fast we could barely track its speed with our eyes. The arm missed but knocked her pink cowgirl hat off her head and it landed next to the closed door to the gym. Alexis ran up the left wall, half-flipped over her attacker so that her feet touched the ceiling, then accelerated her descent by thrusting downward while completing her flip to land on her feet.

Whoa! That move put her behind the man-thing, who growled, his face like an angry demon's below his messy black hair. His mouth hung open, exposing his extended fangs, which were far longer than Lexy's. His fierce eyes tracked Lexy; black eyes with blood lines spreading from the irises out into the sclera and behind the eyelids. He wore no clothes at all, and we had arrived just in time for a full frontal, and he would have just woken up, so, uh . . .

"Gross, Mr. Espinoza!" Kendra shouted and covered her eyes.

Kendra's shout drew Mr. Espinoza's attention. As his eyes focused on her, his tongue hungrily flattened between his two fangs. A few days ago, while visiting O'Brien, the Skull Shadows had shot Alexis twice, and due to the resulting blood loss, she had briefly turned feral and lost her humanity. Mr. Espinoza behaved far more animalistic now than Alexis had behaved then.

Just as he took his first step toward Kendra, Alexis wrapped him in a headlock with her right arm, lifted him off the ground, and pulled him backward. She put the palm of her left hand on Mr. Espinoza's cheek. Her allure battled his as fiercely as she battled him physically. He elbowed Alexis's ribs multiple times. Through the Trinity of Mind, we felt when a rib cracked low on her left side. *Ouch!* He lurched up and came back down, his bare foot smashing her pink hat flat. Had he always had such hairy toes? He reached around and grabbed the side of her black blouse, his claws ripping a section of material away above her right hip. Didn't he know that stripper shirts had snaps and ripping wasn't necessary?

He thrust backward and slammed Lexy against the wall opposite the oak door, knocking down a large, framed picture that depicted various famous athletes' caricatures. Lexy grunted in pain as the frame hit the floor, shattering glass. Mr. Espinoza slammed Lexy against the wall a second time, and as he did, his heel kicked through Muhammad Ali's face, and the broken glass cut the bottom of his heel. Lexy grunted in pain again.

A part of me wanted to erase Luiz's dad. I pulled in magic, but I couldn't justify doing that to Luiz unless he escaped Lexy's grip and came at Kendra. So instead, I reached out a hand and sucked the magic from Mr. Espinoza's allure just as Eldra had sucked magic from us. His allure faded to nothing more than a mild scent of soap, allowing Lexy's still magic-infused pumpkin spice to become the dominant allure.

One, two, three, I started counting to see how long it would take Lexy's allure to overcome Mr. Espinoza. As I counted, he left bloody footprints on the floor while Alexis absorbed a few more hits to the ribs, which made all three of us wince. *Eight, nine, ten.* Mr. Espinoza didn't look anywhere near ready to give in. He thrashed and spun. He bent forward, lifting Lexy's feet off the ground, then jumped backward, trying to come down on his back on top of Lexy, but she twisted, and they landed on their sides. *Fifteen, sixteen.* Mr. Espinosa struggled to get free, but Alexis took the hit from the floor without loosening the headlock, though her other hand no longer touched his cheek. He rolled over Lexy and onto his feet, but she rose with him and restored her palm to his cheek. She augmented her allure, forcing it into him. Kendra and I felt our protection stones warm. *Twenty-one*, I counted just as Mr. Espinoza's body went still. As Lexy held him, his eyes faded to a solid red, and he surrendered control.

Why did he take so long to submit? Lexy wondered.

Neither Kendra nor I had an answer for her.

The door to the mansion's workout gym remained closed. All the doors in the house—actually, all doors in each of the Vampire King's mansions—were cut and carved from two flat slabs of solid oak glued to each side of a metal sheet. Had this door been hollow or soft wood, it would have been in pieces. Two fist-sized dents marked the middle of two large cracks. Another crack in the doorjamb ran down its entire length. The sheetrock on each side had multiple fist-sized dents. Metal sheeting also lined the walls under the sheetrock due to an every-room-is-a-panic-room mentality.

Ariel rushed to the door, pulled down the bent handle, and pushed, but the door didn't budge. She knocked and shouted through the door with her high-pitched, nine-year-old girl voice, "Alexis subdued him."

We heard movement, including the sound of weightlifting bars hitting the floor before the door swung open. Kendra and I followed Ariel inside while Alexis pulled Mr. Espinoza away.

Jody, Carolyn, and Gina each held a weightlifting bar, the kind used for a bench press, vertically, as if they were monks with quarterstaffs, ready to spin them in defense. Arcs dented both the foam puzzle floor and the inside of the oak door where they had wedged those bars. The two former Skull Shadows—Pasha, the Russian, and Sajid, the Middle Easterner—kneeled in the middle of the room, their AR-15s tight to their shoulders, aimed at the door. Seeing us, they stood and lowered their weapons. From behind them, Carl ran to his mom and hugged her hip. Lillian glanced toward Alexis then looked down to the ground. A rope tied each of Mr. Espinoza's six thralls to the universal gym.

Sweat glistened on Jody's forehead, and a few strands of her red hair stuck to it. She wore a cheap, sleeveless blouse with a teardrop opening revealing her cleavage, and a hem that ended two inches above her bargain-brand, low-rise jeans to show off her midriff. Gray socks covered her shoeless feet.

Gina wore Gucci sneakers and jeans. The jeans hugged her hips in a perfect fit. A red camisole with white lace at the top stretched around her chest. Decorating her neck, a simple chain with a pendant read *"Daddy's Girl"* in silver cursive. I'd almost forgotten she came from Texas oil money.

The thralls each dressed in similar outfits: calf-length leggings and a tunic that hung to the top of their thighs, though the colors varied. Star had chosen maize-yellow for her leggings and an ash-gray for her top.

I mentally forced myself to stop analyzing everyone's outfits.

Through the wall of windows, the crest of the sun dropped behind the western mountains that rose above the Great Salt Lake. As the day died, the sky bled a pool of red that spread across the sky, making the few cirrus clouds look like giant claw marks. Had we arrived any later, we might have found the wall of windows splattered, blood spreading across the floor to match the sky, and dead bodies as clawed as the cirrus clouds. The last vestiges of the sun and the oak door combined with Lexy's fast driving had allowed us—well, her—to save everyone from the very massacre that the sunset predicted.

Alexis held Mr. Espinoza's hand as she stepped inside the door, the subdued vampire leaving a bloody mark everywhere he put his left foot. He was still naked, and since mirrors lined three of the walls, there was nowhere to look to avoid the sight of him.

"He woke before sunset, Princess," Lillian spoke, looking down. "His thralls arrived in this room early, as you requested. We gathered the others to join them when the motion alarm sounded."

What alarm? Kendra and I asked simultaneously.

In my bedchamber, we installed a motion alarm to alert us if Miguel wakes before an hour after sunset. Newly turned vampires can get overly agitated if the sun is still up.

I'd almost forgotten that Miguel was Luiz's dad's first name.

Why are the thralls tied up? Kendra wondered, eyeing them.

To keep them from rushing to their deaths, Alexis answered. *As his thralls, they wouldn't hesitate to offer him their lives. In a frenzied hunger like this one, Miguel would have torn them limb from limb.*

Alexis turned to the Russian, pointing toward the thralls, and ordered, "Untie them." Pasha hurried first to Star and untied her from the universal gym, then moved to the next thrall, Maria, whose wrists hung in a Y from the pullup bars. Alexis calmly turned to Jody and said, "You should take Carl to his room now." Jody didn't move, so Ariel took CJ's hand. Jody opened her mouth as if she wanted to speak, but she hesitated and closed it. Ariel led her friend to the door, giving Mr. Espinoza a wide berth. Carl stopped at the doorway, looking back, knowing Mr. Espinoza was about to feed and morbidly wanting to watch. Had we intended not to tell him about vampires? If so, that ship had sailed. Ariel picked up Lexy's pink hat and tried to pop up the flattened crown, but the permanent creases left it ruined.

Alexis brought Mr. Espinoza further into the room and led him away from the entrance toward Star.

"Bring Miguel some clothes," Alexis ordered Lillian and Carolyn. "Then take an hour's extra sleep and tomorrow morning off for successfully keeping everyone alive." The servants nodded. Both failed to hide their smiles as they hustled from the room.

Mr. Espinoza stopped in front of Star, his body a rigid, naked statue, waiting for Lexy's permission before moving further. Star sat down on the center of a leather-covered workout bench and offered her wrist. Maria sat down next to her as if getting in line for her turn.

"One pint," Alexis ordered Mr. Espinoza. Alexis shook her head at Maria, who flattened her lips in disappointment.

Luiz's dad glanced at Kendra as if wishing he could rip his one pint from her. Instead, he sat next to Star and bit into her offered wrist. With naked Mr. Espinoza's lips against her, Star closed her eyes and sucked in a deep breath as if the two of them were starring in *Fifty Shades of Gross*. I had laid on that leather-covered bench multiple times. Seeing Mr. Espinoza's naked ass on it made me glad I usually wore a tank top when I worked out. Still, I'd have the servants lather the leather with Lysol.

Jody opened and closed her mouth, deciding for the second time not to speak her mind. She walked to the doorway and sternly sent her son and Ariel away but didn't follow them. Instead, she waited in the doorway until they were out of earshot, then turned back to Alexis. She hadn't decided against speaking her mind; she'd simply decided to send her son away before she did.

"I 'preciate yer offer to mother y'all," Jody started, "but I won't put Carl in danger again. Stay'n might not be best."

"Weaning a recently-turned vampire off overfeeding on his new thralls when he wakes is dangerous work," Alexis responded. "It only takes a week. He has woken more than an hour after sunset every night since being turned. His early waking was unlikely. Still, the thralls followed the plan. The alarm notified the servants to lead you to safety. Also, I will be here an hour before sunset for the rest of the week," Alexis assured.

Jody nodded. "I'll consider stay'n then, but all the same, for the next li'l bit, I'll take Carl out at night till y'all call." Jody's red hair flung away from her shoulders as she turned abruptly and headed down the hall out of sight.

Her decision to consider staying surprised me. In front of the bloodred sunset over the smooth, dark abyss of the Great Salt Lake, a naked Mr. Espinoza fed from Star. The mirrored walls reflected that same scene in triplicate, which had been Jody's view from the doorway. It had to have freaked her out. I had expected her to grab her son, rush out of here, and never come back. Alexis chose *not* to influence her in any way. To stay or not was all Jody's decision. Could she really be leaning toward staying?

The doorbell rang. Kevin had arrived.

CHAPTER 11
ELDRA'S MEMORIAL

Killing Eldra's husband forever changed me. I think about it all the time. I have nightmares where I blast a magic missile at him, after which, Eldra holds his lifeless body, crying and asking me why. Despite what I did, Eldra gave her life for us. For me. I feel obligated to repay her somehow, but she's gone, so I can't. I can't help but feel that if I hadn't killed her husband, she'd have found a way to survive. —Kendra

Carolyn escorted Kevin to Eldra's room, where I sat waiting at the desk. I looked up at him and met his nervous eyes. On his forehead, where his hair met his brow, a wet strip of skin shone from left to right where he must have just wiped his sweat.

There was so much that I wanted to say to him, but I said nothing. What could I say? I hadn't faked my death; O'Brien had done that, so apologizing for it didn't sound right. Had I contacted him, I would have put him at risk, so I couldn't apologize for that either without lying. I hadn't known Kevin as long as Luiz. With Luiz and I, we became friends so young that I don't even remember meeting him, while I clearly remember meeting Kevin. He had attended a different elementary school, so Luiz and I met him on the first day of middle school. Back in seventh grade, Luiz and I were scrawny geeks, and Kevin may have out-scrawnied us. We had arrived early to get seats in the back of the class. Kevin had arrived fifteen minutes late. Nobody had wanted to sit by Luiz and me because we were geeks with cooties. The only seats available were the two in front of us, so he sat in one but didn't talk to us. At lunch, Kevin stood nervous and scared in the middle of the cafeteria. Luiz noticed and asked him to sit with us. We'd been friends ever since.

What could I say to a friend who spent the past few weeks thinking I was dead? Well, despite the influence of Alexis and

Kendra, or having lived every detail of Eldra's two-hundred-year life like a one-second movie, I was still a guy. So, naturally, I ignored the issue entirely.

"Eldra used your dad's software, Encrypted Contact," I gestured to the laptop on the desk, "and I don't have her fingerprint."

Kevin grinned a giant grin. "I can help with that."

Nothing fixes a broken friendship between geeks like solving a problem together.

"Dad has a process," he continued, "but one of the developers has to do it. He charges five thousand dollars to reset a fingerprint."

"I don't want anyone else involved." I almost said that I didn't have five thousand dollars, but I remembered just in time that I did. Princess Alexis paid her generals a salary. Still, I didn't want to spend it. "Can *you* do it?" I asked.

His grin widened. "Not here. I would have to do it at Dad's work. First, I need to get a debug version of Dad's software and turn on developer logging. Then, you need to create your own account using the debug software and set it up with a new cryptographic certificate pair and your fingerprint. After that, we can log in as Eldra with the incorrect fingerprint, breakpoint the code at the right place, and update the expected values to match yours. Once in, we can add a second fingerprint, make it primary, and then remove the old fingerprint."

Kevin continued explaining the interesting tech using many acronyms that, even being a geek, I was unfamiliar with. Kevin worked part-time for his dad and could already code at a professional level.

"I can take the laptop to my dad's work and bring it back when I'm done?"

"You want me to let you take it?" I hesitated. I had to decide if I trusted Kevin, and if so, how much did I trust him? Would he look at Eldra's data? Of course, he would investigate Eldra's secure messages, wanting to know what I was hiding from him. Even if I asked him not to, he would. Not to betray me, but to look for a way to help me. I did trust Kevin. Fully. He had my back. He would break my trust to try to help me, which could get him in trouble. I needed him to help me without me putting him at risk. Still, Eldra needed someone who could be a board member, run a large corporation, and make critical decisions. I was a lot of things, but not that.

"No. I'll bring the laptop another day," I decided. "I need to talk to your dad."

"My dad?"

"Yep," I answered. "Once you get me into Eldra's messages, I'll need your dad's help. Can you set up a meeting?"

"Who do I tell him he is meeting with?"

"He has to know some of it," I answered. "But don't you tell him. Just get him into a conference room with me, and I'll tell him what I need him to know."

"Jake," Kevin laughed. "If you tell him too much, he won't believe a word of it. I don't even . . ." he trailed off, as if realizing he had admitted too much.

Kevin had listened to the story of the Cabin Battle of Bear Lake that I'd read to O'Brien, but since he was under Lexy's control, it never occurred to me that he wouldn't believe it. The story would sound far-fetched without evidence. I considered casting fire light, but in the corner of Eldra's room, Robin's—Robier Locksley's—staff, Raijin, called to me with its reservoir of power.

"Raijin." I stretched out my hand and called for the staff, like Luke Skywalker calling for his lightsaber. It didn't flip end over end like Luke's lightsaber's pommel had. Instead, the staff lifted, remained vertical, and then flew quickly and smoothly into my hand.

I hadn't taken time to truly examine Raijin. It rose about a foot taller than Eldra's staff, Astrapí, and it fit my palm better. Etched boxes surrounded each rune, while on Astrapí, the runes had been carved without them. The boxes clarified the symbol, defining the spell. Locksley had been more powerful than Eldra, but he struggled with control. His magic would morph and change, often a single spell split in two parts, each part weaker than the intended spell. The boxes were a control aid to prevent that flaw. I didn't need the boxes around the runes, but perhaps Kendra should carry Astrapí from now on, as I would be carrying Raijin.

Kevin's jaw hung open with a partial grin, and he blinked at the staff in my hand. His nervous sweating had stopped, replaced by a glowing awe.

"It's all true. The magic. The druids. All of it. It's all true," I quoted Han Solo with appropriate modifications.

"So what about this Trinity of Mind?" he asked.

I looked at him. How would I explain this to a total computer jeek? "Imagine three computers without internet. The Trinity Mind is like networking them together."

"So you can talk to each other through it?"

"More than that. We have unlimited access to each other's thoughts and emotions. Like hard drives, the data in our brains is still ours, but we can look at each other's data any time. Of course, it is easiest to see the thoughts or memories that are in the front of my mind because, unlike data files on computers, our thoughts and memories aren't laid out in well-named folders or indexed for easy searching."

"That's weird. And you mentioned in your story to O'Brien an old guy's memories."

"Caradoc's," I confirmed. "Caradoc's memories are like hidden files except they randomly pop up unexpectedly. That's not the worst of it. A two-hundred-year-old druid downloaded all her memories into my head. Her memories are different. Imagine I had a ten-terabyte hard drive in my brain, and I'd only filled up half a terabyte so far, then she downloaded her memories into me and filled up the rest, so now my hard drive is out of space from her memories and ninety-five percent of my memories are hers." Hearing myself explain grew my worry. Was I only five percent me now?

"That's insane."

I noticed his comment could be taken as a double meaning. While having two other sets of minds and two other sets of memories sharing my head *was* crazy, he might think I was literally insane right now. Of course, with Eldra's memories, I was going crazy. It was a good thing she'd dumped her memories only into my brain. Kendra and Lexy could browse Eldra's memories any time through me, but her memories hadn't been downloaded into them.

"Cool crystal," Kevin pointed at the large red ruby hanging around my neck.

"You don't think it is a bit girly?" I asked.

Kevin shrugged. "I like it."

"Good. I have to wear it because it's enchanted."

"Really?"

I nodded and explained to him how a protection stone protected the wearer from vampire influence and other forms of mind control. I didn't mention that Alexis had her influence wrapped around Kevin and could control him at will. Would he guess that on his own?

"What else can you do?" Kevin asked.

Again, I considered showing Kevin fire light, but a knock came at the door.

"Maybe later," I answered. "Right now," I found my eyes watering and my voice choking up as I said the next words, "we are having a memorial for Eldra."

"Eldra?"

"The two-hundred-year-old who gave me the brain dump. She died. I'll explain another time." I stood and walked Kevin to the door. I considered inviting him, but he hadn't known Eldra. He wouldn't fit in. Being a jeek wasn't enough to include him in this. Both Kendra and Alexis agreed with my decision and were already waiting for me upstairs.

"You should probably get home," I suggested. "We'll swing by in the morning after . . ." I almost said after football practice. Eldra had registered me for high school at Woods Cross under an altered name, and she wanted me to start football practice in the morning with a school that would, later this year, compete with West Jordan High, the school Kevin would play for. Kevin probably started practice tomorrow as well. Practice would be six to eight, followed by a shower and drive time. We'd be to Kevin's dad's work by ten or so. "After ten."

I opened the door. Carolyn stood outside. If Kevin wondered why she wore servant's attire, he didn't ask. At least she no longer wore that obnoxious bonnet.

"Would you walk Kevin out, please?" I asked her, ignoring the fact that she'd been eavesdropping on us.

"Of course, Protector," Carolyn answered.

Kevin's eyes squinted when Carolyn called me a protector, but again, he didn't ask.

"See ya, Kev," I said the words like we were still close friends. The same way I had said them for years. In my world, where nothing seemed like it would be the same again, ever, it was nice to do something the same, even if it was the way I said a temporary goodbye.

"I'm still freaking out you're alive." Kevin started following Carolyn. "Don't forget. Tomorrow at ten."

I didn't want to walk with Kevin and Carolyn, so I took a different route through the mansion. I first went to my room and changed into the formal black tuxedo the servants had laid out on my bed. It had a bowtie? I could tie a regular tie, but not a bowtie. Not being a girl, it took me only a minute to change, after which, I made my way to the top floor of the house and to the large banquet room where Mr. Espinoza's thralls were helping the servants set up large dining tables. I passed through the large room and out to the balcony that overlooked the city of Bountiful.

The balcony was about twenty-five feet wide and twelve feet from the inside wall to the banister, which consisted of three-foot-high concrete walls separated by slightly taller and intricately decorated pillars every four feet. The balcony curved, shallower at the ends and arching further out in the middle. A potted spruce tree rose at each end. Large sliding glass doors separated it from the banquet hall. Three sets of matching outdoor patio sets, each two chairs and a table, were set up against the handrail, one on each end by the spruce trees and one in the middle.

Kendra and Alexis stood in the center of the balcony, their backs to me, surrounded by what looked to be a crowd. Andrea, Luiz, and Mr. Espinoza—now in control of himself—stood just to their left. Jody, Carl, and Ariel stood to their right. They'd each donned formal attire. I made a conscious effort to ignore the Eldra-inspired desire to scrutinize every article of clothing they wore and instead looked up to the dark, starry sky. I couldn't find the moon. Perhaps the mountains behind me hid its light. Or maybe the moon had simply donned the mountains like a black dress to join us in mourning Eldra's loss.

I walked out onto the large balcony and felt a slight breeze of August night air run over my stubbly scalp, warmer than the mansion's air-conditioned air. "Can one of you tie my bowtie?" I asked the girls. With the Trinity of Mind, Alexis had already turned toward me. I hadn't needed to ask verbally. She stepped close and tied it. As she did, I realized Eldra knew how to tie bowties. Had I had a moment when I was too much me for her memories to come through?

Lexy looked mesmerizing in her black leather dress. The last time she and I had stood together on this balcony, we had watched the fireworks on the Twenty-Fourth of July, a Utah state holiday that was a mini clone of the Fourth of July, only it celebrated the pioneers. The usual background buzz of Lexy's and Kendra's constant mental catfight had become smaller and smaller over the past couple of days. However, it flared back to life and rose to the forefront of the Trinity of Mind. Kendra's scathing eyes supported her raging thoughts.

You watched fireworks with Alexis! Her lips flattened to match her eyes as she clenched her teeth. *You ditched me for fireworks on the Fourth of July!*

It was true. Kendra had hoped to watch fireworks with me, but I'd blown her off. I'd ditched Sis, too, and she had scolded me good afterward.

Those are two completely unrelated holidays, I defended.

As Alexis finished tying my tie, she wore a mischievous grin that matched her emotions. It brought her so much pleasure that she had watched fireworks with me while Kendra hadn't. She couldn't hide her joy as it lit up both her face and the Trinity of Mind, which made it even that much more painful for Kendra. Lexy didn't even want to hide her joy. Instead, she focused on it, intentionally rubbing Kendra's nose in it.

It's Eldra's moment, I reminded both girls. But all the progress toward minimizing the mental buzz of their bickering had disappeared. Their catfighting was back in full force. It seemed petty to me, but not to Kendra. She and Sis had conspired for three months on plans for the Fourth of July, and it had been important to her. She knew she shouldn't be mad, but still, she was furious. This wasn't something she could hold in.

I pulled up the memory of the Lost Rhoades Mine. I focused on the scene where Eldra saved us from certain death as the surrounding water babies charged us. The aged woman leaped from the containment and her body lifted in the air. I shared with the girls my memory of how her body ripped itself apart and the memory of the pain, immense pain like nothing I'd ever felt. I focused on the image of her body as it split into pieces. Her clothes, skin, muscle, and organs—all but her bones—dissolved into magic to provide the spell needed. Eldra's every bone separated. Her ribs straightened, and the bones in her arms and legs split longways into dozens of shards. Her pelvis and skull both cracked into pieces. Each bone shard became an arrow, and we needed every last one of them to save our lives.

"It's Eldra's moment!" I raised both my voice and Locksley's staff, Raijin. Inside, I mentally growled at the girls, demanding they put aside their differences. *She earned it!*

Between my reprimand and memories, they should have stopped bickering, but they didn't. No. They couldn't. The Trinity of Mind wasn't something we were instantly experts at. It was a magic so complex we should have gone insane. Perhaps the bickering was just another form of unfiltered thoughts, echoing between them like the feedback from microphones too close together.

I shot three balls of fire from Raijin, and they launched into the air like fireworks, only they never exploded. They remained visible for over twenty seconds as they rose unimpeded toward space. The sight was enough to distract the girls. In fact, fireworks right now might be the perfect solution to stop their mental catfighting.

I stepped to Kendra and reached for her hand, but she pulled it away. "Hand," I snarled vocally and gave her a stern look. She reluctantly gave me her hand. As our fingers intertwined, I felt the loop that connected her fingerless glove to her middle finger. Those black lace gloves extended to her elbows. Her sleeveless dress left her arms bare while a matching black lace choker wrapped her neck, connected to more lace that continued down in a V that dove between her breasts, well below where she felt comfortable. Her three-inch heels added to her stature, so she only had to lift her eyes a few inches to meet mine.

My solution annoyed Alexis, but she acquiesced by stepping behind us and out of our view, tapping her separation stone.

I raised Raijin and shot four more fireballs, only this time different colors: red, yellow, green, and blue. We watched them until they, too, faded away.

"Yesterday, Eldra gave her life to save us," I elevated my voice, even giving it a hint of magic, so everyone on the balcony and in the large banquet hall would hear me.

Kendra raised her hand and created a glowing bubble about the size of a volleyball. It floated above her hand in the night air before lifting on the light breeze. She created more until five of them drifted off the balcony, but they didn't rise.

Like fire light, the glowing bubble was an easy spell. Kendra was testing whether she could cast a spell that Eldra had known, using Eldra's experience. As candles had lost popularity in favor of lightbulbs, so had the fire light spell lost popularity in favor of the bubble spell. Eldra and many other druids had been using the glowing bubble as a potential's first spell for the past few decades. If O'Brien had tried to get me to cast bubbles instead of fire light, I doubt it would have worked for me.

Let's combine both spells and warm the air inside, I suggested.

She created another bubble while I cast fire light, as small as I could, in the center of it. The bubble became a floating lantern. Together, we made another five of them.

At last, Kendra stopped clenching her teeth, and her tension released.

You see the lights, I chuckled as I finished her sentence in mental song. *Floating lights. Alexis is the princess, but these are for you.*

There is no fog to be lifted, Kendra mused.

Your ire is like a fog, and it's like your ire has lifted. Again, I thought those last words in the tune of the song we were thinking of.

You're reaching, Kendra shook her head.

You're probably right. No one else is even thinking of that song, I shrugged.

Yeah, definitely not.

You already have short hair anyway, and a witch didn't capture you and lock you in a tower.

Two witches captured me and locked me in a round dirt room in a mine. Does that count?

No, I lied. It more than counted.

Then how about the fact that I'm stuck in this mansion with Alexis and she can be a total witch.

Now who's reaching? I let her mentally vent at me about Alexis as we watched our luminescent bubbles drift upward from the balcony. The second to last one popped against the roofline, extinguishing the candle-light center while the others continued to lift upward.

Just steps from us, Luiz's phone started blaring "I See the Light" from the *Tangled* soundtrack, and he and Andrea began serenading each other with exaggerated theatrics.

Kendra and I laughed. *OK, maybe it wasn't just us,* we thought together.

We watched the bubbles travel upward. The glowing, bulbous forms distorted the stars behind them. By the time the song ended, they were too small to see but still hadn't popped.

"Luiz," I called. "Robin—er, Eldra's husband—would always play "Unforgettable" by Nat King Cole for his wife. Luiz pulled that song up on his phone, and we listened to it next.

Alexis created marble-sized orbs, similar to my magic missiles, only not meant to cause harm. She sent them twirling upward toward the bubbles. Kendra and I cast a few more bubbles filled with fire light.

Just as "Unforgettable" ended, I raised Raijin and lit up a lightning bolt rune encased in a square. I shot lightning into the sky. Then I did it again. The third time, I split the lightning, sending multiple zigzags of electricity humming up and out in different directions—the grand finale.

Now we'll always remember that we watched fireworks together at Eldra's memorial, I offered to Kendra. She smiled and lay her head on my shoulder, approving of my solution.

After the lightning, silence settled over the balcony. The silence lingered until Luiz jumped up onto a chair near the railing. "I'm going to miss the way her wrinkled leather face scared us when she chortled in a death cough at my jokes," he laughed. He took a breath and continued. "I'll miss her terrible jokes. I did my best to pretend to laugh at them."

"Those were real laughs," I challenged.

Kendra teared up. She wiped at her eyes. I didn't cry. Neither did Alexis. Mr. Espinoza looked like he was going to say something but didn't. He didn't show much emotion. Jody, Carl, and Ariel remained silent. Jody had never met Eldra, but she sobbed the most. Her tears were for someone else.

Even though Jody didn't know Eldra, she didn't feel out of place like Kevin would have. I was glad I sent him home and that Mr. Espinoza's thralls remained in the banquet room.

Lillian, the older servant, stepped onto the balcony and signaled to Alexis that they'd served dinner.

"She is with her husband," Alexis stated. "Eldra is exactly where she wants to be."

"Have a happy eternity," Kendra whispered.

We made our way from the balcony into the banquet room and sat at one of the large dining tables. Mr. Espinoza's thralls already occupied a table, and he walked over to sit with them. He grabbed an unopened bottle of wine from the center and popped the cork with his fingers before pouring a glass for each of his thralls.

Kendra, Alexis, and I sat with Luiz, Andrea, Jody, Carl, and Ariel. A bottle of wine sat in the middle of our table.

"We are all underage," Alexis lifted the bottle and handed it to Jody, "so this is all yours."

Alexis had no problem drinking wine with dinner, but she had chosen to refrain as a symbol of solidarity for Kendra and me, as neither of us would drink wine even if we were over twenty-one.

After dinner, Kendra and I found ourselves conversing with Pasha and Sajid, whom Lexy had invited to eat with us. It turns out they were both fathers. It hurt me to know that their children were fatherless while they remained here. We didn't talk long, but long enough that Kendra and I mentally asked Alexis to send them home to their families. Alexis understood our feelings but disagreed.

We moved on, conversing with others until ten-thirty when an alarm on Kendra's phone went off, reminding her that we had to get up wicked early. She and Alexis had drill team at six in the morning. I had football practice at the same time. Had Eldra still been alive, Kendra and I might have argued against her plan to enroll us in school. Since she had given her life for us, her act motivated us to fulfill her wishes. We still wrote in our journals for the same reason.

I wish I only needed four hours of sleep, Kendra complained to me as she stood to leave. "Good night," she excused herself from the table. However, she left her separation stone disabled.

"I'll put Carl to bed," Jody stated, trying to speak formally despite her rural accent, "then I'll be back." She followed Kendra with Ariel and Carl in tow. Since Ariel went willingly, Carl didn't argue either.

"*Con permiso,* your *mage*-esty," Luiz laughed as he stood and bowed to Alexis, "Andrea has a curfew."

"Eldra would have loved that pun!" Alexis nodded back to him.

Andrea stood and curtsied, then took Luiz's arm. Luiz paused to tell his *papá* goodbye, and then we watched them leave.

After a few minutes, Jody came back. So did Ariel. About that same time, Kendra enabled her separation stone, cutting her off from the Trinity of Mind in an effort to try to sleep.

All of us in the banquet hall spent a lot of time chatting and getting to know each other. Well, Ariel didn't say much, but the rest of us did. Each of us took a turn sharing different memories of our past. We were up until about two in the morning before Mr. Espinoza escorted his thralls, all drunk, from the banquet hall. The whole room cleared shortly afterward.

That left Lexy and me alone.

Do you feel up to hurting Kendra's feelings some more? Lexy winked as she joined my mind.

I both did and didn't, and Lexy was privy to my every thought. Not hurting Kendra won out.

Too bad, Lexy stepped forward and embraced me. I returned her embrace. Wearing three-inch heels, she didn't have to look up to meet my eyes; she only had to turn her head. Her lips were right there.

Take them, she offered.

I wanted to accept her offered lips, but I froze. The other day, Kendra had been in a voodoo trance, and I had kissed Lexy so we could send jealousy across our emotional rope-bond and wake her. It had worked. It had also hurt her deeply. All I could think of was how Kendra's heart broke after that.

She can barely stand to look at you.

You think I'm ugly, too, I countered. *You're now only attracted to my powerful magic.*

Ah, but I am still attracted to you. Lexy lifted her chin toward mine. Only a few inches separated our lips.

So is Kendra. Remember how she kissed me after the Lost Rhoades Mine Melee?

I do. I let her kiss you without argument. Can I not kiss you without argument now?

Perhaps. I put my hands on her cheeks. I leaned forward until my lips were millimeters from hers. Then I tilted her head down and kissed her forehead.

"Good night," I spoke, trying to drown out the maelstrom of conflicting thoughts and emotions.

How do you do that? she asked.

Do what? I had to ask because her thoughts weren't clear enough to explain her question to me.

Desire one thing so strongly, yet choose another?

I didn't have an answer for her. She couldn't find one in my mind, and our dual confusion became too much, so Lexy tapped her separation stone, leaving me mentally alone with my own confusion. I stepped back and turned, looking down off the balcony toward the road instead of at Lexy.

"They don't come inside thresholds, right?" I pointed at a handful of transients that looked up at us from underneath a streetlight. They looked like nothing more than a few homeless people, but I could sense the difference. I recognized one of them. He had shoulder-length hair and a scraggly, homeless-guy beard. I'd seen him the night I left Club Exposed after battling the voodoo witches.

Lexy shook her head. "They must have sensed the magic in our fireworks. Does Eldra know what they are?" Lexy didn't get Eldra's memories instantly downloaded to her like I had. They were in my head, not hers. With the Trinity of Mind disabled, she didn't have access to them all, just the few she'd already perused.

"Not really," I shrugged. "Could they have hijacked Luiz and Andrea? Maybe we should have escorted them home. Should we check on them?"

Again, Lexy shook her head. "Whatever transients are, they never bother people without magic. Had one of us with magic escorted them home, we may have put them in danger."

"Still, I'll text him."

"No need," Alexis closed her eyes. Luiz wasn't her thrall, but by controlling him, she had formed a mental bond. Distance had only a minor effect on the bond. As long as he wasn't a thousand miles away, she could tap into it. "Luiz is making out with Andrea in front of her house."

I chuckled, nodding.

"Good night, Lexy." I walked through the glass doors into the mansion and headed toward my room. Lexy remained alone on the balcony behind me. The transients had almost been a welcome reprieve to the emotional night. I walked away thinking of them, which almost distracted me from the confusion that had occurred between Lexy and me.

Eldra's memorial was over. I'd thought of the phrase I always heard. Those who pass on are never gone as long as we remember them. I sighed and chuckled. For me, Eldra would never be gone.

CHAPTER 12
PRACTICE

Today, I plan to outdance Kendra on drill team. At grandfather's demand, I practiced ballet until I turned thirteen when mom and I ran away to California. After he found us, I still danced often but for a more adult purpose. I will enjoy every minute of watching Kendra and the other girls stare in jealousy at the way my body moves. —Alexis

I tried to breathe, but the air wouldn't come. I stopped running, briefly resting my hands on my knees to catch my breath. Practice had started with a one-mile warmup. We didn't practice on the football field, but just to the west in a large grassy area that was approximately the same size and doubled as a baseball outfield. As I ran, the damp grass seemed to grab at my cleats, slowing my steps. Only the frontage road separated the field from the I-15 freeway. The loud hum of early morning traffic pounded in rhythm with my rapid heartbeat.

I could no longer see the frontage road on the west, nor the tall Rocky Mountains on the east, which still blocked the sun. It wasn't the dim, early morning light that hid them from my view; my light-headed tunnel vision just couldn't see that far. I could only see the grass directly in front of me. Everything else was hazy.

My ankle ached less than it had yesterday. I wasn't sure if I could even feel it anymore. Could I feel anything but exhaustion?

As I ran around the grass field, I tried my best to make sure that I wasn't last, but I was in the last group. Others had stopped and put their hands on their knees before me. I pushed for as long as I could. But I just didn't have any more energy to give. Last season, I used to run the one-mile warmup with the front group, usually leading. This season, I was already exhausted, with stitches aching in my side, and I still had a whole other lap to go. Practice would last another hour and a half.

104

Calling the first week "practice" is a misnomer, which is why it has been renamed "hell week." We wouldn't practice running a single play. We wouldn't even touch a football. The coaches' sole purpose for morning practice during hell week was to push their would-be players to the brink of exhaustion and beyond.

Well, for me, they'd already succeeded.

Besides being exhausted from only the warmup, two things bothered me. First, I wore nothing but shorts, a sleeveless shirt, and cleats, leaving too much of my splotchy skin exposed for all to see. Second, I didn't have Luiz, Kevin, or Ethan to banter with. The jeeks had been part of every one of my football practices until today. Here, I didn't know anybody. Well, that wasn't accurate. I knew *of* a few players. I studied my opponents last year, so I could name the starting quarterback, one receiver, and a couple defensive linemen. I would have known of more, but the other players I had studied had graduated.

I could hear the coaches talking about cutting me—or maybe I just imagined it in my head.

I dug down deep for the final lap. I wouldn't say I was still running. I forced my body to perform the running movements, despite moving at a pace slower than walking.

I'd been third from last when I'd started the final lap. My head spun. As I looked up with a hundred yards to go, I was no longer third from last. In fact, the second-to-last runner crossed the final orange cone and collapsed. I was dead last. The coaches and the entire team of players stared at me. Most shook their heads at me, and I had to approach them in shame as I finished my prolonged, last-place run. I could feel their eyes and hear their judgment.

"Well, he's cut," I heard from somewhere among the players. Another player said, "What's an albino freak like him doing here?"

What *was* I doing here? Why had Eldra registered me for football? I knew the answer. I needed to work out and rebuild my muscles. It might take years, but I had to start somewhere. Dazed from my run, I didn't feel the merits of that answer.

Near the end of practice, the coach had us pick the position we planned to play. When I walked over to the running backs, I heard the snickers and saw the smirks. I was too thin, and I had just proved to everyone that I couldn't run well. Perhaps I chose poorly by joining the running backs as we lined up for shuttle runs—sprinting twenty yards from one orange cone to the next and back four times. I was only halfway through my first shuttle run when I vomited. A half dozen kids had expelled their stomachs today, but I hadn't expected to be one of them. It just wasn't something I was accustomed to. I hadn't hurled since, well, I couldn't remember ever throwing up. As far as I knew, this was the first time in my life. When I finished, my esophagus ached and burned like never before. Then I had to experience the awful stench and the chunky brown sight of it splattered over green grass. The coach yelled something, and two of my teammates shifted the orange cones five yards to the side so no one had to run through my mess.

Coach Douglas was in his second year at Woods Cross High School. Sometime after the shuttle runs, I felt his eyes on me and knew he would single me out.

"You're Jake, right?" The coach asked.

I nodded.

Eldra had registered me as Jake Estevan. It wasn't much of a pseudonym. But Eldra's logic was sound. First, I wouldn't need to remember a new first name. Second, I likely wasn't going to stay dead forever, so in a few years, it would be easier to merge my prior records with my new ones if both sets were variations of the same name.

"You chose the running backs' line."

I nodded again.

"I'm not sure you . . ." he hesitated and started again. "You're not the size we need to play that position."

I didn't nod. I just stood there dumbfounded. How had I not expected this? It was obvious in hindsight. I wouldn't be able to put on enough weight in the next three months to play running back. Even if I did, I would probably draw unwanted attention to myself and get tested for performance-enhancing drugs.

"Can you kick?"

I didn't answer. Last year, I had kicked a few pooch punts. Could I still kick? I didn't know, but that didn't really matter. Kickers were not real football players. Well, they were. They just didn't play much. They sat on the bench for almost the entire game. The coach had just hinted in a big way that the best place for me was on the bench. Worse, the coach wasn't wrong.

The girls' separation stones were enabled, dimming the Trinity of Mind. I could feel Kendra's worn-out body through her emotions, but not much else. I was too tired to try to break through. Part of me felt grateful for the mental separation because they didn't share my humiliation. Another part of me wished they were listening and could console me.

When practice ended, Coach Douglas blew his whistle. "All right. Gather around," Coach called. I probably moved too close to the coaches. "We have a new special teams coach. This is Coach Kale. He coached the junior varsity team at West Jordan High but now coaches our varsity special teams."

I knew Coach Kale very well. I found myself staring at him. His eyes met mine. They softened with pity. He nodded, then he looked away. He hadn't even come close to recognizing me. Yesterday, I'd been certain my mom would recognize me, but now I wasn't so sure. I'd been doubting that I could get away with Eldra's plan for me to attend another high school with only a different last name, but seeing a coach who knew me so well fail to recognize me, my doubts evaporated as surely as if I'd hit them with a magic missile.

"Let's all welcome him into our fold," Coach added.

The team gave him a big welcome.

"Practice isn't quite over. You are a team," he bellowed. "For the next ten minutes, I want you to get to know each other. Make friends. Become a team!" He and the assistant coaches walked toward the school building.

The team separated into various groups. I tried to join two groups, but in the first, one guy told me to keep walking, and the clear leader of the next group simply shook his head at me. I started toward a third group, but before I'd taken two steps, a lineman with a military cut scowled at me. It seemed none of the groups wanted to include me. How cliquish. The word *cliquish* is something Kendra would say, not me. Still, it fit. How many kids in my previous high school looked at us jeeks talking in a group and thought we were a clique? Had we unknowingly been exclusive?

I sat alone on the curb between the practice field and the parking lot for about five minutes before Alexis tapped off her separation stone. I needed Luiz, but he wasn't here. I tried to imagine what joke he'd tell to cheer me up, but I couldn't think of anything. Without Luiz, the humor in my misery eluded me.

Would you like me to cheer you up with a view of the girls locker room? Lexy offered mirthfully as she walked across the gym, not yet at her destination. Of course, that question ignited a bunch of unfiltered thoughts, most of which I would typically get to hide before choosing the appropriate response. Alexis witnessed all my thoughts. *You seem torn. Such contrasting desires. Again, you desire one thing, yet choose another. It would cheer you up, but then you would feel dirty and the "sin" word. Your church has odd views on nakedness. It is not a sin, Jake.*

Nakedness is normal. Everyone gets naked daily to shower, change clothes, or sleep.

Not in public, I answered, a*nd most people sleep dressed. Besides, what about Kendra?*

I have almost convinced her. She only sleeps half-dressed now.

You know that's not what I meant!

OK, I can let you watch Kendra change, too.

Alexis!

Kendra would be vexed with you for days. Maybe weeks. I like this idea more and more.

Alexis walked into the girls locker room. The lockers alternated colors between dark blue and red. Light wood benches ran between the rows of lockers over a floor of tiny, gray tiles.

No! I tried to think of something else and not focus on what Alexis could see.

Stop worrying. I am the first one here. Nobody is undressing. Yet. Lexy turned around and watched as other girls walked in. *Wendy is cute,* Lexy thought as she looked a long blonde up and down. She shifted her eyes to a girl with dyed black hair. *Kat is trouble.* As Lexy's eyes traveled over Kat's body, she added, *Trouble would be good for you.*

Still, no. I didn't have control of the situation. Alexis wore the separation stone, not me.

If you insist. Lexy tapped her separation stone, but I could still feel her mirth.

Again, I found myself once again completely alone, staring at cliques that I didn't belong to. Nobody talked to me as I waited for the girls. At least twice, a group looked my way, clearly talking about me. Not only was I alone, I was a laughingstock. I tried to remember how long it had been since I was last picked on in school. It was the end of eighth grade when I was still a scrawny geek. It had been a while.

Where was Luiz when I needed him? Well, he would have just ended practice at West Jordan High with Kevin and Ethan. They'd banter for a few minutes before heading home. What I wouldn't give for a moment of that. It hurt to not be with them.

Finally, after long minutes, Kendra and Alexis exited the Woods Cross High School's doors. They tapped off their separation stones and got a front-row view of my despair.

I'm proud of you, Kendra offered. The background catfight between Kendra and Alexis hummed in full force.

None of the girls changed anyway, Alexis shrugged. *All the girls go home in their dance clothes.*

Lexy just wanted something to distract her from being outdanced by me, Kendra reveled in victory. *Mrs. Spinwell told Lexy she wasn't in a strip club. Twice.*

I did not expect drill team dancing to be so stiff, Alexis defended.

I stood, intending to walk over and meet them. I didn't want to remain sitting lonely on the curb, ostracized by a bunch of cliques that secretly mocked me.

Stay there, Lexy ordered. She did not like how the guys on the football team treated me and formed a plan to alleviate that, which Kendra surprisingly decided to go along with.

You don't have to, I started.

Oh, yes, we do, they both answered in unison. Working together, focusing on me instead of themselves, their background bickering ended.

I sighed and sat back down on the curb, waiting for their plan. I couldn't help but grin.

Alexis turned on her pumpkin spice allure. Seconds later, each member of the football team, starting with the closest, turned his head toward Lexy. She wore only a small pair of black Lycra shorts and a black sports bra with red lining. Kendra had a plain white tank top over her black and light blue sports bra—West Jordan High's colors—but had Lycra exercise leggings that went to her ankles.

Kendra's sports bra colors comforted me. At West Jordan, the colors were black and light blue, with the jaguar as the mascot. At Woods Cross, our colors would be red and navy, and we would be the wildcats. Despite having finished my first day of practice as a wildcat, I still felt like a jaguar. Unfortunately, the mascots were a metaphor for my recent change. Jaguars were big and strong like I used to be, while wildcats were much smaller like I was now.

I watched as confident guys from three different cliques stood and stepped toward Alexis and Kendra, trying to talk to them. The girls ignored them as they walked toward me. When they reached me, Kendra sat on the curb to my left and Lexy sat on the curb to my right. Each grabbed one of my arms. Lexy leaned her head on my shoulder while Kendra kissed my cheek. Every single football player on the team went from being glad they weren't me to wishing they were.

My body smelled like grass and sweat, and my breath smelled like vomit, but Alexis pretended my stench didn't bother her. Kendra couldn't smell me. Lexy's pumpkin spice aroma overpowered any other scent around.

"It is hot," Alexis stated loudly and glanced at Kendra, mentally urging her to further torment the obnoxious boys on the football team. It wasn't really that hot, but Alexis wanted Kendra to help make me look good. The sun was just now peeking over the Wasatch Mountains as if it had waited until now to properly spotlight Lexy and Kendra.

"It is," Kendra agreed. Surprising herself as much as me, Kendra grabbed the hem of her tank top and pulled it over her head. She took time to stretch her hands over her head as she pushed her chest out so all the boys could get a good look at her in only her sports bra. She fanned her face with the tank top.

Rescued by boobs again, Kendra giggled. Alexis hadn't been privy to the first time but found it hilarious. I wrongly expected her to feel jealous, but she didn't. Instead, she promised that the next time I needed such rescuing, it would be her turn. However, she shared with Kendra her concern that Eldra's memories might overwhelm my mind and turn me into her. Eldra had warned me that losing myself would be possible.

Good thing we are both *here,* Kendra thought to Alexis. Without the Trinity of Mind, I wouldn't have understood her comment. *We made a pact,* Kendra explained. Kendra and Lexy had had a conversation early this morning about how Lexy made a move on me at Eldra's memorial, well after Kendra had gone to bed. In their pact, if both girls were with me, like now, there were no rules. However, if they were alone with me, neither Kendra nor Lexy would try to get me to choose between them unless planned, like a date, and the other girl was forewarned.

"Shall we go?" I offered, my grin widening. Every guy on the football team stood gawking with an open mouth, glancing between Kendra and Alexis and wondering what two hot girls were doing with a monstrosity like me. Honestly, I had no idea myself. We stood and walked together toward the parking lot. Thank goodness they each held one of my arms; otherwise, my tired and trembling legs might have given out. We made our way toward the silver BMW 440i convertible. We'd switched from the BMW 335i so that Lexy's new Russian bodyguard, Pasha, could take it to the body shop early this morning. Which made me think of Jody.

"Body shop" makes you think of Scarlett? Alexis teased.

No. The Skull Shadow damaged it with their black SUV at Jody's house. That made me think of Jody, I defended, to no avail.

110

Kendra had suggested the metallic blue convertible. She thought it would be the best choice to comfortably fit the three of us and make a strong high school first impression. She had chosen wisely.

Alexis tossed me the keys and started toward the passenger seat. *If I drive, it will emasculate you in front of them*, she shared. Before she got in, she turned to the boys on the football team, every one of which still stared at her. "Bye, boys," she waved. Then she ducked into the BMW. All the boys' eyes switched to Kendra, who waved as well before getting in the back seat.

Lexy's other new bodyguard, the Middle Easterner named Sajid, pulled out of the parking lot behind us in a Ford F-250. Princess Alexis no longer went anywhere unprotected. Ariel sat in the passenger seat. I guess I didn't go anywhere unprotected either.

Hey, about Pasha and Sajid, I asked Alexis. *Can they go see their families?*

They have kids, Kendra added. *Kids that need their father.*

Perhaps a visit would not hurt, Alexis contemplated. She liked their protection and did not want to be without it.

You should tell them to visit their homes for a week first thing in the morning, Kendra urged.

I shall consider it, Lexy replied.

"How was practice for you two?" I asked verbally as we pulled out of the Woods Cross High parking lot. I almost lost my breath just asking the question.

"Alexis used her allure on Mrs. Spinwell to keep us on the team," Kendra grumbled.

"I only used it to convince her to rate us honestly based on the first week," Lexy explained.

"She said our dance skills put both of us in the top five," Kendra grinned extra wide. "And she called Lexy a stripper," Kendra again reveled in victory.

Alexis let Kendra have her triumph and changed the subject.

"Friday, Mrs. Spinwell will speak to the drill captains and come to a final decision," Lexy explained. In her mind, Lexy considered how in a week, every girl on drill would be begging Mrs. Spinwell to keep her. *Do not gloat, or you are out!* Alexis warned Kendra.

Lexy's phone rang. The touchscreen on the dash offered to answer it but listed the number as unknown. Lexy didn't answer it through Bluetooth, but instead, she tapped on her separation stone and put her phone to her ear. Before her mind cut off, I got a thought about Gina, Club Exposed, and that vampire in Las Vegas—the one Lexy said was the most powerful in the United States.

"Now is not a good time," Lexy didn't even bother to say hello. She listened for a minute, then said, "Yes, I can call in one hour." Then she hung up.

The silence crowded the car as Lexy hadn't been able to avoid the fact that she was clearly hiding something from us. What did it have to do with Gina, Club Exposed, and a powerful vampire?

"Can we check on Sis?" I interrupted the awkward silence.

Alexis had set up the convertible's Bluetooth to connect to her phone, so she asked the car to call Mr. Brandt. He answered, and after a quick hello, Alexis asked, "What is the plan for Justine?"

"I have bad news," Mr. Brandt answered.

I gripped the steering wheel and started counting.

CHAPTER 13
BEAR

I'm wary of Ariel. Coyote said she was the worst of them all. She claims not to remember anything before she was trapped and frozen in the well. The other water babies had their memories. Why not her? Is she lying? Can I trust her? —Jake

I showered and ate—the servants had a late breakfast ready—then I went back to bed, despite it being just before 9:00 A.M. The fresh gray sheets felt smooth on my skin. Every muscle ached. I'd overdone it at practice, so Lexy and I had swapped our protection stones. Lexy's necklace had two pendants. The first pendant was a pear-shaped, black diamond protection stone that was also a healing stone. As a dhampir, she could already tolerate a little sun, but with a healing stone, she could walk around in broad daylight like a normal person. The second pendant was a silver trinity symbol with a two-carat diamond, enchanted as a separation stone, mounted to its center. She'd put a clasp on both my protection stone pendant—a large red ruby—and her black diamond pendant, so we could easily swap them. She needed the healing stone during the day, and I needed it at night. I'd have made my ruby a healing stone, too, had O'Brien not reprimanded me for making the one that Lexy and I swapped. Now that I knew a healing stone allowed a vampire to walk in the sunlight, I didn't want to risk making another.

I fell asleep quickly and had two nightmares. Both were memories of Eldra's life more than they were dreams. After the second nightmare, my dreams drifted into something that felt far more real. I found myself standing in damp mud under a dark night sky, rain pounding on me. The entrance to Carre-Shin-Ob emanated magic light in the familiar figure-eight shape. I didn't want to go inside, but I knew I was supposed to, so I did. Would Coyote be in there?

113

I walked down the mine's entrance and past where Caleb Rhoades's name was scrawled into the tunneled wall. The trickle of water still ran down the middle of the tunnel. I curved around with the tunnel and into the cavern. Bright light lit the room, though I couldn't find a light source.

Someone had cleaned up the mess we had left, which couldn't have been easy, because we'd left dead bodies, blood, and gore spread out all around the area inside the nine pillars. More than fifty splotches had dotted the stone floor where water babies had turned to goo. I had blasted the altar to nothing, which had left a hole leading to the well that had imprisoned the water babies. Burned bodies and a blackened floor had surrounded both sides of the pillar we had used to defend ourselves. I had erased sections of the cavern's walls.

Now, the floor and pillars shined. A new altar—this one made of gold—covered the well, and gold patches covered both the erased sections of the walls and the chips in the pillars.

"I cleaned the carnage cluttering the cavern," the words echoed around the pillars and seemed to come from every direction at once. The voice had a strangely British accent. I had expected Coyote's Ute accent. Either he changed, or this wasn't Coyote. I spun around looking for the source of the voice but saw no one. I walked to the new, golden altar.

"Pleased to present my person to a protector," the voice spoke again.

I turned and found an Englishman in front of me. He stood between me and the pillar we'd used in our defense. He dressed as if he'd just stepped out of Downton Abbey. A dark-brown top hat covered his head, and a matching frock hung to his knees. A cravat tie wrapped his neck and tucked under a double-breasted, burnt umber vest. High-waisted pants extended down to his low-heel, pointed-toe boots. Robin had worn boots just like that. No, I wouldn't have known the names of all his articles of clothing if not for Eldra's memories. Nobody had dressed like this man outside of theater since the 1800s, and why were his boots on the wrong feet?

"You wonder at my wardrobe?" His voice contained a challenge in it. He expected me to accept the challenge and try my best.

"You alliterate a lot," I answered.

"Very well voiced," he complimented. "Forgive my fetish for verse."

For half a second, his sentence didn't make sense. The word *fetish* had taken on a sexual connotation toward the end of Eldra's life. Fortunately, his voice carried with it the older, intended meaning, which included only his devotion to alliteration.

"You voice vapid verse very vehemently." Wow. That just left my mouth.

"I can't compete with such complex composition," he continued. "It annoys Coyote. So, I seek to salt his senses with similar sounds."

This guy had to be the oddest man I had ever met. Coyote had described the keeper of this mine as a big, ugly frenemy. Eldra knew of multiple other Native American deities, such as Bear, Rabbit, and Porcupine. According to her, Rabbit was the odd one. "Are you Rabbit?"

"Ha! Rabbit? I am Bear."

"In a vintage Victorian vest?" I asked. I probably had Eldra to thank for the vocabulary, but I hoped some of the alliteration skills came from me.

"You are yet young, yet you win with words."

"Well, why waste words when I can waste you with words," I answered, trash-talking with alliteration, which was a first for me. I smiled.

"You're a protector with powerful prose," he shook his head in disbelief, almost causing his top hat to fall off. He grabbed it and put it to his chest.

"And you're an antique Englishman who adlibs with antique English," I countered.

"I concede this contest."

I considered asking him why he was an antique Englishman, but I held my tongue and waited for him to speak. It seemed he had plenty to say without my questions.

"Last century, I focused on rhyme. This century, alliteration. Do you recognize me?"

I started to shake my head, but then his face triggered one of Eldra's memories. Eldra had met this man at a party held by Robert Peel at Number 10 Downing Street. Peel was Prime Minister of England at the time, serving in the early 1840s. William Gladstone had invited Locksley to accompany him to this party. Naturally, Locksley had taken Eldra. This man—or the man that Bear had cloned—had also attended at Gladstone's request.

Wow! History was so much easier to remember with Eldra's actual memories of it.

"Sir Alfred Tennyson?"

"I quite took on his appearance. Splendid chap." He returned his top hat to his head. "However, I shan't keep this appearance much longer. I expect I'm getting bored of this look. Perhaps I've begun watching for a new face already. On a visit to Brooklyn, I heard tell of a new poet who surpasses even Tennyson. I introduced myself to this man they call Jay-Z. Unfortunately, with the return of global technology, his face is far too famous."

Return of global technology? That phrase spawned so many questions that I would have liked to ask, but instead, I asked a dumb one that I already knew the answer to. "So, you're like Ariel?"

He frowned. "I have little in common with Coyote's most devilish descendant."

"I meant, are you a doppelganger?"

"Doppelganger?" Bear—or Sir Alfred Tennyson—cocked his head to one side as if in thought. "Perhaps. Perhaps not. I can be whatever I choose to be, but I will always be Bear."

"Is Bear a name, or is a bear what you are?"

"Both. I was born a bear on my first world, and our first shape forever defines who we are."

"Does every world have bears? I mean, habitable worlds." I asked, intrigued.

"Have you paid a visit to a habitable world without bears?"

"I've only been on this one," I answered.

"If every habitable world you have been on has bears, why would you assume one doesn't?"

I shrugged. Should I argue with Bear about the flaws of extrapolating from a sample size of one?

"All worlds were created the same way with the same life." Bear continued. "Some worlds require alterations for alternate atmospheres." Bear smiled. "Alterations for alternate atmospheres," he repeated. "That alliteration was unintentional, I assure you. You inspire me, Protector."

I wasn't sure how to respond. "Thank you?"

"Ah," he raised his eyebrows. "Your 'thank you' reminds me of the reason I brought you here for this rendezvous," Bear answered. "I've been avoiding my home for centuries. I wholeheartedly blame Coyote for imprisoning his granddaughters here. They would whisper constantly. I'll be happy to hibernate at home this winter."

"You still hibernate?"

Bear ignored my question. "Also, the Nuchu need me. I've left them alone with Coyote for far too long. As a protector, you require no reward, but my debt to you must be paid." He held out a golden ring. "This is not just gold. It is a piece of the sun. You

can sail its power back to Carre-Shin-Ob. I've never met a
protector that hasn't been slaughtered. This will save you one
time."

He'd never met a protector that hadn't been slaughtered? That
was less than encouraging. "How many can come with me?" I
asked as I took the ring.

"None," he shook his head.

"How do I use it?"

Something tickled my foot. The cavern went black, and I could
no longer see Bear, the pillars, the altar, or anything. Had the light
turned off? My spirit flew through the darkness at a hundred miles
a second. I opened my eyes, waking as Alexis lifted me from my bed
and onto my feet. The afternoon sun blared through my window.

"Where were you?" Alexis snapped.

We lost our connection to you, Kendra informed me. *We're
going to be late.* The drill team also had practices twice a day for
the next two weeks. Both girls, once again, wore their practice
outfits. The servants had washed them. I could smell both the
laundry detergent and fabric softener—or maybe Lexy smelled
them? I looked at the clock: 2:41 P.M. I'd fallen asleep just before
nine, almost six hours. Kendra was right. We were going to be
late for afternoon practice if we didn't hurry.

I jumped out of bed. It didn't even occur to me that, wearing
only boxers, I had exposed my hideous skin to the girls. Perhaps
my self-esteem issues were healing more quickly than my skin?
The servants had washed my practice clothes and laid them on
the foot of my bed. As I grabbed my shorts, I noticed the gold
band on the ring finger of my right hand. In my dream, only my
spirit had traveled to visit Bear, so how did something physical,
the ring, come back with me?

I slipped into my shorts, my sleeveless sports shirt, socks,
and cleats. Meanwhile, I let the girls peruse my mind. They
digested my strange reality-based dream. Even though Bear had
cloned Sir Alfred Tennyson, the dream-based rendezvous had felt
more like a story from Lewis Carroll.

"I rescheduled with Kevin for you," Kendra added.

I blinked at Kendra, taken aback. I'd told Kevin we'd come by
after ten today. Missing an appointment wasn't like me. After this
morning's practice, I'd collapsed into my bed, too tired to think. I
was out the second my eyes closed. Kevin hadn't even come to
mind. After my nap, however, I felt refreshed.

During the ten-minute drive to Woods Cross High, I dreaded
practice and a repeat of this morning's overexertion. After we

parked at the school with less than a minute to spare, Kendra and Alexis went inside while I stayed outside and headed toward the grass field. A few football players had arrived in a rush like us, while the rest already waited on the grass. As I arrived, over a hundred pairs of eyes, freshman to senior, delivered a look of either pity or of mocking.

The sun hung high overhead, more on the west than the east of the blue sky. Its light abolished the tall Wasatch Mountains' shadows that had draped over morning practice. The sun's summer rays warmed the top of my splotchy albino shoulders and the back of my neck. The grass smelled dry, whereas this morning it had smelled wet. It also felt more solid under my cleats. If only the sun could erase the unfriendly looks like it had erased both the shadows and the morning dew.

I wanted to test Coach Kale, so I walked up, introduced myself as Jake Estevan, and told him I was new, too. He wore a gray shirt, black shorts, and a whistle. He looked me in the eyes and thanked me for the kind welcome, then ambled on, placing orange cones on the field. He had no idea he'd coached me as Jacob Stevens.

Coach Douglas wore a white shirt with a red whistle hanging from his neck. He blew it loud enough to briefly drown out the hum of the afternoon traffic on I-15. Then with a shout, he had us warming up with a one-mile run again. It wore me out again. However, as I came around the last hundred yards, this time, I ran at a pace slightly faster than a walk. I wanted to increase my speed, but I couldn't. Still, my pace beat out two oversized linemen who walked to the final orange cone behind me. Third to last felt much better than last! Coach still sent me to practice with the kickers. I stayed there for the first hour, then, for the second, I snuck over to run drills with the running backs. The running backs coach was a short, stocky guy with a bald head who couldn't be thirty yet. He noticed me but didn't say anything. I managed to complete the shuttle run without throwing up.

With wobbly, tired legs after practice, I dropped on the same curb as before, waiting for Kendra and Alexis. My tank top stuck to my sweating body. This morning, my tunnel vision had prevented me from noticing much. This afternoon, I noticed the clear, blue sky, the summer heat, the mountains, and the sound of traffic, as well as the yellow and red paint on the curb I sat on. A group of five guys—one that I recognized—came and sat on the curb surrounding me. They sat too close, invading my personal space.

The guy I recognized was Collin Jones. He sat on my right. Last year, he started as quarterback in the final three games after

Ted Aldridge broke his thumb on his throwing hand. His messy blond hair fell like icicles cutting into his chiseled face. I had to look up at his eyes, putting him about three inches taller than me—the quintessential quarterback. Collin was a senior this year. He had a high probability of starting this season. Unfortunately, he already had the inflated head that everyone wished wouldn't come with the position.

"I'm Collin Jones," he put his left arm around me and shook me with feigned cordiality. I wasn't sure why, but his arm hurt my shoulders. He gave me a very fake smile and offered his right hand for me to shake. I looked at it. I probably should have taken it, but I didn't. Instead, I shrugged out from under his unwanted arm.

"Don't pretend to be my friend, Collin." I shook my head. "Are you hoping to be sitting by me when Kendra and Alexis come out?"

He pulled back his offered hand, and his brow tightened. His smile faded for a second but then returned, even faker than last time.

"Oh. Are those their names? I was hoping you would introduce me, but I can introduce myself."

I stood and started walking away, not because I couldn't handle a bully, but because I couldn't handle the temptation to erase him from existence. The desire surged through me unexpectedly, and I wasn't ready for it. Magic poured into me from all around. I could erase his bully ass in a second. The part of me addicted to the ecstasy of erasing a soul argued that the world would be a better place without this creep. I pushed that thought away as best as I could.

"What are they? Your sisters or cousins or something?" Collin called after me.

I clenched my fists and kept walking, fighting against my unhealthy magical appetite, but losing. I could feel my will slipping and knew that I wasn't going to be able to control myself for long. *I need you,* I pushed through to Kendra and Alexis. I felt their separation stones holding me back, but with great effort, I forced my way through their stones' magic. *I need you, now.*

Uh, we're in the locker room! Kendra protested, but then my overwhelming craving released into both Alexis and her. They tapped off their separation stones, fully letting me in. Each of them shouldered part of my addictive desire, making its weight not so overwhelming.

I warned you that none of the girls change in here, Alexis reminded me. *Most just go home in their practice clothes. We only use the lockers to hold our phones and car keys. But Kendra and I can change if that makes your craving go away.*

No, we won't, Kendra argued.

Thanks, anyway. I'm fine now. My craving is fading.

Or maybe seeing us in the locker room replaced your craving with another, Alexis teased suggestively. Kendra flooded with mixed emotions as one part of her laughed while the other snapped at Alexis. *Which of us do you crave most?* Alexis asked. With that question, Kendra's snapping won out. *What? We are together. This doesn't break our pact.*

Ugh. I didn't want to listen to the background noise of Kendra and Alexis catfighting. At least the wave of addictive desire had dissipated. I ignored the part of me that felt annoyed that my unplanned glimpse into the girls locker room had not included a visual bonus. Maybe that was just an unfiltered thought. I'm not sure how well I filtered it, though.

A few minutes later, Lexy and Kendra met me at the high school doors.

"Wow! You're sunburned," Kendra touched my bright red shoulders.

I shrugged. Perhaps that is why it hurt when Collin shook my shoulders? Lexy's healing stone would have me better by morning, though.

Both girls took an arm and let me walk them to our BMW convertible. As we walked through the parking lot, Collin stood by his yellow Dodge Charger with a group of thick linemen. He eyed us mischievously as we walked by. This time, Alexis had not enabled her allure. Even though she walked close, holding my arm, I could barely smell her pumpkin spice.

"Tale as old as time," Collin whispered in song to the linemen surrounding him, not realizing Alexis could hear him clearly. The lineman all laughed.

Ignore him, Kendra urged.

Someone should shoot him, Alexis thought.

A red laser dot appeared clearly visible on Collin's forehead, just below his spiky, icicle bangs. Sajid had him in his sights, and all Alexis had to do was will it, and he'd pull the trigger. Alexis quickly looked Sajid's way and shook her head. He lowered the laser sight rifle and handed it to Ariel, who watched from the passenger's seat. Collin never even knew he had been a quarter-inch finger squeeze away from having his brain spread all over his linemen. I shouldn't have, but I entertained the idea of Sajid shooting Collin, but the thought faded quickly. That wasn't something I wanted in real life. Sure, Collin was going to make my life hell this year, but as much of a cocky bully as he might be, he didn't deserve to die.

As we drove away, my dread of football practice lifted. I had never dreaded football practice before today. I sighed. I hoped we could visit my sister tonight before O'Brien's surgery. Halfway home, Lexy got a call from the hospital. They'd moved up O'Brien's surgery to 6 P.M. The clock on the dash read 5:07 P.M. We were going to be late. I wouldn't get to visit Sis tonight.

CHAPTER 14
GAME ON

Jake has a deep connection to O'Brien that I don't understand. He has only known him for a few days. The guy shot Jake. He faked Jake's death and dragged him into this mess, pulling me into it as well. There is something about O'Brien, though, that has me curious. He makes everyone around him feel safe—even paralyzed and lying in a hospital bed. How does he do that? —Kendra

Alexis refused to go straight to the hospital. She acquiesced to drill-team practice's dress needs, but after being caught without her body armor at the Lost Rhoades Mine Melee, she refused to go anywhere that might be dangerous without her leather body armor again. And since the Skull Shadows had attacked at the hospital once already, she considered our destination highly dangerous. Also, the three of us had just sweat buckets at practice, and we needed to shower for sanitary reasons if we were going to enter an operating room.

We showered quickly, and Alexis didn't even mentally taunt us this time. Despite being the most worn out and taking the longest to shower, I dressed and made it back to the garage first. Kendra and Alexis had hair to do and makeup to apply. Even with short hair, they took longer.

Kendra arrived next. While we waited for Alexis, I pushed magic into Kendra's hair, urging it to grow at an accelerated rate. Lexy arrived a minute later. Both wore black leather from neck to wrist to toe. Lexy's leather was new. Vertical lines of sewn pink thread patterned her top. The lines ran from neck to hip, except where a fleur-de-lis pattern stitched with pink thread curved over each breast. The same pink thread traveled down her pant seams, and matching fleur-de-lis decorated each rear pocket under a silver zipper. Kendra wore the same leather outfit she'd recently borrowed from Alexis. It still bunched at the joints, not fitting as snugly on her as on Alexis. I didn't have a leather outfit myself. And since wearing a bulletproof vest would draw too much attention, I dressed in a black hoodie and jeans. For half a second, I wished I had a black leather ensemble to match the girls. Mine would have slanting seams that—Eldra! I forced myself to stop analyzing the girls' outfits while designing a matching set for myself.

We all jumped in the BMW, but before we had a chance to leave, Ariel opened the back door and sat by Kendra. Carl stood at the garage door and waved goodbye.

Alexis tried to race to the University of Utah hospital. Unfortunately, it was traffic hour. Luckily, we traveled in the opposite direction as commuter traffic, so at least we weren't gridlocked. Pasha followed us in the same F-250 Sajid had driven earlier.

Lexy's phone rang as she drove. *It is the Bishop again.* Kendra picked it up for her.

"We're not home again," Kendra informed him. "Yes, she is still planning to meet with you tomorrow night." It was a short conversation.

We arrived at the hospital and parked. I checked my phone for the time—6:07 P.M. Hopefully, we wouldn't be too late. And hopefully, the surgeon, doctors, and nurses already under Lexy's influence hadn't been replaced with alternates.

Instead of the seventh floor, we made our way to the spinal surgery operating rooms on the third floor. It took us longer than I wanted, and the minutes ticked by. A nurse—already under Lexy's influence—waited for us with scrubs, masks, and hairnets. Two sets pink, one set blue. I almost reached for a pink set before remembering that I wasn't Eldra. I grabbed the blue ones. The nurse eyed our druid staffs.

They will be too intrusive and diminish my allure, Alexis worried.

Kendra and I handed our staffs to Ariel. The nurse didn't offer a set of scrubs to our mythic mermaid monster. She did not look pleased to be babysitting our staffs, and her lavender eyes raged when Pasha escorted her toward a waiting room. In her anger, she didn't notice a nurse coming our way and bumped into her.

Feeling rushed, I pulled off my sweater and put the scrubs on over my t-shirt and jeans. I transferred the magic vial from my hoodie pocket to the scrubs. The girls put their scrubs on over their leather clothes, but they took their time doing it. Kendra's and Lexy's leather-clad arms poked out of their scrubs, looking very out of place. Alexis didn't seem worried, but Kendra eyed one of her arms and twisted her lips in disapproval.

The nurse under Lexy's control introduced us to the approaching nurse that Ariel had bumped into.

"This is Kelly. She'll take you to the OR 3."

Kelly gave her fellow nurse a questioning look.

Lexy pushed at Kelly with her allure. Lexy had spent a lot of time at the University of Utah hospital influencing everyone who would participate in O'Brien's surgery, including Kelly. There were too many for her to actively control at once, like Kelly, so she turned on her control for them as needed.

Kelly escorted us to a scrub room and forced me to wash from elbow to fingertip for a minimum of three minutes. Alexis and Kendra got away with pulling their leather sleeves up a couple of inches, as far as the leather could move up their forearms, and only washing that much. More minutes ticked by. What if we arrived too late to give O'Brien the vial of Bones of Steel? Finally, after the longest handwash of my life, the nurse escorted us into the surgical operating room.

A red digital clock on the wall read 6:27—almost a half-hour after the surgery was supposed to have started. O'Brien lay face down on a bed, covered by a blue medical cloth. A bright spotlight on a mechanical arm hung over him. I couldn't see his back or an incision as a half dozen men and women in various colors of scrubs stood around him. Were they already done? Had I missed my chance? I hurried around to get a better view.

Three stainless-steel rolling carts held trays lined with sterilized instruments. Four tablet-like screens connected to medical devices that attached to the head of the bed. Tubes and wires traveled under the blue medical cloth that covered O'Brien. That cloth had a long rectangle opening taped to his skin, providing access to O'Brien's back. The white skin tone didn't look like O'Brien's. Of course, his back, which never saw the sun, wouldn't be the same tanned color as his hands and face. As for my worry of being late, I shouldn't have stressed. Not only had we made it in time, they hadn't even cut O'Brien open yet. The anesthesiologist verbalized his every move as he inserted the epidural.

The anesthesiologist stopped and looked at me.

"Ignore us." Lexy's allure once again flared, sending the scent of pumpkin spice throughout the operating room. The anesthesiologist obeyed.

Sit down and relax, Alexis popped into my head. Three chairs lined the wall to the right, on the other side of the room from the door, and she and Kendra sat down, leaving the seat in the middle for me. *This surgery will last almost five hours.*

I should have realized that, but I hadn't. I'd stressed out about being late for nothing. The final bone setting likely wouldn't occur for hours. We'd do nothing but sit here. I *should* have visited my sister first. Justine needed me every bit as much as O'Brien did. I even considered going now and coming back, but the stress of potentially missing the moment would be too overwhelming.

Each girl took one of my hands, Kendra on my left and Lexy on my right. The ring that Bear had given me—the piece of the sun—felt strange as Lexy's fingers pressed against it.

Just before seven o'clock, Lexy leaned over to me. "I almost forgot. I cannot stay," she whispered through her pink mask.

"What?" I asked, confused. "Why not?" Kendra leaned over, sharing my confusion.

"I promised Jody," she whispered. "I am already late. It is almost an hour before sunset." Mr. Espinoza might wake up out of control again, and she needed to be there.

"Will your influence over them last?" I asked, nodding toward the doctors and nurses around O'Brien.

"I will come back as soon as I can," she added, noticeably not answering my question, as she stood and walked out of the operating room.

Kendra's gloved hand took hold of mine, and she tapped off her separation stone.

It's your plan, she encouraged. *She was just here to watch anyway. You've got this.*

I appreciated her encouragement, but I still felt vulnerable without Alexis. Her absence affected my confidence. I had to consciously replace Eldra's analogy that Alexis was like my go-to purse, giving me confidence for any fancy night on the town. I forced myself to pull out a replacement football metaphor. Alexis was like the starting left tackle, who I could always count on to make a good block. But I had to run cautiously when the left tackle was not on the field. Even with Kendra in my head, Eldra's memories tried to take over.

Kendra giggled inside, laughing at how I replaced Eldra's analogy. She gave my hand a comforting squeeze.

This is serious, I worried. *Eldra's memories are constantly pushing for control.* How could my almost eighteen years withstand her two hundred? How could I possibly keep being me? My worry ended Kendra's giggle.

I didn't mean to laugh, she apologized. *I know this is serious,* she worried with me.

In Eldra's room, when her memories had almost succeeded in overwhelming me, Kendra had rescued me by accidentally flashing me a view down her shirt. Even though she'd giggled about that after practice earlier this morning, she couldn't bring herself to let me see down her shirt on purpose. She'd stretched her modesty beliefs far enough already by wearing a white string bikini for me and stripping her tank top off this morning. Even though her current bra covered as much or more than the white bikini had covered, letting me see down her shirt broke her moral code.

How about I spend the next hour remembering your life with you while ignoring Eldra's, Kendra offered. *It can be like therapy, but with memories.*

Memory therapy? It sounded way more fun than the word "therapy" should sound, so I agreed. Kendra started by sharing memories of my childhood, and she worked her way up. When we reached our early teenage years, we found a surprising number of shared memories where Kendra visited Sis and we both tried to avoid crushing on each other. Kendra and I had been into each other for a very long time.

Our shared memories reached the high school years. Kendra had cringed each time I went on a date. I'd only had two steady girlfriends. My first was Ally, who moved away at the end of my sophomore year. We never kept in touch. The second was Teresa.

What happened between you and Teresa?

Uh, oh! I'd dated Teresa for a few months last year. We'd gone on many dates. Unfortunately, her question had focused on the one date that I did *not* want to share with Kendra.

Kendra's mood changed with that memory as she explored it for the first time. She snapped her hand away from mine and pursed her lips.

Second base, huh?

I told her no, I assured Kendra. *I stopped it from going further.*

Not until after her shirt was off, Kendra fumed accusingly. Her hand flattened, and she imagined herself slapping me. *If your stupid skin wouldn't start bleeding, I would slap you for real.*

She wouldn't let the memory go. Her jealousy-driven, morbid curiosity kept her focused. At first, she explored that whole date. Every moment that led to Teresa standing in front of me topless. There was nothing I could do as Kendra replayed the memory.

Teresa had taken me back to her house after our last home game my junior year. Her family owned a large house on half an acre with a separate pool house in the back yard where we could be alone. The pool house had a game room and a guest bedroom. Teresa and I made out on the couch in the game room for an hour. Teresa lifted the bottom of my shirt, then stopped, looking at me questioningly. I answered her question by raising my arms, allowing her to pull my shirt off.

Kendra, don't do this! You don't need to analyze every detail, I warned. She didn't need to torture herself, or me, any further. I reached over to try to tap on Kendra's separation stone, but she grabbed my wrist, gripping it with an ocean of rage that threatened behind her fierce blue eyes.

Despite my warning, Kendra continued focusing on this memory of Teresa and me.

After a few minutes of further making out, Teresa seemed frustrated that I hadn't tried to remove her shirt, so she removed it herself. She turned her back and asked me to unclasp her bra. I obeyed. Then she twisted back around and jumped on top of me. Minutes had passed, during which she led my hands from her back to her front.

The blue in Kendra's eyes darkened like the blue ocean darkens in a hurricane. A hint of magic—emotional magic—traced around her pupils. Kendra had a special ability with emotions—Eldra had first spotted it—and I could both see it and feel it now. If she wanted to, she could destroy me right now with the power of her emotions.

I'd never harm you, Kendra affirmed with a distracted part of her mind. Still, her fingernails dug into my wrist as she continued to turn my memory into her own personal theater.

Teresa sat up and smiled. "There is a bed in the guest room," she offered. She stood and faced me. It took me a few seconds before I could lift my eyes from her breasts to her face. Still smiling, she took both my hands and pulled as she backed up toward the door to the guest room. I let her lead me two steps, but then I stopped. Her arms extended as she tried to continue backward while I remained in place. She tugged. I took two more steps, but I stopped again. Why was I hesitating? A beautiful girl stood topless in front of me, offering to share with me something special. Something every guy wanted, right?

"Come on, Jake," she urged, tugging me another two steps.

Teresa now stood in the guest room, and I stood just outside it. The bed had rose petals on it in the shape of a heart, proving that her intentions were premeditated. I wouldn't be taking

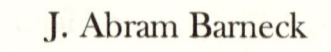

advantage of her. This was an unmistakable *yes* moment. Why wasn't I saying yes back?

She tugged again, but I planted my feet. A long minute passed, and neither of us spoke. She let go of my hands and undid the snap at the top of her tight jeans. "I want you to be my first."

Was that my problem? I'd imagined my first time often, but I'd never imagined it with Teresa. I'd always imagined it would be with someone else. Teresa wasn't taking no for an answer. She shifted her hips as she slowly unzipped her fly, revealing red lace. My desire rose. I considered Teresa. She was beautiful and intelligent, which is why I had first asked her out. I desired her. But was the desire strong enough?

Teresa wasn't that *someone else.*

I watched, struggling as Teresa slowly slid her pants off her hips. Could I really do this? My mouth opened and the words that came out were, "Teresa, I'm sorry." Saying those words broke me from the trance that her undressing had put me in. I managed to shut off my emotions. I turned away. I walked numbly to the game room couch, grabbed my shirt, and put it on. I walked out of the pool house, ignoring her pleas for me to stay. I didn't have a car, so I ran home.

Kendra stopped prying, allowing the memory of that night to end because now she knew.

Why had I refused Teresa? I'd walked out on Teresa, not because there was anything wrong with her. No, I walked away because she wasn't Kendra. I'd imagined my first time so many times. For as long as I could remember, Kendra had been the girl I'd imagined.

Kendra's grip on my wrist loosened. Her cheeks flushed at the memories of me imagining my first time with her. Usually, I would imagine us on our wedding night. Her eyes, a moment earlier threatening like a hurricane above a raging ocean, now calmed like the clear ocean in Maui—a beautiful, secluded beach where Robin had taken Eldra. Kendra and I imagined we would honeymoon there, and she would wear her white bikini for me— at least until she took it off.

We both blushed as we shared our daydream.

Alexis chose that moment to jump into our heads.

Mr. Espinoza woke viciously and was again difficult to calm. I left Sajid to protect—she stopped as she found herself interrupting the two of us. Instantly, her dhampir heart shook. It didn't break. Her past had made her heart so strong it wasn't breakable, or perhaps her past had broken it down to pieces so small it couldn't break further. Still, I'd never felt her heart hurt so deeply.

Mr. Espinoza is calmer than the two of you, it seems. Her reprimand echoed loud and clear in the tone of her thought.

Kendra tried to explain how it had just happened. Her emotions had quickly shifted, and she'd been caught off guard. She'd felt concerned and came up with the memory therapy idea to keep me from turning into Eldra. That had led to her sliding into a jealous rage at the memory of my previous girlfriend. She hadn't expected the reason that I'd turned down Teresa, and that had brought up our mutual love.

You broke our pact on the first day? Alexis snapped back.

That isn't what I was doing, Kendra defended. As unintentional as her thoughts were, she *had* broken her pact, and she knew it. Guilt rose up through her insides. She gulped. Unfortunately, she couldn't stop her unfiltered thought. *Besides, I've already won.*

Is that so? Alexis forced her mind to calm, like the eye of a hurricane. *If you want to play this game, fine. Game on. First to bed Jake wins,* she challenged. *See you in twenty minutes.* Then Alexis tapped her separation stone on.

Kendra's eyes widened at the unexpected challenge. *Could Alexis win?* Kendra wondered, more to herself than to me. Still, my unfiltered thoughts answered her, imagining ways in which Alexis might win.

"Don't you dare," she grimaced in a whisper.

Unfiltered thoughts, I countered. *Besides, I'm saving myself for marriage,* I threw out.

Kendra didn't believe me for a second. That night with Teresa, I hadn't once thought of my religion or saving myself for marriage. Afterward, I'd refused to acknowledge my feelings for Kendra, so I'd convinced myself that I'd done it because of my religious upbringing until I believed that lie. However, now that Kendra had forced me to relive it, it was clear that my feelings for Kendra had been the sole force that stopped me from following Teresa to that bed.

Kendra felt confident that I loved her more than Alexis, yet at the same time, she felt sure that if she didn't find a way to restore their pact, she'd quickly lose this game. Lexy's powers of temptation extended off the charts, while Kendra truly planned to save herself for marriage. She wasn't just stating that goal meaninglessly as I had done. She'd held to that goal for years and refused to throw it away, even for me. Even her shaken faith hadn't affected that goal. Alexis had challenged her to a game she couldn't possibly win.

Kendra tapped her separation stone. "Better we don't share minds right now," she explained. "Maybe I can restore the pact."

I nodded. I looked up at the oversized, red digits on the clock—9:27 P.M. For the last hour and a half, Kendra and I had utterly ignored our surroundings. We'd been lost in each other. But now, it all came back. We sat in a bright, white operating room where doctors and nurses stood around O'Brien's bed, aiding the primary surgeon. The surgeon's constant voice, explaining each action he took to those around him, barely paused, interrupted only by the beeping of equipment or the sound of instruments.

I fiddled with the vial of Bones of Steel in my scrubs pocket. The minutes ticked by, and I knew that they'd soon set his vertebrae back in place. That is when I'd need to put my plan into motion. It suddenly occurred to me that without Alexis, without the power of her allure, I wasn't sure if the doctors and nurses would let me administer the liquid spell.

Over the intercom, a voice paged Kelly—the nurse that had escorted us—from the operating room. She left. Five minutes later, the door opened. I expected it to be Alexis, but it was that same nurse returning. At least, I think it was the same nurse. She looked shorter and thinner than I remembered. She looked at me for a long moment with her lavender brown eyes. Why was she looking at me? Perhaps without Lexy's allure immediately present, she wondered what two teenagers were doing in the operating room. Maybe she'd kick us out. Instead, she looked away and rejoined the group of doctors and nurses around the operating table.

The clock now read 9:57 P.M. Alexis had said twenty minutes, but it had already been thirty. Where was she? I'd arrived here stressed that I'd missed this opportunity, only to find out I had to wait hours. Now that I had waited those hours, I found myself once again anxious and worried that I'd miss it.

Charles needs me, I told myself. I tried to ignore that Eldra was the reason I'd called him Charles instead of O'Brien. Kendra's efforts to pull up my memories—memory therapy—had helped. I would need many hours of her help over the next few weeks, even if it caused Kendra to break her pact with Alexis.

Unfortunately, I couldn't always push Eldra's memories away. As much as they tried to overwhelm me and take over, they also offered me Eldra's knowledge and experience. And with Alexis not here, I needed one of Eldra's abilities.

CHAPTER 15
BONES OF STEEL

Miguel Espinoza is difficult to control after he wakes. He is an anomaly. Usually, with a thrall for every day of the week, a newly turned vampire can wake up, feed, and control himself. Other than the first waking moments after being turned, Vampires do not go berserk with bloodlust. That is a myth. Vampires are not undead. Though my grandfather does like to tell stories of vicious, soulless vampires that existed before his reign. He boasts all the time about how he exterminated them. —Alexis

"**E**verything is in place," the spinal surgeon spoke. He stepped back as if appraising his work. "Time to glue and lock it down."

"Wait," I stood.

The doctors and nurses seemed to see Kendra and me for the first time. The one left of the primary surgeon cocked his head, wondering what we were doing here and why we hadn't yet been escorted from the room. Lexy's prior influence had affected them enough to ignore us while we sat quietly, but now that I'd spoken to them, her influence collapsed.

"You can't be in here," the surgeon stated through his mask.

Kendra was better at both emotional and delicate magic. If I tried Eldra's spell, I'd probably overdo it. I reached over and tapped off Kendra's separation stone for her. She hadn't stopped thinking about the challenge Alexis had issued. It took her a couple of seconds to gather her thoughts and focus on my plan for Charles.

"But he is the specialist you called in," Kendra's voice contained tiny, silk strands of magic. The same magic Eldra had used to convince the old woman working in the Woods Cross High

School office to give her the phone number for Katie Spinwell, the drill team instructor. The magic worked differently than Lexy's allure. It cleared the targets' minds, which left them in a stupor, then replaced all thoughts with a clear understanding of what we wanted. It didn't control them so much as it blocked their mental ability to disagree.

"Right," the spinal surgeon stated.

Alexis joined the Trinity of Mind. *Why did I just feel magic?* she asked as she dried her scrubbed, clean hands in the room next to us, moments away from joining us in the operating room. Our thoughts answered her questions.

We don't need you, Kendra's unfiltered thought lashed at Lexy. She regretted that unfiltered thought, but it was too late. Their catfighting shifted from the background to the foreground.

Charles—I used his first name again, but this time I added his last name—*O'Brien needs us. Focus!*

Alexis walked into the operating room. For the second time, I noticed that the leather arms extending out of her pink scrubs looked out of place.

"Our specialist will examine the spine before you close," Alexis stated, trying to take over. But she hadn't needed to. Kendra's magic had already succeeded. Vulnerability dripped from Alexis into me. We didn't need her, and that realization hurt.

I could ease her emotional pain later. Now, Charles needed me. *Disconnect!* I ordered them. *And focus on O'Brien.* Both girls tapped their separation stones.

I stepped forward, holding the vial of liquid Bones of Steel. I'd assumed I'd be able to pour it into O'Brien's mouth, but he had a tube down it. That wasn't happening.

"Nurse," Alexis touched a woman covered with pink scrubs, hairnet, and mask and pointed to the vial, "can you inject that into the IV?"

The nurse nodded. She took the vial and pushed a long needle on a syringe through the lid.

"He'll only need a bit of it, and please, don't give it to him until I say so," I added.

"A bit?" the nurse asked.

What kind of fake expert was I? The syringe in her hands had measurements on it. "Ten milliliters," I chose the number at the halfway point of the syringe. The nurse nodded and filled it to that mark.

As I stepped to the operating room table, the sight shocked me. A long incision spread down Charles O'Brien's back, exposing his spine from his pelvis to his shoulders. Blood and tissue surrounded the exposed vertebrae. Two metal bars, screwed into bone, lined each side of the spine. I couldn't believe my eyes. If I were susceptible to nausea, I probably would have thrown up or passed out. Worse, I was going to see this even more vividly as I pushed magic into my eyes and turned on my sight. I fought off my revulsion, and instead, I focused on the flow of light traveling up and down his backbone. The flow stopped, blocked by the broken vertebra that the doctors had pieced together.

"This one isn't right," I pointed at the blockage.

"The L3?" the surgeon questioned, pointing at it with an instrument.

"Yes," I confirmed. "Can you adjust it?"

"How do you mean?"

"Uh," I didn't know. What was I supposed to say? "Try to set the broken pieces differently?"

The surgeon requested an instrument from the nurse, who gave him some metal screwdriver-like tool. He already held a large tweezer, and he used them both in conjunction. He worked on the L3 vertebra for a minute, then asked, "Is that better?"

"Not really," I answered. "Keep trying."

He pulled out a large piece of that one vertebra, which let the light travel up and down O'Brien's backbone. Unfortunately, that piece was too big to leave out. When he put it back in, the light's flow stopped. Two more adjustments led to two more failures. O'Brien's spirit still couldn't flow freely past the L3. It had never occurred to me that this wouldn't work. What if we couldn't find an adjustment that allowed the light to flow? What if I had wasted my time?

"The flow is still blocked," I started, but how could I explain to him what I was seeing? If I made myself look like a crazy quack, he might become too agitated, break out of Kendra's magic, and kick us out.

"Can you try something else? What if we put the broken pieces back so that they fit more loosely?"

The doctor cocked his eyebrow. His eyes squinted in doubt.

Alexis upped her allure and said, "That idea is sound."

The surgeon nodded. "Unconventional, but it's worth a try." He requested some thick gel-like solution from the nurse. In moments, he set the broken bits of the L3 again, only not as tightly connected as before. The gel-like solution kept the cracks a hairline apart. The flow of O'Brien's spirit now flowed past the L3 vertebra. As it did, the light in his lower body increased.

"Now, nurse." I pointed at the syringe containing the liquid Bones of Steel spell. The nurse inserted the needle into the IV. I watched as she squirted the glowing liquid—glowing for me at least—into the IV tube. It would hit O'Brien's system in seconds.

I heard the door open and glanced at three men in blue scrubs who entered. They all had blue hairnets and face masks covering some kind of larger head gear that included a visor. With my sight, the light of their spirits looked dim, similar to how Kendra's and Lexy's light currently looked due to their leather body armor. I ignored them and turned back to O'Brien. That mistake would have cost me my life had it not been for Kelly. She jumped in front of me. I mean, literally jumped. Had she kept her feet on the floor, one of the bullets would have sailed over her head and hit me.

At first, I didn't understand what was happening, but Alexis immediately heard and recognized the sound-suppressed gunfire. Skull Shadows? Were they making another attempt on Charles O'Brien's life? Or were they targeting someone else? They hadn't aimed at Charles. They'd aimed at me. Come to think of it, they could have made an attempt on O'Brien's life at any time while we weren't around, but both attempts occurred during *my* presence. Had their previous attack also targeted me, not Charles?

In our hurry after practice, I'd neglected to fill my pockets with small rocks. Perhaps I could pull enough magic from around me to bulletproof my clothes, but I doubted it.

Pasha was in the hospital somewhere with Ariel? Would they come to our rescue?

The nurse who'd jumped in front of me took three bullets to the chest. Another three bullets hit Alexis, but her magic-aided leather body armor stopped them. Alexis and Kendra had refused to carry small rocks because they caused unfashionable bumps and clumps in their leather clothing. Instead, Alexis had one of the servants embed bits of sheet metal into the leather in various places.

The surgeon and another doctor leaned over Charles, offering their bodies as shields to protect their patient. The others panicked. One nurse turned to see the commotion. Once she comprehended that three gunmen were shooting, she lurched backward, falling onto O'Brien's legs and knocking the surgical bed a foot from its original position. The surgeon shouted at her.

The Skull Shadows on the right threw down a vial that shattered on the floor, and magic left the room. We'd left both staffs, Raijin and Astrapí, with Ariel. They were supposed to be our reservoirs of power, but they were too out of place for the operating room, and we hadn't expected to need them. The commotion was loud inside the room, but as the guns had sound suppressors, would Ariel or Pasha hear it and bring us our staffs? Would anyone call hospital security?

I touched the metal chair, and for the first time, my attempt to convert elements to magic failed. I called for the elements a second time, but again, they refused me. The magic wasn't gone. It just didn't work. What was in that vial?

Alexis rushed toward the three men. Nurse Kelly, despite having been shot with three bullets, also rushed forward. She somehow kept pace with Alexis. The Skull Shadow on the right shot Kelly in the forehead, just above her left eye. She dropped. Lexy spun and twisted, dodging potential head shots. Kendra twisted her body in front of me, turning her back to the shooters, ducking, and cringing. Two bullets, directed at me, hit her in the back. My breath caught. The magic in the room had stopped working. However, I breathed a sigh of relief as the bulletproof magic of her leather armor blocked those two bullets. Perhaps the magic still worked because she had cast the bulletproof spell on the sheet metal back at the mansion when she had dressed? Three girls total had now put themselves in front of bullets for me.

Alexis ran two steps up the left wall, leaped off it into a sideways flip—the same move she'd used against Mr. Espinoza—and landed. Multiple bullets hit her leather armor and ricocheted. One hit under O'Brien's bed while another embedded into a wall. One of the doctors shouted in pain. Alexis reached the first of the three Skull Shadows and grabbed his gun. He fired into her chest once before she ripped the weapon from his hands. She pistol-whipped his chin because it was below the helmet and visor. His jaw broke with a cracking sound, and the man collapsed.

The other two Skull Shadows switched weapons, and simultaneously, each hit Lexy with a taser. Lexy's head shook, and her hands stretched out as electricity flowed into her body from two locations. Her body convulsed for long seconds as if Eldra had blasted her with lightning. Despite her enabled separation stone, her pain seeped into me until she collapsed unconscious to the operating room's tile floor.

One of the two remaining men dropped his taser, raised his handgun, and pointed it toward Lexy's head. I grabbed my chair, swung it around Kendra, and threw it at him. One chair leg hit his shooting arm just as he squeezed the trigger. The bullet embedded into the tile an inch to the right of Lexy's head, causing pieces of tile to hit her cheek.

A fourth Skull Shadow entered the room. We had no chance. Not without magic. But the taser gave me an idea. I only hoped it worked. I'd never tried it before, but with my skill at—er, Eldra's skill at casting lightning, it just might work.

I stripped off my gloves. Kendra's leather protected me from a few more bullets as I grabbed two metal instruments, one a scalpel and the other a thin pair of clamps. I put a hand on Kendra's shoulder, and we backstepped to the wall. I let her shield me as more bullets hit her magically bulletproof leather armor. No sooner did we reach the wall than I shoved the ends of the scalpel and the clamps into the holes of the orange electrical plug and let all 120 volts of energy into my body.

I wasn't sure it would work. The magic inside the room had refused me, but I hoped it would work for two reasons. First, electricity is pure energy, and all energy is magic. Second, the electricity didn't originate from this room.

A burning sensation traveled up my arm. Was this going to work? Or was I just electrocuting myself?

I stretched one of my hands out, almost as if to pull Kendra into a hug, except instead of grabbing her, my open palm pointed behind her, targeting a Skull Shadow. My other hand maintained a hold on the two metal instruments sticking into the outlet. I fought to keep my mental control despite the electricity rushing painfully through me. I converted the energy to magic as fast as I could, but was it fast enough?

"*Ligetu!*" I shouted.

The lightning spell hit the closest attacker with a full 120 volts. His jaw locked shut, and he didn't convulse so much as he vibrated. His eyes rolled back into his head. The Skull Shadow that had just entered the room stepped back out the door. The other remaining Skull Shadow tried to retreat as well, but I hit him in the back just as he crossed the doorway.

I pulled the instruments out of the socket and heaved a deep breath.

Three Skull Shadows were down—the one Alexis had pistol-whipped, and the two I'd electrocuted.

Kendra wrapped her arms around me. A sense of relief escaped from her. Not connected to the Trinity of Mind, and with her back turned, she hadn't seen the fourth Skull Shadow that had escaped the operating room. He yelled an order, and another male voice answered. That meant there were at least two Skull Shadows left, both just outside the operating room.

The sounds of screaming from nurses and a doctor finally registered in my ears. The noise hadn't just started, but I had just now noticed.

Alexis twitched, alive but still unconscious.

Nurse Kelly had taken multiple bullets to the chest and one to the head, so seeing her lift onto her hands surprised me. She looked at me with one glassy lavender brown eye and winked.

Ariel?

With my sight still enabled, I should have noticed earlier, but I hadn't. Coyote's granddaughter would live as long as her life source remained safe. She'd hidden it inside a custom bone structure at her pelvis. Ariel had done more than become an exact copy of the nurse; she'd altered herself to protect her life source. We'd fought a cavern full of water babies, and none of them had done this. Perhaps they hadn't had time. Or maybe Ariel had an ability they didn't have. Hadn't Coyote singled her out?

In the cavern, head shots had kept a water baby down for a few minutes. So perhaps their doppelganger bodies still functioned similarly to the bodies they copied. My guess was that Ariel would have to heal the head wound enough to restore her brain's functionality.

If Ariel was here, where was Pasha?

As I leaned back with Kendra hugging me, I felt her pendant slip down my V-neck scrubs and pin against the skin of my chest, so I tried to send power to it directly. It worked.

It's not over, I shattered Kendra's relief.

She released her hug and stepped back, turning to look at the doorway.

That is when the lights turned off, and the monitor screens went black. There were no windows, so the room went completely dark for Kendra and everyone else. I had my sight up. Earlier, the electrical wires in the walls had been lines of light, but now, I couldn't see them.

They'd cut power to the entire room.

CHAPTER 16
SLASHED

I found the complete works of Sir Alfred Tennyson in the mansion's library. I read many of his poems and recognized them. Eldra had already read them all. I expected to understand the poems, especially with Eldra's memories, but I failed. Her memories of the time added context, but despite having met him, she hadn't read Tennyson. She preferred female poets like Emily Dickinson. For me, alliterating and rhyming are far easier than understanding poems from two centuries ago. Sometimes I think I understand a line or two, but each poem's true meaning runs deeper than the text's literal meaning. Tennyson's poems just don't make sense, yet. I hate failing. —Jake

A universal power supply somewhere on the other side of the room beeped to life. Two emergency lights turned on, pushing away the complete darkness. I shoved the scalpel and the thin metal clamp into the orange socket, but as expected, no electricity came out. I grasped at magic, searching for it anywhere, but there just wasn't any.

We are sitting ducks, Kendra and I thought together.

The red clock would have read 10:28 P.M., except the bottom of the first digit had been hit by a bullet, so only the top half of the 1 showed. It was late. Had the Skull Shadows waited until the end of the surgery, when the hospital would have the least amount of people?

A minute went by, yet the two remaining Skull Shadows didn't come into the room. The surgeon and one other nurse had spent the entire time leaning protectively over Charles. They began whispering to each other, asking if it was all over. Other nurses

138

and attendings huddled behind equipment and squatted in the corner of the room. One of the huddling nurses pressed a white cloth to the bleeding thigh of one of the doctors. Blood soaked into the cloth. Some equipment had also been damaged. Cracks spread out like a spider web from a bullet hole in one of the four tablet-like screens.

The light in Charles O'Brien's legs had dimmed to half the brightness of the rest of his body. I took one step toward him but stopped when a Skull Shadow spun into the door, both hands as one gripping his black .45 pistol. He pointed it left, then right, at the doctors and nurses around Charles, checking for threats. The gun turned toward Kendra. A second Skull Shadow entered and pointed his .45 past Kendra and toward me.

I'll stop the bullets while you come up with another idea, she offered.

"End them," the second Skull Shadow stated coldly.

They both fired. Kendra stayed in front of me. This time she faced them, putting her leather-covered arms in front of her face to protect herself from a headshot. The bullets deflected. The Skull Shadows fired again. And again. The bullets continued to bounce off her leather armor as the men emptied their cartridges.

With my sight, I could see the sheet metal sewn in small squares inside Kendra's leather body armor. The sheets dissolved into the magic needed to counter the bullets' momentum until Kendra only had one small piece left.

The two Skull Shadows stayed near the door. They glanced at each other as if asking what they should do, and both seemed to have the same idea. They dropped their clips and popped in new ones. They planned to keep shooting to see how long our magic would hold up. The bullets deflected off us to impact the walls or medical equipment. The cracks of the impacts were louder than the sound suppressed gunshots. Perhaps someone outside the room would hear? Pasha? Hotel security? Anybody?

The shooters each fired, and the last piece of sheet metal converted to magic. The next bullet would kill us.

I love you, Kendra.

I linked the spell to all my metal, she informed me. Earlier, when she had cast bulletproof on the pieces of sheet metal, on a whim, she'd also linked it to the underwire of her pushup bra and to the rivets and zippers of her boots. *We needed it once before.*

The next few bullets, however, dissolved that extra metal quickly enough. The upcoming bullets would slice right through us.

I touched the ring that Bear had given me.

Use it, Kendra suggested.

I could never leave you like this.

They might stop shooting if you're gone. Kendra considered. *If you go, I have a chance.*

Would I be forced to use the ring so soon? I didn't yet know how to use it. How could I ride the piece of the sun? There was no magic around to try it. I could use my clothes again if needed, but I doubted the blue scrubs I wore would provide much magic. I would have tried harder if the ring could have brought Kendra along with me.

Just then, the bullet-ridden nurse—Ariel—leaped to her feet and absorbed the next pair of bullets. She shrugged off her wounds, continuing to step toward the shooters. They fired again. She didn't go down. Fear filled their eyes, and they each emptied their seventeen-round magazines into her. She absorbed all thirty-four bullets as they shredded her upper torso. Almost nothing remained of her pink scrub top, and what little remained absorbed massive amounts of gore. She bled a greasy purple ooze, but it wasn't recognizable as human blood. Finally, Ariel fell to the tile floor, face first. The protective bone she'd formed around her lifeforce took two hits: one a glancing blow, and one direct. The formation shattered, rattling her lifeforce but not extinguishing it. It still gave off light, if barely.

The Skull Shadows' empty magazines clattered to the floor as they reloaded. Another seventeen rounds each were coming our way. They pointed at nurse Ariel for a second to see if she moved, but she didn't. One of them shot her twice more in the head anyway. Then the guns lifted toward us.

I searched for some way to use the ring, but in such a rush and without magic, I had no idea how.

Kendra turned and hugged me. I closed my eyes. Our clothes—mostly Kendra's leather—would protect us for a bullet or two, but they had new clips and thirty-two rounds left.

Two loud gunshots went off—not sound suppressed. The sound echoed throughout the operating room, causing further screams and increased panic. I cringed and waited for the pain. None came. Kendra twitched, too, but from fear, not from being hit.

Blood spattered inside the glass visors, and both the remaining helmeted Skull Shadows dropped lifeless to the floor. Blood poured onto the floor from each of their heads.

Behind the two now-dead men, holding a pistol in each hand, stood Slash Donaldson, wearing a blue policeman's uniform. His eyes locked onto mine. I found myself focusing on the eye with the vertical scar cutting above and below it.

"Jacob Stevens."

Hearing my name sent chills down my spine. He put both guns away into holsters on each hip. "We need to talk." Why did he put his guns away? That didn't make sense. Hadn't he tried to kill me at the police station just yesterday?

"You're not going to kill us?" I asked.

"No," he answered.

I don't trust him, Kendra thought.

"Why should we believe you?" I questioned. No way would I trust him either, but he had put his guns away. If he planned to kill us, all he had to do was shoot.

"I need you alive."

Even though he'd put away his guns and she had no metal left to power her bulletproofing spell, Kendra stayed between Donaldson and me. In a background thread of consciousness, Kendra and I argued over her chivalrous act.

"That's not very convincing," I challenged.

"I have thirty million reasons to keep you alive. Is that convincing enough?" Slash growled.

I remembered the thoughts Lexy had pulled from his mind, lending truth to his words.

"If you aren't going to kill us, then you need to give me a minute." I found myself shouting the last few words.

"You can have a minute," Donaldson nodded.

I rushed over to Charles, moving the doctor to the side. O'Brien's legs gave off only half as much light as the rest of his body. I let my sight travel down his spine and watch his spirit flow down. I nudged the doctor.

"It's too tight," I pointed at the fragment that the surgeon had moved earlier.

Donaldson interrupted my concentration as he started talking loudly and animatedly into his phone, calling in the shooting to the local police. Maybe he planned to continue his charade as a local police officer? What had come of his shooting Alexis in the jail foyer?

The doctor still held his metal instruments. He jumped back into the surgery as if the shooting had never occurred. He tried to adjust a piece of the L3 vertebra, but his metal instrument clinked against the exposed bone. It sounded like steel.

"What the hell?" the doctor swore.

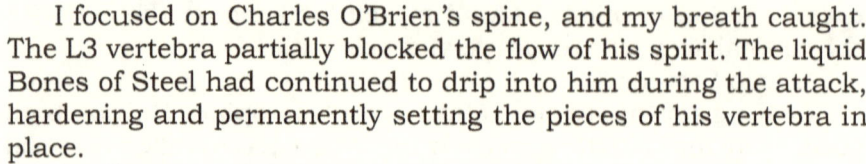

I focused on Charles O'Brien's spine, and my breath caught. The L3 vertebra partially blocked the flow of his spirit. The liquid Bones of Steel had continued to drip into him during the attack, hardening and permanently setting the pieces of his vertebra in place.

"No!" I growled through gritted teeth.

Would he be paralyzed forever now? I reached for a soul-erasing magic missile. I planned to erase the bodies of all the Skull Shadows. The living and the dead. Including Donaldson. In fact, I'd erase everyone in the room. O'Brien didn't want to live like this, so I'd erase him. The doctors and nurses failed us, so why not include them. Why not all of us? None of us deserved to live. In a haze of anger, failure, and addiction, I lost complete control.

Lucky for everyone, the magic was still absent from the room. I called for it, but none would come to me.

"Aaahhh!" I shouted out. O'Brien's spine couldn't be fixed. The Bones of Steel would heal the broken L3 vertebra. It would be solid and unadjustable after the spell wore off. I couldn't undo this. I couldn't erase anyone, either. There was nothing I could do. I clenched my fists, my whole body shaking in anger that I couldn't release.

Kendra's arms wrapped around me from behind. My cheeks dampened. Tears from the depths of some divine despair dripped down my cheeks.

As I'd lost control, her mind hadn't been able to stay connected with mine. I'd used my anger to push her mind away as if it were a separation stone. Now, she pushed back, fighting against my anger with her love for me. Her push worked.

CHAPTER 17
NO ANSWERS

I can't believe I broke our pact on the first day. I didn't mean to. Worse, I stomped on the dust of Lexy's already-crushed-by-life heart. I don't see how she will ever forgive me. She'll want revenge. She is about ten times more beautiful than me. I've seen Jake's memory of the druid's grove. Had Alexis not come across Jake's memory of me using magic, Alexis might have taken Jake's virginity right there on a bed of pine needles. Fortunately, that didn't happen. But if she goes after him, with his self-esteem already collapsed, what will he do? I guess I deserve this. I felt Lexy's pain and added to it. What am I going to do? ——Kendra

Kendra's emotional push didn't just jolt me out of my anger; it also woke Alexis. She blinked open her eyes. She turned her head and scanned the room before her eyes widened, and she sprang to her feet. Slash continued talking into his phone, sounding every bit like an official police officer and not a Skull Shadow fraud masquerading in a blue uniform. She stepped toward Slash as if to attack, but with his phone at his ear, he acknowledged her with a nod, then turned away. She almost punched the back of his skull but stopped, her left arm extended defensively, and her right arm pulled back, fist at her ear. She looked around, confused.

Donaldson had shot her in the forearm yesterday. Her hand slipped to her leg, touching her runed dagger through her pink scrubs. She'd have to reach down into her scrubs to pull out the blade. Had it been readily available, she may not have hesitated to slash off Slash's head.

Alexis turned to me and absorbed my pain and sadness, my failure to fix Charles. She pulled my emotions into her. Just like she could use Kendra and me to divide the effects of her hunger, she used herself and Kendra to divide the torment of my failure.

Alexis walked over and put her right palm gently against my cheek. She didn't intend to use her allure, but it flared to life instinctually, spreading the scent of both pumpkin spice and honey throughout the room. "Calm," she commanded. Everyone in the room calmed down because with Lexy's allure, they wanted to obey her. My protection stone warmed at my neck, preventing her allure from affecting me. However, her palm still touched my cheek, and the touch of someone you love is powerful. I calmed down.

See, Lexy's thought directed at Kendra, *you have not already won.*

Now is not the time, I cut off their spat.

Alexis tried to find Pasha through her connection to him, but she could not reach his mind. She'd tried with the same result just after the attack started.

Slash Donaldson tapped his phone's screen to hang up and turned to us. "We have about three minutes before the cavalry arrives. Do you want to be witnesses, or do you want to make yourselves scarce?"

"Scarce," Lexy and I answered at the same time. "And we need Ariel," I pointed at the bloody bullet-ridden nurse on the ground.

"I can't let you take a corpse," he shook his head.

"She isn't a corpse," I replied. "You know about," I started, not sure what word to use to finish, "about other humanoid species."

"She's one of your kind?" Slash looked at Alexis.

"No," Alexis answered as she knelt by our ancient little girl and turned her over onto her back. "Ariel is something else entirely."

Little remained of nurse Ariel's pink scrub top. She'd taken more than thirty-four bullets, and they'd left it shredded and covered in gore. Alexis made no attempt to cover up her exposed stomach and breasts. To my surprise, Ariel's skin showed only thirty-four circular red marks, one for each bullet. She had already healed. Or was 'healed' the right word? Should I say reformed? She hadn't reformed her body that quickly after the Scarlett Rescue in Ogden. Had she somehow drastically improved her morphing speed? Or was it that she had more matter as an adult?

Alexis lifted Ariel, cradling her and carrying her with ease. Our ancient little girl had saved us. I wanted to be the one to carry her. How I wished I still had my muscles. But that wasn't something I dwelt on much anymore. I'd moved past that concern. I'd made my choice to live with myself as horrific looking as I was, and that choice had been worth it.

While Donaldson ushered us from the operating room, the lead surgeon busied himself with the remaining nurses, discussing the need to close the sixteen-inch incision in Charles O'Brien's back. Slash led us down a hall toward a stairwell.

We passed the waiting room, but Pasha was not there. Our staffs, Raijin and Astrapí, leaned against the wall between two chairs. Kendra hurried and grabbed them before we hustled on.

Not far from the stairwell, a nurse slipped out of an on-call room directly in front of us. Her matted hair and her bloodshot eyes made it clear she had just woken up. Probably from the loud gunshots. She didn't seem to know what had just occurred. She shook her head as if confused, then turned our way. The real nurse Kelly stood in front of us. Her eyes found Ariel, a mirror image of herself—except shorter and thinner—in Lexy's arms with a pink shirt shredded to near toplessness and stained purple with ooze. Those eyes widened. She opened her mouth as if about to scream.

Kelly's shock of seeing herself was too jarring for Lexy's push of allure to control the woman. Perhaps Lexy's allure influenced her just enough to help the nurse swallow her scream, or maybe as a nurse, she was so used to gore that she'd recovered on her own—no allure needed. Lexy turned away from me and handed Ariel to our new Skull Shadow friend. He took her and held her in the same cradle position. Alexis trusted Slash before me? No, of course she didn't. I just wasn't strong enough.

Alexis quickly stepped to the nurse and put her hands on the nurse's cheeks. With her touch, her allure finally overcame Kelly's surprise. They locked eyes and Lexy's face grimaced as she exerted far more effort than usual.

"Kelly," Alexis spoke the nurse's name softly, then removed her hands.

Nurse Kelly nodded. She walked back into the on-call room, laid back down on the bed, and immediately fell back asleep.

"I erased the prior minute of her memory," Alexis assured us. This wasn't something she could do easily. The effort to remove that minute had drained Alexis.

Had Ariel put the nurse to sleep involuntarily earlier? Was this her second involuntary nap of the evening? Maybe she'd wake well rested and thankful to have missed all the commotion. What if the doctors and nurses remembered her being shot up? How was that conversation going to go for her?

Slash handed Ariel back to Alexis, then pulled out a pen and a card. He wrote a time, a place, and his phone number. He gave it to me and said, "Meet me here Wednesday. Call if there is a conflict."

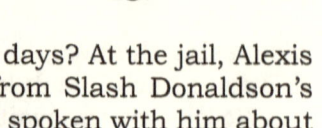

Wednesday? Who wanted to wait two days? At the jail, Alexis had pulled some interesting memories from Slash Donaldson's mind. He knew my biological father. He'd spoken with him about finding me. Now, he was suddenly offering to talk as if he were an ally, and I had to wait two days to get answers. No! I wanted the answers now.

Down the hall, the elevator dinged.

"That could be the cavalry," Slash warned, then turned and shuffled quickly toward the elevator. We hustled into the stairwell and started down.

"What about Pasha?" I asked.

"If he is alive, he will return to the mansion," Alexis answered coldly. Ariel had put Nurse Kelly to sleep; had she done something similar with Pasha?

"Won't we be on the security cameras?" I asked.

"No," Alexis answered. "The security guard turned them off for this surgery."

"Why would he do that?"

"Because I asked him nicely," Alexis answered.

CHAPTER 18
BEAR NECESSITIES

It takes firm concentration to keep my secrets from Jake and Kendra. I thought I would fail once Jake received Eldra's memories, but now, it is easier. He knows how I am protecting my secrets, so he could pry with more success, but now he also knows that some secrets must be kept, so he pries less. There are things about me, and him as a protector, that I would prefer neither Jake nor Kendra discover. Ever. —Alexis

I twisted and turned in my bed. The expensive silk sheets slid smoothly over my rough skin, but comfort wasn't enough to help clear my mind, which replayed the attack. I found all the possible ways to blame myself for failing to give Charles a fully functioning spinal column. Perhaps because of emotional exhaustion, sleep came more quickly than I expected, and at some point, the dreams followed.

Bear spoke to me, still a Sir Alfred Tennyson doppelganger, and still with his boots on the wrong feet. I stood in the cavern at Carre-Shin-Ob, as I had in the prior dream. The nine pillars surrounded me. I stood a few feet away from the golden altar, and above me, the five-foot-wide golden discs still hung from the ceiling.

"You did not use your piece of the sun. Brilliant luck that you didn't use your only one." Bear's 1800s British accent sounded musical.

"Rhyming?" I questioned.

I twisted the piece of the sun—a golden ring—around my right ring finger. Last night, in O'Brien's operating room, I had considered using it, but I hadn't known how. When Bear had given me the ring in our previous dream, I had awoken before he

147

explained how to use it. Had it not been for Slash Donaldson killing his fellow Skull Shadows, I would be dead. I wouldn't leave the dream tonight until Bear showed me how to use it.

"I have decided. I'll change my appearance, as previously confided." Bear nodded. "It is time I modernize before I *antiquitize*." He made up that last word and blinked at me as if wondering if I would notice. I did. He shrugged.

"Jay Z?"

"I think not," he responded. "In your thoughts, I saw a young bloke last time we spoke." He didn't have to tell me which boy he meant. He lined his words with magic just as Coyote had done. He meant the Native American boy whom we'd met after the Lost Rhoades Mine Melee. Bear continued, "I called upon his home. As an apprentice, he is alone. Coyote offered to be his master, so I must step in to save the boy from disaster. No apprentice of Coyote has ever survived to reach twenty." He paused and shrugged again. Perhaps 'Coyote' and 'twenty' didn't rhyme as well as he liked. "Coyote is who he is. I must acquire a Nuchu vibe to be accepted by the tribe."

"You're not going to kill a man to take his identity, are you?"

"What a preposterous notion," Bear looked offended, "to cause a man's family such pained emotion." He paused, deep in thought. "However, technology complicates this life. Choosing has caused a far greater strife."

"Can't you make up your own identity?" I asked. Ariel had turned her seven-year-old form into a nine-year-old with little effort. "You could keep some of Sir Alfred Tennyson and some of a new man."

"A mix?" he questioned. "A quite difficult fix. But I would not have to hide. In the open, I could stride." He had planned to stay hidden on the reservation in areas where technology—such as cameras—was minimal. "I must find one who has technical knowledge. I know of a Nuchu who attended college."

"How much knowledge do you get from someone when you change into them?"

"All of it," he answered, and the magic coating his words detailed what he received—knowledge, thoughts, memories, emotions, and experiences—most everything about them. The knowledge forever became a part of him, part of Bear. However, *all* did not include motivations, hopes, dreams, love, or hate. He would know of those feelings, but he wouldn't share them. I couldn't help feeling like it was very similar to how Eldra had given me all of her memories.

Does that mean that Ariel, after last night, would now be an experienced nurse?

"I will also choose a new mate," Bear grinned. "With the Trapped Ones removed, I need not wait." He planned to marry. He'd married many times. But Bear hadn't married since Coyote had frozen the Trapped Ones in the well as it left his home tainted. He glanced at the base of the golden altar. With the Trapped Ones gone, he could bring a mate into his home again.

"Do you have someone in mind?"

"In the morning, I'll choose." The magic infusing his voice informed me that Bear would pick a girl and take her. It didn't come across as consensual. I stiffened. He had opened his mouth, about to rhyme with a second line, but his eyes thinned into a troubled face. Had he read my thoughts? "Do not be stressed," Bear laughed. "The one I choose shall be blessed. I find a woman of low repute, who has always been destitute. I'll change her life, removing all strife." He shrugged again, "I used that same rhyme earlier," he complained, not trying to rhyme with his complaint.

"So, you won't be like Coyote and fall in love, get a woman pregnant, ditch her by dying and changing forms, and leave your baby girl to be raised by wolves?"

"Coyote is a fool. When did he act so cruel?"

"Uh, he didn't," I chuckled. "It was just a joke. Will the woman you pick be like a thrall?" Alexis had taken Mr. Espinoza to Vegas to choose his thralls. He'd returned with two prostitutes and multiple homeless runaways—some drug addicts and one a schizophrenic.

"My mate will not be a thrall, though neither will she be an equal, but I swear by the sun, I will treat her like one," Bear defended. "Princess Alexis wisely planned for your friend's father. Following her plan would be no bother. But seven is many and one is lonely. Like you, I will choose two." His words continued to be imbued with additional information. Bear had never been a monogamous being. He would pick two regular human women, not one of his ancient alien species. The two women would be inferior to him in every way. When compared to his long life, he would only know them briefly. And yet Bear respected his mates to a level that I hadn't expected. Despite picking from among prostitutes, one of the lowest social classes, he truly planned to love them.

"We are not all tricksters," Bear continued, and with his words came the knowledge of his rivalry with Coyote, a rivalry older than this world. Not a rivalry in which they sought each other's lives, but one in which Coyote brought constant chaos, while Bear worked to reduce chaos and replace it with peace and safety—important attributes for a being that hibernates.

"Is Ariel a trickster? Coyote's granddaughter?"

Bear looked at me but didn't speak. I wasn't sure he was going to answer. After waiting in silence, I added more details. "She says she doesn't remember anything."

"That is true," Bear acknowledged. "Her memories are few. Half a century past, I briefly released her to complete a task. When she returned, her memories had all burned."

"Should I be worried about her?"

"For many millennia, she carried the darkest soul," Bear answered. "Where her darkness went, I do not know."

That didn't sound promising. I had more questions, such as what would happen if her darkness came back, but Bear spoke first. He gestured toward the golden ring on my right hand.

"I shall explain how to use your one chance to flee, now."

I listened intently to his well-rhymed explanation.

I woke up to an early alarm. I inhaled deeply and breathed in Kendra's scent. I opened my eyes and found myself looking at the short but now one-inch longer boy-cut hair at the back of Kendra's head. Had she slept in my bed all night? The alarm woke her, too. She turned and smiled.

Alexis stood leaning against the wall, wearing black, thigh-length spandex shorts and a sports bra. "We have practice." She couldn't hide her annoyance that Kendra had slipped into my room and slept on the left side of my bed. Kendra hadn't wanted Alexis to make a move last night.

"I guess I win." Kendra smiled at Alexis. "I bedded him first."

Lexy's eyes thinned. "Clearly, that is not what I meant."

"Weren't your exact words, 'First to bed Jake wins?'"

Lexy's mouth opened. It had never occurred to her that Kendra would try to bed Jake in such an innocent manner. The idea wasn't even something Lexy could comprehend. I'd seen her in a lot of situations and with a lot of different emotions on her face, but her wide eyes and half-open mouth was a new look for her—a stunned expression caused by Kendra outsmarting her. It took her longer to recover than usual. "Sneaking into his bed after he is asleep hardly counts."

"You should have chosen better words," Kendra challenged.

"The term 'bed him' has a specific meaning," Alexis returned her challenge.

"I won fair and square. If you prefer, we can put the pact back in play."

"I did not break our agreement. You did," Alexis reminded. "Your choice to sleep in Jake's bed hardly makes me more willing to restore it."

Good thing they didn't tap off their separation stones because I didn't want to experience the unfiltered thoughts that surely would be escalating.

Kendra slipped out of my bed and stepped to the door. She wore her usual white camisole but also wore a pair of black sports shorts. Kendra put a hand on her stomach, feeling her bloated, cramping pain, which I felt, too. She opened the door to leave but turned back, glaring at Lexy. "Sore loser," Kendra brushed her growing boy-cut hair as she walked away.

Lexy's eyes blackened from pupil to sclera.

I started toward the bathroom. Alexis followed me.

"How about a shower," Lexy offered. Red streaks of lust cracked through her otherwise black eyes. Before I could answer, she pulled her sports bra over her head and tossed it on my bed. Then she grabbed her spandex shorts at her hips.

A part of me really wanted to say yes. Instead, I shut and locked the bathroom door behind me.

"I'm not showering this morning," I called through the door. I'd failed Charles O'Brien. I hadn't gotten over my anger. The girls just didn't understand. Kendra didn't even know him well enough, and Lexy's brutal upbringing stunted her empathy, so neither mourned with me this morning. When I saw myself in the mirror, my hands balled into fists. I threw a punch at myself in the mirror but stopped an inch before punching my reflection. Practice would be a nice distraction from the girls' crazy competition and from the pain and anger of failing O'Brien. I needed something, anything, to keep me from spiraling into an uncontrolled fury.

CHAPTER 19
BREATHING

There are two ways I can look at life. Option 1. Nothing has gone my way, starting with how I was conceived. More recently, a druid sniper shot me and faked my death, a nightwalker chased me and nearly fed on my soul. Lexy saved then betrayed me, then two gunmen and a vampire nearly killed me while I was saving my sister. After that, I flayed myself with magic, leaving me with road-rashed skin. I woke from a coma only to barely survive voodoo witches, their zombies, and some fierce half-water-baby, half-ancient-alien creatures. Then Eldra died for all of us, blessing me with the curse of her memories in the process. Now my mom and sister are in jail, awaiting bail hearings. Yeah, option 1 sounds bleak. Option 2, Everything is going my way. I have two gorgeous girls fighting over me. I get to play football again. My creeper stepdad is finally out of the picture. I'm getting paid a salary. I live in a mansion now. I can use magic. How cool is that? Am I a glass half empty or half full guy? Maybe I'm the guy who sees both the full and empty halves. —Jake

I breathed in and out with ease. Ten boys—including me—made up the last group of football players running the mile to start practice. There was a big gap between the last ten of us and the next group of runners further ahead.

"Losers!"

I heard Collin's voice and looked up. He'd lapped us and wanted us to know it. Well, maybe I was a loser, but I led the last group of ten, so at least today, I wouldn't be the last loser. I grinned unexpectedly and had no problem breathing while running. I remembered punching my West Jordan quarterback, Mike, a couple weeks back—before this druid mess all started. Collin deserved a fist in the face so much more than Mike did. I decided that, one day, I would punch him. I tried to push myself harder, but my legs just didn't have the muscle. I felt my body exert more energy, but I didn't speed up at all. OK, maybe I wouldn't be punching Collin any time soon.

As I crossed the finish line, I noticed that my ankle didn't hurt today.

Coach Douglas sent me with the kickers again. I snuck over to run drills with the running backs about halfway through practice. The running backs coach stood with arms folded, his tan biceps stretching his gray T-shirt sleeves. He caught my eyes and held them. His mouth opened, then closed, as if about to say something. His lips tightened, then he looked away.

I breathed a sigh of relief, happy that my breath still came easily. I realized that while I'd burned off over fifty pounds of my skin and muscle, I hadn't burned off any part of my lungs. My lungs only struggled yesterday because I hadn't practiced in about two weeks. My "breathers" had bounced back in a day. Hopefully, my muscles and skin would also bounce back someday.

When practice ended, I again took a seat on the curb between the grass field and the parking lot. Neither Lexy nor Kendra tapped off their separation stones. With my back toward the school and a noisy breeze flapping my tank top, I didn't hear Kendra exit until she sat next to me. Lexy was not with her. I scanned the parking lot but didn't see her. Ariel sat in the passenger seat of the silver BMW 440i convertible, watching me. Last night, our mythic monster had shifted back into the form of a nine-year-old girl with lavender hair.

Neither Pasha nor Sajid were around. Pasha had returned last night. He didn't remember anything but waking up dizzy and disoriented in a stall in one of the hospital bathrooms. Lexy detected an unusual scent on him but couldn't place it. She assumed that he'd either been drugged or gassed. When we asked Ariel about it, she had simply shrugged. Pasha's complete failure to assist in the gunfight last night had helped Kendra convince Alexis to send Pasha to visit his family this morning. So, he would be gone for the next week. Sajid would remain. Of course, as her generals, we'd be with her wherever she went, so it wasn't like she needed both of them. Once Pasha returned, she'd send Sajid, and they would trade off.

Kendra sat with me but didn't say anything. A few silent minutes later, the convertible pulled up in front of us with Lexy in the driver's seat.

"Get in," Alexis ordered. Nobody had seen Alexis exit the school. If they had, every boy on the football team would have gawked. That meant she hadn't wanted to be seen. She wore a pair of sunglasses, which wasn't unusual for her to wear in the daylight. She used to always wear them before I made her a healing stone. She didn't turn her head our way. Her sports bra and Lycra shorts left most of her body exposed, and she couldn't hide her rigid demeanor. Adding that to her tone of voice suggested her motives for wearing sunglasses included more than protection from the sun. I'd rejected her advance this morning and locked the bathroom door to keep her out. Instead of letting it go and accepting that I just didn't want to be a part of their competition, she'd taken my rejection personally.

"Today, we're going to Kevin's, right?" I asked.

Alexis nodded but didn't speak. Her stiff shoulders gave her nod a cold, mechanical feel.

"I'm so sorry," Kendra offered Alexis. "I didn't mean to break our pact."

Alexis glanced at Kendra, and her shoulders relaxed and lowered. Then she glanced back at me, and her shoulders tightened and raised again.

Yep. Lexy was angry with me, not Kendra. She did not speak on the drive home. Back at the mansion, after parking in the vast garage, Alexis quickly slipped from the car. She entered the house before either Kendra or I exited the convertible. The two of us walked into the house silently. Lexy's tension lingered between us. We walked down the hall until we reached the stairs, where we paused. Kendra and Lexy roomed upstairs in the mansion. My room was directly below Lexy's.

"I'm excited to visit Kevin," Kendra forced a smile through the tension.

"Me, too."

"Meet you at the car after we shower?"

"Maybe not right after you shower. You should get dressed and ready first." I winked, trying to cut into the tense mood with a joke. Kendra frowned. My flat joke added to her tension instead of easing it. If only I had Luiz's skill at humor. "I'll just be waiting and waiting, then."

"Hey, I don't take that long to get ready." She looked up and adjusted her lower lip to blow her short bangs off her forehead.

"My hair is still short and . . ." she didn't finish, but I knew what she wanted to ask.

The magic that aided her hair growth had faded. I should have noticed sooner. I touched her hair and pushed magic into it. Her bangs, which reached her eyebrows now, fell back onto her forehead. With the magic, her hair looked to be growing a half-inch per day.

"Thanks, Jake," her words matched her grateful emotions and conflicted with Lexy's angry ones. She kissed my cheek—which, as ugly as my skin looked, took courage—then blinked and looked around, realizing that if Alexis caught her kissing my cheek, it would make matters worse. She dashed upstairs.

I made my way to my room. Carolyn leaned over my bed, just barely finishing making it. She'd set up a card table of breakfast a few feet to the right of my bed with a mound of scrambled eggs and bacon and veggies on a plate. I glanced at the bathroom, hearing the hum of the running shower. I stepped toward it, confused, but I was too tired to think about it.

"I started the shower for you," Carolyn answered my unspoken question. She usually looked me in the eyes, but her eyes stayed low, looking at her feet.

"I'll eat first. You can turn the shower off." I sat down and dug in.

I was about halfway done when Carolyn finished with my room and was about to leave. She opened my door. She hadn't turned off the shower.

"Don't leave," I asked, stopping her in the doorway. "Alexis and Kendra are in a spat. I need you to stay here in case Lexy stops by my room. She wants me to pick her over Kendra, and I'm just not going to do that."

Carolyn glanced toward the bathroom, then looked back down at her feet. A sound, not running water, came from the bathroom. So did the change of Lexy's emotion.

Oh.

I looked at my breakfast and wished I could just finish it without drama, but it was clear that my breakfast would have to wait.

I stepped to the bathroom. The door was half-open. Did I dare peek inside? Steam covered the glass shower door. Lexy's naked, sitting silhouette huddled shaking in the corner of the shower. She'd pulled her knees close to her chest, and her arms rested on them and covered her face. The water sprayed down onto her.

She lifted her head and looked up over her arms.

"I heard you," her voice vibrated vulnerably. I didn't expect her to be shaken like this. "You are my only option, Jake. I need you to pick me."

She hung her head back behind her arms.

I didn't know what to say. I stood there, stunned by Lexy's behavior. She was the Princess of the New World. She'd conquered her grandfather. She had escaped every possible terror a girl could imagine, and she'd come out alive and sane, if not unscathed. But when I didn't pick her, *that* had broken her? How? I didn't even reject her. I only chose not to choose yet.

Her shaking stopped. She stood. I couldn't see clearly through the steam-covered shower, but she swiped her hand in a thin line across the glass, wiping away the steam and revealing her eyes. Her pink pupils were damp. Were tears mixing with the water from the shower? Pink also faded into the corners of her eyes. I could see the top freckle where a drop of my blood had singed her cheek. Stark sadness seeped from her into me. I'd felt this level of sadness in myself twice before: when Grandma died when I was eleven, and a couple days ago when Eldra gave her life for us. Why did Lexy feel this level of loss? She hadn't lost me. Even if I didn't pick her and picked Kendra, she would still have me. Our Trinity of Mind was permanent. We would never be separated. How could she feel this loss? I wanted her to tap off her separation stone, which I assumed she still wore, but I could only see her eyes and her steam-obscured silhouette.

"She wants me to pick her over Kendra, and I'm just not going to," she quoted me. The pink in her eyes darkened to red, which further darkened to black. Her sadness didn't go away, but a dark rage accompanied it. Slowly the clear section of glass fogged, obscuring my view of her eyes.

Lexy shut off the shower and popped open the glass door. She grabbed my towel—there was only one. She held it in front of her but didn't wrap it around herself. "Am I just another Teresa?"

I didn't know what to say. My mind was a little short-circuited. Not only was I having a hard time with Lexy's sadness and anger, but she stood barely towel-covered in front of me. It took every ounce of concentration to keep my eyes on her black ones, even though their blackness urged my eyes to look away. What was I supposed to say? Was it better if I didn't say anything?

"I see." She took my silence as her answer.

Great. Not speaking had failed me as bad as speaking might have. My mind was a maelstrom of mixed thoughts. Would it have even helped if she had disabled her separation stone?

Lexy slowly stepped from the shower to the doorway, where I stood, unintentionally blocking her exit.

"Move," she demanded. I stepped back and let her pass. I watched her walk across my room and open the door. She turned and looked at Carolyn, her eyes still black and enraged.

Carolyn stood by the door, looking down and trembling with fear every bit as much as Lexy had shaken with sadness. Did Carolyn think Lexy was about to kill her? The servant seemed to fight against herself as she offered her neck to Alexis. Alexis wrinkled her nose and looked down. Carolyn had peed herself, and it dripped down her leg onto the hardwood.

Seeing Carolyn's fear-caused reaction changed something in Alexis. Concern replaced her angry sadness, and her eyes calmed to their regular red color. "I would never kill you," she spoke softly. She looked at me, and her sadness returned. Alexis didn't look back at Carolyn. She simply walked out.

Carolyn continued to tremble as she stood there in her soiled servant garb. What had Carolyn experienced with her master—whoever that was—to make her that afraid?

I felt awkward standing there, so I hurried to the bathroom. As I showered, I regretted hurting Alexis. She'd overheard me saying I wouldn't pick her over Kendra, but I didn't mean that I was going to choose Kendra over her. I meant that I wasn't going to pick either girl right now. That would have been a much better response than saying nothing. Why hadn't I been able to think of that before she walked out? I slapped the shower wall, causing my hand to sting.

Why had I just let Lexy walk out? I hadn't even taken the opportunity to check out her naked backside. I pushed that unfiltered thought away and focused on how I had hurt her feelings.

I sat in the shower, thinking for a long time. I didn't wash my hair or my body. I just sat there, letting the water pour over me, feeling the magical energy of running water. Twenty minutes must have passed before Kendra tapped off her separation stone and jumped in my head.

I'm ready, where—Oh, my gosh, you're still showering! Sorry.

As she tapped her separation stone, I hurried and thought, *Wait, don't go.*

A few seconds went by before her mind, tentatively, joined mine again. I kept my eyes closed as I told her, *Lexy needs you.* I let her see my memory of what had occurred between Alexis and me. Kendra's anger grew.

You can't be mad at her right now.

Oh, yes, I can! Kendra snapped back.

Well, you'll have to be mad at her some other time. She needs you too much, and she needs you now.

Fine, Kendra conceded. *By the way, I'm the one who has been waiting and waiting this time.* Kendra tapped out of my head. Ten minutes later, I was dressed—yes, in a dark gray hoodie—and looking for Kendra. I didn't have to search. We had an emotional rope connecting us, so I walked directly to the hidden doorway to Lexy's cavern—now Mr. Espinoza's. Just after I arrived, the bookshelf swung open. Kendra stepped out and then closed the bookshelf behind her.

"She's not here," Kendra shrugged. Kendra had dressed in two tops, a white shade shirt under a black camisole blouse with thin shoulder straps and lace and frills arching over each breast. Her jean shorts hugged her hips tightly and extended just beyond her mid-thigh. The jeans' maize yellow matched the color of her converse shoes. *Ugh!* I forced myself to stop analyzing her outfit.

"Where else have you looked?"

"Everywhere."

"Where did she go?" I asked, not expecting Kendra to answer. If Lexy left, Kendra wouldn't know where she'd gone any more than I did.

"Did you call her?"

"Four times. No answer."

"Text?"

"I texted her after each call."

I pulled out the smartphone that I'd only had for a couple of days. I dialed Lexy and waited. No answer. I texted her: We are going to Kevin's. We need you.

Lexy wasn't supposed to go off alone. She had sent Pasha to visit his family, but hopefully Sajid was with her.

"Sajid?"

"I texted him," Kendra explained. "No response."

"So we don't know if he is with her or not?"

Kendra shook her head. Even if Sajid were with her, he didn't have magic. As her generals, Kendra and I were supposed to stay by her side.

"Do the servants or Jody know where she has gone?"

"No," Kendra shook her head. "But I asked both Carolyn and Jody to call me if they see her."

"Did you check the garage?"

"That was my next stop."

We stood just a few steps down the hall from the garage door, just past the two paintings. One painting was all black with swirls around an eye. The other was red-and-black line art that could be either a red-outlined vase or two women's faces with blood spilling from their necks to their breasts. I couldn't force my eyes to see the vase anymore.

Kendra walked over and opened the door to the garage. Each car, or motorcycle, had a spotlight over it. One spotlight illuminated an empty floor.

"The convertible's gone," Kendra shrugged. "Do we find Alexis or go to Kevin's?"

"Well, we need to get to Kevin's, but I don't know if Alexis is OK."

"Can you break through her separation stone?"

I pressed against Lexy's separation stone, but this time, I couldn't break past its barrier.

My phone rang. I quickly pulled it out of my pocket, certain it was Lexy. The phone said: "Unknown number." I answered.

"Jake?" Kevin's voice said my name. "Are you on your way?" We were supposed to meet him at his dad's work just after ten. It was already nine-forty-five, and the drive would take just under thirty minutes.

"Almost," I answered. "We are getting a late start. We haven't left yet. Be there in half an hour," I promised, then hung up.

Kendra stood just inside the garage. Ariel stood next to her, though I hadn't seen her enter the garage.

"We gotta go," I said. "If Lexy won't answer her phone, Jody or Carolyn will text us when she gets back." I turned my eyes to the cars in the garage. "Which one?"

Kendra eyed the various vehicles in anticipation.

"You at least have a learner's permit," I told Kendra, "So do you want to drive?"

"Heck, yes!"

I regretted letting her drive the instant I offered. Now, I would have to sit through a long drive with nothing to do but think about Sis's arrest, O'Brien's spine, and Lexy's emotional devastation.

CHAPTER 20
HACKING

Jake and Kevin are geeks to a depth a drill-team girl like me may never understand. I'm smart. I have a 3.9 GPA. But I'm not into spending my free time on computers or chemistry. I couldn't imagine choosing to learn geek stuff as a hobby. I prefer dancing. I used to spend hours of my free time with Justine studying dance moves and choreographing new dances. —Kendra

"**D**ad has a private conference room booked for us," Kevin spoke in almost a whisper as he led Kendra, Ariel, and me through the glass office building's third floor. Gray cubicles checkered the area where software developers quietly coded away. With fifty people working, the silence surprised Kendra and me. I could hear the clacking of typing and not much else.

The floor-to-ceiling windows gave a similar westward view as Lexy's mansion, only twenty miles further south. Instead of the Great Salt Lake, we could see suburbia extend almost to the Oquirrh Mountains. The famous Kennecott Copper Mine marred the mountain as surely as my self-flaying magic had marred me.

"Just in here," Kevin opened a heavy, wood, conference room door.

Inside was even quieter than outside.

Kevin set his laptop on the conference room table. I expected lots of computer equipment in the conference room, but it only had an empty table, chairs, and a projector.

I sat down next to Kevin and set down my—well, Eldra's—laptop next to his. Kendra followed Ariel to a whiteboard where the doppelganger girl grabbed dry-erase markers and started drawing, properly behaving as if she really were only nine.

"First, let me get a debug build of the email software," Kevin said. "Then we'll copy it over, install a debugger, and—" "Do I have to listen to this?" Kendra asked.

Kevin gave her a grin. "The world does need more girl software developers."

"How many drill team girls become software developers?"

"I don't know, but maybe you could convince the whole team!" Kevin suggested.

Kendra rolled her eyes as she shook her head no.

"Wait here," Kevin stood and opened the door. He walked out of sight for a minute then came back with a tan, brunette woman in light jeans and a gray V-neck. Despite the simplicity of her outfit, she looked like a model.

"This is Kendra," Kevin introduced the new woman to Kendra, ignoring me.

"Hi, I'm Arupta," the woman spoke with a barely noticeable Indian accent. "That is a beautiful top," Arupta complimented Kendra's black, frilly camisole over her white shade shirt. Arupta didn't have magic. She was just a regular human woman. Still, her wide smile almost alleviated my stress. For a second, I forgot that I didn't know where Alexis had gone, that both Mom and Sis were in prison, that O'Brien's surgery had failed, or that Eldra had died. Smiles didn't need magic to be powerful.

Arupta offered her hand to Kendra, who took it and shook it.

"And who is this little girl?" Arupta looked past Kendra, smiling even larger for Ariel, who turned around from the whiteboard, pursed her lips, and turned back.

"That's Ariel," I answered for her after she refused to reply.

"Your hair is beautiful," Arupta offered. "I've never seen lavender hair look so natural. Who dyed it for you?"

Ariel turned back around, gave a wide grin, but again, she didn't answer.

"Uh, we're just babysitting her," I offered in place of an answer.

"Kevin says you would like the tour," Arupta turned back to Kendra. She opened the door and pointed outside with her arm.

I watched Kendra follow Arupta out. Ariel looked my way. She knew she was expected to go with them, but she preferred to stay with me.

"Go with Kendra," I confirmed.

She frowned, but she went. My jaw almost dropped at the image she'd drawn on the whiteboard depicting the face and shoulders of a young Native American woman holding a baby close. While the thick dry-erase markers had prevented detail, the outline was beautiful.

"That will keep them busy," Kevin grinned. If he noticed Ariel's drawing, he didn't comment. "I guess Kendra isn't a jeek like us."

I raised my eyebrows at the comment, but Kevin had already turned back to his computer. Was Kevin correct? Was Kendra not a jeek? I wanted to challenge Kevin and argue and defend Kendra's jeekness. But I had never thought about whether she was or wasn't a jeek, so I had no data to back up my argument. Instead, I simply said, "Maybe not."

Kevin walked me through the process of checking out the source code from their private git repository for their Encrypted Contact software. After he pulled it down, he compiled the code in debug mode.

We worked for about a half-hour until we found ourselves at the point in debugging where the code compared my fingerprint with Eldra's. We tried to make it work, but the security measures in place were too strong.

Kevin left the conference room and a minute later brought in a scruffy-looking nerf herder in his fifties. He had a gray-white beard and white hair. His T-shirt had a picture of Han Solo and said in Star Wars font: "I code Solo." The shirt wrapped unflatteringly around his potbelly. An inch of his fat stomach—with hair—was visible as it lopped over and covered more than half of his leather belt. His outfit needed serious help.

"This is Alan," Kevin introduced the man.

Alan didn't offer me his hand or say anything.

"Is your username Alan1?" I asked.

He cocked his head at me as if confused. "A Tron reference? From your whiny-ass generation?" He glared at me.

"Yes," I pronounced the word 'yes' like the floating bot in Tron.

His grimace disappeared. He didn't smile, but his lips held a flat line. He offered me his hand. "You're all right!"

"I watch a lot of movies," I added. "I lived a life deprived of a streaming service, but my stepdad hoarded DVDs."

"Ah. Your stepdad sounds like a great man," Alan nodded.

I shrugged. My creepy stepdad—now deceased—was far from great, but Alan didn't need to know that. I didn't want to bring up anything that might change his mind about my being OK.

"So, what's your problem?" Alan asked Kevin.

Kevin explained the problem in explicit technical detail that I struggled to follow. I'd taken one coding class with Kevin my sophomore year, but I didn't study coding in my spare time. I spent my free time watching movies and reading books. What personal studying I took involved football and chemistry. I'd always assumed I would become a chemical engineer, working in a field like immunizations where I could protect people from getting sick. Kevin, however, spent every spare moment he had coding. He coded part-time for his dad.

"That's a dumbass idea," Alan spoke matter-of-factly to Kevin. "Move."

Kevin didn't take offense at all. Instead, he looked at me with a smile, and behind Alan's back, he mouthed, "No social skills, but," then he added out loud, "he's the best."

Alan changed tactics from overwriting her fingerprint with mine to adding my middle fingerprint to the list of Eldra's approved fingerprints. He dropped some swearwords as he typed, debugged, and failed a time or two. Ten minutes later, Alan made a fist and shook it in celebration. His upper lip hit his bottom teeth, clearly forming an F sound.

"Don't swear," Kevin quickly tapped Alan's shoulder.

"Freaking A, then," Alan modified. "It worked. But now your dad will set me to fixing this security flaw."

"Is it a security flaw if it requires source code?"

"It doesn't, though," Alan growled. "I did it in code, but all I did was access the private key, apply encryption, base-64 encoding, and inject your friend's fingerprint into the correct place in our cryptsql database. I have to write up a security report on this. I'm supposed to get half the five-thousand-dollar bonus for this. I don't suppose this is a paid gig," Alan grumbled.

I wasn't really listening because I was logging in with my middle finger to *Encrypted Contact*. It worked. Their email software looked like all email programs. The inbox had a red parenthesized number next to it—two hundred twenty-seven. How was I going to get through that many unread emails? Were that many emails sent since Saturday?

The door opened. Kendra and Ariel followed Arupta back into the conference room.

"Oh, my heck, Kevin." Kendra had a grin from ear to ear. "How come you haven't shown me coding before. I thought it was a lame guy thing."

"I solved that misconception for her," Arupta bowed, taking full credit for changing Kendra's mind.

"I didn't know coding could be so awesome," Kendra continued. "Why aren't there more girls coding?"

"Who knows," Arupta answered. "I'm a girl, and I love it."

"Coding kicks ass," Alan added to the conversation. "But we are short on vaginas."

Kevin cringed and Kendra's mouth fell open.

Arupta rolled her eyes. "Maybe that answers your question, Kendra." Arupta scowled at Alan. "Alan has no social skills."

"What?" Alan's face looked shocked. "I was quoting you," the coder defended himself. "I heard you—"

"No, Mr. Eavesdropper." Arupta cut him off and shook her head. "Just no!"

"But . . ." Alan started.

"Different context," the female coder held up her hand, cutting him off again.

"Anyway," Kevin interrupted. "Thanks for your help, Alan," Kevin exaggerated his words as he ushered Alan out of the conference room.

Alan paused just outside the door and looked back in. "We still on for tonight?"

"Yes, Alan," Arupta answered.

"Good," Alan nodded as he left.

Kendra tilted her head at Arupta questioningly.

"I'm giving him social skills training. He likes this lady that goes to his church, and I'm helping him out by teaching him to say the right things and improve his social interaction. He's not very good at that, as you can tell."

"That's OK. I'm on board with getting more, uh," Kendra hesitated, trying to find better words than what Alan used, "more girl power into coding," Kendra winked at Arupta, true girl power rolling off her as Arupta gave her a fist-bump. Eldra would have approved.

"Could you get the whole drill team here for a tour?" Kevin challenged.

"Why stop there? Bring every girl in your school," Arupta added.

"Probably," Kendra answered Kevin. With Lexy's help, she could get the drill team to do almost anything. She shrugged at Arupta, unsure about bringing every girl in the school. "It's a bit of a drive, though."

"It's barely five miles," Kevin pointed west and a little north toward West Jordan High School.

Kendra glanced at me as we both realized that Kevin didn't know we'd registered at Woods Cross.

"What?" Kevin asked, reading our eyes.

"I'll do my best," Kendra offered. "Which girl on drill do you have your eye on?" she changed the subject.

Kevin's cheeks reddened. "Not telling!" A bead of sweat formed below his brow. "Jake, let me install *Encrypted Contact* on your phone so you can read your emails on it, too."

I drifted from their conversation back to the list of emails. I felt Eldra's life taking over mine. The need to go through these emails pushed into me as if it were a person in need of protection. Eldra had dedicated much of her life to these businesses. For the past decade, she'd been on the board of a fashion company. Since the Day of a Thousand Deaths, she'd taken the place of deceased druid board members on over thirty other companies. However, she'd helped the Vampire King infiltrate almost half of those companies by replacing herself and other board members with people under his control. She still held a board seat in seventeen companies.

I glanced up to make sure no one was looking over my shoulder at the screen. Ariel had returned to work on her whiteboard drawing while Kendra chatted with Arupta. Kevin had my phone, setting up the email software app. I adjusted the laptop for just a bit more screen privacy.

I opened the first email, the last of a chain including thirty-three previously unread emails, each one marked as urgent. I couldn't believe who the email was from. Darla—the latest one-name pop singer sensation—had started a designer clothing line. She wanted to add a line of leather clothing for her fans who wanted to dress like her—in leather. It was a ten-million-dollar decision—five million on buying up multiple small leather design companies and another five million investing in growth. The board was split, and I was the deciding vote. I had already decided to vote against the motion, so I quickly wrote my response. I typed Eldra Locksley at the end of the email. Typing that name shook me. Hadn't I died? Wait. I wasn't Eldra, and I hadn't died. Eldra had died. I—Jake—had only pretended to die.

Help! I pushed the thought out past Kendra's separation stone. I needed her. Her memories of Jake—er, me—could bring me back, and I needed her now.

Kendra tapped off her separation stone and told Kevin and Arupta, "Let me check on Jake." She left Kevin and Arupta talking and walked over to me. She put one hand on my back and looked at the screen over my shoulder. Like she'd done at the hospital during O'Brien's surgery, she administered memory therapy. We shared the memory of when she had sought me out earlier this summer on the Fourth of July. About five minutes before the fireworks would start, Kendra had laid on the grass next to me. We looked at the dusk sky together. Sis and the guy she was with that night—Austin—lay on a separate blanket a few feet away. I glanced at Sis, and she nodded. In Kendra's memory, I'd looked to Sis for permission, and Sis had granted it with that nod. In my memory, I'd promised Sis I wouldn't tread on her territory, that I'd find a way to escape. To me, Sis's nod meant that she agreed that I shouldn't make a move on her best friend. Yes, I had wanted to watch the fireworks with Kendra, but I'd assumed Sis had forbidden it. I'd gotten up to use the bathroom and said I'd be back, but I bailed on Kendra and went and hung out with Luiz.

I felt guilt—*my* guilt, which helped me feel like me, not Eldra.

Thanks for fixing that failed fireworks moment at Eldra's memorial, Kendra kissed my cheek. *Lexy would love a new leather designer,* Kendra read the email over my shoulder and offered her opinion. *I'll tell her I convinced you as a peace offering.* After that, Kendra helped me rewrite the email. I quickly changed the wording to say that I fully approved and had a very interested customer, and perhaps, a niche demographic. Typing the answer as me, not Eldra—though still signing with her name—helped keep Eldra's memories from overwhelming mine and taking over my life.

I clicked send.

How does it feel to have just spent ten million dollars together? Kendra asked.

Did we really just spend ten million dollars on a new leather designer for Alexis?

At that exact moment, a wave of fear flooded into us, coming from Alexis. I pressed my mind at Alexis, trying to push past her separation stone. It hadn't worked earlier. This time, I noticed it felt different. As if her separation stone were reinforced with a containment. Kendra's worried eyes met mine. This time, I didn't give up. I pushed pinholes into that containment, slipped through it, and then pushed at her separation stone with more force.

Alexis's fear collided with us like a blitzing outside linebacker hits a quarterback. Worse, her agonizing pain shot into Kendra and me.

CHAPTER 21
TAKEN

Jake doesn't know the effort my mom went through to get pregnant and carry me to term. The symbiotic protist that creates a vampire, sometimes misnamed a virus, makes giving birth impossible. The protists prevent an egg from attaching to the uterus wall. A vampire male can get a human woman pregnant, which results in the birth of a dhampir. A dhampir has altered DNA and is a carrier of the symbiotic protists. I don't want Jake and Kendra to know the pain my mother went through to lower the protists count and keep it low long enough to give birth to me. —Alexis

Lexy's right arm throbbed unbearably above her elbow, where it bent awkwardly. Blood dripped down her arm from where the point of her broken humerus poked out of her skin. A half-dozen strong hands held her down. Other vampires? Between her anger and anguish, I couldn't grab many of Lexy's thoughts. I got the sense of a dark warehouse. Sajid's lifeless body lay beside her. The separation stone pushed me back out before I could get more information. I tried to force my way back into Lexy's mind but couldn't get through a second time.

I stood quickly and snapped shut Eldra's laptop, drawing Kevin's and Arupta's attention. "Sorry to cut our visit short."

"We're late for . . ." Kendra tried to come up with a fake excuse, but Lexy's fear flustered her, and she couldn't come up with a good lie. Why had six vampires taken Lexy and killed Sajid?

I grabbed my phone from Kevin as we pushed past him and Arupta. We almost forgot Ariel, but she followed us, leaving behind a near masterpiece on the whiteboard. We hurried toward

167

the elevator, our loud, hurrying feet causing developers to pop up like prairie dogs to see the cause of the noise.

"But the lunch meeting with my dad," Kevin shouted.

"Reschedule," I shouted back.

I looked for a sign that directed me to the stairs but didn't see one, so we continued to the elevator. Kendra and Ariel ran more quickly than I could. The ancient little girl pushed the down button with childlike enthusiasm.

What do we do? Kendra asked as we waited for the elevator. Her face had turned pale and she was clearly shaken.

Ariel glanced from Kendra to me with curiosity.

I don't know.

Who might know who took her?

I don't know, I repeated, and I hated that I'd answered that way twice.

I thought about that. Who *might* give us an idea?

Carina? Slash Donaldson? Or could we find Alexis ourselves, using the spell Eldra had recently tried to use to find Kendra?

Didn't that spell fail? Kendra asked, which reminded me that it had, indeed, failed.

Still, we'd try.

The elevator arrived with a ding, and we rode it down, mentally discussing our options. We didn't find many. Kendra agreed that if the spell failed and neither Slash Donaldson nor Carina knew anything, we would be out of options.

We exited the elevator and ran out of the building. It felt good to run, even if my run was slower than Kendra's and Ariel's. Kendra rushed to the driver's side of the silver Porsche 911. It had a removable hardtop, but we hadn't had time to remove it. Ariel slipped into the back from the passenger side and left the door open for me. Kendra started the Porsche before I arrived at the passenger door. I was barely seated when she shifted into gear. Quickly, I grabbed the door handle and pulled it closed. I took out my phone. I didn't have Carina's number, but I pulled out the paper Slash Donaldson had handed to me. I had a feeling he could contact Carina.

As Kendra drove toward the mansion, I dialed Slash's number. The phone errored, and the error message read: "Direct calls are forbidden. Use the *Encrypted Calls* app." I felt annoyed and simultaneously grateful that my secure phone didn't allow me to invalidate its security.

I redialed using the app. It took longer than usual for the call to connect.

"Officer C. J. Connelly," Slash's voice answered.

I'd forgotten he used that pseudonym.

"You know who this is, right?" I asked.

"I do," he answered. "Is there a conflict?"

"Sort of. Alexis has . . ." I stopped because I didn't know what to tell him. "Did Princess Alexis call you?"

"No," Slash answered.

"Do you have Lexy's mother's number?"

"Carina is no longer Alexis's mother," Slash didn't answer the question, but his response was surprisingly filled with concern. Perhaps he wasn't concerned with us so much as he was concerned we would miss his meeting. He wouldn't want to lose his chance at thirty million dollars.

"I won't be calling her in a motherly fashion," I replied. "It's an all-business call."

"I don't know her number, but I can text someone who can have her call you. What's your number?"

I didn't know my phone number. That was part of the security on our phones. Instead, there was an app that provided either a one-time number or a good-for-the-day number. I clicked the app and selected the good-for-the-day option and read it off to Slash.

"Thanks."

"Will you make our meeting?" Slash's voice faded as I pulled the phone from my ear to hang it up. I ignored his question and pressed the red phone-shaped hang-up icon.

"If I'm to keep you safe, I may need to know what is going on," Ariel's nine-year-old voice suggested from the back. I glanced at Kendra. She shrugged. I turned back to Coyote's granddaughter, explaining Lexy's broken arm and the rest of what I'd seen through the Trinity of Mind.

"Sajid is dead?" Ariel questioned.

I nodded. Eldra's death still hurt. With Sajid's death, I just felt numb. I barely knew him. We'd had one conversation at Eldra's memorial. Kendra felt sad, but not for Sajid. She felt it for his family. Pasha went home to see his. Sajid would never go home again.

Ariel asked a few follow-up questions, but I didn't have answers for her.

We made it to the mansion just after one o'clock. We would have less than two hours before we had to go to practice again. Would we make it to practice today?

Ariel ditched us to look for Carl.

Who were those other vampires who had Lexy? How do we find her? This is worse than when you were taken. We knew who took you and how, and we still had Eldra. We don't know anything about who has taken Alexis, and with Eldra gone, we have to find her alone. Should we start with Eldra's tracking spell?

I'll get Lexy's hairbrush, Kendra ran upstairs.

I watched her go, then wandered toward the dining hall.

I could still feel Alexis on my list of protectorates. I hadn't had a vision of Lexy's impending demise, so perhaps she wasn't about to die, but she already had a fractured humerus. I kept touching the bone at my right bicep when hints of Lexy's pain slipped through to me. Were Lexy's captors torturing her? Or had the broken arm occurred during her capture?

As I entered the dining hall, I nearly ran into Lillian.

"Oh," Lillian gasped. "We'll prepare you lunch immediately," she recovered. She turned and headed around the long dining table toward the kitchen. I followed her.

I should have known you'd go looking for food, Kendra jumped in my head after finding I hadn't waited for her at the bottom of the stairs. *Where should we be when we cast this spell? I'm not casting it in the kitchen in front of the servants.*

Eldra's room, I answered, and moments later, we met there.

Kendra held up Lexy's brush.

"How do we cast this spell?" she verbalized the question, even though she was already rummaging around my mind for the memory. I didn't need the memory. I'd cast this spell so many times in my two-hundred-year life.

You're not Eldra, Kendra reminded me. *You were only born this century. We do need to learn from Eldra's memory, though, Jake. Will you be OK?*

I had lots of memories of casting this spell, but I pulled up the most recent memory, which was my own, not Eldra's. In the memory, Eldra had held Kendra's hair in her palm and had asked Alexis and me to put our palms under hers.

Kendra held out the brush, and I pulled some strands from it and cupped them in my palm. Kendra put her palm underneath mine. She returned to the memory, noticing how Eldra had felt the magic around her, and then breathed it in before pushing it into the strands of hair. Kendra and I each took a simultaneous deep breath, pulling magic inside us with the air.

My memory became the equivalent of a YouTube tutorial. "Wait until it is so intense you can't push anymore," Eldra had told me.

We compressed the magic into the strands of Lexy's hair. As the power intensified, a sphere of red and blue lines began to flow around the strands.

I wish I could see magic like that, Kendra mentally voiced her jealousy, repeating the phrase Alexis had used.

"*Sécan*," we spoke an Old English word in unison to invoke the spell.

Our hands warmed, then became hot. Too hot. The strands lit up in flames and burned away.

"Ouch!" Kendra yanked her palm from underneath mine.

"What happened?"

"You burnt me," Kendra shook her hand, then looked at it. "I mean, it isn't really burned. It just got hot."

"That should have worked," I scrunched my eyebrows together.

"Maybe you can't use Eldra's memories and experience exactly the same way she did. Your magic is way stronger than hers. Wouldn't it work differently?"

I considered that for a moment. Did that make sense? My magic was stronger than Eldra's. Why hadn't I noticed before? When I cast Eldra's lightning spell to kill the remaining water babies, I had wanted the spell to be more powerful, so would I have noticed my extra strength?

"OK. Let's try again."

I pulled more hair from Lexy's brush—there was plenty—and again cupped it in my palm. Kendra cupped her palm underneath mine. I watched the magic spread around the strands of Lexy's hair in a perfect, glowing sphere made up of red and blue lines. I remembered the brightness of the magic light in Eldra's palm. Instead of pushing the magic until it was so intense that I couldn't push anymore, I held it steady at that same brightness. Kendra was right. I wasn't Eldra, so I didn't have to push hard.

As the sphere elongated its shape, the points began to bounce like a compass. The magic shaped itself into a definite arrow and the bouncing stopped. It pointed firmly in one direction, south, not wavering in the slightest. This spell wasn't struggling like it had when Eldra had found traces of Kendra at her home. There was no mistaking that if we followed this arrow, we would find Alexis. It also provided distance. Lexy was forty-five minutes south, which would put her in Provo. Eldra's memories took over as I let the magic arrow give me more details. She moved further south every second, traveling fast. That meant the freeway: I-15.

What's south on I-15? Kendra asked, and she answered her own question, listing the cities. *Spanish Fork, Payson, Santaquin. Nephi, Fillmore, Beaver,* then *Cedar City, St. George,* then *Las Vegas.*

When she thought Las Vegas, my head began to spin. I staggered backward and collapsed on Eldra's bed. My spirit lifted from my body. Through the Trinity of Mind, Kendra reached out and held onto me, either to keep my soul in my body or to hitch a ride; neither of us was sure which. I panicked, not because I was astral projecting again, but because astral projecting usually meant someone needed protecting. Was that someone Alexis?

Despite Kendra's efforts, my spirit broke free from her mental grip and lifted straight up out of the house and high into the air. I traveled south at a rapid pace. I didn't follow I-15, but instead, I took a direct path over the curving earth.

The beauty of Utah unfolded below me as I traveled the length of the state. The Rocky Mountains rose majestically to the east and seemed to shrink as I flew slightly west, distancing myself from them. The dry, flat land of eastern Utah held a unique beauty in the evening light. The sky dimmed as I traveled. Was I moving forward in time? I arrived in Vegas to behold a beautiful red sunset.

I had traveled from Bountiful to Las Vegas in just over a minute.

I continued to fly, only more slowly now. I astral projected directly over the strip, which wasn't really that glamorous compared to the vivid red sunset that drowned out the flashy lights. The many buildings looked small from so high up—at least, they did until I started descending.

I approached just west of the Stratosphere. In the distance, I could see other casinos and hotels, including the Luxor, the one that looked like a pyramid. Just past the Stratosphere, I descended rapidly. Too rapidly to be sure enough of the location to find it again.

I slipped down through the roof of an old building and passed a few dark, unused floors before reaching the basement and stopping in a large room.

The light in the room was dim but not dark. Girls dressed in almost nothing wandered the room or sat on various sofas entertaining a dozen guests. A wood-topped bar with stools lined one end of the establishment. Shelves holding various liquor bottles decorated the wall behind it, except in the center where a mirror reflected a reverse duplicate of the room. My reflection wasn't in it.

I found myself next to a man who was sitting on a couch. He looked familiar, but I couldn't quite place him. In front of him stood a Native American girl dressed in just enough to cover the essential parts, her outfit decorated in an offensively stereotypical

Native American style. A beaded headband wrapped her forehead and dark brown hair, which half-covered her tiny dreamcatcher earrings. Her bra was made of brown leather, and from the top of each cup, a row of leather fringe ended with a dangling feather. Matching fringe hung all the way around her barely-there bottoms. Despite looking at her feet, she maintained a forced smile. A chubby man stood next to the girl, a hand on her shoulder. He had light hair and a face dotted with pockmarks and freckles. His hand did not rest lightly on her shoulder. Instead, it gripped firmly in a claim of ownership.

The man I could almost recognize handed a gunnysack about the size of a grocery bag to the pockmarked man, who took it. He must not have expected it to be so heavy because he almost dropped it. He opened the sack and pulled out two six-inch-tall glass cylinders holding gold coins. He took the lid off one and tipped a coin, three inches in diameter, into his hand. The imprint of a bear stared up at us.

Bear? I turned back to the man on the couch. A few of Sir Alfred Tennyson's features remained. While the shape of his nose and mouth were unchanged, he now had deep brown eyes and black hair over a more prominent forehead. His darker skin now looked only a shade lighter than the Native American girl's. His hiking books were on the wrong feet. He'd changed back to a Native American but kept some of Sir Alfred Tennyson, becoming a hybrid of two people.

The pockmarked man signaled to a thin old man who stood to the side of a bar. The old man walked around the couches, glancing at the patrons' interaction with the girls, as he brought over what looked like a voltmeter. The instrument had the words *Gold Analyzer* branded on it. The man tested the coin, then half-grinned. "Pure twenty-four karats, boss."

"Shanna is yours," the chubby pockmarked man declared, pushing the Native American woman's arm forcefully toward Bear. Bear took the young woman's hand, gently lifted her wrist to his lips, and kissed it. He didn't see her as a woman he had purchased, but as a woman he had rescued.

"Shanna Chegup," Bear included her last name, which the seller hadn't yet provided him. Up until he spoke her name, the young woman had refused to meet Bear's eyes. The sound of his voice speaking her full name carried magic and drew her eyes to his. His eyes offered peace to her. "It's a pleasure we could meet up," he rhymed with her name. Her fake smile transformed into one that reached her dark brown eyes.

I wasn't sure why I was witnessing this scene. I didn't feel the burning desire to protect either Bear or Shanna. Bear led the woman from the busy room toward a steel door, behind which a dark hallway stretched for thirty yards. Many of the ceiling tiles were missing, exposing pipes and cut wires that hung down like long fingers, ready to grab an unsuspecting victim. Most of the lights were out, and sharp-edged shadows swallowed all but the center of the hall. The shapes of the shadows brought back recent disturbing memories. If I were in my body, I might have had a panic attack.

The Native American deity led the woman he'd rescued down the hallway and safely past the shadows and wires. The benign shadows never lashed out, and the wires hung impotently, never grabbing a victim. After a turn, a stairwell led up to another set of steel, windowless doors. Bear and Shanna exited through the doors into a now-dark alley. The sun had set. A glowing darkness had taken over the sky, blocking any view of the stars. Bear hustled toward a large, four-door Dodge Ram.

My protector magic made me aware of the danger that hid in the shadows. Halfway to his truck, Bear sniffed the air, sensing the threat as well—perhaps too late.

Twelve silhouettes—vampires—left their hiding places with inhuman speed and attacked. Two men and ten women.

Bear responded with equally inhuman speed. He spun Shanna behind him, deflected the first male vampire's claw, redirected a short blonde vampire's bull rush, and stopped a strong, stilettoed kick an inch before it pierced his ribs. The second male vampire's fist crashed with full force into Bear's left cheek. The hit twisted Bear away from Shanna. A fifth vampire swiped Bear's legs, dropping him to the ground.

"I thought I felt a protector's soul," an unexpected voice spoke just to my right, startling me. Without a body, I didn't jump, per se, but my spirit lurched. "I followed so I, too, could know," Bear's spirit explained, with a slant rhyme.

I turned and found Bear's spirit in the illuminated shape of a massive bear bending down to put his maw close to my ear. Bear had a round head with light brown fur that turned reddish around the eyes and ears. He looked like a Kodiak bear except even more enormous. My entire head could easily fit into his mouth. His appearance startled me as much as his unexpected voice had. Seeing Bear's spirit beside me reminded me that the vision before me would occur in the future.

Before I could respond, Shanna screamed. I turned back to her in time to see a woman—a vampire with long straight red hair wearing an emerald blouse and black pants—shove her hand into Shanna's chest under her left breast. When she pulled out her hand, she brought Shanna's heart with it in a vicious *Temple of Doom* moment. She opened her hand and watched the heart as it beat three times, then stopped. Who was this vampire woman, and why was she impersonating Mola Ram? The redheaded vampire grinned, then bit into the heart as Shanna's body collapsed to the asphalt.

The other vampires worked to tear limbs from future Bear's body. They left him for dead, but I could see his lifeforce left unharmed in his limbless torso. One vampire found Bear's key fob and clicked a button on it. The truck's lights flashed, and its four doors unlocked.

Vampires darted to each door, then opened them.

Inside, a second Native American woman hovered low. She had black hair cut in a jagged pixie style around high cheekbones. Her slick, thigh-high boots and black, side-slash mini dress suggested she had been working a corner before Bear picked her up. My protector magic flared to life even before I saw the boy. The prostitute held him in a tight hug as if she could hide him beneath her bosoms. The boy from the reservation—the young new shaman—was on my list. Bear had promised to train this boy in magic so Coyote didn't "ruin" him.

"The boy's mine," the redhead laughed, then she took another bite of Shanna's heart.

The vampires pulled first the young woman, then the boy, from the truck. The boy didn't fight or scream. Instead, he closed his eyes and trembled in terror. The vampires didn't use their allure to control either victim because they didn't want them to be willing. No, these vampires wanted them flavored in fear.

The redhead moseyed toward the young shaman and gave him a bloody smile. "This heart is getting cold," she laughed and dropped the shredded organ. Blood covered her hand and dripped past the tattoo of the letters MK on her wrist. I turned my head, refusing to watch as the horde of vampires descended on the woman while the redhead went all come-in-heart, Temple of Doom style, on the boy.

I turned to my right and looked Spirit Bear in his large round eyes. "I have to save him. I will save him," I promised.

"Thank you, Jake, for showing me this mistake," Spirit Bear replied. "I will move up my rendezvous and rescue these two lost Nuchu. I must leave Sin City before dark." He didn't rhyme with his last sentence. He simply spoke his truth. Bear didn't need me to save him or the boy. He was a being that had survived the lifetime of multiple worlds. He wasn't even worried about saving his future self, because it was clear, the Bear in my vision still had his lifeforce intact. Despite the deaths of all those around him, had he not shared my vision, he still would have survived to morph another day. Of course, now that he was forewarned, this event would never take place. The need to immediately drive to Las Vegas to stop this atrocity left me.

As my spirit started to rise, a black SUV pulled up. Bear's eyes widened as he looked at the vehicle. Perhaps he could see inside it? Bear grabbed my astral projection's ankle and held me from rising further. My protector vision had ended, but a Native American Deity had decided I would stay longer, so I did.

Four doors opened, and six large vampires—all men—slipped out. Two more vampires, females, exited the back doors. One was Asian, Chinese maybe, and the other was blonde with fair skin. The two female vamps pulled a chain-bound Alexis out of the back. Her broken arm had healed out of place, giving her right bicep a bent look.

Lexy didn't struggle as the two women hauled her toward the four shredded bodies. The vampires had already dragged the dead bodies into a pile about ten feet from the truck. The two female vampires that held Lexy looked to be about half her size. Both wore black leather, but not like Lexy's. Theirs was not genuine leather, but a shiny material as fake as the Asian's blue hair color. While Lexy's leather armor was handmade to her exact measurements, their pleather counterparts were tacky, mass-produced, off-the-shelf trash. Perhaps these vampires didn't have Lexy's resources or taste.

The two vampire women would be stronger than they looked, but Lexy had them by at least five inches. She also had magic that they didn't have. How had they captured her? Perhaps all eight of them had jumped her. Had Alexis entered that dark warehouse willingly? On a sunny summer day like this one, they couldn't have grabbed her outside.

The Asian vampire put one hand on Alexis's head and tried to push her down. Alexis held firm, so the blonde kicked her in the back of her legs, dropping Lexy to her knees on the aged asphalt. Her chained hands rattled loudly. The blue-haired woman grabbed Lexy's black hair, using it to direct Lexy's eyes at the four shredded bodies.

"Look," the Asian leader commanded. "This is what happens to those that steal *kenzies* from Master King's territory."

"Her arm is healing," the fair-skinned vampire warned.

"Henry," the Asian called.

A thick-necked, tan vampire with brown hair and a bodybuilder's physique walked up and grabbed Lexy's elbow in one hand and her shoulder in the other. He lifted his knee, and with a quick yank, he rebroke Lexy's arm around it.

Lexy hissed in pain. She began bleeding again out of the compound fracture.

One of the vampire men, a short, stocky man with curly black hair, lifted out a rusty propane tank from the SUV. A short hose connected the tank to a long metal pole. I heard a click and saw a spark and yellow flames with a blue-green center spit from the pole's wide end.

The stocky vampire walked over to the bodies and held the flame on their feet, slowly moving the fire up to their torsos until the bodies burned on their own. Flames illuminated the otherwise dark back-alley parking lot.

I had been wrong. My eyes widened. Had Bear not joined my vision, he would not have survived. I watched his lifeforce burn away.

My soul, pulled by protector magic, fought against Bear's hold, trying to return home. Bear's spirit dimmed. Holding me in place sapped his energy.

"In America," the Asian woman grinned, "the vampire king is not your grandfather." Still holding Lexy on her knees, she leaned into her ear, her blue hair draping over her cheeks. "He no longer rules here." She nipped the top of Lexy's ear. Blood dripped down the rim of her ear until it formed a droplet at her lobe as if it were a ruby earring. Just before the droplet fell, the blue-haired woman licked from Lexy's lobe to the top of her ear, savoring the blood.

"You taste better than they claim." She touched her tongue to her fangs and lowered her lips closer to Lexy's neck. She snapped her fangs inches from Lexy's jugular. "Too bad Master King forbids it," she whispered in Lexy's ear. "Maybe I bite a drink anyway."

Lexy whipped her head sideways into the cruel woman's face, breaking her nose and sending her flailing backward. Lexy twisted and punched the blonde woman with her left fist. Before Lexy could stand, the musclebound vampire wrapped around her, pinning her arms and squeezing like a boa constrictor right where her right arm had broken.

Alexis cried out in pain.

"Drake," the Asian vampire called, her voice muffled by her hand, which held her nose as it gushed blood. The man with the torch turned and walked toward the Asian. She removed her hand from her nose and briefly looked at her bloody fingers before turning her eyes to Alexis. "Badger, record this."

Another vampire with black badger lines tattooed over his eyes came forward, pulled his phone out, and started recording video.

The Chinese vampire signaled to Drake, and he lifted the torch and stepped toward Lexy. "Master King said to eliminate you if you were going to be a problem."

Drake pushed the fire toward Lexy's face.

"No! Start low," the Asian woman spat, "so she screams longer before she dies."

I watched as Drake brought the propane torch lower and put it right between her kneeling legs. The leather began to shine. As it caught fire, it scorched and pealed. The flames rose over her torso and spread around her breasts.

Bear's grip on my spirit failed. Had he not held my spirit in place, I never would have seen Alexis. I wouldn't have known her captors had brought her here.

"Pay attention to when you were pulled home," Bear shouted as I launched up into the sky, "It's important that . . ."

But the sound of his voice faded too quickly. Whatever his important words were, he hadn't spoken them in time.

CHAPTER 22
WHERE IS SEXY?

Without Kendra, I think I'd go insane with Eldra's memories. Or perhaps I'd simply become Eldra. How would I dress if her memories took over? Would I become a crossdresser? A drag druid? I'm a teenage boy that likes girls—a lot. Hopefully, with Kendra's mental memory therapy, I can stay that way. —Jake

T traveled back over the landscape of Utah, now terrible and frightening. This time, I saw Utah for not only its beauty but also its threat. Harsh weather, dry wind, snow, and floods had mercilessly cut the beauty from the eastern Utah desert and the Rocky Mountains.

The Great Salt Lake seemed a falsehood and a lie. With a promise of plenty of water, the lake spread wide and long, like a con artist's conniving smile at knowing that the water hid a salty poison that would sicken all who drank of it.

The safety I felt in Utah had stemmed from the cities built by the pioneers, who'd broken this terrible land with their blood, sweat, tears—and even their lives. Mobs had forced the pioneers to flee Missouri to Nauvoo, Illinois, a deadly, mosquito-infested marsh. But that hadn't been a terrible enough choice of land. Angry mobs continued to slaughter the oppressed pioneers and forced them to flee the United States in the 1840s. They fled to the worst, most unlivable, and driest land possible—a land I could now see for the terrible conditions it provided. It wasn't just a desert; it was a salty, barren wasteland that sought out and killed all life that tried to live here. Never before had I seen Utah in this way. The ability to build a city in this wasteland was a miracle that proved a higher power.

My astral-projecting spirit lowered through the mansion roof, past the top two floors, and into Eldra's room. Kendra sat on the bed next to my motionless form as I slipped back into my body, breathed in deeply, and sat up.

"I'm so glad your back," Kendra spoke verbally, while with the Trinity of Mind, she ingested the memory of my vision. The magic arrow we had used to find a direction to Alexis was gone.

Kendra stood up from the bed and faced me. I grabbed her waist, pulling her into a desperate hug, using Kendra to fend off the fear that I had been left with after seeing the vampire burning Lexy's body with a torch. The hug helped significantly. And not just because I was sitting on the bed and Kendra was standing, so my face ended up hugging her soft breasts. The hug provided just enough distraction for me to remember that my vision would take place in the future. Nobody had burned Lexy—yet.

Kendra's heart sped up as the embrace turned more intimate than she expected. Neither Kendra nor I wanted to end the hug, but we did. Kendra sat back down next to me on the bed.

"We have to save her," Kendra spoke first. "I . . ." she didn't finish, but I could feel her emotions. Despite Kendra's constant catfight with Alexis, she cared for her like a sister, or perhaps, like a twin. The Trinity of Mind had created a bond stronger than blood between the three of us, a bond that could never be broken.

"Your vision took place just after sunset." Her hand trembled as she pulled up her phone and opened the weather app. "Sunset is at 8:34 P.M.," she added, then pulled up her phone's map. "It takes over six hours to get to Las Vegas."

I touched Kendra's hand to calm her down.

"Call Pasha," she suggested. Could we rip him away from his family the very day Alexis sent him home for a visit?

I dialed. A few seconds later, Kendra and I stared at my phone, listening as the other side rang and rang without an option to leave a voicemail. Kendra texted Pasha but he didn't respond.

"Why did we have Alexis send him home?" Kendra said as she slumped her shoulders.

I shrugged. Did we really regret that? Or were we just stressed that we couldn't find Lexy? Had Pasha not gone home, would he be just as dead as Sajid?

"Or maybe, with twice the protection, Lexy would have escaped," Kendra argued.

"Let's make sure to take both Raijin and Astrapi." The staffs were reservoirs of magic, so I took a moment to draw magic from my surroundings, filling both till they were full.

I called Luiz. He didn't answer, but I got a text from him saying he was at work. As I started texting him, I wondered what if it had been him, not Sajid, who had died? I decided against texting him.

A knock came at the door to Eldra's room. We both jumped off the bed as if we had been caught doing something wrong on it.

"Come in," I called.

"The servants said you wanted lunch," Jody held a tray of warm, roast beef sandwiches.

I hurried over to Jody and took two sandwiches. Kendra followed and took one, too.

"We gotta go soon," I told Jody. How much could we share with her? She'd seen a lot recently. I didn't think telling her that Alexis had been kidnapped would help the distraught woman.

What about when Mr. Espinoza wakes up? Kendra thought.

"Hey, Alexis might not make it back by dusk. So . . ." I started, but I didn't know where to tell Jody to go.

"I should take Carl to the hotel tonight," Jody finished my sentence for me.

"The hotel?"

"Alexis booked a long-term room at the Comfort Inn & Suites by Woods Cross High School. She said we can use it on nights that she can't make it back by eight."

"Yep. Go there tonight."

"We really have to hurry," Kendra shrugged apologetically. Then we dashed back toward the garage, sandwiches in one hand, druid staffs in the other.

Coyote's granddaughter must have had some type of sixth sense because she stood at the garage door waiting for us. She wore a stuffed backpack and held a large bag of jerky. She bit into a large piece just as we arrived.

Carl stood with her. "I want to come with you," he stated firmly.

"Another time," Ariel put her nine-year-old hand gently on the boy's cheek.

He nodded.

The three of us jumped back into the Porsche 911. CJ watched from the door to the garage as Kendra drove us away. Ariel frowned in the back seat as if she knew she would have to save my life again. The staffs barely fit in back at an angle over her legs. Ariel pulled out a phone that looked like mine and put in earphones, a behavior that almost convinced me she really was just a nine-year-old.

The protector magic shook in me. It didn't want me to go to Las Vegas. I ignored the feeling. Saving Alexis was too important.

No sooner did we hit the freeway than Kendra floored the gas. It was just before 2:00 P.M., and she wanted to be well out of the Wasatch Front traffic before four. The speedometer went up to 200, but Kendra evened out when the needle pointed between 100 and 110. The car was small enough that she could easily weave from lane to lane to maintain our speed.

We were already in Provo when my phone rang. I answered.

"Jacob Stevens?" the voice sounded just like Alexis.

"Lexy?" Had she escaped? I hoped.

"No. This is Carina."

I should have noticed the slight difference in Lexy's mother's voice. Her voice was not quite the same pitch as Lexy's, and she had spoken my name formally. Lexy would have called me Jake.

"Some vampires took Lexy," I explained.

"When?" Carina asked.

"Almost two hours ago."

"Do you know who?"

I pulled up the memory of my vision. "They're taking her to Las Vegas. There was a bunch of them. One was an Asian woman with blue hair. She seemed in charge. She mentioned Master King multiple times. Is that a name or a title?"

Carina swore, but not in English. I didn't recognize the language. It hadn't occurred to me until just now that English wasn't Carina's first language. Alexis spoke without an accent, and nothing in her memories suggested she had grown up speaking anything but English.

"First name Master, last name King. It is not a title, though he wishes it were. He claimed Nevada as his territory back during the wild west. I don't know a lot about him."

"Any idea why he would take your daughter?"

"I'll call you back," Carina hung up.

The protector magic's urge not to go to Las Vegas came back. I did my best to ignore it.

Kendra drove on. She had her separation stone turned off. She passed the time by sharing memories with me to keep Eldra from taking over. Without Kendra and our connection through the Trinity of Mind, I would have become Eldra by now. I wondered how long I would need her memory therapy.

Speaking of therapy, when was the last time that I let my pitiful, albino, road-rashed looks use my self-esteem as a punching bag? Perhaps protecting others didn't give me time for self-esteem issues.

We passed a sign advertising gas and food options in the city of Nephi off the next exit. I'd have to try the One Man Band Diner someday, when we had time to stop and didn't have to go all Super Mario Brothers and rescue a princess. The phone rang.

"Carina?"

"I didn't know," Carina responded. "I thought Alexis had bested Father."

"What didn't you know?"

"Master King defeated Armon Jeffries in New York, then let him live and keep New York if he stood by him in a new Declaration of Independence. Jeffries had already conquered most of the United States. When he backed Master King, so did everyone else."

"The 1776 Declaration of Independence?" I asked, confused.

"No. This was quite recent. Master King sent it on July 4th, last month. They copied much of the wording of the original 1776 Declaration of Independence, but cleverly altered it. It includes signatures from all the powerful vampires in the Americas. They declared independence from my father's rule. Master King declared himself King of the Western Hemisphere."

"Was *King of America* taken or something?" I jested. "How does this . . ." I let my sentence trail off as I realized the ramifications of what I'd just heard. "The Vampire King answered Master King's declaration of independence by declaring Alexis Princess of the New World."

"Exactly. But there is more," Carina explained. "The more Alexis refused to kill, the more Father wanted her dead. Father is strong. Controlling him is difficult. Sometimes his desire presses on me," she paused. "By naming her Princess of the New World, he was making another attempt on her life, an attempt so subtle that we missed it. He gave his granddaughter her title after never refusing to recognize the new Declaration of Independence. Master King cannot let this stand. He will kill Lexy."

"Or Lexy will kill him," I argued in Lexy's favor.

"Either way, Father wins. He always wins. Even when we think he hasn't."

Lexy's Grandfather *was* an evil genius. We were fools to think we had beaten him. Could we ever be safe while he lived? Carina was supposedly controlling him, but what if he broke free?

"I cannot help you, but perhaps I know someone who can. I will ask."

"Who?"

"Better that you do not know." Carina hung up.

Eldra excelled at politics. She had served for over a hundred years as a druid ambassador. Could I lean on her memories to help diffuse this situation? If I did, would I risk losing myself? I remembered the propane torch lighting Lexy on fire. Maybe it would be better to erase anyone who threatened Lexy from existence?

Fyr Leoht. I imagined burning them, flames shooting from my hands, but as I thought it, I remembered spending days reading the druid manual. I'd poured over the spells. *Fire Light* was only one fire spell, but it was supposed to be a small flame, like a candle. It was *not* an attack spell, even though I'd used it as one. I had read an attack spell that used flame—or at least, Eldra had. The book had been an old but thin leather book. It had belonged to Caradoc's protector brother and was a handwritten list of protector-only magic spells. Caradoc had lent it to Robin for research, but I—er, Eldra had taken it from Robin and read it herself. It was a death spell that only worked on vampires.

Fæcele heorte. Torched heart.

It involved shoving masses of magical energy into the protists inside a vampire's heart and then lighting them on fire so that the heart burned from their chests.

Kendra shivered. She didn't approve or disapprove of the spell. She was more worried about me becoming Eldra. She stopped me from reading Eldra's emails on my phone and began reminiscing about our past. She brought up a memory of Sis, herself, and me riding our bikes down Sugar Factory Road to the West Jordan swimming pool. We would ride to the pool dozens of times each summer wearing just our bathing suits. Kendra chose the memory of the first time our parents let us ride alone. I was ten, Sis was nine, and Kendra was eight. Sis wore a blue one-piece that she was growing out of. Kendra wore a worn-out pink one-piece that I only now realized had been handed down through at least three of her older sisters.

You never wore a white bikini back then, I mused. I felt more myself and less like Eldra with the help of her memory.

I didn't have boobs back then. What would I have done with a bikini? She glanced at me with red cheeks, having realized what she'd just thought.

My phone made a very loud ding. I'd received a text message. The last time it had done that, the sound had given away our presence to a pair of voodoo witches in the Lost Rhoades Mine. My sister was the only one who texted me and . . . I just remembered she was in jail or juvenile detention. I hadn't even tried to visit her yet. *What kind of brother forgets his sister for two days?*

The kind who is in survival mode, Kendra consoled me. *She's my best friend, and I haven't thought of her either.*

I read the text. It wasn't Sis.

Can our secure phones get a text from a wrong number? I showed the text to Kendra.

It read: I can help. Where is Sexy?

She glanced away from the road to read it and shrugged, which caused her to turn the steering wheel slightly. The Porsche jerked just over the white line before she pulled us back into our lane.

Another ding signaled another text: My apologies. Autocorrect. Where is Lexy?

I texted back: Who is this?

Response: No names. Where is Sexy?

Another text followed immediately: Damned autocorrect. Where is Lexy?

I held the phone so that Kendra could glance at it while driving.

"Should I answer?" I verbalized the question because the car's jolt had alerted Ariel, and I could feel her eyes behind me, reading the text as I held the phone for Kendra.

"Last time we got help from someone we didn't know, we ended up babysitting a nine-year-old," Kendra teased.

"I currently look twenty-one," Ariel spoke from the back seat in a more adult-like voice.

I looked back, and Kendra adjusted the rearview mirror so she could see our now not-so-little doppelganger. A dozen empty bags of jerky and butter stick wrappers littered the seat and floor. Ariel sat higher in the seat than she had before. She still held her phone, but one earbud hung down, so she could hear us from her right ear. Her legs, which previously had fit easily in the Porsche's tiny backseat, were now forced to turn to the side to find space. The clothes that had fit her when she was a nine-year-old lay folded on the seat next to her.

"Why are you naked?" Kendra's voice jumped a few octaves.

Ariel's naked body didn't look twenty-one so much as it looked thin and emaciated. I could see her ribs where there should have been breasts, and her collar bones jutted out eerily. Her skin had plenty of color; otherwise, she would have looked like a starved-to-death corpse. The two druid staffs still crossed at an angle from the corner of the floor to the corner of the roof, adding to Ariel's discomfort.

"I'm too thin. I need more food," Ariel answered my look. "And no, you shouldn't trust this contact." She put her second earbud back in, turned back to her phone, and started using the thumbs on both. Was she playing a game?

"But why text us if not to help?" Kendra wondered. "Didn't Carina say she knew someone who might help? Maybe this is them."

I considered both their thoughts. They were both valid. However, did I have to fully trust this person to provide information on Lexy's location?

I replied: Las Vegas.

Another text came to me: Will be there in four hours.

I looked at the clock on the dash. It read 3:03 P.M.

"What are you playing?" I asked, but Ariel didn't answer.

"Lexy only installed one game for her so far," Kendra answered. "Mortal Kombat."

Another text: Try not to kill me.

I showed it to Kendra. Ariel touched my shoulder. She'd removed an earbud, interested again. I showed her the message, too.

"Strange," Kendra reacted. "Who do you think Carina would send?"

"I have no idea," I replied.

"Drill team and football practice started at three," Kendra reminded me.

"I'll text our coaches."

"Don't lie," Kendra suggested. "Tell them that a life and death situation came up out of town. Alexis says it is easier to manipulate people with her allure using the truth rather than using a lie."

I couldn't help but wonder if Lexy would survive to help manipulate our coaches.

"I'll also ask if they have a workout plan that we could follow to make up for missing practice."

I made a plan to try to call my sister as soon as I finished all these other calls.

CHAPTER 23
SHIVER

Is it my fault Alexis took off this morning? Would she have been captured if I hadn't broken our pact? Now that I've had more time to think about it, I feel less guilty for breaking the pact. Lexy acts like I did it on purpose. Jake simply needed therapy, and those other thoughts just happened. It's difficult to stop a thought pattern once it's started. However, I also pressured her to send Pasha and Sajid to their families. Though she'd only sent one, my thoughtless actions made her vulnerable. Then again, it also saved Pasha's life. Still, this is my fault. I treat her like a villain, but she's not. The bond we share through the Trinity of Mind is strong. I'll do whatever it takes to save her. —Kendra

As we traveled south on I-15, I scanned the Utah terrain, this time in slow motion. The Rocky Mountains loomed to the east. South of the Wasatch Front, they didn't look quite as majestic and tall. The barren land looked more cultivated than it had when my astral-projecting spirit flew over it earlier. Tiny towns dotted the interstate every dozen miles or so, with larger-but-still-small towns about every half-hour. It didn't look quite as inhospitable as I remembered.

We passed Fillmore, then Beaver. Later we passed Parowan, then Cedar City, followed by Hurricane and St. George. With each city, the protector magic reminded me that it didn't want me to go to Las Vegas. Perhaps I was interpreting the feeling wrong. Lexy was on the list.

Kendra didn't understand the protector magic either. She sped on. Twice Kendra slowed when the radar detector—standard in each of the Vampire King's cars—had beeped at us, but besides that, she kept a speed well above 100 miles per hour.

The red rocks of southern Utah often jutted out from crags, and sometimes made up entire cliff faces. The rust color continued into the northwest corner of Arizona and into Nevada.

We rolled into Vegas at 5:54 P.M.

I'd been to Las Vegas twice before, both times around Christmas for a college football bowl game—a Utah Ute's game and a BYU Cougar's game. Kevin's dad took us each time. We stayed at the Stratosphere the first time and the Luxor the second. Both times, our team won. After each game, we drove up and down the strip once before going to the hotel room. Kevin's dad sent us straight to bed and drove us straight home first thing in the morning, protecting us as much as he could from Sin City. Las Vegas looked surprisingly tame in the afternoon light.

Kendra tried to glance around while keeping her eyes on the freeway.

"Take the next exit," I suggested, pointing at a green freeway sign. "Let's pull over somewhere and get a direction on Lexy."

"And some food?" Ariel reminded.

"We're early enough. I guess we have time to order something," I agreed.

"But she isn't even dressed," Kendra once again complained in a high-octave voice.

Ariel yanked out her earbuds, set her phone aside, opened her now almost empty backpack, and pulled out a black skirt, a white blouse, and high heels that all looked like they belonged to Jody. She struggled in the confined space to pull them on. Once she did, they looked loose.

The protector magic didn't like that we'd entered Las Vegas. *You gave me a vision,* I mentally spoke to it, confused, but the protector magic didn't speak back.

Kendra pulled off the freeway and turned east toward the strip. She pulled into a parking lot across the street from a pizza place. A few people on the sidewalk stared at our Porsche.

"Let's get some pizza, then seek Lexy in the bathroom together," Kendra suggested as she exited the Porsche.

"Did you hear what you just said?" I chuckled.

"Yep, that sounded wrong." Kendra blushed.

Our grins didn't last. The worry for Lexy flattened our smiles as we crossed the street.

Do you feel the magic? Kendra asked through the Trinity of Mind. Magic brushed across our skin like a breeze, changing directions frequently as if hundreds of people nearby were continually casting magic spells.

A lot of minor magic users perform here, I answered her from Eldra's memories. As Druid Ambassadors, she and Robin had been stationed for five years in the nineties, living in various casino suites. Our last year we—er, Eldra and Robin had lived in the newly finished Stratosphere.

Outside, the restaurant looked to be just a corner building off 3rd Street. It was a great location, but nothing special. Inside, dim lights and the red and black color provided a romantic-ish atmosphere—if a pizza joint could be romantic. The cab of a shiny black semi with painted fire on the hood and wheel wells stood out as the main decoration. Somehow, it didn't clash with the atmosphere. The expansive dining area extended the distance of what could have been two more restaurants. It wasn't just a corner store.

More people than we expected, mostly couples of all different ages, filled the dining area. I glanced at Kendra. She shrugged. Going somewhere else would take just as much time as eating here. Only a few glanced our way, but those that did gawked at Ariel. She wore a black miniskirt that hung far too loose. The white shirt looked a bit short but still drowned her thin frame. Her entire appearance looked off—wrong.

This pizza place sold by the slice, which meant we wouldn't have to wait to eat. I wasn't going to have a slow dining experience while the image of Lexy being burnt alive loomed over me. Some of their pizzas had the usual toppings, but I'd never had a purple potato pizza before. I used the pay app on my phone to buy us eighteen slices, three each of the popular toppings. Our doppelganger girl, however, wanted four of their meatiest pizzas to go. We had to cast a spell, so maybe we had time to wait for four freshly cooked pizzas.

We ate quickly. Well, Ariel and I ate quickly. The oversized slices filled an entire plate. Kendra finished her second slice after both Ariel and I had finished our eighth each. I'd thought Kendra would only eat one piece, but perhaps the past two days of drill team practice took a lot of energy and left her hungry. Ariel asked for a pitcher of water, drank it all, then asked for a refill and drank that too, reminding me that an adult body is over sixty-percent water. Her skirt and shirt still didn't fit but looked less loose.

The three of us headed to the bathrooms—they weren't the small restaurant bathrooms with locks, but busy, multi-person bathrooms with stalls, so we couldn't lock one to cast the spell. Kendra and I split up to use the facilities anyway since we had just driven over four hours and then had dinner. I finished first and waited with Ariel for Kendra. Ariel didn't need to use the bathroom despite the amount of pizza and water she had consumed. I guess all those calories went straight to her figure.

"Let's find a back alley or something?" Kendra suggested. "We left the druid staffs in the car."

My premonition came to mind. My back tensed as I remembered the sight of Bear and the two native American women and the boy burning in a pile in front of Lexy as a vampire pushed a blow torch toward her.

"We won't need them for this spell," I glanced toward the sky, "or while the sun's out."

"We still need to go to the car for Lexy's brush."

"I need my pizzas," Ariel reminded.

"Wait at the table, and we'll come back for you after we cast the spell," I suggested.

Coyote's granddaughter eyed me.

"We're safe for now," I promised.

Ariel nodded in agreement. "I'm thirsty anyway." She pulled out her phone and earbuds and started playing Mortal Kombat.

Kendra and I walked out of the pizza place. After grabbing Lexy's brush, we found an alley behind the pizza joint. The evening summer sun hung low and didn't directly shine into the alley, but the late evening sky shared plenty of light. We didn't see anyone around. Still, we hid between two dumpsters.

Kendra tapped off her separation stone, then pulled out a few strands of Lexy's hairs from her brush. This time she held them, and I put my hand under hers.

Let's do this, she urged.

Wait. We need a containment. We were out in the open. I didn't want to broadcast to the entire city that two druids were in town. Maybe Las Vegas's magic "wind" would hide us, but I got the feeling that our combined power would stand out. Kendra wrapped a containment around us, using her imagination as there was nothing to mark a barrier with.

Would it be cliché if we started carrying chalk? I asked.

Both our phones chimed at the same time. It was a text from Jody that said: Your Bishop stopped by. Since Alexis stood him up, he talked to me. I want an hour of my life back.

Deal with it later, we both thought. We'd completely forgotten that Lexy had a meeting tonight with our church's bishop, but it wasn't important now. Of course, Kendra wanted the bishop to be important. The fact that she couldn't place any importance on his call just further added to her crisis of faith.

Where were we? Kendra asked, trying to focus.

You were creating a containment, I answered.

190

With the containment in place, we pushed power into the black strands.

"*Secan,*" Kendra whispered as, this time, she led the spell. The blue and red lines came to life, spreading out in a sphere before elongating into a six-inch arrow pointing due west.

The back door to the restaurant on the other side of the alley opened. Kendra and I froze in place. A thin guy with a nose ring and giant ear studs stepped out, holding a garbage sack in each hand. He seemed startled to see us. His eyes fell on the glowing item in Kendra's hand.

"Whoa!" He set down the garbage sacks and held up his hands. "You need to take that," he pointed at the glowing arrow, "and whatever you plan to do with it to . . ." he didn't finish but gestured a bit southeast. "This isn't the right area of town for that type of thing. You need to leave." He motioned with his hands for us to leave the alley.

Oh! That looks like a—I started.

No! Kendra snapped, trying but failing to cut off my thought. Kendra turned beetdigger red. I grabbed her hand and led her from the alley, unable to contain my smirk.

"This is a family part of town," the guy yelled at us. "You keep that away from here."

Where do I put this? she asked, holding up the red and blue glowing arrow awkwardly in her hand.

I laughed, unable to keep my unfiltered thoughts from answering her.

You're as bad as Luiz! She hit me with the glowing arrow. It felt like being hit with a Nerf dart filled with static. She tapped on her separation stone to avoid more mental embarrassment.

She didn't have pockets to hold the glowing arrow, so I took it from her and put it in my hoodie pocket. As I did, I realized I'd left my head uncovered. I now had normal eyebrows and an inch of hair on my head. Still, I looked like I was healing from crashing a bike and scraping off all my skin, ugly enough to hide under a hoodie, but I hadn't considered covering up in a while.

Ariel walked out holding four massive pizza boxes just as we reached the doors. She looked at me, saw my wide grin, assumed it was for her, and smiled back. I offered to carry the pizzas for her, but she shook her head. We made it across the street and back to the Porsche. Kendra had to slide her seat forward beyond what was comfortable just so the pizza boxes could fit in the back.

Kendra drove us west as we followed the magical arrow toward Lexy. As we drove west, the arrow turned more north. Vegas roads were mainly laid out in the grid system, so northwest wasn't an option. She turned north on Rainbow Boulevard.

"Keep going north till it is pointing directly west," I suggested. I pulled up the map app on my phone. "Actually, take Summerlin Parkway. It sort of curves northwest."

After a few miles, the arrow pointed north enough that we exited on Rampart Drive, but we found the arrow wanted us to cut through a golf course. We backtracked and got lost in a wealthy neighborhood and spent twenty minutes trying to escape. The clock read 7:03 P.M. We were wasting time.

We found ourselves back on Summerlin and followed it until the arrow pointed directly north. By the time we reached the next exit, it pointed northeast. We drove through multiple neighborhoods of mansions and by various golf courses before we found her. As we drove by one particular white mansion, the arrow turned and stayed pointed directly at it.

Kendra pulled over. "At least, driving a Porsche, we fit in," she gestured toward the millionaire estates around us.

"I fit in better, too," the now twenty-one-year-old-looking Ariel cut in.

Kendra and I looked back at our adult-looking doppelganger. No phone or earbuds. She'd eaten all four of the pizzas. The now-empty boxes still provided a strong aroma. We found her using her hands to adjust her breasts. The white blouse now stretched around them. Her lavender hair hung long and full. Her miniskirt now hugged tight to her thighs and left her legs bare down to her high heels. Did she think we were going clubbing?

"No bra," she informed. Her eyes took on a faraway look. "I didn't remember," she whispered, as if that explained everything, though it seemed she was talking more to herself than to us. As far as we knew, Ariel had very few memories. She'd told us that she only remembered a frozen sleep in the well, then waking for a few days before I freed her. She was hundreds, perhaps thousands, of years old. Where were all her memories? The other water babies hadn't lost their memories. Why had she?

"Maybe stop looking," Kendra gently put a hand on my chin and turned it away from Ariel's chest.

"My density is still low," Ariel mumbled. "I'll need more food and water soon."

I tried to ignore Ariel and Kendra by analyzing the mansion.

Kendra took the arrow from me and held it up, looking down it as if it were a rifle with a sight. "It points below the mansion."

"Underground?"

"I guess so." Kendra shrugged.

"I'm going in," I decided.

"How?" Kendra asked.

"Remember when I found Eldra and . . ." I started but stopped. Kendra wouldn't remember when I had used my senses to find Eldra, Carolyn, and Lillian, because she hadn't been there. Voodoo witches had captured her spirit, and she'd let them into the mansion. The voodoo witches had killed most of the servants and animated them into voodoo zombies, which is why Eldra, Carolyn, and Lillian had been hiding. I'd found them by partial astral projection—sending out only my senses.

I reached over and tapped off her separation stone to let her see my memory. She scowled at me but left it off. Until now, she hadn't fully grasped the servants' gruesome deaths or the brutality they showed after being turned into zombies. Nor had she seen Alexis's brutality at severing their undead heads. She began to tear up, as she blamed herself.

I closed my eyes and pushed my senses toward the mansion, leaving Kendra to experience her emotional pain without me. Unlike when I astral projected, my spirit didn't leave my body. Instead, only my senses and my focus left—it was still a form of astral projection, but I was still aware of being in the car, just not able to respond.

My senses traveled between two tall, white pillars, looking up at the huge mansion looming over me. The white columns made me think of the Parthenon, except there were only two of them, and the marble stood smooth and shiny instead of cracked and crumbling.

I traveled forward—not walking but not exactly floating either. My senses passed through the double-door entryway without opening the doors. The grand entrance hall didn't surprise me, but only because I was expecting immaculate elegance, and it lived up to my expectations. My eyes followed a narrow but lengthy carpet to a round staircase that rose to a balcony. Princess Alexis would not be upstairs in the tallest tower. This was not a fairy tale. It was real life.

I seeped through the floor's travertine tiles. I felt my senses find tiny pores and microscopic gaps within the tiles and slowly lower through them. Tall windows with deep window wells let enough sun into the basement to discern shadowy shapes. I spread out my senses, searching for but finding no evidence of a hidden room.

I let my senses once again seep into the floor. There had to be another area below the basement. I felt damp earth and sensed tiny living creatures crawling in it as I traveled deeper. It didn't take long before I encountered a stone barrier—or perhaps a cement wall. I slipped through it far more slowly than I'd slipped through the tile. For a few minutes, I thought my senses would be stuck in the dense wall forever before I found a crack and drained out of it into a lightless space.

My senses spread out again. This subbasement continued for some distance beyond the mansion, and multiple carved tunnels hooked into it. A dozen vampires slept in the first tunnel, nine of which were women. Fourteen more in the second tunnel—only two men, the rest all women. Two of the women stood awake, talking. A third woman rose from a sleeping space carved into the tunnel wall. I spread my senses to the next tunnel. The third and fourth tunnels held human thralls so tightly quartered that I couldn't count them all. There must have been more than a hundred in each tunnel. To my surprise, some weren't thralls. Their fear trembled in the air, vibrating my senses.

Alexis had urged Mr. Espinoza to choose his thralls from among those whose lives would see an improvement by it. His thralls were safer and more protected than they had been before he chose them. This was not the case here. The people I sensed shied away from corpses of those who had survived the vampires during the night only to die during the day—perhaps from blood loss? They didn't want to be here.

Every last thrall had a tattoo of the letters MK on their arms. Did Master King mark his humans like ranchers marked their cattle?

Free them! my protector magic whispered to me, but I didn't know how to obey. I also didn't want to see the dead bodies or feel the fear of the living, so I started down the fifth tunnel.

I'd never been inside a *crypt* of vampires before. Vampires considered any term associated with the grave the equivalent of a racial slur. Often a single vampire's home would vulgarly be called a grave, tomb, or coffin. Eldra and the druids called the home of multiple vampires a *crypt*—offensive, yes, but that was the druid's intent as there was no love lost between them and vampires. Druids also used *crypt* for a group of vampires, like *flock* was used for birds. Alexis, however, called both a group of vampires and their home a *shiver*. A clear memory of Alexis's tutor lecturing her came to mind.

"Shiver is the American term," her tutor explained to Lexy. "In Europe, a group of vampires is called a *colony*, which is the term for any community of one kind of species living close together."

"Is it not the term for a group of bats, too?" Alexis asked.

"Vampires have nothing in common with bats," the tutor snapped at Alexis. "Explorers of the new world encountered a new species of bat that sucks blood, and the feeble-minded assume a relationship. No, the term 'colony' didn't come from bats. Bats got it from vampires. The word's meaning as a group of vampires predates its first usage for bats. The British also used this term as they conquered nations around the world, did they not? But we called our groups colonies well before the rise of the British empire."

"Why do groups of vampires in the United States call themselves a shiver?" Alexis asked.

"In America, the thirteen colonies made using the British term too confusing. The vampires fled to the United States for the same reasons as everyone else; to escape oppression. They chose the term 'shiver' after the group name of another creature that can smell blood as well as we can. A creature that represented the ocean between them and we who had oppressed them: the shark."

I took comfort in knowing that Alexis had decided to never create vampires. She never planned to start her own shiver.

I wasn't quite sure why I had unrestricted access to Alexis's memories until I found her at the edge of my senses. She stood chained to a cement wall in the fifth tunnel. This close to her, I had somehow pulled that memory as if her separation stone weren't enabled. Was it because the edges of my senses shared the same physical space?

She shifted her head and breathed deeply, pulling in part of my senses. The rest of my spirit traveled from the car to Alexis almost instantaneously and followed my senses into her body.

CHAPTER 24
FIRE ALLEY

Did my mother betray me to Master King? I should be used to betrayal by now. My grandfather betrayed me, along with all the other vampires who pretended to care for me before I turned thirteen. Kendra betrayed our pact. Jake betrayed my feelings for him by not choosing me. Is there anyone left who has not betrayed me? —Alexis

Jake?

I convulsed for a second, causing the thick steel chains binding my wrists to rattle. Why was I wearing thick steel chains?

Give it back. Get out of my body! Alexis snapped.

Kendra hadn't liked it when I'd taken control of her body, but she hadn't been furious. Alexis didn't behave as I would have expected. She didn't seem relieved that I'd come to rescue her. Instead, she thrashed at my spirit, causing it to vibrate and pulse, making it impossible to think or communicate with her. My soul felt like it was being hit from all sides. Like when my coach called a hard run up the middle for short yardage, and linemen, linebackers, and safeties all hit me from different directions.

The last time I'd been in Kendra's body, I'd learned how to give up control, so I did that for Alexis. Even still, she wrenched control from me with fury and shoved at my soul.

You chose her! she shouted the thought and shoved me out of her body with a pulsing power far more potent than I was prepared for. My spirit launched from her. Before I came to a stop, I passed through a wall. My spirit shivered as a vampire walked through me, followed by a second vampire. I shivered again. It happened eight times as a shiver of eight vampires walked through my soul to enter Alexis's room. The shivering had to be a coincidence, right?

I didn't know all their names, but I'd seen these eight vampires in my premonition. Henry, the tan bodybuilder. Drake, the one with the torch. One was the blue-haired Asian, and another was the blonde. The other four had also been there, lurking behind their leaders. Again, the familiar MK tattoo marked their wrists—so it wasn't just for thralls.

"Bring her," the Asian woman commanded.

Alexis grinned mischievously. "Jié Shù," Alexis thinned her eyes at the woman. "You promised torture before these came off?" Alexis glanced at each manacle as the muscular Henry unlatched them from her wrists but left the ones on her ankles.

"Disappointed?" the Asian smiled back. "You won't be." She gestured to the bodybuilder, and he walked behind Alexis. He kicked her behind her knees, forcing her to kneel. He raised her right arm. I winced and tried not to sense what was happening, but unlike my eyes, my senses could not shut, so I saw him break her arm again.

Alexis held in her scream. I felt her pain despite her enabled separation stone. Why hadn't she disabled it so that we could find her? Perhaps she didn't want us to. Even though I hadn't chosen Kendra over her, she thought I had. In truth, I simply hadn't chosen. Would explaining that calm her down? Was she really that angry at me? Well, her belief that I chose Kendra was her last thought as she'd shoved my spirit out of her body.

That is when I noticed the silver box—the size of a wedding ring box—hanging from her silver chain. Did it cover her separation stone? Maybe she couldn't touch it? Could she turn it off if she couldn't touch it? I enveloped my magical senses around the box and found it let magic out but not in. Perhaps I'd judged Lexy too harshly. Sure, she was *vexed* with me, but she wasn't that petty. Had she been able to contact us, she would have.

The box proved her capture was premeditated and well-planned. Had her captors not done their research, they might have simply removed her protection stone. But with it removed, she would have full access to the Trinity of Mind. Kendra and I would have known everything the moment the necklace was removed. The box informed me that her captors knew about the Trinity of Mind, which meant they also knew about Kendra and me.

I'd occasionally managed to break through Kendra's and Lexy's separation stones, but I hadn't been able to break through to Alexis since her capture. Was that box the reason?

The manacles that had held her wrists now dangled from the cement wall. Henry disconnected the metal rings from that wall and used them to latch Lexy's hands behind her. The manacles at her feet did not need to be removed to disconnect from the floor. Instead, he used a key to unlock an ancient-looking padlock with a three-inch thick bar. Then, he grabbed Lexy by her almost shoulder-length hair and lifted her to her feet. He used her broken arm, chained at her back, to push her forward. With her first step, the chains on her feet caught, almost tripping her. She shuffled quickly to keep her feet and shortened her next steps.

As Alexis ambled past Jié Shù, the Asian laughed. "The torture is coming." She emphasized the first syllable of torture with a pause and a glance at Drake, perhaps making a pun by saying "torch-er"?

As I followed them through the underground tunnels, the four-foot-thick cement walls suggested this subbasement had started as a millionaire's underground bunker. The shiver of vampires must have taken it over and dug the tunnels out from it. I followed them up a flight of stairs that led to a secret door in a long garage. They led Lexy to the large black SUV that I had seen in my vision. Two female vampires opened the back doors, and Henry shoved Alexis inside. Was it silly of me to think that she'd be without a seat belt, and seat belts save lives?

I pulled away, letting my soul slingshot back to my body.

"Jake," Kendra's palm felt warm against my cheek.

"I'm back," I answered. The sun had recently set, and the color purple tinted the darkening sky.

The clock on the dash read 8:41 P.M. Ariel, playing Mortal Kombat on her phone again, dropped an earbud from one ear to listen. Her earbud tangled in her charging cable.

"It creeps me out when you leave your body," Kendra voiced, but she'd left her separation stone disabled and already analyzed my out-of-body experience. "It's like you're in a coma or something," she added. Then the car went quiet as Kendra reviewed what had just happened in my mind.

"Uh, um," Ariel reminded us that she couldn't read our minds so I mentally filled her in.

"I just don't understand the way Lexy responded," I shrugged. "She should have been happy that we've come to save her."

Kendra pursed her lips. "I think it fits her personality perfectly," she explained. "She struggles with a death wish, stalled by her feelings for you. But then, this morning, I broke our pact. You picked me."

"I didn't—" I started, but Kendra, shaking her head, cut me off.

"I know, but she doesn't. Is her death wish back? She does everything on her own, including surviving. She probably assumes she will either get out of this on her own or get her death wish."

"Let's cut them off at the gate," I suggested.

"Uhm," Kendra widened her eyes at me. "They have eight vampires."

"So?" I challenged.

"And a guy with a machine gun in the booth at that gate," Kendra added.

The image of Drake pushing his burning propane torch at Alexis worried Kendra as much as it worried me. I wanted to fight them as soon as they reached the end of the driveway. Kendra didn't. We both looked at Ariel for the tiebreaker.

"Wait for them and follow them," Ariel suggested from the back seat. "Just don't let them see you."

Kendra frowned. "We're in a Porsche." She'd never tried to discreetly follow another car before, let alone in a car that stands out.

"I think," Ariel started, then paused. "I think I've done this before. Let me drive."

Kendra didn't even hesitate. "I'll get in back," she said as she opened her door and stepped out. Kendra had to tilt her knees to the side to fit.

Seconds later, adult Ariel, who had looked nine years old a few hours ago, put the Porsche into gear and started driving with surprising confidence.

"What does their vehicle look like?" Coyote's granddaughter asked.

"A black SUV," I answered, remembering that she didn't have access to my thoughts. "But we haven't seen it come by yet. How do you know where to go?" I questioned.

"I just know," Ariel nodded.

The street we followed rounded the neighborhood of mansions with only one intersecting road leaving the circle. Palm trees lined both sides of the intersection. Ariel drove past that street and followed the circling road. Had she continued too far? We couldn't see the turnoff, just the palms on our side.

I glanced back at Kendra. She shrugged.

We waited about two minutes. I started to get antsy. I had no idea what Ariel waited for. Was she just guessing when the SUV with Alexis would come?

"Headlights on the palm leaves," Ariel commented and started driving again.

I raised my eyebrow. How had she seen the headlights? Sure, it was after sunset, and the purple sky had deepened, but it wasn't fully dark yet. I couldn't see headlights on the palm leaves. It left me wondering how much better Ariel's eyes were than mine. It reminded me that she was the granddaughter of Coyote, an ancient alien and a deity. She might not be as old as him, but how old was she? What had caused her amnesia?

Sure enough, as we passed the palm trees and turned right at the intersection, we could see a black SUV about fifty yards in front of us.

Ariel followed the black SUV from a distance for the next fifteen minutes. At first, we headed east, back toward the Stratosphere. With the sunset, the Las Vegas lights had lit up, decorating the skyline. Soon, we turned away from the Stratosphere. As I began to recognize the rundown area we drove through, the Vegas Strip lights dimmed behind us.

Was my vision about to come true?

But how? Why? Bear had promised to complete his business and be far outside of Las Vegas before nightfall. What had he meant to tell me that was so important?

"They are turning into an alley," Ariel informed us as she held the steering wheel with one hand and pointed. She didn't follow. Instead, she passed the alley entrance and continued beyond the boarded-up buildings until we were about a block away. She pulled into an almost-empty strip mall. Of the seven storefronts, three had for rent signs, and one was boarded up. The three stores that remained open were a smoke shop, a tattoo parlor, and a dry cleaner. The tattoo parlor glowed, illuminating tattoo-like window art, almost like stained glass, that prevented a view inside. Two cars sat parked in front of it. Even though a dozen other parking spaces were available, Ariel parked the Porsche between those two cars—perhaps an attempt to hide it?

"Is this area of town safe?" Kendra pursed her lips.

Of course it wasn't safe. Ariel and I treated her question as rhetorical.

We remained sitting in the Porsche. It didn't seem that any of us knew exactly what to do.

"If only Luiz were here." I shook my head. "He'd say something like, 'If we survive, let's get *I saved Alexis in Vegas* tattooed on our asses.' Only, he would say something far funnier."

Kendra grinned. Ariel didn't.

"You said," Ariel began, "that in your vision, the vampire Drake burns Alexis in just a few minutes." She thinned her eyes at me. "I assume you intend a surprise rescue."

I nodded. I glanced at the clock—8:58 P.M.

"Follow me," Ariel slipped from the Porsche.

Kendra grabbed Astrapí and I grabbed Raijin. No way would we leave our druid staffs.

The protector magic's worry returned. This time, I think I understood it better. It no longer cared who was on my list to protect because if I were dead, would the list matter? If the magic worried for me, I'd have to be careful, but I assumed that if I were going to die, I would have a vision, right? What if that wasn't how it worked? What if I only saw a vision if someone other than me was going to die? I pushed those thoughts away and ignored the protector magic. I was willing to risk my life for Alexis.

Ariel led us to the boarded-up building near the alley. The parking lot wrapped between the strip mall and the dilapidated building. We continued following our mythic monster.

"Even in a surprise attack, we will likely die," Ariel grumbled.

Next to a steel door leading into the dilapidated building, a one-inch steel pipe rose up the brick to within a foot of the rooftop, about twenty feet above us. Adult Ariel examined it briefly.

"We climb."

"You're in high-heels and a miniskirt," Kendra reminded Ariel, who tugged off her high heels and threw them up onto the building.

"That was the last thing the nurse Kelly wore on her most recent visit here," Ariel explained as she grabbed the pipe with both hands. "I realize now that she hadn't come to Vegas on a rescue mission." She jumped, put her bare feet flat on the brick straddling the pipe, and started walking up the wall.

"Sorry to throw you, Raijin," I told my druid staff, then tossed it onto the roof.

"They're named, not sentient," Kendra shook her head at me before tossing her staff onto the roof, too.

I grabbed the pipe to follow, but Kendra batted my hand down. "I'll climb behind her, thank you very much." She tightened her face at me, then glanced up at Ariel. The darkness hid whatever the miniskirt didn't, but I chose not to argue with Kendra's irrational moment of jealousy. Who did she think I was? Luiz? Besides, I was too worried about whether I *could* climb the pipe. I remembered the last time Kendra and I had gone rock climbing. I'd had all my muscles, making climbing easy. But now?

Kendra kept her yellow converse shoes on and walked up the wall, hand over hand underneath Ariel. The doppelganger reached the top of the bar, then leapt up, catching the roof ledge with both palms and launching herself the rest of the way up in one smooth motion à la Jackie Chan.

I grabbed the pipe. The metal felt cool in my hands. I yanked, but the sturdy pipe didn't budge. Surprisingly, it wasn't too difficult to climb the first five feet. Sure, I'd lost most of my muscle, but I was six-foot-one and only a hundred and fifty pounds. I didn't weigh much, and it didn't take much muscle to walk up the wall. That changed quickly at around fourteen feet. My fingers began to tremble with a burning ache. I looked above me to see Kendra standing on the edge, looking down at me. Each shift of my grip became painful. My knees shook, and my quads burned. Sure, it didn't take much muscle, but I didn't have much. My Achilles tendons and my calves screamed. I could feel a cramp coming on. It should have been only five more steps, but my hands didn't reach as high with each shift. I focused on not falling. The late evening darkness behind the building hid the ground beneath infinite shadows. If I fell, it seemed I would fall into darkness forever.

The next shift of my hands failed. My left hand grasped at nothing but air because it was dark and I couldn't see that the pipe had ended, elbowing into the wall just below where my hand flailed. I kicked with my feet, which kept me from falling for half a second before my right hand's grip failed. I started to fall.

A hand snatched my right wrist like a vice. I looked up. Ariel lay on her stomach, half her body over the edge and her left hand gripping mine. Without apparent effort, she stood while lifting me, reminding me very much of Alexis.

My feet made a crunching sound as I touched down. A couple inches of pebbles covered the entire roof—tiny playground-sized pebbles. I hadn't expected that. Was that something they did on buildings? I'd never been on top of a flat-roofed building before.

As I picked up Raijin, I grabbed a few pebbles. My pockets already had some, but who knew if I would need more. We were about to attack eight vampires, and I didn't remember any guns from my vision, so maybe grabbing more pebbles was a waste of time? To my left, I saw Ariel eat a handful of the little rocks. I watched her swallow, scoop a second handful, and swallow them, too. Her crinkled face suggested that she didn't enjoy it. Coyote's granddaughter looked up to find both Kendra and me staring at her with open mouths.

"My density, remember?" Ariel stated as if that was all we needed for an explanation. She ignored our stares. "This way." As she tiptoed toward the south corner of the building, she bent low, and her hand swooped down to grab and consume a third handful.

Kendra and I followed her, staffs in hand.

When we reached the southeast corner of the building, we still weren't close to where we needed to be. I recognized where we were. This was the alley where I'd had my vision. While astral projecting, I'd descended from the sky, so I better recognized the area from the roof. I could see the taillight on the back corner of the black SUV that barely stuck out where the alley turned to the right. In that hidden parking lot, I'd watched the vampires kill Bear, the shaman boy, and the two women that Bear had rescued from a life of selling their bodies. I'd watched Drake use his propane torch to burn their corpses. Had that already happened?

"Over there," I whispered, gesturing with Raijin. "We either have to climb down into the alley or jump across it to the next building," I added.

Ariel pointed to her ears. "They may hear us," she mouthed.

Vampires had enhanced hearing, but while this small alley didn't have many people, it wasn't quiet. The sound of cars could be heard, and music hummed from a nearby building, filling the night with background noise.

Ariel led us to the front of the building, the furthest point away from vampires in the alley, near the southwest corner. "Jump here." The alleyway was at least fifteen feet across. Last spring in track and field, before I'd burned off my muscles, I'd been able to jump eighteen feet in the long jump. But now?

"Uh," I started, but Kendra beat me to it by saying, "Yeah, we can't jump that far."

"I'll help," Ariel offered. She grabbed Kendra at her hips and directed her to the edge. "Bend down and jump. Give it your all."

Kendra glanced at me, then handed me Astrapí. I could not only see the fear behind her eyes, but it also seeped into me despite her enabled separation stone.

"You'll be fine," I assured her. "We can trust Ariel." I wasn't sure if I was lying. Could we trust her?

Ariel squatted down, put one hand spread wide on Kendra's stomach, and curved the other under her backside to her pelvic floor like a cheerleader spotter.

"That's uncomfortable," Kendra complained, her voice yet again raising an octave.

Again, I missed Luiz. Oh, the jokes he would make about this scene.

"One." Ariel counted, ignoring Kendra. "Two. Three. Jump!"

Kendra jumped. Coyote's granddaughter lifted and threw Kendra shotput style. Kendra flailed as she traveled over the fifteen-foot chasm between the buildings. She cleared the gap with at least eight feet to spare but didn't stick the landing. With a thud and scrape—no gravel sound—she fell and rolled.

"Your turn," Ariel suggested.

I set the druid staffs down. "Toss these to me once I'm over there."

After the other water babies had changed to human forms, they hadn't had enhanced strength. I studied our doppelganger for a second. From the shoulders down, I recognized the shape of the body she had mimicked, though it was significantly shorter. Her skin also seemed much darker than earlier.

"Are you cloning Alexis?" I asked.

"Yes. No," Ariel answered. "I rarely *clone*. I sampled Alexis to help me adapt."

"Because she is a dhampir and stronger than an average human, right?"

Ariel ignored my question, grabbed my hips, and shifted me into position. Then she put her hand on my stomach and her other curving low under my backside, just as she'd done with Kendra. Yep, that was uncomfortable.

"Lexy's magic?"

Ariel shook her head no, then started counting. "One. Two. Three. Jump!"

I jumped as the ancient doppelganger shoved my backside, and with the hand on my stomach, kept me vertical. For a moment, I felt like I could fly. But unlike Kendra, I hadn't added much strength to the jump, and despite burning off fifty pounds of mass, I still outweighed Kendra by thirty pounds. The edge of the far building came at me quickly. As my toes hit the brick ledge, my heels hung off. The way I landed absorbed most of my momentum. I found myself balancing precariously but slowly tipping backward.

Ariel grabbed me as she flew across the gap. Her right hand pulled me from the ledge and onto the roof with her. That made twice she'd kept me from falling. Had she made the jump with both staffs in one hand? Or had she started with a staff in each hand and shifted one of them mid-air so she could grab me?

Kendra brushed herself off. Then she gripped her elbow. She looked up at me with worried eyes. She held her elbow as she approached us. Blood filled the small scrape. One of the vampires would surely notice if a young teenage girl's blood added its scent to the air near them. I wasn't sure how far away they could smell blood. Could they smell it already? Either the blood had already given us away or approaching with Kendra's bleeding elbow would surely do so.

"The wind blows north," Ariel stated.

I couldn't feel the wind, at least not until she said that. I noticed Ariel's lavender hair flutter slightly and felt the faint breeze on my skin.

"Perhaps if we stay on the north edge of the roof," I suggested, which would put the vampires east of us.

Ariel gave me a look that seemed to say, "Duh, that's what I just said." She handed me both staffs, then grabbed the bottom of her white shirt and ripped it around her waist, leaving a two-inch white strip. She used it as a bandage, wrapping Kendra's elbow with the skill of a nurse. Well, she'd turned into a nurse just yesterday, so according to Bear, she'd have that nurse's skills. She tied off the bandage, held up Kendra's elbow, and nodded in satisfaction.

"It's not just my elbow," Kendra explained. "I'm," she glanced at me again, "I'm on my period. Day three. I didn't think about the scent of blood until this," she pointed at her elbow.

Ariel shrugged.

Why did I feel so awkward every time her period came up? It was a normal part of life, right? Still, I avoided the topic by silently leading the way toward the northeast corner of the building. Fortunately, this roof didn't have pebbles. The crunching sound would have given us away as surely as the smell of Kendra's blood.

Alexis can use a containment to hide her scent, I remembered to Kendra.

I can try, Kendra responded enthusiastically as she followed behind me.

As I peeked over the edge of the roof, I found myself looking down on a lot more than eight vampires. How had I forgotten? Or had I simply expected things to be different because Bear would be long gone? In my vision, there had been a dozen vampires waiting in the shadows surrounding eight more with Alexis. That made twenty.

Sure enough, Bear's truck was nowhere to be seen. A pair of vampire women—one the redhead who liked to eat hearts wearing the emerald blouse and black pants—dragged two men, one the fat pock-marked man, the other the older man who'd tested Bear's gold.

I did the math in my head. I hadn't cast magic today. With the element of surprise and time to concentrate, I could probably make a six-pack of marble-sized magic missiles. Kendra might be able to do two. Assuming all eight eliminated a vampire, that would leave twelve, but could we make that assumption? Once we attacked, I wouldn't be able to focus on more than a couple magic missiles at a time. I could use Raijin to blast them with lightning. But that might not kill them. It might only slow them down. Surely, Alexis would use the distraction to break free and take out those closest to her, or at least force the musclebound Henry to deal with her instead of us. So at least eleven vampires would attack us at full speed after that. With our staffs, Kendra and I might be able to erase eight more by the time they reached us. Ariel could hold off the others long enough to let us erase them, right? Probably not, but I mentally tried to convince both myself and Kendra that it was possible.

The risks were high. Would Henry kill Alexis? She had a broken arm, so how well could she really fight?

One tall vampire wore a dark cloak that seemed to absorb light. Something about him scared me more than the other nineteen put together. I got the feeling that if we attacked, my magic missiles might not penetrate his cloak. Could I use other magic? Could I torch his heart? If I did, how long would that take? Would we survive this?

My phone vibrated in my pocket.

CHAPTER 25
FRIEND OR FIEND

I love both Alexis and Kendra. How am I supposed to choose between them? What do they think? That I'll pick one and stop loving the other? That's absurd! I'm only seventeen. I'm not choosing. Maybe when I'm twenty-something, a choice will have to be made. But seriously, why now? Of course, Alexis and Kendra agree with me. That is why they made their pact. I need Kendra's mental therapy. I hadn't realized Alexis would freak out about Kendra helping me. She's angrier than I was when she almost said yes to Keagan's marriage proposal. —Jake

"We ducked back out of sight. Fortunately, I'd correctly silenced my phone this time, but it had still vibrated, which might have been loud enough for vampire ears. I carefully and quietly pulled my phone from my pocket. Before I could turn off vibration on notifications, I noticed the text message.

The text was from the same guy who texted about Alexis earlier. It read: I see you on the roof. Do not attack.

I showed the message to Kendra and Ariel.

Ariel's altered appearance caught me off guard. First, I'd noticed her darker skin color earlier, but now it was black as night. Second, she'd stripped off her white shirt. It lay wadded up in her hand, against the roof where it couldn't be seen, leaving her wearing nothing but a miniskirt.

"White is too easy to see," Ariel mouthed.

Kendra read the text message and shrugged. Kendra's white shade shirt was visible at the shoulders where the black camisole didn't cover it. "Should I remove this?" she asked Ariel, grabbing her white undershirt's collar.

Ariel touched the hem of Kendra's sleeve, pressing it against Kendra's skin, and shook her head, no. Kendra's light skin wasn't all that much darker than the white shirt.

I peeked over the roof edge again. Our location put us about twenty yards behind the scene below. The SUV parked directly below us. The blue-haired Jié Shù stood behind Henry, who held Alexis in front of the chubby, pockmarked guy who ran the underground establishment.

"Dale," Jié Shù shook her head. "You let a man walk away with two of our girls. We punish stealing!"

"He didn't steal her. He bought her," Dale's voice raised in nervousness. "He paid twice the asking price."

"Who was he?" Jié Shù asked.

"The deal required no names," Dale picked nervously at an especially large pockmark high on his left cheek as he answered.

"Describe him!"

"I don't know. Younger guy, maybe thirty, with brown skin and black hair. He looked Latino or maybe Native American, like the girl he bought."

"Black hair? Latino?" Jié Shù's voice raised, and her accent thickened. "Her spawn. Miguel Espinoza."

Did they mistake Bear for Mr. Espinoza?

The redheaded vampire that I'd seen in my earlier vision stood to the side of Dale. Jié Shù gave her a barely perceptible nod. The redhead smiled, then her clawed hand shot into Dale's chest and pulled out his heart. From this distance, I couldn't see if it beat outside of his chest.

Dale coughed twice. His eyes widened, and his face shook in fear for the last second of his life before he dropped to the asphalt.

"I'm certain you can continue this man's work, Wade," Jié Shù stated coldly to the older man that had tested Bear's gold.

Wade nodded.

"We do not do business with our enemy. Fern will check up on you weekly," Jié Shù gestured to the redhead, who took a bite of the heart, her mouth and hand dripping in blood.

"He paid double," Wade explained, then gulped. "In pure gold." Hesitantly, he held out the gunnysack of gold that I'd seen Bear use to buy the Native American woman.

"Linzi," Jié Shù called to the blonde woman next to her.

Linzi approached the man and took the gunnysack. She brought it to Jié Shù, who took the bag then let out a high-pitched screech and dropped it.

"It smells cursed," Jié Shù stepped back from the burlap bag. She pulled magic into her hands, forming a dark and hazy glow in her palms. The haze looked tainted, similar to the way Voodoo Whoopie's magic had. She pushed the magic at the bag of gold.

Kendra and I shivered as Jié Shù's tainted magic rippled into us with more strength than the ever-present Las Vegas magic wind.

Great! The Asian wasn't just a vampire. She could use magic, too. And she hadn't bothered to hide her magic in a containment. Was she not afraid of transients? Transients would surely come, but they didn't bother those with powerful magic, which meant Jié Shù was either stupid or strong. Then again, perhaps transients kept their distance from vampires.

Worse, I was just about to try to push at that silver box that covered Lexy's separation stone. Could I break through both? I didn't know, but it would take a significant magical effort. Would that ripple magic? Would Jié Shù be able to feel me trying? I didn't know, but could I risk it? I decided against it.

"She has magic. I don't." Ariel mouthed. "Take her first." Her eyes, thinned in worry, seemed to say more.

I nodded. During the Lost Rhoades Mine Melee, we'd defeated the half-water-baby half-ancient-alien shapeshifters because we used magic sight. Before using sight, our attacks only appeared to work. After a few minutes, the water babies had recovered. Once we'd used our magic sight, we learned where to attack to kill them. Jié Shù might not turn on her sight, but even an attack that took our ancient alien shapeshifter out for a few minutes would be enough to ensure that we would lose.

With magic on the vampire's side, our chances of survival just decreased significantly. I'd have to hit the Asian witch first while we had the element of surprise.

Jié Shù grimaced as her tainted magic wrapped the gunnysack of gold. After a minute of struggle, she dropped her spell and beckoned to the blonde vampire, Linzi. "The curse is strong. I can't break it. Throw it in the dumpster."

As Linzi obeyed, I remembered what Coyote had said about the gold in Carre-Shin-Ob. If we took any, we'd be visited by his big ugly frenemy—Bear. I doubted Bear cared when he spent the gold himself.

Kendra tapped off her separation stone and asked, *Should we attack or not?* Her stomach ached uncomfortably. Her desire to save Lexy contrasted with how her period left her demotivated. She didn't feel like a fight. She just wanted to sit at home on the couch. Despite feeling terrible, she'd made the decision to give her life to try to rescue Lexy.

We let the magic build up inside us.

"Drake," Jié Shù called.

I slid back behind the cover of the roof's ledge as Drake stepped around a dark-cloaked vampire who hid his features and started toward the SUV. Kendra and Ariel ducked back, too.

He's going for his propane torch.

My phone vibrated again, and another text read: Trust me. Do not attack.

But I don't trust you, I thought.

I don't trust him, either, Kendra agreed.

I heard the SUV door open and close. I didn't hear the spark light the torch over the ambient city noise, but propane fire lightened the shadows on the building wall on the far side of the alley parking lot.

My body filled with enough magic, ready to form a six-pack of magic missiles. Kendra filled her magic reserves as well. Ariel's fingers had lengthened into claws, and she no longer looked topless, even though she still didn't have a shirt. Scales now covered her shoulders, chest, upper arms, and thighs.

I turned to look back over the edge. Drake was burning the pockmarked man's body. Why hadn't I had a desire to save him? He wasn't just a strip club owner, giving women like Jody a job. No, he bought and sold women like cattle, forcing them into this life. A man who dealt in human trafficking was unworthy of protection.

Alexis, however, had always been on my list. There was no way I could let her die.

One vampire woman caught my attention. I hadn't noticed her during my vision. She was one of the twelve that surrounded the other eight who stood near Alexis. The fire illuminated her face, beautiful, dark-skinned, and surrounded by long dreadlocks. Her red eyes reflected the torch's yellow flame, making them look orange. I couldn't make out her outfit—something all black. I probably wouldn't have picked her out now, except her red eyes met mine. She'd seen us.

I started forming my magic missiles. Kendra created a containment around us so our magic didn't ripple and warn Jié Shù. I had to attack before Dreadlocks alerted the others. Except, the woman shook her head, no, at me. Her silent lips moved, forming a single word. Eldra's skill at reading lips far surpassed mine, allowing me to make out the word.

"Friend."

Three times, she glanced toward the SUV, or perhaps to the alley, and repeated the mouthed word. Kendra and I hesitated.

Just then, Drake laughed as he turned from Dale's burning body.

Jié Shù stepped to Alexis and grabbed her shoulder-length hair to steer her eyes toward the burning man. "Look!" the Asian commanded, shaking Alexis by the hair. "This is what happens to those that let our enemies take *kenzies* from Master King's territory. In America," the Asian woman grinned, "the vampire king is not your grandfather." Still holding Lexy on her knees, Jié Shù leaned, putting her lips close to Lexy's ear. "He no longer rules here." She showed Alexis the tattoo of the letters MK on her wrist. Then she nipped the top of Lexy's ear. Blood dripped around the rim of her ear until it formed a droplet at her lobe as if it were a ruby earring. Just before the droplet fell, the Asian woman licked the blood from her lobe to the top of her ear. "You taste even better than they claim."

I wasn't sure if I actually heard Jié Shù's words or if I remembered them from my vision.

The blue-haired witch slid her tongue to one fang and seemed to consider biting into Alexis. "Too bad Master King forbids it," she whispered. "Maybe I'll drink anyway."

Lexy whipped her head back and sideways into the Asian vampire's face, breaking her nose and sending her flailing backward. Lexy twisted and punched the blonde woman with her left fist, but before she could leave her knees, the musclebound vampire had her. He wrapped his arms around her, pinning her arms and squeezing exactly where her right arm had broken.

I would have attacked the moment Alexis had if not for the vampire with dreadlocks. She kept her eyes on mine and shook her head. She mouthed, "Friend is coming," every few seconds. If any vampire glanced at Dreadlocks, they would have seen her communicating with us. Fortunately, the surrounding vampires had their eyes glued to Alexis as she managed to stand, despite Henry's grip around her upper torso. Standing didn't free her, though. The manacles still locked her hands behind her back. A short chain connected her hand to additional manacles around her ankles. Still, she twisted and dropped, slipping down out of Henry's grip, and despite her chained ankles, spun one leg and swiped his feet, chopping his legs and sending him flipping to the ground. Then Lexy jumped, tucked, and looped her arms below and around her legs. Chains still connected her wrists to her ankles, but with her hands in front, her range of movement increased.

The vampire with black badger lines tattooed over his eyes, Badger, rushed Lexy. She grabbed him and tried to throw him, but his fingers gripped the chain linking her wrists. She struggled to pull free, but Henry grabbed her from behind again. Unlike in my vision, Henry didn't easily subdue Alexis. Instead, it took Henry, Badger, and Linzi struggling together to subdue her, and not without difficulty.

Kendra didn't want to wait any longer. She hadn't witnessed my vision firsthand, so instead of reading the dreadlock woman's lips, she watched Lexy struggle. *Why are we trusting that vampire?* Kendra asked. *And who is this friend?*

Ariel looked at me and shrugged, evidently agreeing with Kendra, despite not being privy to her thoughts. The shapeshifter dug her razor-blade claws into the edge of the roof in anticipation of a fight.

I won't watch Lexy burn, Kendra promised.

I won't either, I returned her promise.

Yet we continued watching the scene below. To my dismay, it continued to follow my vision.

"Master King offered to let me eliminate you if you misbehaved." She signaled to Drake, and he pointed his torch toward Lexy's face.

"No! Start low," the Chinese vampire spat, "so she feels it longer."

I watched as Drake brought the propane torch lower and put it right between Lexy's legs. The leather began to shine, then blackened, catching fire and burning upward. Flames rose up her torso and spread around her breasts. Alexis struggled, but Henry, the strongest vampire I had ever seen, held her in place.

I formed my six magic missiles. Kendra formed two. A hint of magic—not ours—rippled into us—so gently that, had I not had Eldra's experience, I wouldn't have detected it. It was not our magic. I recognized it as Lexy's.

The woman in dreadlocks looked nervous. She no longer looked at us but instead glanced from Lexy to the alley as if hoping her friend would arrive in time. Oh, great! Was Dreadlocks doubting that her friend would come?

We have to attack now! Kendra thought, rising to her knees. Ariel and I rose to our knees as well. If all the vampires hadn't been watching Alexis burn, they'd have seen us kneeling on the roof, our chests and heads in clear view. But they didn't see us. Watching Alexis burn was too mesmerizing. I kept the magic missiles below the roofline because their blue light would surely attract attention despite the other entertainment option.

As I lifted my hands to cast them, I saw the fire wrapping around Lexy's body, burning off her leather armor. But the fire wasn't the only light I saw. A thin layer of magic wrapped Lexy's skin. I dropped my magic missiles and put a hand on Kendra and Ariel, pulling them back down off their knees and onto their bellies.

Of course! I smiled. *How had I not realized this?*

Kendra pulled the knowledge from my mind before I mouthed to Ariel, "Alexis can protect herself from fire." Alexis had taught me to control the temperature around my body. Hadn't I picked up a pizza pan straight from the oven and redirected the energy so that my hands didn't burn? Also, while I watched the flames engulf Lexy, my protector magic hadn't ignited in the slightest. That was the important information Bear had been trying to tell me. The reason I'd seen the vision was to protect the boy that would grow up to be the Ute Tribe's new medicine man. Had Alexis been in danger of death, my protector magic would have kept the vision going longer, but it had sent my spirit home. It had been Bear's power, his curiosity, that had kept me in the vision longer and allowed me to see beyond the need to save the boy.

I peeked over the edge again.

Alexis remained kneeling as tall flames burned her leather outfit. The fire lasted minutes. Henry had been forced to let go of Alexis and back away as the fire burned the leather at her back. Drake walked around Alexis, making sure every piece of her clothes was on fire—except her necklace and silver box-covered pendent—then he, too, had backed away and turned off his torch. As the fire burned, pieces of Lexy's leather armor fell off, some as ash and some as chunks of leather that continued to burn on the asphalt around her. The soles of her boots dropped into a melted rubber goo that Alexis shifted her feet to avoid. Soon, the flames fell away from her. The light from the flaming chunks on the asphalt cast upward shadows on Lexy's exposed figure. Her silver necklace still hung from her neck, and the silver box locking her pendants away rested just above her breasts.

Ugh. Alexis found a way to get naked again. Kendra complained.

I raised an eyebrow at Kendra? *Are you victim-blaming? She just survived a burning like a true Targaryen.*

No, Kendra defended. *It was just an unfiltered thought. Besides, she's clearly not a true Targaryen. No dragons have hatched.*

That's too bad. Dragons would be helpful.

Smoke and ash blackened most of Lexy's exposed body. It also tarnished the silver box hanging from her chain. Sweat ran down her skin in various places, forming driplines on both her torso and thighs. The few patches of skin free of ash glistened on Lexy's kneeling body. Her perspiration gave warning that the fire had almost outlasted her magic. If Drake knew, he would light the torch and burn her till her magic gave out.

Lexy's laughter echoed from the asphalt below, followed by her voice. "Is this what you meant by torture?" She pointed at the end of Drake's torch. "Torch," she paused, "er."

Jié Shù's back stiffened.

"You should *end* the puns." Lexy emphasized the word 'end' with such an exaggeration that it clearly had a meaning beyond the obvious.

Jié Shù lunged forward and slapped Alexis, knocking her head so far to the side it almost looked like her neck broke.

"You dare dishonor my name," Jié Shù's Asian accent thickened.

My phone buzzed again. I looked at it. The *friend* had been right to warn me against attacking. We would have died. I knew it. Kendra knew it. Even Ariel knew it. While I admired our willingness to give our lives for Alexis, I couldn't help but shake my head at our foolishness.

The text read: It's time. You will want to kill me. Please refrain.

"Linzi," the Asian woman held out her hand. "Your blade."

Linzi lifted her shirt and pulled a knife from a sheath concealed inside her belt. The blade was only six inches long, but Alexis, who kneeled, naked and chained with a broken arm, couldn't defend herself.

Why hadn't my protector magic shown me this?

"Jié Shù," a man's voice shouted from the alley. Hadn't I heard that voice before?

All twenty of the vampires, including Linzi, still holding her blade, turned toward the voice.

"Master King prefers her alive," the Scottish accent hit me like a dagger. I could only see his silhouette, but I knew who he was.

Jié Shù gestured to Linzi to put her blade away and walked toward the silhouette.

"I didn't expect to see you here."

"Who is this?" Fern, the redhead, demanded.

"This is Keagan," Jié Shù replied.

CHAPTER 26
KEAGAN

In the last few days, Jake has really struggled to deal with me being on my period. Since day one, he gets all awkward every time it comes up. Well, he'll have to figure out how to deal with it because it's going to happen every month. In fairness, I'm a bit embarrassed that every month he will not only know but feel my discomfort through the Trinity of Mind. Perhaps I need to figure out how to deal with him knowing every detail about me and my girl things. Lexy's reaction surprised me. She avoids the subject, and Jake and I can tell she's hiding something with those mental lockboxes of hers. Usually, Lexy teases me about any topic related to sex. Why not this? ——Kendra

I clenched my teeth—the desire to kill Keagan pulsed through my soul like my blood pulsed through my veins. The temptation to erase him pulled at my willpower, begging me to give in. I couldn't find a part of me willing to fight it.

Kendra grabbed my hand. Her simple gesture destroyed the temptation and allowed me to breathe.

"What are you doing here?" Jié Shù frowned. "Think you can save this wannabe princess's life, do you?"

Keagan kept stepping forward until he stood a few feet from the thin, Asian woman. He smiled at her. "Actually, I came to save yours."

"Mine?" Jié Shù tilted her head. I had forgotten Keagan's foreboding demeanor and the effect it had on others. He hadn't become the Vampire King's general by mistake. There wasn't a vampire here that was his match. Perhaps Henry had more strength than Keagan, but if those two fought, Henry would be the one to end up dead. Jié Shù could use magic, so maybe she had an edge, but if Keagan feared any of them—or even if he feared all of them together—he didn't show it.

"You don't know how close to death you were?" Keagan's Scottish accent sang the question.

Jié Shù no longer looked sure of herself. She glanced around nervously at the other vampires.

"Alexis saved you all," he looked, for what seemed the first time, at Alexis. He nodded at her. She glared back with red eyes and lifted her manacled hands over her chest to give herself a semblance of cover. She did not demonstrate any gratitude at his unexpected arrival. "You don't know how lucky you are that she is invulnerable to fire," Keagan continued as if Alexis had not given him a death stare.

Did Keagan know the limits of her invulnerability?

Jié Shù continued to glance at different vampires.

"Not from your own," Keagan grinned and gestured to the vampires that failed to be subtle as they formed a circle around him. "I doubt any of your vampires would betray you. Besides, they are lucky, too." Keagan lifted one finger in the air and twirled it around. "You are all lucky. You all almost bled your last drop."

Nineteen of the vampires began looking around. Only Dreadlocks looked unconcerned.

"Why?" Jié Shù tried to gain her confidence back. "Because *you* would have killed us?"

"Me?" Keagan smiled. "I'd likely as not have tried. I'm a formidable foe, certainly. I'd probably have taken a dozen of you, maybe even fifteen."

"I doubt you could even take Knight Time," Jié Shù gestured toward the dark-cloaked vampire that Henry had stood behind earlier.

"The infamous Knight Time?" Keagan grinned. "I've hoped luck would allow me to try my skills against yours for a century. My luck has landed."

Before seeing the cloaked vampire, I'd thought Henry was the most powerful here. He looked it. How strong was Knight Time if he was more powerful than Henry?

Knight Time slipped a long, thin sword from the folds of his dark cloak. The cloak reminded me of a nightwalker, but his hands were visible, clearly human. The sword's silver-gilded handle wrapped around his hand.

Keagan shifted slightly on his feet.

"Knight Time doesn't fail, Keagan. Leave now, and I'll call him off," Jié Shù offered.

"I'll stay."

Knight Time approached Keagan. I expected him to provide a display of blade skills, but he didn't. He simply lifted his rapier, holding it in front of him, ready. The fact that he felt no need to display his skills concerned me more. Knight Time wasn't concerned with flash. He had no intention of intimidating his enemy. He fully believed he would kill Keagan in seconds.

The first swing of his rapier happened so quickly I missed it. It appeared Knight Time's blade had almost instantly switched positions. Keagan shifted just as quickly, moving to the left in a blur. Knight Time swung again. Keagan blocked with his forearm, and sparks flew, indicating he wore metal vambraces under his leather jacket. The rebounding blade left Knight Time unbalanced. Keagan swung his fist, but Knight Time retreated and gathered himself for a second attack. He sliced low and left at Keagan's legs, but Keagan stepped aside. Knight Time continued his motion and returned his blade in a fluid swipe at the right of Keagan's torso. Keagan blocked again with his forearm. Instead of losing balance this time, Knight Time used the rebound, turning it into a high arcing swing down at Keagan's head. Keagan blocked it with his left arm, but Knight Time pulled his swing down, sliding his blade off Keagan's forearm and impaling Keagan through the chest. Keagan grabbed the blade with his left hand, lunged forward, forcing the rapier deeper through his body and yanked Knight Time toward him. He shot his right hand forward through Knight Time's neck, ripping off his head. The head fell back into the cloak's hood, which caught it like a sack before the rest of Knight Time's body collapsed.

Almost in unison, the remaining vampires took a step back. Only Fern, Jié Shù, and Henry remained in place.

Keagan pulled the blade from his chest and smiled toward Alexis, saying, "I stole your move, love."

My first thought was, *Lexy is not your love.* My second thought was, *you both stole the move from the Uruk-hai Lurtz from the movie version of* Lord of the Rings. My third thought was that Keagan had left the Bear Lake cabin before Lexy pulled that move. Unless he'd watched from a window? Had he? It dawned on me that he had never fled the Cabin Battle of Bear Lake. He'd waited to see if we would be victorious, because if not, he would have returned.

"Nobody's ever beat Keagan in a fight," Dreadlocks told a tiny blonde vampire next to her, loud enough so everyone could hear. She then turned to a dark-haired vampire dressed in a sheer gothic dress, who stood on the other side of her. "He took out a whole shiver in Brazil all by himself." The gothic vampire gulped while the tiny blonde vampire widened her eyes over her button nose, then glanced toward her Asian leader.

"Quiet, Jace!" Jié Shù hissed at Dreadlocks.

"What Jace says is true," Keagan pointed Knight Time's blade at Dreadlocks. "Hell, with luck, I might be able to take all twenty of you. Nineteen now. You should have attacked while I was injured." He opened his leather jacket and used his fingers to spread the hole in his shirt to show that his wound had already closed. "Was he really your best?" With the rapier, Keagan pointed at the cloaked and lifeless form of Knight Time. "*Whit's fur ye'll no go by ye!* What's fated to happen will happen," he translated the Scottish phrase. He let his words hang in the darkness for a few seconds, then continued. "But you're mistaken, Jacy," he kept his gaze at Dreadlocks. "I've lost twice," Keagan pointed the rapier at Alexis, "to Princess Alexis's general. I fled both times to save my skin and blood." Keagan raised the rapier into the air. "Don't kill us, Jacob, First General to Princess Alexis," Keagan shouted into the air, his Scottish accent almost making it a song.

What's he doing? Kendra asked. Ariel tensed to my right. She glanced our way questioningly.

Keagan's conning them, I suggested.

Keagan's Scottish voice turned pleading. "If, as Master King's generals, you issue an official Blood Rule Challenge from Master King, perhaps Lexy's general will follow the laws of the challenge and let us all live."

What's a Blood Rule Challenge? Kendra and I thought simultaneously.

Sounds like some type of formal duel, I added. *Keagan must think that is the best way to avoid an all-out fight.*

Can we trust Keagan's plan? Kendra asked.

No. I replied. *But do we have a choice other than trying to fight? Maybe with Keagan, we'd win?* Kendra wondered.

Keagan strutted into the circle of vampires—a brave move—then came to a stop next to Alexis, rapier still in hand. None of the vampires tried to stop him. He reached for the chain that connected the manacles at her wrists. "Do you have the key for these?" he asked. "It's time we set her free, so Master King isn't charged with breaking the rules of a challenge."

"We have issued no Blood Rule Challenge. And even if we did, we don't follow the oppressor's laws," Jié Shù lifted her chin.

Perhaps Keagan had said the wrong thing, because suddenly, most of the vampires lifted their chins. He'd touched on a subject that hit their pride. They had declared freedom from the Vampire King—from European vampire rule. I recognized their American patriotism.

"The Vampire King's laws? I wasn't talking about his oppressive laws. I was talking about the laws Master King put in place. I believe changing the laws of the Blood Rule Challenge was one of your first actions after you declared independence, was it not? What does your new law say about preemptive attacks?" He rested both his hands on the sword, cane-like.

The vampires that formed the circle surrounding Keagan nodded almost in unison. Keagan *hadn't* said the wrong thing. He had intentionally puffed up their patriotism to use it against them. They *wanted* to obey their own law.

"Did you feel that, Jié Shù?" Keagan shivered. "I'd hurry and declare Master King's intent to challenge Princess Alexis before her general, Jacob, unleashes the spell he's forming that just gave me the chills."

I didn't start a spell.

I know, Kendra answered.

My magic reserves were full, and earlier, I had created magic missiles, but I'd dropped them once we had decided not to attack.

"You have a problem now," Keagan growled with unexpected anger. "If you don't invoke the Blood Rule Challenge, you will face not only her generals, which includes the man that sent me running twice, but you will also face me." He raised his clawed right hand above his shoulder, just above Lexy's head, still bloody, and then pointed again toward Knight Time.

Seconds passed in silence. Nothing happened. Keagan didn't attack. Jié Shù looked around as if waiting. Someone had to move first, but I knew it wasn't going to be Keagan. He was waiting for me. He kept stealing glances at the rooftop. He knew I was here, but he didn't know exactly where.

"I think you're lying," Jié Shù smiled nervously. "There is no one else here but you, is there?" Her accented words came out choppy and quick. "We had inside information, Keagan. As long as we leave Alexis's pendants in place and functioning, but keep her from touching them," she pointed at the silver box that hung from Lexy's silver chain, "her generals can't find her." She smiled as if she'd won. "End him!" she ordered her vampires.

"Jacob?" Keagan called.

Jace looked me in the eyes and mouthed, "Help him."

I swore under my breath. I doubted Keagan could take nineteen vampires. If he could, he would have just done it instead of conning them. I already had as much magic as I could hold, so I was as ready as ever.

"Keagan's on Lexy's team, so," I didn't finish the whisper.

I used Raijin to help myself to my feet, then I lifted the staff high and shouted, "*Lígetu!*" A lightning rune lit up as I shot a thick bolt into the twilight. I let the magic pour out of me, trying to cause the strongest ripple of magic that I could so Jié Shù could feel my power. The lightning split into three, spreading out and illuminating the dark night. Thunder exploded with such audible force that it shook the buildings within a one-block radius and echoed from one end of Sin City to the other.

"Oh, I'm here," I shouted. "And I'm not alone."

Lexy's eyes found mine. Her jaw tightened.

Kendra and Ariel stood as well. Kendra used Astrapí to shoot her own burst of lightning into the air. Her lightning lit up the night, and her thunder cracked with far less force than mine had, though it was still impressive.

Ariel must have donned her white shirt during the lightning show, but she'd kept her scaly, dark-as-night skin. She jumped from the roofline, landed on top of the SUV, then ran down the windshield. She jumped off the SUV's hood with a front flip that landed her next to Keagan.

"Alexis has four generals," Ariel stated flatly. The trickster's granddaughter had caught on quickly enough. She understood that the goal was to avoid a fight by showing off our power. If we forced Jié Shù to issue a challenge instead of attacking, then everyone would walk out of here alive.

The blue-haired witch glanced at Alexis, who nodded, confirming Ariel's statement. Did Alexis recognize the twenty-year-old woman with black scales for skin?

"Linzi?" Jié Shù asked.

"I'd go with issuing the Blood Rule Challenge," Linzi shrugged. She didn't look like the type of girl—or vampire—who liked to get her hands dirty fighting.

"Fern?"

"There are twenty," her eyes darted to Knight Time and back, "nineteen of us and four of them," the redhead seemed to be the only vampire other than Jace not scared of Keagan and us. Blood still painted her hands and chin. If it were up to Fern, the fight was on. "You felt his magic," Fern continued. "How strong is he?"

Jié Shù didn't answer Fern. Instead, she glanced at me, Kendra, and Ariel before turning to Keagan and Alexis.

"Master King will challenge Alexis for rulership of the Americas. I, Jié Shù, First General to Master King, invoke the Blood Rule Challenge on his behalf."

"The key?" Keagan lifted Alexis's manacled wrists.

"We left the key back at the shiver," Jié Shù explained. "Bring her along, Henry."

Henry stepped forward, but Keagan put a clawed hand on the body builder's chest. Henry looked down at the hand as if he intended to rip it off. He grabbed Keagan's wrist, but Jié Shù stopped him. "No, Henry. The challenge has been preliminarily issued."

"Princess Alexis will ride with her generals," Keagan spoke as if there were no threat to his words. However, the way he positioned the rapier to strike with one hand and spread his claws in the other, combined with his jet-black eyes, held nothing but threat.

I hung down from the ledge of the roof and then kicked away from the wall and dropped onto the top of the SUV. Kendra followed behind me. She didn't hang. Instead, she hopped off the edge, twisted in a one-eighty, palmed the ledge till her feet hit the wall, then bounced off and landed on the SUV roof as if it were a practiced drill team move. She couldn't hide that she intentionally did it to show me up.

Together, we slid to the hood then jumped to the ground. Alexis eyed us as we approached her. I made a considerable effort to keep my eyes on Lexy's and not below. I couldn't read the emotions that slipped through her separation stone. Was it sadness? Anger? Shame? Love? Hate? Perhaps it was all of them.

Keagan stepped back out of the way as Kendra and I rushed to Alexis. We knelt next to her and wrapped her in our embrace. It surprised me when Ariel joined in, making our three-way hug a four-way. Again, I missed Luiz. He was missing all the opportunities at humor.

We held Lexy, but she didn't hug us back. Why not? Kendra reached up to tap off Lexy's separation stone but found the silver box blocked her. Only a rotating clip held the box closed, so she popped it open. The box separated into two pieces that fell to the asphalt. Kendra tapped Lexy's separation stone.

Her maelstrom of emotions and thoughts flooded into us.

I can't hug back. I am manacled, Lexy's mind answered my question. *And my arm is broken.*

As we absorbed what we could from her thoughts and emotions, I touched and focused on the manacles, converting two lines of the metal's elements into energy, essentially slicing the metal apart by erasing molecules. The manacles dropped from her wrists as if slit by a knife. As soon as the manacles fell, one of her arms wrapped around me and the other, despite being broken, wrapped around Kendra.

I repeated the process with the manacles at her ankles. The four of us stood, unwrapping from our hug.

"Keagan," Alexis stretched out her broken arm. "Will you set my bone before it heals again?"

Kendra immediately stripped off her black lace camisole covering her white shade shirt and helped Lexy put it on. She put it over her broken arm first. The camisole covered up her top half—mostly. It barely stretched around Alexis, clinging tightly to her every curve. Being four inches taller than Kendra, the camisole ended just above her navel. Her tattoo remained clearly visible.

A gift from the Vampire King!

As Keagan took Lexy's arm to set the bone, Kendra surprised both herself and me by unbuttoning her maize-yellow shorts. I pulled my eyes from Lexy's tattoo to watch her slip them off. Her need for modesty mixed with her desire to help Lexy, creating an interesting emotional mix of embarrassed resolve. Underneath, Kendra wore white Lycra dance shorts—ready for drill practice in case we had managed to make it back. We hadn't.

Lexy screamed in pain as Keagan yanked her arm. Kendra and I felt her agony through the Trinity of Mind as if it were our own.

Kendra helped Alexis put on her shorts. The shorts' material had some stretch, but not enough. Kendra tried to button them for her, but she couldn't stretch them enough. She managed to zip them up halfway, but that still left the top two lines of Lexy's tattoo visible.

I met Kendra's eyes, then looked down shamefully. It hadn't even occurred to me to offer Alexis my hoodie. I didn't have a T-shirt on under it, and it would have exposed my road-rashed skin. Perhaps I wasn't entirely over my ugly looks.

A lot of the vampires eyed Kendra.

"The Blood Rule Challenge is not yet official," Jié Shù reminded Alexis. "You and Master King must meet to formalize it."

Can you explain this Blood Rule Challenge? Jake asked.

It is exactly what you think it is, she answered. *A formal duel between Master King and me. Often to the death but sometimes only until submission. Someday soon, we will meet with Master King, make the challenge official, and set a future date for the duel, usually a few weeks to a few months after the challenge is issued.*

"Follow us to the White House," Jié Shù ordered.

"White House?" I raised an eyebrow. No way were we going to drive all the way to Washington D.C.

"Master King's mansion," Lexy explained verbally as she held her broken right arm tight to her body. *It is here in Las Vegas,* she added through the Trinity of Mind. *The mansion under which I was being held when you astral projected into me,* she snapped at me with her thoughts. Now that our hug had ended, and Alexis was covered, her mood switched from the happy, "Yay! You saved me" mood into a bitter, "You didn't pick me, so why do you care?" mood. Behind the bitterness directed at Kendra and me lurked a fury that her grandfather had tricked her into one more mission to kill his rival. Hunger also boiled through her. Her arm had been broken multiple times today. The effort to heal had left her ravished, which would have been obvious even without the Trinity of Mind. She hadn't had food or water, let alone blood, and she could smell Kendra's blood, both from her elbow and her period. She wanted to tear Kendra to pieces and feed on her.

Lexy stiffened, tapped on her separation stone, and took a step toward Keagan. She gathered herself before turning to Master King's First General.

"I am the challenged," Lexy spoke formally. "I have no obligation to go to him. Master King must come to me."

"You will meet with him before dawn," Jiè Shú stated flatly.

"I think not," Alexis raised her voice.

"We have the girl," Jiè Shú reminded.

"Gina?" Lexy asked.

The Asian woman shrugged and glanced at Fern, who grinned wickedly.

"If you don't come before dawn," Fern demonstrated an exaggerated breath of pleasure, "I'll bathe in her blood."

"We have to be back by six in the morning," Kendra reminded. To her, drill team practice was a priority that rivaled vampire politics.

Lexy glanced at Kendra, then at me, then at Keagan. "What do you think?" she asked Keagan.

"I'd tell you to go home and let Fern bathe in Gina's blood," Keagan shrugged. "But I know you, love. You won't do that, will you?"

Lexy shook her head.

"The challenge has been issued." Keagan continued. "Until your duel, he can't touch you. Still, I don't trust him. I'll come with you. My presence should dissuade him from subterfuge." His words sounded confident, but his eyes fixated on Lexy in worry.

"We will meet with Master King in ninety minutes. That will be midnight," Lexy decided. Her hunger overwhelmed her separation stone, flooding into Kendra and me. "Gina is mine. Harm her, and I will consider it a breach of the Blood Rule Challenge laws."

Jace collected Knight Time and put his cloaked body and head into the back of the SUV—laying him on his back and putting his head in place—before she, Jiè Shú, and five other vampires filed gracefully into the SUV.

The remaining vampires' continual hungry glances at Kendra proved they could smell her blood, too. Those glances didn't cease until the twelve other vampires faded into the night. They somehow managed to disappear before they actually moved out of sight. I didn't know vampires could do that. My experience with them involved little more than a parking lot surprise attack, the Cabin Battle of Bear Lake, and my time with Alexis. Alexis had kept a tight lid on what she knew about vampires, despite the Trinity of Mind.

"Can we go now?" Kendra asked. She wanted to leave as soon as possible. I didn't blame her.

"One sec," I walked over to the dumpster, set my druid staff aside, and jumped up. I failed to jump high enough. Pathetic. I tried again, this time using my hands to pull up as I jumped. I managed to get my belly up to the edge and lean over. Fortunately, the dumpster was full. I grabbed Bear's gunnysack from the top of a black bag—it wasn't even dirty—and dropped back down. I tested it with my magic, and sure enough, it wasn't cursed but instead had tendrils of magic similar to a locator. The curse wasn't a curse; it was just a tracking spell. Growing up with no money, I took notice when gold was tossed in a dumpster. Bear spent this gold, so he wouldn't be coming after it. Maybe he'd let me keep it?

"Now we can go."

It felt good to walk out of the alley without fear. At least until I realized I was walking steps away from Keagan. He also glanced repeatedly at Kendra, his eyes streaked with hunger. I'd sooner erase him from existence than see him again, and his glances at Kendra added to my addictive temptation, but I tried to hold off. Without him, the rest of us would have taken on the twenty vampires and likely died trying, and failed to save Alexis. With him, we'd walked away without a fight. However, I couldn't help but worry about the challenge. The battle would still take place someday in the future.

When?

CHAPTER 27
LOVELY LEATHER

I have been burned so many times by so many people. The past few weeks, with Jake and Kendra, I let my heart heal. Why did I do that? So that it would hurt when Jake and Kendra burned it again? Speaking of burning hearts, Jake found the spell. Does he know a protector's purpose yet? How will he feel about me once he knows? He already burned my heart figuratively. Will he burn it literally? I guess it matters little since he chose Kendra over me. —Alexis

We walked around the corner of the strip mall without speaking. The Porsche now sat alone in front of the tattoo parlor, which was now dark. The tattoo art decorating the windows had become nothing but shadows on the glass.

"You drove this?" Alexis scowled at the puny Porsche. There were five of us now, and the Porsche hadn't fit three very well.

"I have my bike up the way," Keagan gestured up the street. Just two buildings past where we parked, a lone motorcycle stood out in the darkness.

"You can ride with me to see this MK dobber," he offered.

Alexis took Knight Time's sword from Keagan and tossed it to Ariel. "Bring this." Then she grabbed Keagan's hand and said, "I will drive."

"Not with a broken arm," Keagan shook his head. "Sit behind me and tell how you acquired that pair of freckles."

My anger flared as Alexis and Keagan held hands as they walked away from us. Keagan pulled her closer and she let him. I put my hands together to form a magic missile, but Kendra grabbed me and hugged me. I didn't hug her back. Instead, I stared over her shoulder at Alexis and Keagan as they walked the

226

distance to his motorcycle and mounted it. We had just driven hours to save Alexis and nearly took on a shiver of vampires for her. She thanked us by driving away on a motorcycle, sitting behind Keagan with her left arm wrapped around him.

I noticed movement from an alleyway across the street from where the motorcycle had parked. A homeless person stepped out. At least, the transient was dressed like a homeless person. Where there was one, there were many. I sensed more of them behind this one. Sure enough, a couple more stepped out. They usually didn't bother those strong in magic. Could they feel my strength? They didn't charge us. They just watched. They let us get in the Porsche and drive away.

We didn't know what to do for ninety minutes, and Alexis had driven off, not telling us where she was going, so we texted Keagan and Lexy but didn't receive an immediate response. We didn't want to sit around and wait, so Kendra drove Ariel and me down the strip. We looked at the lights, the cars, and the people. Las Vegas was unlike any other city in the world. Beams of light shot into the night sky from various hotels. A few minutes earlier, I'd shot a powerful display of lightning up into the sky, and the thunder had shaken buildings. Only the transients had noticed.

We passed the Luxor, the miniature Statue of Liberty, and a dozen other sights. People of all sorts lined the streets. We passed Sonic the Hedgehog, the entire cast of the Simpsons, and a white and dark angel—all people in costumes, of course.

Shortly after we reached the end of the strip and turned around, a Caradoc memory hit me.

"I know where to go while we wait for Alexis," I explained to Kendra. She liked my idea. It would only take five minutes.

It actually took twelve minutes. We'd just finished at that destination when Alexis jumped into our heads just long enough to tell us where to meet her.

We arrived at Lovely Leather at 10:57 P.M.

Kendra, Ariel, and I entered to find Alexis standing on a platform trying to pull on leather pants that were too small, her body now clean of ash and her hair damp. Next to Alexis stood a slightly overweight, fake-redheaded woman in her forties sorting through a rack of hanging leather articles of clothing. Alexis had already changed into a black and red leather bustier with a jacket over it.

I felt Eldra's two-hundred years try to take over my mind. It wasn't lost on me that I'd just made the decision to overpay for a leather design company. I wanted to judge every outfit in this place. I took a breath and tried to focus on Kendra.

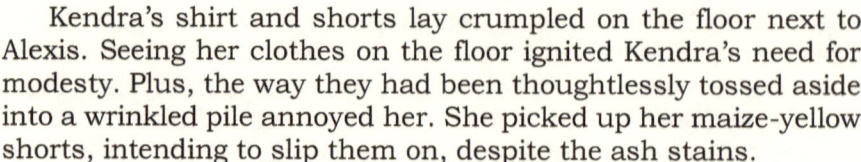

Kendra's shirt and shorts lay crumpled on the floor next to Alexis. Seeing her clothes on the floor ignited Kendra's need for modesty. Plus, the way they had been thoughtlessly tossed aside into a wrinkled pile annoyed her. She picked up her maize-yellow shorts, intending to slip them on, despite the ash stains.

"Kendra," Alexis shook her head. "Leather. You, too, Ariel."

Kendra, with one leg already in her shorts, looked up at Alexis and sighed.

"Undress and try those on," Alexis pointed toward the right side of the rack of leather items. The fake redhead immediately pulled a dark gray bustier and pants and offered them to Kendra. The lady wore a black leather tube top that didn't go down far enough to cover her midriff. Her black leather pants fit too snuggly, causing her love handles to muffin-top over her pants.

I took another breath, trying to keep Eldra's memories from taking over, and focused back on Kendra. She thinned her lips and sighed at the thought of trying on leather. She let her shorts drop back to the floor, stepping out of them, before bending over to untie her yellow converse shoes.

Kendra looked around for a dressing room but couldn't find one.

"Go wait outside, Jake," Kendra ordered.

"No," Alexis contradicted Kendra. "He needs leather, too." Alexis turned toward the store's lone worker. "One size larger," she requested and started the slow process of shimmying out of the too-small leather pants, moving each side down an inch at a time.

Kendra thinned her eyes at me. "Turn around, then."

For over a hundred years, I'd helped women dress. I'd even delivered babies. And she thought I needed to turn around?

"Jake?" Kendra questioned.

Hearing my name brought me back. I turned around.

Keagan chuckled. I hadn't noticed him sitting on a sofa watching Alexis try on various leather outfits. My anger at him had calmed some. I didn't need Kendra to hug me to keep myself in control enough to avoid erasing him from existence. Still, I filled myself with enough magic that I could erase him if I changed my mind later.

"How does this go on?" Kendra asked.

"It has a built-in bra, honey," I heard the redhead explain to Kendra. "You'll have to take yours off."

Keagan's smile widened.

"Turn around," I growled, my jealousy pushing Eldra's life away from the forefront of my mind.

Keagan looked at me, the right side of his mouth twisted in ridicule. He started to speak. "You—" I didn't wait for him to finish his comment. I shot lightning from my hand to the floor. "I said turn around!"

Keagan nodded and obeyed.

I ignored the fact that lightning was Eldra's favorite spell, not mine.

Thanks! Kendra tapped in and out too quickly to notice I was losing myself to Eldra.

The worker brought me a leather jacket and a pair of pants decorated with four buckles, two above the knee and two below. The pants fit perfectly. I hesitated to remove my hoodie to don the jacket. It had a lot of zippers and a half dozen small buckles of its own. I had only thought of my unsightly skin a few times today, as opposed to every few minutes. Was I overcoming the hit my ugliness had delivered to my self-esteem? Maybe not all the way. I tried to slip on the leather jacket over my hoodie. It didn't fit, so I gave in and pulled the hoodie off. Hopefully, the Lovely Leather lady wasn't staring at my bare chest with pity.

I jiggled one of the buckles on my left leg and felt all the zippers and buckles on my jacket. The number of zippers and buckles was no accident. Alexis had made sure I had access to plenty of metal in case I found myself unable to pull in magic.

Ariel came and sat by me, having chosen a perfect-fitting leather outfit immediately. I tried not to analyze it as she slipped her earbud in and started playing Mortal Kombat on her phone, again.

Over the next five minutes, I lost myself in analyzing the leather outfits.

"You don't fill this one out," the worker told Kendra behind me.

A splash of Kendra's raw humiliation hit me. The rope of emotion between Kendra and me flared to life, made of thick strands of mortification because *I* heard that comment. The rope of emotion gave me an anchor, helping me slow Eldra's two-hundred years of life from taking over mine.

Alexis giggled. I started to turn around to shout at her, but Kendra's embarrassment signaled the removal of her bustier, so I stopped half-turned, facing Keagan.

Keagan didn't look at me. His eyes fixated on a rack of leather clothes. It was a good thing *he* hadn't laughed. I would've wiped him from existence.

I ambled away from Keagan and turned so I didn't have to look at him while still keeping my back to Kendra. Except I found myself staring directly at a tall mirror, reflecting a clear view of

Kendra. She stood topless but for one arm covering her breasts as she waited for the redhead to bring a bustier a size smaller.

Oops, I was staring. Kendra wore black leather pants with a silver-studded belt. I watched her take the bustier from the woman. She wrapped the bustier around her back, no longer covering herself, then pulled the bustier closed in front. I should have looked away, but I couldn't. Partly because seeing Kendra that way, I completely forgot Eldra existed. The Lovely Leather lady turned Kendra slightly, pointing her directly at my mirror. Kendra's reflected eyes met mine.

Double oops. She caught me. I quickly turned away.

If Kendra knew she'd rescued me by boobs a third time, she might giggle again. But her separation stone dimmed the Trinity of Mind, so she didn't know. I waited for her fury to hit me through the emotional rope connecting us. It didn't. Instead, I only felt gratitude and relief, neither of which matched my expectations. Why wasn't she furious?

Unfortunately, I found myself with nothing to do but analyze the outfits in the store again. As the long minutes slipped by, Eldra once again began taking over. I pulled out my phone and emailed Darla, telling her to add Lovely Leather to the list of small leather stores to acquire. By the time I sent the email, Eldra was battling me for control again. Kendra and Lexy were now dressed but still needed time to pick out shoes, jackets, and other accessories.

Forty-five minutes later, we all stood at the checkout counter dressed in leather as Alexis paid. Adult Ariel's leather pants had small silver chain loops around the waist and a studded belt that matched Kendra's. The shapeshifter's skin remained unnaturally dark black, far darker than Manouchka—a Haitian voodoo witch that we'd recently both fought against and freed. Her scales ended at the backs of her hands, the only part of her body other than her face not covered in leather.

Alexis hoped we'd meet with Master King and drive home through the night. But she liked to be prepared for the unexpected. What if we ended up staying the night? She'd had the redhead pick the three girls out some sleepwear. Lexy usually slept naked, but if, for whatever reason, she had to room with Kendra and Ariel, she decided wearing something would be proper. This place stocked a small section of sleepwear that wasn't leather.

While running Alexis's card, the woman apologized profusely that the only pants they had in stock that fit Lexy's five-foot-ten frame had been pink pleather. Alexis had replaced her black and red bustier with a black one with pink laces and stitching that matched her pants. Her distaste for her pants exuded past her separation stone. Despite choosing a matching ensemble, the tacky pleather had no business on a body like hers. Lexy's black leather bustier and matching heels put the pink pleather to shame. Still, she looked hot and filled out the back of the pink pants perfectly. Alexis and Kendra had bought leather jackets but didn't wear them in the Vegas heat. They could have used magic to push away the heat, but the leather jackets still would have looked odd.

I analyzed Lexy's top, realizing that the pink stitching suited her. Yes, the pants were terrible, but every famous female needed a brand. Her mother, Carina, always wore black with red accents—usually in the stitching but sometimes in the pattern. What if Lexy branded herself the same way, only with black and pink. The metaphor pink provided would add to the brand. Pink was a mix of red and white, just as Lexy was a half-dhampir, a mix of vampire and human. My two-hundred-year-old mind continued to work on her visual brand.

Kendra misunderstood my odd look at Alexis and smiled mischievously at me as she mouthed, "Pink. I know, right?"

We turned to go, but Keagan grabbed Lexy's left arm and pointed to her right arm, which she held tenderly.

"You need a pint," Keagan suggested, his Scottish accent making me think of a pint of beer, but of course, Keagan meant a pint of blood.

Lexy's fangs extended. Keagan glanced at Kendra again, making clear he also wanted a pint. As I stepped protectively closer to Kendra, Lexy took the fake redhead's willing wrist and bit into it.

Shortly after Lexy finished, the five of us stood in Lovely Leather's parking lot between the Porsche and Keagan's bike. A parking space divided us. Alexis leaned on the bike, and Keagan stood behind her on the other side, while Kendra, Ariel, and I stood by the Porsche.

"We should have recorded that shopping spree for a *Pretty Woman*-like movie montage." Kendra smiled, trying to use a joke to close the gap between us. Ariel looked at Kendra quizzically, clearly not catching the reference.

I pulled out my phone. "Can I have a picture of you in pink pants?" I could use it to work on outfits that would become part of the Princess Alexis brand.

"Me, too," Kendra asked.

Lexy's red eyes met mine. The corners of her mouth almost turned up. Instead, she forced her eyes to harden and compelled her emotions to hold onto her anger. She still chose to be vexed with me. "You want to make a joke of me? Now? The most powerful vampire in the United States captured me, had his minions break my arm and try to burn me alive, and then through her general, issued a Blood Rule Challenge, and you want to be funny? You two are not Luiz!"

Click.

"Next time, don't ask permission," Keagan suggested as he held his phone pointed at Lexy's lower half.

Alexis turned to Keagan, leaned over the bike, and with her left hand, slapped him. The separation stone barely dimmed her anger as it boiled into my mind.

Click. Click. Both Kendra and I took a picture of Alexis in her pink pants leaning over Keagan's motorcycle. Alexis whipped back around to us, seeing us both with our phones out.

She stiffened. Her red eyes could have burned us up with lasers if only she knew a spell for that. Ariel stepped between Alexis and me and lifted her leather arms protectively, her scales visible on the back of her hands.

"Someday, Lexy, when we are old and gray, we'll sit around laughing about this picture," I suggested.

"Damn you, Jacob Stevens." Alexis rarely swore, so taking her picture in pink leather pants must have crossed a serious line, but why had she sworn only at me, not Kendra? Kendra had taken a picture, too. On the plus side, Lexy's use of my full name pulled me back in the lead for control of my own mind.

"Sorry, I—" I started, but Alexis held up a hand, so I stopped. Her emotions felt confused. There were too many emotions to pick out one. I pushed hard against her separation stone and barely broke through long enough for one phrase.

I will not pardon Jake for one perfect comment, Lexy promised herself.

I wanted to get more, but the separation stone pushed me out. What did Lexy mean? How was what I had said "one perfect comment?"

"Did you check the boot for weapons?" Keagan pointed at the Porsche.

Without Eldra in my brain, I might not have known that "boot" was the British term for "trunk." "It doesn't have a trunk."

"The boot is in front on a Porsche," Keagan explained.

"Kendra. Keys?" I held out my hand, and Kendra gave them to me. Sure enough, the key fob had a button with a trunk icon. I clicked it, and the front of the Porsche popped open. I walked over and looked in.

Inside, weapons decorated the tiny trunk. A short shotgun hung from under the open roof. If it hadn't been sawed off, it wouldn't have fit. Two HK45s and a dozen clips fit into a custom wooden box. Four Ruger 9MMs inside hip holsters lined the inside of a second custom box. A pair of clips fit into slots above each gun. A belt hanging from the right side of the trunk held a dozen blades. The front half-dozen consisted of military utility blades in black sheaths. The back half-dozen consisted of throwing knives. Two sais held by rubber hooks hung at the back. I unclipped the sais and lifted them out. The Vegas lights glistened off the foot-and-a-half long blades.

"Alexis," I extended the pair of weapons toward her. "With these and your pink pleather, you could be Mileena."

Ariel glanced up from her phone, once again playing Mortal Kombat. She *was* playing as Mileena at the moment, which is why Kendra noticed the similar pink. Kendra changed her voice to sound like the Mortal Kombat video game and said, "Mileena wins! Fatality."

Alexis eyed the sais, ignored them, and looked into the Porsche's front storage herself. She moved the HK45s and grabbed black leather hip holsters from underneath, still in the package. She ripped open the package and hooked each hip holster to the outside of her pink pleather pants, which were too tight for her to try to fit the holsters inside. Next, she grabbed a pair of magazines and put one inside each side of her leather jacket pockets. Then she loaded each HK45 and holstered them.

I lifted the sais and ran my fingers down the flat of the blades. I touched one of the tine tips and found it sharp as a needle. The urge to mark the blades rose inside me. Robin had taught me how to mark blades a century-and-a-half ago. A magic symbol can aid the metal in many ways beyond merely keeping it sharp. I pinched my thumb and pointer finger opposite each other and let the magic augment between them like electricity between two Tesla rods. A tiny welding torch of magic lit up the blade and reflected off my face. Into the blade, I burned an arc with three straight supporting lines that symbolized increased blade strength and a sharp edge. Magic infused the steel elements of the blade. I recognized the steel's unique quality as well as the carbon fiber nanotubes, a telltale sign of Damascus steel, a forging methodology thought lost since around 1750. The newness of this blade confirmed what we druids had suspected for centuries. The knowledge of Damascus steel remained among the vampires. It only took one symbol to strengthen the steel, a square with a pillar inside it. I added a second rune in the shape of a teardrop, then I added two bones crossing below it. The rune added a magical poison that would prevent wounds from healing quickly if cut, even for vampires.

Lexy's runed dagger would likely be magic-infused Damascus steel as well. Where was her blade? Did she have it when she'd been captured? Drake had burned everything except her necklace off her body, so she certainly didn't have the blade now. The skull-hilted blade she'd taken from Manouchka was also missing and I'd sensed magic in it as well.

Since Alexis ignored the outstretched sai, I handed it to Kendra. She glanced at it, then offered it to her dark-skinned doppelganger. Adult Ariel pulled out her earbuds and put away her phone before taking the sai and slipping it into the silver-chained loop on her right hip. I put my fingers on the other blade and added the same steel strengthening symbol. Then I burned in a shield with a circle inside it, which would create a defense against magic. I added a third symbol, the shape of a boomerang with three lines, that three times would bring the sai back when thrown. I also handed it to Coyote's granddaughter, and she put the second sai on her left hip.

Alexis held a throwing knife toward me, handle first. It was small and well made but would still break easily, so I pinched the blade between my thumb. With the same tiny but intense magic light, I etched the symbol of strength, the square with the pillar, then the teardrop and crossbones, and on the other side, I added an arrow that would magically aid in throwing accuracy. She slipped the throwing knife into a thin sheath designed to be concealed inside her pants and clipped to the waist. She somehow managed to fit the thin blade inside those tight pink pants.

I looked up, and Keagan had three of the throwing knives in one hand and Knight Time's rapier in his other. Should I give one of the most powerful vampires in the world runed blades, making him more powerful? I shook my head at him. He looked disappointed but leaned the rapier against the Porsche so he could use both hands to conceal the throwing knives in their sheaths, then slid them inside his belt, one on each hip and one at his back. Then he stole another glance at Kendra.

The sawed-off shotgun remained, hanging from the lifted hood.

"We should have brought Luiz," I frowned.

"He will be here in five minutes," Alexis responded.

CHAPTER 28
LUIZ

I can feel the protector magic calling to me, and with that calling, a sense of purpose already weighs on me. It is more than just protecting. Strange that I don't fully understand that purpose yet. It is a secret that only protectors know. It feels like I should know about this purpose, as if the protector magic has tried to tell me, but I've refused to listen. —Jake

"**L**uiz is almost here?" I tilted my head at Alexis and blinked.

"I summoned him to bring Mr. Espinoza," Alexis explained. "My intent was for him to negotiate my release." Her tone suggested that our efforts to save her had interrupted her other plans.

"But he isn't a thrall," I wondered, "and they couldn't have left until dark, could they?"

Alexis ignored me, not offering answers to my questions. I pulled my eyebrows together in annoyance that she'd called Luiz. Sure, she had him bring his dad, but dragging Luiz here still meant putting him in yet another life and death situation. She had no right to pull my friend into her political problems. Of course, another part of me missed Luiz terribly and would be happy to see him.

Hopefully, we'd get to see Gina again tonight, too.

Kendra tapped off her separation stone. I breathed in, and my shoulders relaxed as her mind melded with mine.

We should apologize, Kendra suggested. "Jake didn't pick me," Kendra turned to Alexis and explained.

Alexis shook her head, tight and quick, and mouthed, "Not now," trying to shut us up.

"She meant I am not going to pick either of you right now," I added, ignoring her plea for our silence.

Alexis glanced at Keagan, who already looked at her with mocking bemusement. Her red eyes returned to mine, then rolled in exasperation. I wanted her to tap off her separation stone, but she wouldn't. I could still feel her emotions, but it took me a bit to recognize her current emotion: defiance.

"You turned me down for this flayed radge?" Keagan's Scottish accent thickened. He shook his head. Then pointed at Kendra, his eyes hungry, as he added, "And he picked this quine instead?"

Kendra feared Keagan's constant looks.

I didn't know what "radge" or "quine" meant, but I assumed they were Scottish insults. Add that to his hungry looks, and my patience collapsed. Anger flared inside me.

"Watch your mouth, you blood-leeching parasite," I dipped into the vampire insults that Eldra knew of.

"Careful, child," Keagan's eyes turned black. "You're only alive because twice I let you live," Keagan grabbed the rapier from where it leaned against the Porsche, stepped toward me, and lifted the blade to point it at me.

"No, you're only alive because twice you fled like a coward!"

"I'm not scared now!" He lunged at me with Knight Time's rapier, but I stepped back and Lexy grabbed him, so the point came up short. Ariel's leather- and scale-clad forearm had appeared out of nowhere to block the strike had it not fallen short.

"Fæcele heorte." Torched heart. Both Keagan's and Lexy's eyes turned white. The magic formed in the shape of a hand inside Keagan's chest, and its fingers wrapped his heart and paused its beating. To me, the hand glowed with smoky, translucent light. To Kendra and everyone else, the hand was invisible.

Keagan turned away with inhuman speed, trying to flee, but he only managed two steps before he collapsed.

Jake, Alexis tapped off her separation stone to plead with me. Her thoughts and emotions exploded into turmoil. She wondered how I'd learned this spell—one that usually must be taught to a protector. Part of her feared me, while another part feared for Keagan.

I had Keagan's heart wrapped in my imaginary hand, squeezing it but not yet igniting the torch. The pressure prevented his heart from pumping the blood through his body. All I had to do was augment the heat, ignite the protists, and light up his heart like a torch. It would take only a thought.

No. Please.

Keagan *had* killed Lexy's mother. He was also the first person her grandfather had gifted her to. He deserved to die. Alexis ignored her bad memories of Keagan and focused on the good memories, where he had treated her with care and respect. She pleaded with those memories.

He has protected me. He has saved me. Alexis forced me to see her memories that showed how Keagan had changed his behavior toward her. For centuries, he had hunted and killed humans to feed. In the last three years since falling for Alexis, Keagan took on thralls, treated them well, and alternated feeding on them—rarely killing. All because she had asked it of him. When Keagan had proposed, he had let Alexis read his mind, and now, she showed me the thoughts he'd shared with her. At the Cabin Battle of Bear Lake, he could have returned and saved the Vampire King. He should have. We'd barely won. If he had returned, defeating us would have been easy. Carina only chose our side when it was clear that we had gained the advantage. Had Keagan regrouped and returned to the fight, Carina may have chosen the Vampire King's side. But no, Keagan had watched through an outside window, waiting. He never returned to help, even though he'd known there was a chance he'd be exiled and perhaps hunted for the rest of his life. He'd taken that risk for Alexis. And now he *was* exiled. Since Bear Lake, he'd already survived two discreet assassination attempts. He expected that, soon, the Vampire King would put an open price on his head.

When Keagan told Jié Shù and Master King's vampires that I had sent him running twice, he was conning them. Did he know that I was as powerful as his con suggested? Well, I'd just made him flee a third time. I tightened my grip on his heart. I wanted him to be certain of my power. Still, I couldn't bring myself to ignite the flames of my magical hand, but I couldn't release its grip on Keagan's heart either.

Alexis put her palms on my cheeks. Her scared, white eyes pleaded every bit as much as her words did as she asked one more time, "Please, Jake?"

A honk sounded behind me, startling me.

I released the magic hand, letting the torched heart spell evaporate, freeing Keagan. I pulled away from Lexy's palms and turned to see two bright headlights glaring. I noticed with the corner of my eye that Alexis rushed to Keagan's side. I stepped back, ready to jump out of the way, but the black SUV came to a complete stop. The lights turned off, and the front door opened. I expected to encounter more of Master King's vampires.

"¡Diantre! Jake," Luiz shouted as he stepped out of the vehicle. "Thanks for the Vegas invite!"

The passenger door opened, and Andrea stepped out. She wore jean shorts, rolled above her knees, and a plaid button-up with a pleat over each breast. She'd left her hair curly.

"Help me get *papá* out of the coffin in back," Luiz asked, yanking me from the Eldra-instigated clothing critique of Andrea's outfit.

"Andrea, check out the pink," Luiz looked toward Alexis. "*Pretty in Pink*, huh? I'm not sure Andie ever wore leather."

"That's an oldie but a goodie," Andrea laughed.

Alexis grinned but didn't respond. She caught the movie reference through Kendra, as it was Kendra's mom's favorite movie.

I liked her pink pants. Eldra wanted to try them on.

I'll give you one hour of memory therapy when we get back, Kendra offered.

I bet you will, Alexis replied angrily, then shut her mind off from ours. I didn't need to look back to know that Keagan had sat up. I hadn't done him any permanent harm. Should I have? Would I regret letting him live again?

"Jake, my *papá*?" Luiz asked again.

"Sure, Luiz," I answered and walked to the back of the SUV, but Luiz paused by the Porsche, seeing the open trunk full of weapons. He grabbed the sawed-off shotgun and followed me to the back of the SUV.

The seats in the back of the Lincoln Navigator had been folded down. A coffin rested inside, offset just to the right, allowing one of Mr. Espinoza's thralls—Maria? —to fit sitting cramped on the left side. She knelt, trying to shimmy out, but the coffin wedged her in tightly. Her cream-flowered blouse didn't match either color of the striped pattern on her leggings, not to mention that the two patterns would have clashed even if the color hadn't. Flats were probably a wise choice, but white flats with a cream shirt? Really?

Being a young twenty-year-old didn't help Maria exit the cramped space. It took her a good ten seconds to shimmy on her hands and knees toward the back of the SUV. Luiz's eyes fixated on Maria's chest. On her knees and bent over, Maria's loose cream-flowered blouse hung low, exposing her entire bra-covered chest. Kendra caught Luiz's eyes and shook her head, but to her surprise, he looked away. Was this thing he had with Andrea getting real? Instead of noticing what the state of Maria's shirt exposed, as a seventeen-year-old boy normally would, I'd let Eldra almost take over and completely missed it. Instead, I'd criticized Maria's outfit.

OK, maybe two hours of memory therapy? Kendra blushed as her unfiltered thoughts imagined more than just therapy in those two hours, but her imagination wouldn't translate to reality. Those were just unfiltered thoughts. Her—*our*—religious morals gave us firm boundaries we wouldn't easily cross, boundaries that, despite Kendra's shaken faith, hadn't moved yet.

Maria finally escaped the cramped space in the back of the SUV. I offered her my hand, helping her step down onto the asphalt. Ignoring more mental criticisms about Maria's outfit, I turned back to the coffin. It was taller than I expected and nearly touched the ceiling. I grabbed the two side poles and tried to lift the end of the coffin. It didn't budge. I tried harder, hoping to slide it out at least an inch. It still didn't budge.

"Alexis," Luiz shouted. "I forgot Jake can't help lift heavy things anymore."

"Glad to help," Keagan answered, his voice inches from my ear.

I whipped around and found Keagan's face, eyes furiously black, inches from mine. Alexis stood behind him, holding both his forearms. His claws hung sharp, twitching at the ends of his fingers. He didn't say anything, but by extending his claws, his threat came through loud and clear.

I felt compelled to respond. "That makes three times that you've run from me now."

His arm twitched, but Lexy's grip didn't allow him to hit me, if that was what he intended. The effort to hold Keagan back reached her eyes. I'd pushed him too hard. Without Lexy here, he would have killed me on the spot. Could he kill me? Had he conned Jié Shù and the other vampires? Or had he simply told the truth. Could I have defeated all of Master King's vampires with Keagan's, Ariel's, and Kendra's help? Would he have risked his life if he thought winning wasn't a sure thing? He had risked himself for Alexis before, at the Cabin Battle of Bear Lake, right? Then again, he fled because the risk of staying outweighed the risk of running. Was he really here because he loved Alexis—as tainted as the love might be—or because he had some ulterior motive that benefited some scheme for power?

"Hi, Alexis," Andrea interrupted. Alexis dragged Keagan with her to greet Andrea. She offered Andrea her hand, but Andrea hugged her instead. Alexis tensed but allowed the hug. Andrea stepped back, smiled, fluttered her eyes past Lexy to Keagan, and asked, "Who's your hunk?"

"I'm Keagan," Keagan's black eyes glanced back at me, then returned to Andrea. As he took her palm, the black started to fade from his eyes, and by the time he kissed the back of her hand, his pupils, once again, were ruby red.

"Back off!" Luiz had moved to stand next to me, the sawed-off shotgun from the Porsche's boot in his hands, pointing at Keagan's face. "If you ever touch my girl again," Luiz spun the shotgun, loading a shell with the lever-action in one fluid movement, "I'll blow off your *maldita* face!"

Keagan let go of Andrea's hand, grinned, and strolled toward Luiz and the shotgun. When he reached the back of the SUV, he turned his back to Luiz and the shotgun as if not at all bothered. "Alexis, the other side, please?" Keagan gestured to the coffin.

Alexis and Keagan gripped the poles on each side of the coffin, lifted it out with the ease of a dozen pallbearers, and set it on the asphalt. The decorated coffin's exterior was made of smooth dark wood that looked black except where it reflected the city lights. Silver trimmed the coffin and formed four short rings on each side through which the pallbearer poles were inserted.

Alexis popped open the lid. Luiz's dad lay inside, as motionless as a corpse, his skin significantly paler than Luiz's. The inside was surrounded with cream-colored silk. Mr. Espinoza didn't breathe. He rested there, dead stiff. There was no evidence he was going to wake up. At least until his red eyes popped open.

"*Hola, mi niña,*" Mr. Espinoza gave a fanged smile at Alexis. "*Tengo hambre por sangre.*" He closed his eyes and breathed. "*La aroma. Ella está cerca.*" Mr. Espinoza leaped from the coffin and turned toward Kendra, completely ignoring Maria. Red lightning streaks shattered his otherwise black eyes.

Alexis grabbed one arm and Keagan grabbed the other, just as Mr. Espinoza lunged at Kendra. As he had the other night, Mr. Espinoza went berserk with bloodlust. He could smell Kendra's blood, either from her elbow or her period. Probably both. He thrashed, flailing his arms and kicking. Had it only been Alexis holding him, he would have escaped, but Keagan bear-hugged him and lifted him up, preventing him from going anywhere.

"Bolt, ya bloodied fud!" Keagan shouted at Kendra through a grimace, his accent extra thick.

Ariel grabbed Kendra and led her to the Porsche before shoving her into the driver's seat and closing the door.

Luiz rushed to his dad. At first, I thought he was going to defend him—perhaps help free him. Instead, he offered his father his arm. Mr. Espinoza stopped thrashing and grabbed his son's forearm, biting into it high by the elbow.

Neither Keagan nor Alexis released their hold. Instead, Alexis spoke, clear and calm. "One pint." She repeated the order every few seconds until she estimated he'd drank a pint, then she put one hand on Mr. Espinoza's cheek. "Let him go!" He dropped his son's arm with more obedience than he'd shown a few nights ago.

Maria quickly offered her wrist to replace Luiz's. As Mr. Espinoza sucked down his second pint, the red lightning streaks in his eyes faded some, but not completely. Once he released Maria's hand, his eyes found the Porsche and stared at it—at Kendra—for long seconds before Alexis used her hand on his cheek to turn him away.

I was getting sick of vampires looking hungrily at Kendra.

"I have not received a Blood Rule Challenge before," Lexy turned to Keagan. "What should I expect tonight?"

"Just negotiating a date. Usually, negotiations last less than an hour." Keagan explained. "The Blood Rule Challenge is confirmed. You haggle over a duel date and a location and go your separate ways until then. However, the date and location are vitally important."

"Will we be in danger?"

"Always," Keagan answered. Then he looked around. "The larger your entourage, the safer you will be."

Great. That meant all of us would have to go.

Alexis met Mr. Espinoza's eyes, making sure he listened and focused. "We need a plan for negotiating. We need your mind."

CHAPTER 29
WHITE HOUSE

I'm struggling with who I am versus who I was. Modesty used to hold a high importance in my life. Now, at least with the Trinity of Mind, modesty has disappeared, and I'm becoming numb to its absence. When I caught Jake looking at me at Lovely Leather, all I could think about was how glad I felt that he chose to look at me instead of Alexis. It wasn't until well after he looked away that I remembered I was supposed to be furiously mortified. —Kendra

I sat behind the driver's seat as Mr. Espinoza turned the SUV into the White House driveway and stopped at the checkpoint booth. A lantern-shaped light sat on a pole that rose above the booth, illuminating the driveway. A short woman sat inside the booth attending the window, and a man holding a machine gun stood behind her. The woman stepped out of the booth to knock on the driver's side window. Mr. Espinoza rolled it down. I recognized the woman's blonde hair and button nose. She had stood next to Jace in the alley.

The blonde spoke with a perky voice. "Park just west of the house. I'll meet you there and lead you inside."

Mr. Espinoza nodded at the instructions.

The tiny blonde looked up at the top of the SUV. "Nice daybed," she clearly avoided using the word "coffin." Did Mr. Espinoza even know that the word coffin offended vampires?

Mr. Espinoza smiled. "It's my coffin."

Nope, he didn't know yet.

The blonde scrunched her eyebrows together, then returned to the booth. The boom gate rose, and Mr. Espinoza drove forward. The driveway continued in the shape of an S for a quarter mile before bright lights illuminated the pillared White House. The SUV's headlights cast tall, palm tree shadows onto the white, three-story exterior. Luiz's dad turned right at the

242

paved circle leading to the mansion's main entrance and pulled into a parking area in front of a building with four garage doors.

We'd let Luiz and Andrea drive the Porsche alone. They parked next to us.

As we got out, I noticed the size of Princess Alexis's entourage. Kendra, Ariel, Luiz, Andrea, Mr. Espinoza, his thrall Maria, Keagan, and me. What if Pasha were here? And Jody, Carl? That made eleven. Add in Mr. Espinoza's six other thralls, and the count rose to seventeen. If we managed to get Gina back, it would be eighteen—nineteen had Sajid not been killed. Perhaps Alexis *was* forming her own shiver.

The blonde with the button nose already stood under the light between two garage doors. She held the doorknob of a small entry door behind her. She eyed the weapons we each carried. Kendra and I held our druid staffs. Ariel's sais hung from the chains at each of her sides. A holstered HK45 was clipped to each of Lexy's pink pleather hips. Luiz carried the sawed-off shotgun. Keagan had kept Knight Time's rapier. Andrea and Maria each had a 9mm handgun. If Mr. Espinoza had a weapon, I couldn't see it.

"Follow me inside," the blonde opened the entry door. "Remember, you have the right to bear arms, not use them." She glanced at Lexy's pants. "Pink, huh?"

Lexy gave her a death stare, but Kendra and I barely stifled our laughs.

The blonde shrugged, and without waiting for us, she walked inside.

Of course, we would bring our arms. This was a meeting with a rival. Sure, the meeting was supposedly protected by the laws of the Blood Rule Challenge, but laws can be broken.

I stepped to the side and let the others go first. I had two rings, the one Bear gave me on my right ring finger and the one pulled from the Skull Shadow in my pocket.

"Luiz." I pulled him aside, and Andrea paused with us as well. "Wear this." I slipped the Skull Shadow's magic-absorbing ring into his palm.

Andrea cocked an eye at Luiz.

"*Diantre*, Jake." Luiz gave an exaggerated pout. "Aren't going to get down on one knee first?"

"Very funny," I shook my head.

"*Lo siento*, Andrea," Luiz grinned. "Even though he didn't kneel, I'm going to marry Jake. Thanks for helping me keep up the appearances of being straight while I waited for my best friend to finally come out."

"Shut up!" I shook my head and laughed.

"You can't joke like that!" Andrea punched Luiz in the shoulder.

I turned and headed inside, leaving Luiz and Andrea to follow.

We all followed the blonde through the pitch-black garage before entering a dimly lit hallway of the White House. We passed a maid, who entered a bedroom, not to clean it, but as if it were hers.

"Why are you bringing us in through the servants' quarters?" Keagan's Scottish accent thickened at the end of the question. He didn't sound happy at all.

Should we be offended that the blonde brought us inside through the servants' entrance? Eldra's memories suggested so.

"Have you never visited our shiver before?" the blonde raised an eyebrow at Keagan. "This is the way everyone goes."

Keagan moved to argue further, but Alexis put a hand on his shoulder, stopping him. Still, his demeanor stiffened. I already knew he was a predator, but suddenly, as his walk changed to a prowl, he now seemed to move like one. His change worried me.

We exited the servants' hallway into a massive open space, which we crossed, then walked down a flight of stairs. The basement at the bottom of the stairs mainly consisted of an open floor plan. The tiny blonde led us through a great room, then into a small room. She tapped a tablet-like screen by the doorway, and across the room, a massive bookshelf slid forward. Behind it, a cement stairway led downward into the darkness and into Master King's shiver. Speaking of shivers, I felt them rise through my spine and into my hair follicles as I walked down into the darkness. The sense of evil rippled under my skin.

I recognized the cavernous home of the shiver from my previous tour via astral projection. The tunnels cut into the earth and rock below the White House. However, this time, I noticed much more than when I was astral projecting. Four pillars, each at the point of a large square, held up the ceiling—and perhaps held up the White House above. Beyond the pillars, I found the entrances to the tunnels, some of which my spirit had explored. A single, low-power electric line traveled down each tunnel with a single LED light every ten feet. The tiny LEDs provided enough light to barely see where to step while leaving most of the tunnel walls shrouded in shadows. Vampires could hide in darkness yet see clearly with their red eyes. I glanced down the tunnel where people were held like cattle.

Free them. I both heard and felt the urge again. The protector magic didn't demand that I save them now. Instead, it urged me to plan and do it soon. Was Gina with them?

"Mindy," I heard Jié Shù's accented voice call. "Take them to The Cage."

The little blonde that we followed stopped and looked toward Jié Shù, who stood in the shadows of one of the tunnels. An LED above her illuminated her hair just enough to detect its dyed-blue hue.

"Of course," Mindy replied.

Jié Shù eyed our weapons. She lingered for a moment on Luiz's shotgun before she stepped back into the shadows, and her dark silhouette turned away and faded into the tunnel.

The Cage? Kendra popped into my head with nervous curiosity.

Doesn't sound good, I agreed.

"You try to cage us, and I'll blow off your head," Luiz's shotgun now pointed at Mindy's face.

"It isn't that type of cage." Mindy rolled her eyes at Luiz.

Neither Alexis nor Keagan seemed concerned with our destination. We wished Alexis had her separation stone disabled so we could get some information from her. I'd expected us to walk in defensive formation, with Kendra in front of Alexis and me at her rear. Instead, Alexis walked next to Keagan, her arm in his elbow, allowing him to escort her. Luiz similarly escorted Andrea while his dad escorted Maria. Kendra and I came next. Only Ariel walked behind us. She still seemed more interested in protecting me—for selfish purposes—than protecting Alexis.

"This way," Mindy nodded, pointing with her blonde head toward the last opening—two tunnels to the right of the one which Jié Shù had disappeared into. Kendra and I followed the procession into the last opening, our staffs clacking loudly. An extra light, a full incandescent bulb, illuminated the first five yards, shining on the walls and revealing two textures: the first, a natural sandstone of rust and tan; the second, a rippled pattern. The sediment lines did not match the rippled shape. Instead, the ripples looked scratched out, not with tools but with fingers—or maybe claws. Finger-sized lines suggested that vampire claws, perhaps owned by some of the vampires still in this shiver, had carved out these sandstone walls. A clear image came to mind of a vampire feeding from a Latino woman's forearm with his bloodied, nubbed fingers gripping her wrist and elbow. His fingers slowly healed and extended as he fed. Hours later, his fingers fully healed, he would return to work to shred his fingertips to nubs again, in a repeated process, until completion of each tunnel. The image felt like a memory, but not mine.

It must be Lexy's memory, Kendra suggested.

Maybe. But her separation stone isn't enabled. Had the memory come from protector magic? From Caradoc or Eldra?

I reached my fingers out and found they fit perfectly into four of the finger-shaped lines. Kendra shivered.

The tunnel curved to the right, descending slightly, leaving the incandescent light behind, until only the glow from the tiny LEDs remained. Then it opened into vast darkness that gave me the sense of a large cavern. I couldn't see more than five feet in any direction. Unlike the tunnel, the cavern did not have any LEDs. Water trickled from somewhere deep in the darkness.

"Lights," Alexis spoke the word as if it were a command.

Mindy gave a barely perceptible nod to Alexis and then disappeared into the cavern's black void. The soft tap of her feet on the sandstone floor remained audible. A second later, the room lit up like a boxing arena. Long fluorescent lights, two dozen of them arranged in pairs around a large, hexagonal fighting cage, flickered to life and reflected off the metal. The surrounding stadium seating remained dim. The hexagonal enclosure rose from floor to ceiling and looked twice the size of an MMA arena. The chain-link looked old, with dents and bends throughout the walls, including one hole about eight feet up, big enough to crawl through. On one side, however, the chain-link glistened new, apparently recently replaced. Unlike an MMA cage, the floor did not have any padding. It was the same hard sandstone as the tunnels, except dark stains deepened the red stone in more than a dozen spots. The stains worried me, so I looked away. The walls of the cavern looked natural, not carved, with water-created divots in apparently random locations.

"Welcome to The Cage," Mindy smiled.

I don't like this, Kendra worried.

Mindy glanced at a watch on her wrist. "At midnight, we open seating to our shiver. First fight is at 12:30." She glanced to the south side of the room at a set of elevator doors we hadn't noticed until now. "And to a few special guests."

"Special guests?" Alexis raised her eyebrows.

"This *is* Vegas," Mindy answered, as if reminding us what city we were in—or under—was explanation enough.

Keagan frowned, his eyes thinning in concerned thought.

Mindy didn't wait around for us to ask more, but instead walked back the way we came. With my eyes adjusted to the bright fluorescent lighting, the tiny tunnel LEDs were not enough. Mindy disappeared the moment she reached the tunnel shadows.

"Can you disappear in shadows like that?" I asked Alexis, who thinned her eyes at me and didn't answer.

"It is a primal instinct of ours to slip quickly into the shadows," Keagan answered for Alexis with his Scottish accent. "The shadows are our friends. We embrace them, and they protect us from the light."

"Creepy much?" Luiz mocked Keagan fearlessly.

"Mr. K-Creepy, right?" I smiled, recalling Jody's name for Keagan. Keagan shifted out of the corner of my eye, drawing my vision back to him. At the same time, adult Ariel stepped in front of me protectively. He smiled back at me enough to show his fangs, but the smile didn't reach his eyes, which looked as black as they looked red. Alexis stood firm, her posture stiff and fixed. Her leather-clad arm still wrapped around Keagan's as if he gently escorted her, but her trembling hand betrayed her effort to hold him back.

Luiz chuckled, not noticing the tension until Andrea, holding his hand, tapped his hip.

I was about to ask Keagan if I'd touched a nerve.

Stop, Jake! Kendra mentally reprimanded me.

I didn't notice that I'd instinctually filled myself with magic until I felt ready to burst with power.

"We have this meeting with Master King to deal with," Alexis spoke.

Keagan relaxed—or at least Alexis no longer struggled to hold him back—and his eyes lightened back to red as he put aside his anger.

I breathed out, letting my tense body settle down and allowing the overwhelming amount of magic to flow out of me.

We huddled together and discussed where we would like the challenge to take place and how best to negotiate. I suggested Rice Eccles's stadium after midnight. There was plenty of room to move—a whole football field—and there were plenty of seats for spectators, and the surrounding stadium would hide it from prying eyes. But Lexy reminded me that bringing vampire spectators inside the line wouldn't be a great idea. Mr. Espinoza's ideas were superior to mine.

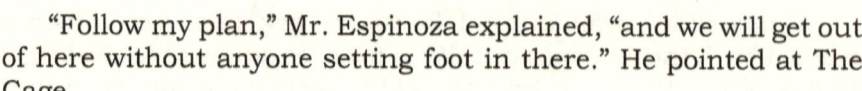

"Follow my plan," Mr. Espinoza explained, "and we will get out of here without anyone setting foot in there." He pointed at The Cage.

Keagan didn't appear to have been paying attention. He seemed to be looking around, distracted. When there was a break in conversation between Lexy and Mr. Espinoza, he cut in. "Something doesn't feel right. I think we need a backup plan in case this veers off course." He looked around at the arena. "I have an idea if you would like to hear it."

Shut up and listen. Kendra pre-empted another snide remark from me.

"*¿Papá?*" Luiz asked.

"I'd like to hear his idea," Mr. Espinoza smiled at Keagan as if he were a child allowed to speak only so everyone could hear the cute little idea from his cute little child brain, "before I reject it."

Keagan's eyes darkened again, clearly aware of Mr. Espinoza's tone.

CHAPTER 30
MASTER KING

Gina wants to become an entrepreneur. She has a rich daddy and her own trust fund. The opportunity for an investment came up, buying Club Exposed, so she called me. I agreed to meet her and the owner of Club Exposed. Master King set me up. He owns the club and mind-controlled Gina to lure me to a meeting. —Alexis

After a short planning and brainstorming session that didn't go Keagan's way, the first vampires arrived—two college-age-looking guys and a girl. All three wore matching yellow V.I.T. T-shirts. On the back, the acronym boasted the letters vertically with a few meanings for each letter in small print on the right. The first item in each list stood out in bold.

V	**ampire**
	ery
	iral
I	**nformation**
	mportant
	nternet
T	**echnology**
	echnican
	rendsetters

Vampire Information Technology was the company name. *Very Important Technician* and *Viral Internet Trendsetters* were the other phrases on the shirt.

The two boys wore cheap black cotton pants and black shoes, but the girl's outfit caught my attention. She wore Doc Martin shoes and a black miniskirt that ended mid-thigh and accentuated her feminine hips. She wore black knee-length leggings under her skirt, which allowed her to bend over and connect cables under tables without worrying about exposing herself. Her black hair hung straight to her shoulders, and she'd dyed the very tips of it yellow, which blended with her shirt. I couldn't decide if her outfit was genius or a fashion faux pas.

They started connecting wires, sound systems, and ethernet. A part of me chuckled at the idea that someone would have created a tech support company specific to vampires. Of course, this was real life, not fiction, and in real life, things like sound systems and networking didn't just work magically.

As the three geeks eyed us warily, it dawned on me that these technicians were not the stereotypical bloodthirsty, murdering vampires, but real people who also happened to be vampires. The protector magic did not ignite with the need to kill any of them. In fact, the protector magic in me sensed that not one of these technicians had ever killed or even harmed another person. They needed to drink living blood to survive, but they must have found ways to do it without killing. They were no different than Kendra or me. Well, we were druids, so I guess they were no different than Luiz and Andrea. I had given Alexis the benefit of the doubt, and even after she drained Mr. Espinoza, my best friend's dad, I still stood by her. I treated her not as a vampire—er, half-dhampir— but as a young woman, pretty much my age, who deserved every chance in life. These three vampires were just trying to live their lives like any regular Joe—or Jane. Wake up, go to work, go home.

The V.I.T. geeks did not have the MK tattoo on their wrists, indicating they were outsourced workers, not from Master King's shiver. The young woman kept starting a sentence, stopping with a glance at us, then closing her mouth.

My phone dinged. I checked it. There was a text message. It read: I watched with worry.

Seconds later, another text message came through, saying: This video is vicious and violent.

I didn't have to ask who the texts were from. The alliteration made it obvious. Before I could respond, a third text came through—a video. I clicked it.

Just before I finished the video, Keagan grabbed my phone.

"Hey," I complained.

Keagan forwarded the video to himself, then handed my phone back. He glanced at a tech and media station that the three V.I.T. workers were setting up before walking over to Lexy and Mr. Espinoza. He whispered in Lexy's ear. He looked determined.

I texted Bear back: 👍 . Sure, a thumbs up didn't rhyme or aliterate, but it was still word art—sort of.

Others from the shiver began to arrive. I hadn't noticed additional entrances to the cavern at the top of the stadium seating until people entered through them. It didn't take long for the stadium seating to fill. Would I be scared if I had to fight in The Cage? Probably not. I didn't fear The Cage. Had I wanted to, I could have burned Keagan's heart from his chest in a second, and there wasn't a vampire here that even compared to him. I didn't fear any of them. Except perhaps Jié Shù, who had a hint of magic and could possibly create a containment, but I'd be able to slip through it. But saying you aren't afraid of one vampire is easy. I glanced from The Cage to the stadium seating. Could I say that I didn't fear all of them?

I could create quite a supply of marble-sized magic missiles all at once—maybe ten now. Could I also cast torched heart at several vampires at the same time? If so, how many? I'd already decided that with Ariel, Kendra, and Keagan, I couldn't take twenty. How many were here?

I looked around at the increasing number of vampires in the stadium seats. I started counting them because, when nervous, I like to count things. I planned to count one section and then multiply it. Kendra ignored my counting, mostly. I must have been counting for a few minutes because I was nearing five hundred before Alexis surprised Kendra and me by dropping into the Trinity of Mind.

They are not all vampires. Most are thralls, and not just high-ranking thralls. A battle to the death in The Cage increases the adrenochrome in the blood.

What's adrenochrome? Kendra asked.

It is produced by your adrenal glands. Blood with adrenochrome gives us a euphoric high so powerful that all other blood tastes bland without it. The more frightened you are, the higher the concentration in your blood.

Adrenochrome harvesting is real, then? I asked. Ethan was the conspiracy theorist among the jeeks, and he'd discussed it multiple times.

Alexis didn't answer. She'd already closed off her mind, again.

I stopped counting. Looking at the crowd that continued to grow, could I even tell which of these people were vampires and which weren't? Why had I assumed they were all vampires? Because I was in the depths of a shiver. Because without Alexis in my head, I didn't know near enough about the situation I was in. Why didn't she leave her separation stone turned off?

Mindy, the tiny blonde vampire, returned and walked over to us. "Master King is on his way. Follow me." She turned and walked toward one of The Cage's hexagonal sides that had a dugout of sorts, where a fighter could enter The Cage but still be separated from the crowd. I noticed most of the bends in the dugout area pushed outward. Perhaps The Cage wasn't to protect the fighters from the crowd, but to protect the crowd from the fighters.

Alexis joined the Trinity of Mind. She never expected the duel to take place in an MMA-style cage, but she felt certain Master King would want to schedule it to occur here. She shared with Kendra and me one of her memories of a Blood Rule Challenge duel, and there hadn't even been fighting, just a battle of mental control. But she'd never negotiated a challenge time or location before.

Mr. Espinoza thinks Master King may have mind control beyond allure, like my ability to read minds. If he can use it at full strength while fighting, he will be hard to beat. By creating a mixed martial arts cage, he forces his challengers to play to his strengths, Alexis explained.

Home field advantage? I wondered.

Most vampires cannot protect against mind control while battling, so if he hit their minds hard in the midst of a melee, they'd succumb to his will with little resistance.

Alexis tapped her separation stone.

I felt grateful that Kendra kept her mind connected to mine. The weight of Eldra's memories—her thoughts of Robin, her children, her grandchildren, her careers, one as a Druid Ambassador, another as a board member on various corporations, and more—pressed against me like a reservoir pressed against a cracked dam. Without Kendra's mental aid, the dam would collapse, and Eldra's memories would wash over and consume me.

Eldra wanted me to wipe vampires from existence. Until just a few minutes ago, I'd never disagreed with her. But after seeing the three V.I.T. geeks just doing their jobs, and feeling their normalcy, which was very different from the other vampires I'd met, I no longer felt sure. However, I remembered the tunnel in this very shiver, filled with people for the vampires to feed on. The dead I encountered on the tunnel floor suggested that I'd be forced to kill plenty of vampires. Eldra wasn't wrong; she just wasn't entirely right either. Perhaps the younger vampire generation, like the three young, college-age members of the V.I.T., had learned to live without evil brutality.

Minutes passed. We had planned for the negotiations—and for the unexpected—as best we could. Now to wait. The anticipation left me tapping my foot and glancing between the tunnel entrance and the elevators, wondering from which direction Master King would enter.

Kendra turned on her sight to see if, with it, she could tell a vampire from a human. I did it, too. We looked at Mr. Espinoza and compared him to Luiz and Andrea. Mr. Espinoza's inner glow looked fragmented and dim, like a million tiny particles of light instead of a solid spirit. Mindy, who stood at the doorway to our dugout, had the same light as Luiz and Andrea, solid but dimmed by clothes. We'd expected her to match Mr. Espinoza. Perhaps the shattered particles of light had nothing to do with being a vampire? Maybe he'd always looked like that. Looking around, we found only one other vampire whose spirit shared that same dim fragmented light—Fern, the redhead who liked to rip out and eat hearts. She sat next to blue-haired Jié Shù in a dugout on the opposite side of the hexagonal cage from us. When had they entered? We hadn't noticed. Linzi and Henry also sat in the dugout. Sitting on the row behind them, I spotted Drake, Badger, and Dreadlocks—Jace.

Kendra and I wondered at the connection between Dreadlocks and Keagan. We understood enough not to give away her allegiance, but would she join our side if things got ugly? What if the entire stadium turned on us?

The lights suddenly dimmed. An excited voice came over the loudspeaker, "Welcome to The Cage!" the announcer shouted, walking in from one of the upper cavern entrances, holding a wireless microphone. A spotlight followed him.

"It has been months since the last Blood Rule Challenge duel, but tonight, Master King fights again!" the announcer paused, and the crowd cheered. "Are you excited?" he shouted the question. The crowd cheered again, but this time louder, the sound pounding on my ears as it reverberated around the cavern. "Master King is undefeated in challenges," the announcer continued.

What's he doing challenging Alexis if he already has a challenge tonight? Kendra asked, but I didn't have an answer other than momentary confusion as our joined minds started to piece together what was really happening tonight.

Keagan swore. He stood up and walked to the dugout's exit, distracting me from hearing the announcer as he spoke of Master King's victories. Mindy stepped in front of Keagan at the dugout exit. He gracefully lifted her out of the way with what seemed like no effort at all. He walked around The Cage. Mindy followed behind him, looking all around as if unsure what to do. Keagan found the stairs in the crowded stands leading up toward the announcer and started climbing.

"The challenger is Alexis Kaloyan!" the announcer shouted.

Wait, Master King challenged Alexis. Tonight was just supposed to be the negotiations. Our joined minds finished piecing together what was happening. Master King was taking his shot now.

"Perhaps giving Master King ninety minutes to prepare was too generous," Mr. Espinoza told Alexis with a slight grin, impressed by this move.

The crowd booed, and the announcer nodded, encouraging the boos to last longer before continuing. "Yes, you would recognize that last name. She is the granddaughter of the very man who oppressed us for centuries. The very man who drove us to flee to the Americas. The so-called Vampire King." The announcer spoke his name in a mocking tone, and the jeering of the crowd doubled. "He has sent his granddaughter to force a monarchy back onto us. He wants us to let her be our ruler." More boos. "He declared her the Princess of the New World. Are we not free?" the announcer asked the crowd. "Master King. Will you save us from this oppression? Will you once again defeat this tyrannical monarchy?"

A second spotlight flashed to life, pointing at the open elevator doors and illuminating a man dressed in a black gi and holding a pole with the American flag. Both Kendra and I instantly became his biggest fans. He stood tall with curly brown hair. His demeanor reminded me of Sylvester Stallone's, or perhaps a combination of Rocky Balboa and Bruce Lee mixed into a true American patriot. He looked nothing like those actors, though. His celebrity lookalike would be Mark Ruffalo. Was he secretly a hulk? His allure affected the entire crowd. My protection stone warmed. No, it heated up. It had never felt too hot on my skin before. This time, it was clearly overworked at the attempt to push away Master King's allure. Enough of his allure made it through the protection stone that I worried whether Alexis could even keep her entourage on her side.

Then a second allure hit me, not quite as strong, but strong enough I took notice. Under the announcer's spotlight, Keagan stood holding the microphone in one hand, and gripping the announcer's neck with the other, holding him down on his knees.

"I am Keagan," he spoke with no hint of his Scottish accent. Many in the crowd cheered as Keagan's allure urged them to do so, and they eagerly complied. "And this announcer has made a couple of grievous errors, which I will now rectify."

"You claim freedom, and yet you bow to a man who calls himself Master King? How ironic. Alexis did not challenge Master King. No. You," Keagan pointed at Master King with the microphone, "challenged her."

The crowd hushed, shocked to hear the news. Jié Shù stepped slowly from the dugout, trying not to be noticed, to make her way to Keagan.

"He's gone rogue," Mr. Espinoza growled and stood up. "This is not the plan," his Spanish accent came out thick and heavy.

"We're switching to his plan now," Alexis put her hand on Luiz's dad, urging him to sit back down. He sat but didn't look happy to do so.

"You speak of the oppression you have escaped," Keagan continued. "Then you share with Alexis a piece of that oppression, but don't pretend the Vampire King oppressed you more than her. Look at Alexis. Where have you seen her before? Humiliated each year on All Soul's Day. Forced to dance and undress in front of all of you. Her oppression ran far deeper than what you were allowed to see. She came to this country for the same reason as you. To flee the oppression of her grandfather.

"Master King!" Keagan shouted. "You have broken your own laws of the Blood Rule Challenge. Is it not true that you have tainted any chance for a duel to occur tonight?"

"Lies," Master King answered calmly into a microphone he'd just acquired from one of the V.I.T.

"Why did you have her kidnapped? Why did you steal one of her thralls?"

"I did no such thing!" Master King shook his head. "Alexis has no thralls."

"Why did you have Henry break her arm today?"

"More lies."

"He broke her arm thrice!" Keagan told the crowd. "Worse, you helped her grandfather oppress her. Three times you accepted Alexis to your bed as a gift from the Vampire King. And underage all three times."

The crowd gasped. Keagan paused to let his statement sink in, his eyes fixed on Master King. He didn't see Jié Shù walking up the steps toward him. Her hand lit up with amber light, magic that only I could see. The magic launched from her hand. Keagan grabbed the pommel of his rapier, surprised by the attack. He'd been ready to defend himself from a physical attack, but not a magical one. The spell looked like some type of poison. It collided with a containment a foot in front of Keagan and spread around the invisible barrier, leaving him untouched.

I got him, Kendra confirmed, her hand extended, supplying the magic forming the containment.

Mr. Espinoza no longer stood with us. I hadn't noticed him leave.

Keagan removed his hand from the rapier's pommel, looked down at Jié Shù, shrugged, and then pointed upward. Four stadium televisions, hanging from the cavern ceiling in a square, turned on. The four screens displayed an angled view of the security camera feed from the back alley where we'd rescued Alexis—the video Bear had texted me.

Yes! Kendra and I mentally cheered together.

The video was dark but not grainy—not in today's high-definition age. No, it was crisp and clear for all to see. The date and time displayed on the bottom right, confirming the video took place barely two hours ago. In the feed, Jié Shù spoke to Henry, who moved to Alexis. The crowd watched silently as the video showed Henry grip Alexis and break her right arm over his knee.

The crowd gasped again, but it was much louder this time.

"You dare call my words lies. Do you cheat before all of your fights?" Keagan called out.

A few people in the crowd shouted similar questions at Master King. The sound of the grumbling crowd created a low hum.

"Where is your Scottish accent, Keagan?" Master King asked. "Where is your oppressive leader? Surely the crowd recognizes you, Keagan, as the Vampire King's former Second General. One of the primary oppressors that drove us from Europe to the Americas."

The crowd turned on Keagan, shouting obscenities at him. Keagan ignored them. He simply pointed again at the screens.

It seemed baffling that they spoke of coming to the Americas like it just happened. Perhaps the older a vampire was, the more recent two or three hundred years ago seemed. Or perhaps, the Vampire King was still driving them to flee?

A clamor sounded from near where the V.I.T. had set up their equipment. Between the noise of the crowd and the darkness, the clamor was quickly ignored.

The video reached the point where Drake tried to burn Alexis alive. The crowd silenced, watching in awe as Drake lit Lexy's leather clothes on fire.

"You tried to burn her alive?" Keagan asked it as a question because doing so had more effect on the crowd, which remained silent, eyes fixed on the screens. The video continued, showing Alexis covered in flames, her leather armor burning off her body as Drake walked around her with his blow torch. Pieces of Lexy's leather armor fell to the asphalt, leaving her exposed.

A second clamor, this time a loud crash near where the V.I.T. had set up their equipment, caused the TV screens to go black. Dozens of vampires in the crowd shouted obscenities, some at Keagan and some shouting at Master King. How many of Master King's shiver had just become disenfranchised with their leader?

Master King's eyes thinned, the first sign that his subterfuge regarding this challenge wasn't going the way he had expected. He wanted to duel Alexis tonight. Now. Before she had time to prepare. Did he know that with time to prepare, she had check-mated her grandfather? Or if not beaten him, at least reached a stalemate?

"Jié Shù," Master King spoke into the microphone. "Start the entertainment." Away from the microphone, he looked at Mindy and mouthed, "Bring them."

"Looks like you get a private meeting after all," Mindy pointed with her head for us to follow.

Keagan tossed his microphone to Jié Shù and quickly descended the stairs to join us.

"¡Bien hecho! Papá," Luiz put his hand on the shoulder of his father, who joined us from the direction of the V.I.T. equipment. A cut under Mr. Espinoza's left eye was already healing. Had he not defended the equipment, the video would have gone black before the crowd had seen Drake try to burn Alexis alive.

"Keagan's plan worked," Alexis told him.

Mr. Espinoza's eyes went black. "I helped," he growled between his teeth, "but I prefer plans. Not winging it."

"Keagan did not become one of the top vampires in the world by accident," Alexis reminded.

Mr. Espinoza looked ready to object further, but since we hadn't followed Mindy, she returned, so he closed his mouth.

"Come," Mindy beckoned, and we all followed her to the elevators.

Behind us, Jié Shù announced an opening fight, naming two fighters I didn't know. We crowded into the elevator, but Andrea ended up stuck too close to the door, so a warning tone began beeping. Seconds passed as the elevator doors spread open at a snail's pace. Luiz grabbed Andrea and pulled her close to him, but it didn't matter. The doors continued to close painfully slowly. Finally, they closed, the beeping stopped, and we started rising.

"You see, love," Keagan whispered to Alexis, with a subtle glance at Mr. Espinoza. "I step in, and now we get the special guest elevator."

Mr. Espinoza's eyes remained black and fixated on Keagan.

We entered the mansion, where Mindy led us down a hall, through a large door, and into a large room. Master King stood at the far end, his back to us. He faced an empty fireplace and still wore the gi. It had an American flag on the back. His feet were bare, and he adjusted the thick, curly brown hair that topped his head. A tinge of gray lined the sides of his hair.

Master King turned around, and Luiz spit out, "¡Dios mío! It's the guy who plays the Hulk." Up close, Master King looked even more like Mark Ruffalo than from a distance. Until he smiled. His lines were different. They were wider on his cheeks and far deeper. He'd been smiling for so many centuries that the creases in his skin were unnaturally deep. He also had green eyes, not red. Was he wearing contacts? Because I'd never met a vampire with eyes any color but red.

"I get that a lot," Master King looked genuinely pleased with the comparison. He lifted his chin to glance behind us, seeing Jié Shù, Fern, and Linzi, his generals, entering the large room. They gathered to our left. The bodybuilder, Henry, followed behind them. As Master King had lifted his chin, a leather strap necklace with multiple crystals peeked out from the collar of his gi. What magical stones did he have? One of them must augment allure because there was no way his could be naturally that powerful. Eldra, however, had no knowledge of the existence of such a stone.

"The guests are entertained," Jié Shù assured him.

"For now," Master King sighed.

"If you force the Blood Rule duel on Alexis tonight, you'll cause a war," Keagan started right in, his Scottish accent no longer suppressed.

"First things first," Master King smiled, turned to Alexis, and looked at her pants. "Can you please explain the pink?"

He spoke to Alexis like he knew her well. It bothered Kendra and I that the Vampire King had gifted Alexis to both Keagan and Master King. His allure made it hard for us to dislike him, but we managed.

"Go watch the sunrise," Alexis responded.

"Testy."

"Where is Gina?"

"Don't worry. Fern is here," Master King nodded to his redheaded general. "She isn't off bathing in Gina's blood."

"Return her to me. Now!" Alexis spoke as regally as she could, but somehow, her usual regal tone failed in Master King's presence.

"Excellent posture for giving orders." Master King smiled but ignored the demand. "Did your grandfather teach you that?"

"Enough with the small talk!" Keagan cut in. "I'm trying to help avoid a war."

"What if I want a war?" Master King shrugged.

"Then you're a dobber. It's a war you can't win."

"I can beat the Vampire King," Master King's anger dripped with each word. Whether he was angry at being called a dobber or being told he couldn't win, or both, I couldn't be sure.

"At what cost? Afterward, will enough of your followers survive to defeat the next challenger?"

Master King didn't answer.

"If you honor the laws of the Blood Rule Challenge and defeat Alexis when it is fair," Keagan explained, "there will be no war. Your rule here won't be questioned. You know John Kaloyan can't stand the New World. You will have complete rulership to yourself, have time to build your power, and then time to take over the rest."

"Perhaps," Master King's eyes thinned. "Then again, perhaps dueling tonight is the better option. Are you certain there will be a war? The Vampire King put Alexis in my path intentionally. Two-to-one, all he does is thank me for killing her."

"What if he set this up?" Keagan countered.

"Why would he do that?" Master King shook his head.

"So you're to blame, not him, when he declares war on you for killing her?" Keagan explained. "Are you certain those on your side will stay that way? This is high risk."

"Perhaps it is a risk I'll just have to take."

"You know it isn't." Keagan shook his head. "The risks are more than war."

"I know the risks!"

"We are in Vegas, so, how about a gamble?" Keagan suggested.

"What do you propose?" Master King smirked.

"Princess Alexis's best against yours." Keagan sounded confident. "In The Cage, tonight."

"Keagan," Alexis cut in. "No!"

"I have this handled," the Scottish vampire shrugged off her concern.

Mr. Espinoza's black eyes glared at Keagan.

"If I win, you and Princess Alexis fight in an official challenge for the rule of all of North and South America in front of all the vampires on All Soul's Day."

Master King glanced at Keagan, then at his four generals. Keagan could take any of them, and he knew it. He focused on Alexis.

"I'll accept this wager with one change," Master King smiled. "The best out of three fights decides whether the Blood Rule Challenge takes place tonight."

"Agreed," Keagan remained confident, but Alexis gripped his arm, trying to get him to stop. He ignored her. He could take any one of Master King's generals. Could he take three in a row? Probably. He'd made short work of Knight Time, but what about Jié Shù's magic?

"I pick your three generals," Master King added.

"That's not the bargain," Keagan spat back. "You pick yours, and Alexis will pick hers."

"Are you so certain you could take three of my generals in sequence?" Master King read Keagan's intentions like a book.

"And I could still take you after," Keagan boasted.

"Hah! Then why would I agree to a best of three against you?"

"If we can't make a deal tonight, then we walk out of here with nothing more than a future date to continue negotiations."

"A future date to continue negotiations?" Master King smiled. "You are in my house and in my shiver. There will be no walking out of here unless I say so! I'm done speaking with you," Master King returned his eyes to Alexis. "I will fight you in the Blood Rule Challenge. I choose to fight tonight, the risks be damned, or you will agree to this wager. What do you choose, *Princess*?" His tone turned mocking as he spoke her title.

Mr. Espinoza had warned Alexis against fighting Master King tonight, as he was too much of an unknown. We didn't yet know his secret to victory. He had beaten the best of the best throughout the United States. Perhaps Keagan could take him, but could Alexis? We needed time to research the man and find out how he behaved during his past challenges. Fighting Master King tonight was not an option.

"Neither," Alexis answered, trying to regroup and fall back to Mr. Espinoza's plan.

"Then you will remain here, under my 'protection' until such time as you agree to the challenge."

"The laws for the challenge forbid incarcerating a challenged opponent," Alexis scoffed.

He gave a sly smile. "Incarcerated? Such a nasty word. I will do no such thing. You will simply be under my protective care."

"She's already under my protective care!" I snapped, but Alexis put a hand on my shoulder to silence me.

Do not, under any circumstances, reveal to Master King that you are a protector, Alexis thought.

"As he said," Alexis nodded to me, "my generals protect me. I thank you for the offer of additional aid, but politely decline."

"I must insist."

"Enough of this. Offer another time and place. Where would you like this challenge duel to take place?"

"I choose tonight, in The Cage."

"I cannot agree to that. I believe our negotiations are at an impasse. We are leaving," Alexis stood.

"Looks like Gina is yours," Master King told Fern.

"Do it, and we'll make sure every vampire knows of your treachery!" Keagan shouted as he, too, stood. "We can't save Gina. Let's go, love." He took Lexy's arm, and together, they took a step.

"Try to leave, and I cannot guarantee your protection."

Two men stepped into the doorway and pointed machine guns at us. I had my staff and my Smith & Wesson. The two machine guns trumped both. If I had a wall of sheetrock between us, that would be different, but I didn't.

"I've been on both sides of a dozen Blood Rule Challenges and seen two dozen more. Nobody has so brazenly ignored its laws," Keagan tried to cut back in, but Master King ignored him and kept his eyes on Alexis.

"You will cheat?" Alexis asked.

"Me?" Master King's eyes widened in feigned innocence. "I will do nothing but obey the laws of the Blood Rule Challenge. These men are not my thralls nor under my control. They are a rival's thralls. It would be unfortunate if they made an attempt on my life and you and your generals died in the crossfire." He smiled, knowing he had us.

Alexis glanced at Mr. Espinoza, clearly reading his mind. Luiz's dad looked furious with the turn of events. He'd said earlier that if we followed his plan, we'd leave without a fight. He clearly felt that Keagan had ruined that chance. I wasn't so sure. Give Luiz's dad a day or two and he'd outthink Keagan every time. But he'd had only ninety minutes to plan, with limited information. Keagan hadn't made a mistake in negotiation. No, the only mistake was made by all of us. We assumed Master King would obey the laws of a Blood Rule Challenge. We should have never even come here. Had it not been for Gina, we wouldn't have.

It seemed we had three options. One, try to walk away and die by machine gun and let Master King get away with it unpunished. Two, let Alexis fight and die against Master King tonight. Three, we generals fight, and if two of us win, Alexis gets to wait until All Soul's Day for the challenge.

Whether Mr. Espinoza liked it or not, Keagan had given us a chance. He'd played on Master King's desire for a wager to get us three fights we could win instead of one Alexis would surely lose. In The Cage, Keagan would win, and I'd win. What about Kendra or Ariel?

"My Generals will fight," Lexy chose option two, "but not to the death. That is non-negotiable."

"Sorry, little girl," Master King shook his head, "all fights in The Cage are to the death."

"Master," Fern spoke up. "May I have the blonde child?" She gestured toward Kendra. "I want her heart."

I am not getting in that cage with her. Kendra's fear burned into me. *I have magic and Astrapi, but vampires are fast. If I attack and miss, Fern will pull my heart from my chest in a second.* The possibility of dying felt all too real to Kendra.

"Jié Shù will fight ugly-boy," Master King pointed at me.

"*Aye,*" Luiz defended. "It took a lot of magic to make Jake look this good!"

Master King ignored Luiz. "Fern will fight the blonde child. Linzi will fight the lavender-haired woman with scales." He'd left Keagan out of the fight entirely.

"Keagan," Alexis looked him in the eyes, demanding he interject in some way.

"This is Las Vegas," Keagan offered. "We roll a four-sided die. You and Alexis each rank your generals one through four. We role the die and the two generals at that rank fight."

"I don't have four generals," Master King shrugged.

"Use Henry as your fourth," Keagan suggested.

"No, Keagan." Alexis challenged. "I cannot agree to put my generals' lives at risk for a gamble."

"Little girl," Master King's diminutive patronization continued. "If you wish, you and I shall fight instead. When I win," he glanced at us, "by law, your generals and thralls are mine. I'll let your generals live." His grin widened. "That is, I'll let them live if they survive The Cage." He blinked as if rather pleased with himself. He'd outwitted Alexis, Keagan, and Mr. Espinoza, and he knew it. "You see, either way, they risk The Cage."

"You would not! Killing generals and thralls after a challenge is forbidden on penalty of death."

"Who is to say they didn't freely and bravely choose to fight in The Cage? Welcome to America, the land of the free and the home of the brave."

"Best of three," Keagan demanded. "After two fights, the third fight will only take place if there is a tie."

Master King nodded to Keagan, then fixed his eyes on Alexis.

Alexis closed her eyes and took a breath. "Agreed," she nodded.

"Excellent," Master King rubbed his hands together in excitement. "Rank your generals, please."

"Ariel, Jacob, Keagan, Kendra," Alexis answered without hesitation.

"Interesting," Master King's smile fell. He glanced at Jié Shù.

"You put your weakest at the top," Jié Shù accused, "hoping to have an advantage with three out of four."

"Did I?" Alexis asked with a perfect poker face.

Master King and Jié Shù stared at each other for long seconds. I recognized the silent communication. I wasn't sure how they communicated, but they did.

"Jié Shù, Fern, Linzi, Henry," Master King ranked his generals in order.

Oh, no! Kendra and I thought. *What if Jié Shù uses sight against Ariel?*

"Shall we return to The Cage?" Master King grinned. "I'd like to let a special guest in our crowd—a friend of yours, Alexis—roll the four-sided die."

CHAPTER 31
UNPROTECTED

My mom and sister are in jail. Master King's minions captured Alexis and nearly burnt her to death. I'm willingly letting Keagan live, again. Worse, he's on our side. I'm sitting writing this journal entry on my phone. I don't feel in control. I just need something to go my way. —Jake

"Wait." Jié Shù stopped everyone from leaving the large room. "We must bind this with Blood Rule Challenge oath magic," she insisted in her accented voice. "You two," she pointed at Master King and Alexis, "must take an oath," she paused, "no, two oaths. The Blood Rule Challenge oath, and one of not cheating or helping with magic in The Cage." She glanced between Kendra, Alexis, and me. We out-magicked them three to one, and she knew it.

"My generals are not fighting without magic," Alexis countered.

"Apologies," Jié Shù shook her head, her blue hair swinging. "For themselves, yes. I meant help another. The blonde," she pointed at Kendra, "can't put a containment around Keagan."

"And there will be no spells that harm the audience," Master King interjected.

"What can they bring into The Cage?" Alexis questioned.

"Nothing more than whatever they can wear," Master King suggested.

"Your honor is absent. Bind both agreements by magic," Alexis spat.

"My honor is always good in a bet," Master King smiled.

"Include protection from them," Alexis pointed to the men with machine guns. "I want special protection until we leave this city!"

Master King chuckled. "No. Until noon. No more."

"The standard Blood Rule Challenge oath, first. The wager oath second." Alexis demanded. "I assume the challenge oath is the same. Or did you change it?"

"Laws improved. The oath is unchanged," Master King assured. "Together, then."

"Watch how this is done," Alexis told Kendra and me. "You may need to know how to do it," she tapped her separation stone. *Make certain that she applies the oath magic to Master King.* She tapped her separation stone again.

I could easily see the glowing magic, a silver light, in Jié Shù's hands. Alexis took one hand, and Master King took another.

Master King and Alexis spoke in unison. "As the master of me and mine, I take an oath of peace until the Blood Rule Challenge duel begins. Neither me, nor any that serve me, nor any under my control or influence, shall harm you. Nor shall they harm those that serve you or any under your control or influence." Jié Shù glanced at the doorway, now empty, where the two men with machine guns had stood.

The visible, silver-colored magic first rippled into both Master King and Alexis, then it rippled through all but a few of us in the room. It bound Luiz, Andrea, Mr. Espinoza, and Maria, but it didn't touch Keagan, Kendra, Ariel, or me. We were here by our own choice. None of us were under Alexis's control or influence, so the oath magic failed to bind us. However, it continued spreading outside the room and bound everyone in Master King's shiver.

"The second oath will mean no interference and a fair fight tonight," Jié Shù explained. "Neither me, nor any that serve me, nor any under my control or influence will interfere with the fights tonight. And we offer a special provision of protection from our rivals until noon."

Master King and Alexis repeated her words. Again, oath magic spread around the room, and again, it failed to bind Keagan, Kendra, Ariel, and me.

Jié Shù's eyes blinked, confused that four of us remained unbound by the oath magic. She turned her eyes to Master King. Their silent communication happening again. I didn't like it. It gave me a taste of how Kendra, Alexis, and I might make others feel when we communicated mentally.

"My generals will need to take both oaths themselves," Alexis explained before Master King could accuse her of trying to cheat. "My oath cannot bind them."

"Interesting," Master King thinned his eyes, pulling the wrinkles on his forehead together.

"My generals are free. I am surprised at you, Master King," Alexis accused. "You speak of freedom and patriotism, yet you don't trust anyone in your shiver to be free. All my generals are free. You don't deserve to rule the Americas."

Master King's green eyes darkened. No doubt they'd turned black with anger under his green contact lenses. I could tell he regretted taking the oath, but it was done.

"Take my hands," Jié Shù held out her hands to Kendra and Keagan. Each took one of her hands and quoted the same two oaths. Then she offered her hands to Ariel and me.

As I reached forward, time stopped.

Jake, Kendra called to me just before my soul slipped from my body, and I lost connection to the Trinity of Mind. I found myself traveling through the floor back into the underground tunnels. Two men fought in The Cage while the crowd shouted, but my spirit sped by the arena so fast that I didn't see or hear much of the current fight. In a second, I found myself in the tunnel with the people captured and held like cattle.

The tunnel was almost empty compared to when I'd been here before. Where were all the thralls? Of course, many would be in the arena watching the fight. Were others having the blood sucked from them somewhere else? And where was Gina? I didn't see her. My protector magic didn't have her on my list, but I wanted to protect her anyway.

An artistic sign hung on the tunnel wall. A painted image of grapes and a wine bottle decorated the right side of the sign while the left side held a list of names matched to wine measurements. One of the amounts was circled in blood: McKenzie = 5.0 liters. A phrase I'd heard Jié Shù say to Alexis repeated in my mind. "This is what happens to those that steal *kenzies* from Master King's territory." The average human had five liters of blood. They'd named these people "kenzies" after a five-liter container of wine.

I found myself drawn to a man with short, tightly curled hair and stubble on his dark face. I could feel something powerful, not in the man himself, but directed at the man. Then in a flash, I witnessed hundreds of prayers all for this one man, begging God and Jesus to bring him home to his family.

The protector magic turned my attention to a large, overweight woman with stringy, blonde hair and a pockmarked face. Far away, a woman with similar features but two decades older begged God in prayer to bring her daughter safely home. She'd prayed the same prayer a thousand times in the past week alone.

I moved to a black-haired man with tan skin and a black beard. Multiple people—no, multiple families—all kneeling on a rug, prayed to Allah for his safe return. He had family praying for him here in the states and others all the way in India.

The protector magic moved me to about ten different individuals, not deeming the person worthy themselves, but instead showing me their loved ones, begging and pleading in prayer for them. It didn't matter whether these people were individually worthy of being saved because the sheer number of those who pled to a higher power had deemed them so. Their loved ones were worthy. It felt like it took ten minutes to witness each person and their loved ones.

I ended on a small woman who looked a bit like Kendra, only a few years older. She had long, golden-brown hair that looked like Kendra's had before her current boy-cut. She had similar facial features, with her cheekbone placement and blue eyes. However, her belly jutted out like a basketball—only much bigger. The baby would come by morning.

"Save us," a short, brown-haired girl who couldn't have weighed a hundred pounds looked directly at me as she spoke the words. I wasn't sure she'd really spoken. Then a rough, tattooed man next to her looked at me and repeated her request. How could they see my spirit? How did they know I was here? It wasn't just those few. All of them turned toward me—even those the protector magic had skipped. Their eyes bored into me, pleading as they repeated, "Save us." In seconds, the entire group of people pressed toward my spirit, seeing me and begging me to save them.

"Fern wants my baby's heart," the pregnant woman who looked like Kendra cried. "Please, save my baby from Fern!"

I flashed back to my body in an instant.

It took me a second to reorient myself to being in my body. Kendra sat on the hardwood floor, holding me in her leather-clad lap. Alexis and Keagan argued loudly with Master King and Jié Shù, but I couldn't tell what they argued about. All I could hear was a loud buzzing in my head, drowning everything else out.

I took a deep breath, and the arguing stopped.

Jake. Kendra and Alexis both joined me in the Trinity of Mind. They both absorbed the vision I'd had. They felt the strangeness of this vision, too. It was so different from the other protector visions that I'd experienced.

I can't take the oath, I explained, but there was no need. Kendra and Lexy shared my mind. They already knew. The problem was that Alexis didn't know what to do about it.

"I can't take the oath." I found Raijin next to me. I grabbed the staff and used it to stand. My eyes glared at Master King. "You are letting your shiver kill on a whim," I accused.

Ariel's face tightened as her eyes widened on mine. "I took the oath," she spoke simply. Ariel couldn't protect me. She blinked with fury in her eyes.

Master King stepped forward and backhanded me. He hadn't swung hard, but he was strong. I fell back into Kendra, and Robin's staff clattered to the floor. I would have taken Kendra down with me, except Alexis caught us and held us up. I remembered being punched by Gunther, the center on my football team. That punch had rocked my world. Despite taking it easy, Master King's backhand felt ten times that hard. My head spun. My right cheek throbbed, and blood dripped down and hit the corner of my mouth. I tasted my own blood. Certainly, the vampires in the room could smell its coppery scent. Could they smell my unique and enticing blood type? Maybe I'd get lucky and they'd try to bite me, drinking enough to burn them to death before they realized their mistake.

"The oath magic did not protect him from me," Master King wondered. He tried to backhand Kendra's cheek. Kendra flinched away, but she hadn't needed to. The oath magic bounced his hand back and he nearly hit himself in the face. He looked back at me, then at Alexis. "What is this trickery?"

Whatever was in Lexy's eyes, it was enough for Master King to decide he'd be better off with me dead. "He is not part of any oath and therefore, by law, he is not protected. Kill him!"

I closed my fists, magic hands already spreading from me.

"Fæcele heorte." Torched heart. My grimaced shout came out a bit quieter than expected. The backhand had done a number on me. If not for the seconds Master King had delayed, I would have been too punch-drunk to have countered his order. But as it was, Master King, his three generals, and Henry choked and grabbed at their chests.

Fern fell at my feet, having almost arrived soon enough to obey Master King's command. However, while by oath, Alexis couldn't harm Master King's minions, nothing had prevented her from stepping in the way.

I'd wondered, *Could I cast this spell on more than one vampire at a time?* Well, I currently had a magical hand around five. However, each hand was weak, and I could barely keep that many hands alive.

Jié Shù's containment wrapped and freed her heart. She pulled in magic, and the air tingled as she prepared a spell of her own. "Stop him, or I will," Jié Shù ordered Alexis.

Kendra prepared to cast a containment around me. She couldn't harm Jié Shù, but outside of an official fight, nothing in the oath prevented her from protecting me from Jié Shù's magic.

"Jake," Alexis pleaded verbally, so Jié Shù could hear. "If you do this, I will be executed for breaking the laws of the Blood Rule Challenge." Her mind begged me with far more than words.

"Why?" I questioned, and her mind answered me with the Vampire King's laws. Her grandfather wanted her dead. If my actions as her general gave him a reason to execute her by law, he'd take it happily.

That was all it took. My fists opened. I left the magic hands in place, but I released their warm grip. "Master King," I elevated my voice, trying to sound powerful. "Feed. But stop killing people. Make it a new law."

Every vampire in the room, Alexis included, had white eyes that fixated on me with their fear.

"A protector!" Master King shouted.

Fear rolled from Alexis into me. Fear *for* me, which was a nice change from her fear *of* me. She hadn't wanted Master King to find out what I was.

"You brought a protector into my shiver!" He grabbed the fire poker next to the fireplace and swung it at Alexis. I had been about to grip his heart again but hadn't needed to. Instead, the fire poker slid off to the right, missing Alexis by inches. Oath magic flared to life, shaking Master King's body. Agony twisted on his face.

"You have made an oath by magic to do me no harm," Alexis reminded.

Master King turned his angered gaze at me, perhaps considering whether to try to kill me again or not. "I want him gone. I don't want his oath. He will leave now, or his presence will end our oath."

I didn't move. Could I leave my friends?

"If he doesn't leave now, I'll call my entire shiver to rip him to shreds!" Master King shouted. He reached for a wall phone, but Alexis stepped forward and put a hand on his wrist. Touching with no intention to harm didn't appear to bother the oath magic.

"If he leaves, then he becomes part of your oath of peace," Alexis continued negotiating. She didn't tell him it would be one-sided. I couldn't offer him the same.

"I'd never let a protector be part of my oath of peace," Master King spat. He shook off Lexy's hand and pushed a button. "Bosley," he spoke into the phone. Alexis heard the man on the other end respond.

"Do you want him to leave or not?" Alexis questioned, trying to get the upper hand. "How many in your shiver are you willing to call to the slaughter? Will you watch them all die again?"

"I'll kill him myself then!" Master King turned toward me with black, furious eyes. He wanted to kill me. He'd closed his fists, and when they opened, his claws burst out.

Alexis wrapped a hand around Master King's waist just as he lunged. Master King tried to backhand Alexis, but with the oath magic preventing him from harming her, his hand rebounded. The room sprang to life with action. Keagan had one arm around Fern's sternum and another around Linzi's, both of whom wanted to join Master King in killing me. Ariel bear-hugged Henry's thighs, lifting him off the ground with surprising strength. Jíe Shù and Kendra stared daggers into each other's eyes. With the oath, the blue-haired Asian was unsure how to attack, while Kendra was unsure how to defend. Luiz had his shotgun held horizontally across his chest and stood shoulder to shoulder with Andrea, creating a wall to block them from me—not that they could have blocked any of the vampires for more than a half-second.

Jié Shú must have finally decided to act because she darted forward and pulled Kendra out of the way. Kendra wasn't strong enough to stop her. Simply moving Kendra's position clearly wasn't against the oath magic. The vampire witch extended her left hand at me, and said a phrase I didn't quite understand. A black haze extended from her hand and formed a smoky-like katana. She thrust the ethereal blade, targeting me through the space between Andrea's and Luiz's heads. Luiz reached to grab the blade, trying to save me. The smoke broke its form and absorbed into the ring I'd just given him. Jié Shù's eyes widened and she stepped back.

"Include him in your oath of peace, and he will leave!" Alexis almost ordered Master King. Now with both hands wrapped around him, she used every bit of her allure to help in her persuasion.

Master King struggled to get free but couldn't. I didn't know how the oath magic worked. Alexis gripped Master King tightly, but her intentions were to keep him from killing me, or me from killing him. Master King's intentions, however, were clear. He wanted to rip me to pieces with his claws. The oath magic allowed Alexis's contact but stopped Master King's. The same dynamic seemed to apply to Lexy's generals and Master King's generals as well. Does oath magic understand intent?

"It was not him!" Lexy shouted. "It was my grandfather who did that to you. Besides, the protector will burn out your heart where you stand if you try."

Master King put his clawed hands on his head and pinched his eyes closed. He stopped moving for two full seconds. His generals stopped moving as well. When he opened his eyes, they had changed back to red. Lexy had touched a nerve. Was he concerned for his shiver? Or just for the power his shiver gave him. He seemed to be getting angrier.

"Let him leave with your oath," Lexy urged again.

"Never! He'll never be part of my oath! I curse him and his kind. Now and forever!"

"He will leave if I ask him to," Alexis assured again. "You will not kill him."

"*If* he leaves," Master King spat, "we let him go, but not by oath. Send him away before I change my mind. But if his number is rolled, I get to pick his replacement from any of your generals."

"Agreed," Alexis nodded, even though Mr. Espinoza grabbed her, shaking his head. She ignored him. In her rush to convince Master King not to call his shiver to kill me, she'd agree to anything.

You have to leave, Alexis informed me.

"No!" I shook my head. I wanted to take the oath, but I couldn't. I had too many people to save. I didn't understand what I was going to do next. I wanted to stay put, to refuse to leave, but the protector magic urged me to exit. I fought against the urge with all my strength. How could I walk away from Kendra and Alexis? Or Luiz and Andrea? Leaving was not an option.

I'm not under oath. I can kill them! I reminded her. *Let me do it and we all walk out of here.*

Then my grandfather will sentence me to death for breaking the laws of the Blood Rule Challenge. You have to leave, she pushed with all her allure.

The protection stone already felt hot, overworked by Master King's allure. Still, it mostly blocked Lexy from controlling me; however, I took an involuntary step back. I fought against my legs, willing them to stay put.

Luiz handed me the keys to the Porsche. "*¡Diantre!* Jake, you gotta go."

Alexis grabbed the protection stone and yanked it from my neck, letting her allure hit me full force. "Go!" she ordered again.

"Leave now!" Master King shouted, also using his allure. I felt the fury in his allure, an aged fury that shook me unlike anything I'd ever felt before.

Do not fight it, Alexis urged. The Trinity of Mind gave me just enough mental strength to stay put. However, Alexis and Kendra both tapped their separation stones.

Without the protection stone or the Trinity of Mind, I couldn't fight back against both Alexis's and Master King's allure combined with the will of the protector magic. That combo took complete control of me, turning me into a robot unable to choose my own actions. I found myself walking out the door. My mind became numb and empty, devoid of feelings. I found myself following Mindy out of the White House; a tiny part of me fought against the outside control. By the time I reached the Porsche, that tiny part of my mind that fought back had doubled in size. I vaguely remember starting the Porsche and driving. I fought on, trying to regain my own will. I couldn't feel or see anything except the road before me.

As I drove, I fought against the forces controlling me. It took time, but I won the mental battle. As I regained my self-control, I found myself on the freeway heading north, almost leaving the Las Vegas city limits.

How long had I been driving? I pulled over immediately. The clock read 1:13 A.M. The protector magic still pushed against my will, urging me to continue fleeing the shiver for now and prepare to go back later to save the kidnapped people. I pushed the urge away, fully in control of myself.

Kendra and Lexy still had their separation stones blocking the Trinity of Mind. *Kendra?* I tried to push past her separation stone. It didn't work. Maybe I didn't have the mental strength. But I didn't need it because Kendra joined my mind. She'd sensed the change in my emotions.

Jake? Are you OK? Are you safely away from here? Despite the distance separating us, Kendra's palpable excitement mixed with fear reached me through the Trinity of Mind as she watched the first cage fight: Ariel vs. Jiè Shú.

CHAPTER 32
ARIEL CAGED

Ariel: Hi, CJ. Playing Mortal Kombat. U R right.
Very realistic! It's late, so you won't answer.
Meeting you has been amazing. Hope to see you
soon.

Yes, I'm safely away, I answered, but that was not where I wanted to be. I wanted to be back with Lexy and Kendra. No, I *needed* to be back there.

Kendra stood next to The Cage in one of the dugouts. Through her eyes, I could see the fight.

The third round had already started. Adult Ariel danced barefoot near Jiē Shù, wearing the outfit from Lovely Leather that covered most of her dark, scaled skin. Her long lavender hair tossed with each swing of her sai. Her Asian opponent wore a white wushu uniform with long sleeves. Blue thread, the same color as her hair, lined the crossing ties in front as well as the embroidered shape of two dragons: one at her right shoulder and one at her left hip. Her pants started white at the waist, but beginning at the knees, faded to a solid blue. Looking through Kendra's eyes, the martial arts outfit didn't glow, but it must have been magic-infused because the cloth deflected most of Ariel's slashes, but not all. Jiē Shù's forearms were tattered and stained red with blood. Three slashes, one bleeding, marked her right thigh. Another slash on her left knee appeared to be healing. Most of the slashes on her left arm were healing as well. The blade I'd marked with the teardrop and crossbones didn't allow the vampire to heal.

Master King's First General appeared to be struggling. And yet she ignored two of Ariel's vicious swings that bounced off her uniform. She then punched Ariel in the face, knocking her backward and to the ground.

A lock of blue hair fell to the sandstone floor. Jiē Shù glanced at it, then touched her head behind her right ear. Her hand came away with blood.

273

Ariel rebounded as if the punch hadn't affected her at all. She lashed at Master King's First General with fury. Jié Shù's forearms were no longer covered with enough material to defend with, so she let the blades hit her silk outfit, then kicked our mystic monster, sending her flailing backward. The Asian vampire witch threw two black, shadowy shuriken with three curving points. Ariel held up the sai in her right hand and the shuriken collided with the magical shield.

Why was she allowed to bring her sais? I asked.

When she walked in with those hanging on the chains of her leather pants, Master King asked her to remove them. She told him no. He insisted. She didn't budge. She said, "No. I'm wearing them."

Mr. Espinoza stood and reminded Master King that during the negotiations, he had given the rules that anything they could wear, they could bring in.

I grinned as I hit the gas, pulling back onto the freeway. I needed to return. I couldn't leave my friends to fight without me.

Ariel slashed with her sais again. Her left sai hit Jié Shù in the right collar, slicing the silk wushu top from collar to arm just as Master King's First General kicked again, catching Ariel in the neck. A piece of the wushu top fell forward, as did the strap of her bra. For a split second, it didn't look like it had cut skin, but then a line of red formed, and a second later, blood ran down from the wound.

Jié Shù fell to her knee with agony in her grimace. She reached out a hand and two more shuriken appeared and launched at our scaled ally. Her shield blocked the first one, but not the second one. The shield magic had run out. The second shuriken cut right through Ariel's leather shirt at her right collar bone, and one curved point sunk deep, unhindered by the scale it hit.

Jié Shù touched the corners of her eyes with her middle fingers and her eyes turned white—magic sight white, not frightened vampire white.

She's using sight, I worried with Kendra.

The shadow shuriken dissolved, leaving Ariel with an oozing wound. Her eyes widened and one hand shifted to cover an area around her left pelvis.

The Asian vampire grimaced and stood. She formed another shuriken in her right hand and pitched it at Ariel, right toward the left of her pelvis.

Ariel tried to dodge, but the triple-pointed blade curved to stay on target, so she slashed at with her sai, but with the shield magic exhausted, the spinning shadow went right through it. She twisted so it hit her hip. A second later, she blocked another one with her forearm. Ariel had been winning, but the blue-haired vampire witch now knew how to kill her.

Ariel's obsidian-like face grimaced. She rushed at Jié Shù again, only this time, instead of swinging her sais, she defended her lifeforce from more shuriken with her scaled arms. Once the next wave of shuriken ended, rather than swinging her sais at the vampire, she threw them at her. With blue hair tossing, Jié Shù dodged the first one but was forced to knock the second away with her elbow before it could impale her.

Our shape-shifting ancient alien surprised Jié Shù by jumping onto her and wrapping her arms and legs around her as if giving her a hug. She bit into the witch's neck. One of the thrown sais, the one with the boomerang spell, curved in the air and came spinning back. But Jié Shù, not Ariel, caught it in the air and stabbed the blade through Ariel's pelvis.

Ariel's grip loosened. The Asian vampire grabbed Ariel's black, scaled arms and peeled her off, dropping her body in a clump, motionless on the red sandstone floor. Her body remained completely still. Jié Shù walked to the center of the ring, her face bloodied, with only shreds of her shirt remaining, hanging from her white wushu pants. Her straight blue hair stuck together in sweaty bunches. The cut piece of her wushu top hung down on her right side and her cut bra strap dangled, a drop of blood ready to drip from it. Dozens of blood-red cuts lined Jié Shù's body, all over her arms and ribs, only half of them healing. Ariel's other sai lay on the sandstone floor.

Fern jumped into The Cage, microphone in hand. She had changed her outfit, replacing her emerald blouse and black pants with short black spandex shorts and a bikini top with a word over each breast: *The Cage*. The spotlight glistened off rhinestones decorating the ankle cuffs and toe straps of her four-inch platform sandals. Despite her precarious footwear, she gracefully walked across the sandstone floor to Jié Shù. She lifted the blue-haired woman's hand up in the air and shouted, "Jié Shù wins!"

Ariel's faking, right? I hoped. *Look with sight.*

Kendra pushed magic into her eyes and scanned Ariel's altered body. The scales she added to her black-as-night skin hadn't saved her. Despite all those alterations, her facial features remained that of the little girl who we'd spent the past few days with since the Lost Rhoades Mine Melee. Her lavender eyes lay wide open. I expected one of them to wink at me, but they didn't move.

Kendra's eyelids pushed drops of tears down her cheeks. There was no sign of Ariel's lifeforce inside her body. Kendra blinked her eyes, releasing her sight. *She's gone,* Kendra's chin quivered. We'd just gotten used to the half-ancient-alien shapeshifter. I'd almost stopped seeing her as a monster.

Two men entered The Cage and lifted Ariel's body to carry it out. Jace collected the pair of sais and brought them to Keagan. Before the two men could carry the black, scaled corpse far, it began to shake until it split apart at the molecular level, separating into a mix of elements and dropping to the floor of The Cage as goo.

Was this all my fault? Probably. Why had I driven away? Of course, I knew why, but that didn't stop me from asking or from slapping the steering wheel in frustration. My chest ached. I'd felt this twice in my life before. When my grandma died and when Eldra had shattered herself into a spell to save us from the water babies. This pain reopened those wounds and added to it. The agonizing weight in my chest pressed at my lungs. Why had I let all of this happen? I felt a second pain in my chest. My lungs begged for air.

I vaguely heard Master King announce a special guest. He named some big company from China before an Asian man walked into the chain-link arena holding a large, foam, four-sided die. Unlike a six-sided die, which was a cube, a four-sided die was a pyramid. A pyramid didn't land with a face up, it landed with a point up. Each point had a number written on its three sides. He tossed it in the air. It tumbled end over end, as it went up, then down. It bounced off the floor, changing direction at random for almost a dozen bounces before it came to a stop. The Asian man bent over and picked up the pyramid and held it high.

Help, I begged, unable to get my breathing under control.

The number four marked each side of the peak—Kendra's number.

"Our esteemed guest has rolled a four," Master King's voice echoed over the speakers.

Around the arena, all eyes turned to Kendra.

CHAPTER 33
ANTICIPATION

Do you know what it is like to walk into a shiver of vampires with blood on your elbow? And on your period? Every pair of red eyes glanced first at my elbow and then at, well, you know. It's bad enough that Mr. Espinoza can't take his eyes off me, but having a whole shiver behaving the same way, there are no words. Fear? Terror? They don't even begin to explain how I feel. Hopefully, I don't freeze up in fear like I've done before. —Kendra

Lexy didn't know who to console mentally, Kendra or me. *Kendra,* I told her because I no longer needed help. The moment the pyramid die landed with Kendra's number at the top, my breathing jolted back to normal, just like hiccups are jolted back to normal by fear. Make no mistake, I was scared. I couldn't lose Kendra like I lost Eldra and Ariel. Anger mixed with my fear. My addiction flared to life. If I were in the shiver's arena, I'd erase every last vampire there. Could I make a magic missile big enough?

I'm coming back, I promised, but it was a hollow promise. According to the clock, I'd been driving in a protector-induced daze for over twenty-five minutes. I'd made the decision to drive back near the end of Ariel's match, but I hadn't even been able to turn around until the next freeway exit. I was just now starting to head back. If I floored it, it would take me at least twenty minutes to get back, and there was no way I'd be allowed past the gate and the guards with machine guns, let alone allowed back into the mansion and down into the shiver. Fighting my way through would take another ten minutes.

Before Alexis had asked us to meet her at Lovely Leather, we had made a stop at the Las Vegas Druid Cache. It had been three times the size of the one in Utah, but most of the shelves were out of stock. We'd picked up a handful of vials—seven total—but

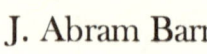

only two of them would help Kendra survive. Bones of Steel and Flesh of Steel. If she drank those, she'd be invulnerable. I reached into my hoodie pocket and felt four vials. Two were night vision and disguise, and the other two were Bones of Steel and Flesh of Steel. My heart sank. I carried the two important vials with me. Kendra had the wrong three vials: night vision, truth, and healing. Those wouldn't help her.

Torched Heart, I suggested.

I can't cast torched heart, Kendra informed me.

I knew she was right as soon as she said it. Torched heart wasn't a druid spell. Neither Eldra nor Robin could cast it. Even Caradoc had tried and failed. Torched heart required protector magic, which is why casting it had revealed me as a protector to Master King. Had I just ruined my anonymity? I remembered Carina's words after the Cabin Battle of Bear Lake. "If anyone finds out what else you are, nothing will slow the legions that will hunt you." I pushed that memory away. Kendra needed me. She fought against her fear, and it was everything she could do to not freeze up. So far, the fights we'd survived over the past few weeks had given her more post-traumatic stress than experience.

There is nothing I can do to stop this, Alexis disabled her separation stone long enough to share that one thought.

This night had spiraled out of control. How did we get into this situation? We'd come to rescue Alexis from being torched to death, and succeeded, only because Keagan convinced Master King's generals to declare a formal Blood Rule Challenge. At no time did we think Kendra would end up being asked to enter an underground MMA cage in a fight to the death. There was no way we could have predicted this. Yet in hindsight, it seemed so obvious that we should have.

Kendra struggled to take her first step, so Keagan took her left hand and led her into the ring. Her leather jacket covered her leather bustier and hung a few inches over her leather pants that ran down to her leather boots—all purchased an hour before at Lovely Leather. Sure, that was a lot of leather, but would it provide much armor against a vampire such as Henry?

"Cast something powerful and fast," Keagan encouraged. "And don't miss."

Prepare a magic missile, I urged her. Even with the Trinity of Mind, it took a few seconds to goad her past her fear into action. She let magic fill her as the announcer read a message from a sponsor. At least Kendra had escaped having to fight Fern. Fern scared Kendra far more than Henry. If Kendra were any more afraid, no amount of coaxing would keep her from freezing up.

A ring girl entered the hexagon arena. She dressed in the same The-Cage-logoed bikini top as Fern but also wore bikini bottoms. The ring girl held a large sign that listed the over-under on the fight. She strutted around the chain-link hexagon showing the sign to everyone in the crowd. The odds were against Kendra seventeen to one. Kendra gripped Astrapí with white knuckles, her trembling right hand also shaking the staff.

"You are going to win!" Keagan let go of Kendra's left hand, leaving her standing alone on the side of the arena closest to our dugout. "Twenty thousand on Kendra," Keagan yelled. He didn't honestly think Kendra would win. From what I understood from Alexis, Keagan had millions of dollars under various pseudonyms he'd created. The vampires had learned from the Great Depression, and investing was something they were mandated to do by the Vampire King. Even small investments became massive nest eggs after a couple lifetimes. If he really thought Kendra was going to win, he would have bet much more. He'd chosen a number that he wouldn't miss, but to Kendra, would be just enough to boost her confidence. Kendra heard my thoughts through the Trinity of Mind, which ruined his attempt.

I almost missed the next exit, but I swerved and nearly hit some barrels meant to protect me from crashing into the cement barrier. It was hard to concentrate on driving while trying to focus on Kendra and see through her eyes. I felt frustrated at the protector magic. Why had it taken control of me? Why had it helped Alexis and Master King force me to leave? What protector purpose did this serve? To save all the thralls but lose those I loved?

"This is a rare treat!" Fern spoke into the microphone with a high, girly voice. "A treat I wanted for myself," she licked her lips. "Kendra is a druid." She paused to let the crowd gasp. "On the Day of a Thousand Deaths, we killed all the druids we could find, didn't we?" She paused to let the crowd cheer. "We hate druids. They always side with the protector against us, don't they?" The vampires booed and hissed. "Tonight, you get to watch Humongous Henry, a vampire weighing two hundred and ninety pounds," the lights dimmed except for two spotlights, one on Henry and another on Fern, "fight one of the last living druids." Fern turned from Henry and walked toward Kendra. "The little blonde, Kendra Duncan, weighing in at one hundred and eighteen pounds!" Another spotlight lit up above Kendra. "Kendra is sweet sixteen. An innocent little virgin," Fern laughed. "See why

I wanted her for a treat?" She made a sucking sound with her mouth as if tasting something delicious.

"Bets on the outcome must be placed in two minutes," a male voice spoke over the speakers.

"Humongous Henry," Fern strutted from the center of the ring. "What do you think of this special treat Master King has given you?"

"To be honest," Henry shook his head, "I prefer a challenge. This girl. She won't be a challenge. I am going to toy with her. I'll strip her clothes, layer by layer, until she is exposed for all to see. Then I will drink this virgin girl's blood as I defile her," Henry exaggerated a hip thrust, "in front of the crowd." Then Henry leaned over to Fern's ear and whispered into it.

"That would be some entertainment," Fern spoke into the microphone again. "What do all of you think?" Fern gestured to the crowd, and about two-thirds of them erupted in applause. "Who thinks that Henry can back up his strong talk?"

The crowd started chanting: "Henry, Henry, Henry."

Those in the crowd closest to The Cage began shouting vulgarities at Kendra. Fern walked over to Kendra and asked, "What do you think of Henry?"

Kendra didn't answer. She just stood there frozen. The crowd laughed at her.

"You heard him offer to defile you. Does that tempt you to let him win?" She winked at Kendra, who remained frozen, unable to speak, unable to gather her thoughts. "I bet it does." Fern leaned in and whispered, "Henry promised to save me your heart."

Fern will die, I swore. Not just because of what she'd said to Kendra—though, at the moment, that was reason enough—but because she was addicted to ripping people's hearts out. She took at least one heart every night. Master King had ordered her to limit herself to one per night, but I knew—or perhaps the protector magic told me—that she took more whenever she thought she could get away with it. She'd never stop. Stopping monsters like her was the reason that the first protector was created.

I tapped the brakes to keep from hitting an old pickup, which drove slowly in the left lane in front of me. I called the driver a few bad words.

"Betting ends in ten, nine," a male voice over the stadium speakers started counting down. The crowd counted down, too. "Three, two, one, zero."

Look at the runes on Astrapí, I coaxed Kendra. *You can do this. You have lightning. He doesn't have magic, so the containment*

280

runes are useless. That tremble rune could be helpful. I once—er Eldra once scared off an entire cavalry by making the earth under their feet tremble.

Lightning might just make him angry, Alexis joined our minds. *You have to hit him pretty hard and sustain it to make him pass out. Even a powerful shock might only knock him out for a few seconds.*

Magic missile, both Alexis and I suggested to Kendra.

Keep them small, I added while Alexis simultaneously contradicted me with, *Hit him a big one.* Our conflicting advice wasn't helpful. Worse, we weren't confident Kendra could win and our unfiltered thoughts kept letting her know that.

You can do this! I tried to force my mind to ignore my doubts and instead pictured her standing in her confidence stance, the half T position that she used before drill team performances. Unfortunately, my unfiltered thoughts imagined Henry punching through her chest, splattering blood all over her sequins, and giving her heart to Fern.

Not helpful, Lexy snapped at me. Kendra's thoughts jumbled and nothing verbal could come out.

The bell rang, and the fight started. I lost hope of returning in time.

CHAPTER 34
118 POUNDS

I spent years planning out how to trick my grandfather, the Vampire King, into making me Princess of the Americas. I studied his behavior and his desires. The situation with Caradoc brought me back to the United States. Mr. Espinoza's strategic mind helped put my plan into action, giving it a chance of success. Still, without the Trinity of Mind, the plan would have failed. Perhaps it did fail? Did my grandfather outmaneuver me? Master King caught me by surprise. I suspected a challenge would come, but not this soon, and not from him. Having been gifted to him, I know him biblically, but beyond that, I know little else about him. It hurt more than I expected to watch Ariel die. Kendra is entering a battle she has no chance of winning. How will her death affect me? I must not dwell on that. I must mentally prepare to fight Master King immediately after Kendra's death. Keagan does not believe that I stand a chance. If Kendra dies, perhaps following her is for the best. I have teasingly imagined Kendra's death in the past so that Jake does not have to choose between us. The unfortunate truth is, if Kendra dies, Jake will never forgive me, and I will lose them both. —Alexis

Kendra clacked her staff on the red sandstone ground. Astrapí's rune of trembling lit up with a warm brown light. The cage rattled.

Henry hesitated as the ground trembled beneath him. Sandstone cracked around the room. Dust fell from the walls and ceiling, some landing in the ring and some landing on spectators. Five seconds after it started, the trembling stopped. Henry eyed Kendra. He smiled, perhaps realizing she didn't know what she was doing. Could he tell she hadn't been sure what that spell would do? His eyes suggested that he'd read her inexperience like a road sign. He'd have no problem arriving at his destination. His intended destination was not something I wanted to let him reach. How could I stop him while driving twenty minutes away?

Henry sprinted at her. He wasn't as fast as Alexis, but he was still vampire fast. She tried to dodge, and it looked like she succeeded. Too late, she realized that he had let her move to the side so he could get behind her. With ease, he grabbed her leather jacket, yanked her shoulders back and stripped the jacket off, then kicked her in the lower back, sending her flying forward.

Kendra lost her handle on Astrapí as she fell, but the staff bounced and rattled its way back to her. She grabbed it, rolled to her feet, and stood up.

Astrapí's lightning rune flared to life.

We said, "No lightning." Alexis and I both pushed the thought at her, but to no avail. She was lost in fear. Not frozen, but unable to think coherently. Unable to do anything but grasp at the next thought, whether right or wrong. The Trinity of Mind wasn't helping—especially with our less-than-confident, unfiltered thoughts. Lexy and I weren't inside The Cage, only Kendra was. Her fear poured into us. Eldra had said that such a bond between three people should have driven us insane, and we better understood why as Kendra's debilitating terror fed our doubt. We would have disconnected except we were even more afraid of leaving her alone.

Lighting shot at Henry, but he tossed the leather jacket over his head like an umbrella, catching the lightning with it, then darted out of the way. The lightning hit the jacket, leaving it steaming as it fell to the sandstone floor. Leather doesn't conduct electricity, so the tiny edge of the lightning that hit Henry only gave him a minor shock.

"That's one article of clothing down," Fern spoke to the microphone. "Should we take bets on how many articles of clothing he will strip off in round one?"

The crowd, not all vampires, renewed their betting frenzy.

Magic missile, Kendra. Hit him hard, Alexis urged.

No, hit him small, in the legs, I suggested, but she'd already taken Alexis's advice.

I pulled off the next exit and pulled into the first parking lot at a Subway sandwich shop, finally giving up hope that I'd have time to drive back. I didn't want to stop, but I needed to—not to get a sandwich, of course. Yes, I eat a lot, but not at a time like this. Besides, it was well after one in the morning, so Subway was closed. No, I parked because if I didn't have to focus on driving, maybe I could think of a way to help Kendra.

Henry sprinted at her, and she blasted him with a magic missile. It was a direct hit, right in the center of his chest. It lifted Henry from the ground and knocked him backward. He collided with the far side of the hexagonal cage and fell forward.

Yes! I fist-pumped in the driver's seat while stopped in a Subway parking lot. I smacked the steering wheel in excitement. She'd won! She—.

Henry jumped to his feet. A glow emanated from below his neck. He wore some kind of stone that absorbed magic. The Vampire King had survived my magic missiles with the same type of crystal at the Cabin Battle of Bear Lake.

Alexis stood and shouted at Master King. "You have broken the rules and assisted Henry."

"Henry entered the ring with only what he was wearing," Master King laughed.

Henry glanced at Master King, giving him a nod.

Alexis unleashed a tirade of mental curses. She rarely swore out loud, but in her head, she had a growing glossary of vulgarities.

Henry smiled at Kendra. He lifted one finger in front of his face and swayed it back and forth like a basketball center who'd just blocked a dunk. He darted left. Then right. Approaching her as he shifted side-to-side to keep her unsure of which direction he'd attack from. Then he rushed toward the area behind her. She turned to keep him in front of her, but he ran up The Cage wall, launched off it, flipped over her, and landed behind her. He gripped the tops of her leather pants, one claw on each hip, his fingers curling down inside the waistband. He pulled his claws outward, shredding and ripping them down to midthigh. The shreds left nothing holding the front and back of her leather pants up, so they folded down, exposing her white spandex shorts.

"*Fyr leoht,*" Kendra screamed. Fire shot from her left palm and burned Henry. In fact, half the crowd could feel the heat. Henry dove to the sandstone ground and rolled away from the flames, putting his back toward it. Too quickly, Kendra's spell faded and extinguished.

That was Kendra's first time casting that particular spell as a weapon. Was I not close enough to feed Kendra magic, or was the oath magic preventing it? I tried, but while distance didn't seem to matter with sharing thoughts, I found it mattered for sharing magic—either that or her oath magic prevented her from accepting help, even from those, like me, not under oath. Oath magic prevented Alexis from feeding Kendra magic but allowed communication through the Trinity of Mind. Of course, communicating verbally was allowed, so why not communicating mentally? I'd have to go to her to help. But I'd already stopped driving toward her, and sat a twenty-minute drive away in a Subway sandwich parking lot. Henry would have his way with her, and Fern would have her heart before I could drive back.

Like Kendra, I couldn't think. I couldn't come up with any clever idea to help.

Blood dripped from Kendra's hips. Henry's claws had shredded the tops of her leather pants and left a few bleeding cuts.

Henry stood, his eyes black. He shot forward and slapped Kendra across the face, the force tossing her to the ground. Astrapí rolled away from her. She lay on her stomach, trying to shake off her dizziness. Henry walked slowly toward her, and just as she tried to push up, he stepped on her, pushing low on her back with his foot.

He could kill her anytime. I trembled. I had to do something but what? Staring at the yellow and green Subway logo wasn't helping Kendra.

I couldn't see much besides stars through Kendra's eyes, but Alexis had a disturbing view. With his claws, Henry severed the laces on one of Kendra's leather combat boots and yanked it off. He held it up and let the crowd cheer him on. He threw the boot to the crowd through the one hole in the chain-link. Then he clawed through the laces on the other boot, stripped it off, and threw it to the crowd, too.

Kendra cannot think, Alexis worried. *That slap knocked her senseless.*

Never before had Alexis regretted letting someone get so close to her. She'd thought—no hoped—to have Kendra as a sister. She'd hoped that her grandfather would declare her free from Blood Rule Challenges until after she finished school. She'd hoped to extend that declaration to include four years of college.

None of that was going to happen because she would watch Kendra die. With the oath, there was nothing she could do about it. Her grandfather had set her up. He'd played her beyond anything she could have ever imagined. He wanted both her and Master King dead, so he'd pitted the two against each other. He'd have half his wish.

I shared Lexy's dread—an overwhelming amount of horror and trepidation swelled in my chest, causing anguish more overwhelming than I'd ever felt. I spiraled into an abyss of despair, not sure there was anything I could do to save Kendra, but trying anyway, grasping at any idea but coming up empty.

Henry knelt, replacing the foot pressing into Kendra's lower back with his knee. Using both hands, he gently slid off one sock as if undressing a lover. For the second sock, he tore it off viciously with his claws, leaving cuts around Kendra's calf and ankle. Next, Henry grabbed her shredded leather pants and ripped them down her legs, using his claws to strip them all the way off.

Kendra twisted and kicked her heels at Henry, who didn't budge. She might as well have kicked a telephone pole for all the good her kicks did. He grabbed her left lower leg and threw her across The Cage. She hit the fence, which had plenty of give. The chain-link pushed outward five inches, probably saving her life, before rebounding and tossing her onto the hard sandstone.

The bell rang. Round one ended.

Keagan and Alexis leaped into the ring, Alexis rushing to Kendra's side and Keagan rushing to her druid staff before Henry could think to grab it and break it.

I love you, Kendra. Lexy's mind shivered in pain. *I am sorry.*

Keagan knelt by Kendra. He took her hand and put Astrapí into it. Then he eyed Kendra's wounds. His fangs extended like he was about to taste her blood. Instead, he turned away.

The oath prevents us from using our saliva on her, Alexis explained, reading a positive intent into the way Keagan's hungry eyes focused on Kendra's exposed and bleeding hips.

Don't use the healing vial, I shared. *At least not unless you survive the match. It saps your energy as it heals.*

Kendra now wore only her leather bustier and white spandex undershorts. Alexis slipped out of her leather jacket and slipped it over Kendra's shoulders. *Whatever you can wear is fine,* Alexis shrugged when the oath magic didn't prevent Kendra from accepting it.

"Don't stop throwing magic at him," Keagan suggested.

Like Jake said, Alexis now agreed with me, *use many little marble-sized magic missiles. Try to injure his legs.*

Keagan and Alexis lifted Kendra to her feet. The crowd's noise elevated as Fern, standing in the center of The Cage, spoke into the microphone, sending her voice over the speakers. She held up three fingers and started walking out. "Round two begins in three, two, one."

The bell sounded, starting round two.

Henry darted at Kendra. Kendra held her hands cupped together like she was protecting an egg. She opened them and a small magic missile the size of a marble shot from her hand and hit Henry in the left shin. Her magic missiles didn't have the erasing power that mine did, or he'd have lost his leg. The crystal pendant once again lit up at Henry's neck. Still, the missile blasted his shin backward. Combined with his forward momentum, the instant shift in direction snapped his tibia. Henry fell but caught himself with his hands.

Kendra retreated to the other side of The Cage. She watched as Henry grabbed his broken shin. He grimaced and pulled, setting the bone in place.

How long does it take a vampire's bone to heal? Alexis's broken arm hadn't healed instantly. It still wasn't fully recovered.

The more excess blood he has, the faster he will heal, Alexis answered. *Before the fight, he fed well. He will be mobile by the end of round two.*

Keagan had fed well before taking a blade to his chest, and he'd healed rather quickly. Perhaps it was a coincidence, but Alexis caught sight of Jié Shù, sitting in the dugout feeding on the wrist of a short, fat white guy. She hadn't changed out of her tattered clothes. Half the cuts and holes in her skin had closed, but the skin of those wounds remained discolored.

Henry stood on one leg and hopped a few times to get his balance. "That hurt," he shouted at Kendra. Then he berated her with a slew of vulgar words and promises.

Luiz raised his arm and shouted, "*¿Que conejo?* Watch him hop! You've made him a bunny."

Kendra glanced at Luiz and smiled. His cheer cracked and weakened Kendra's fear, settling her nerves.

Kendra flicked another missile at Henry's other leg. He tried to dodge but couldn't, so instead, he squatted down close to the ground. The glowing orb hit him in the shoulder, knocking him rolling back, but he simply hopped twice and caught The Cage's chain-link to stay upright. The crystal once again glowed at his neck. The first attack on his leg had only worked because he had lunged at Kendra with speed. Now, moving carefully, her magic missile wouldn't break his other leg.

Can you hit the crystal? I asked. Kendra threw another small missile, this time directed at the stone pendant. The missile hit it, but the crystal absorbed it without Henry even taking a hit.

Henry slowly hopped along with the chain-link, moving toward Kendra. She backed up, trying to stay on the other side of The Cage from him. Immediately after absorbing her next magic missile, and before she could form another one, his hops quickened. With just a few rapid, one-legged leaps, he nearly caught up to her. He lunged at her with inhuman speed.

She darted toward the center of The Cage while swinging Astrapí at him, hitting him as hard as she could in the head. The blow did nothing to slow or hurt Henry. He continued forward as if the staff were a Nerf toy. However, the blow worked like a stiff arm in football, keeping the defender an arm's length away, allowing Kendra to barely escape his grasp.

Henry, his lunge coming up empty, slid on his stomach across the sandstone. Half of Eldra's staff rolled next to him while the other half remained in Kendra's hand. Magic lifted from the broken staff like a spirit lifted from a body at death. Astrapí died. The runes' light ceased like the lifeless eyes of a corpse.

Kendra flicked another magic missile at Henry, this time attacking his spine as he sprawled out prone. Could she paralyze him? The missile hit him in the center of his back like an oversized fist, compressing his torso between it and the arena floor. Having fed, his lungs were filled, so the magical blow forced out a gross spurt of crimson that spread over the sandstone. Henry twisted and rolled to the chain-link at the side of The Cage. He grabbed it and lifted himself to his feet. Apparently, she hadn't succeeded in damaging his spine. He coughed as blood dripped down his chin, his eyes still angry black.

He made two more well-timed lunges at Kendra, but she dodged both. They danced around for the next two minutes—well, Kendra danced, and Henry hopped—until the bell ended round two.

With that stone on Henry's neck absorbing your magic, your spells are not doing enough damage, Alexis told Kendra.

Kendra didn't respond. Her blank mind couldn't think. She stood next to Alexis and Keagan in her white Lycra undershorts and a leather jacket over her leather bustier.

On the other side of The Cage, Fern stomped away from Henry, angry. Something about that interaction set off warning bells in my head. Something had changed. A certainty that Kendra would not survive round three shook me.

I needed to be there. I had to be there. I hadn't even expected Kendra to make it to round three, but she'd caught a break—literally—when she'd broken Henry's shin. Had I continued to drive, would I have made it back in time? I glanced at the clock. No. Only six minutes had passed since I'd pulled off the freeway and parked in a Subway parking lot. I needed to be there.

What else can you try? I asked.

I'm trying everything, Kendra responded. However, a subtle memory hit her, reminding her of something her mother had once told her. She was thirteen at the time. She had been crying over an argument with Justine—Sis—who hadn't talked to her for days. She couldn't remember what the argument was about, but she remembered how her mother had hugged her and asked, "Have you tried everything to make it better?" Kendra had nodded. Then her mother asked. "Did you pray?" Kendra shook her head. "If you didn't pray, then you haven't tried everything."

Kendra's faith had taken a hit lately, but despite that, Kendra closed her eyes on the side of The Cage and said in her mind. *Dear Lord, please help me.*

Alexis and I added an *amen* to her prayer. I didn't really think her prayer would be that beneficial. What could God do? As Henry beat her down then drank her life away while possibly defiling her, would God send His spirit to comfort her in her final moments? Nothing about that sounded comforting.

Finally, an idea hit me. I wasn't sure if it would work, but I'd try it anyway. I took the vial of Flesh of Steel and drank it, then I drank the Bones of Steel potion. Trying something I'd never done before was better than trying nothing, right?

The bell signaled the start of round three.

Henry walked out on both legs. His broken shin was not fully healed but no longer hindered him.

Kendra didn't hesitate to flick a marble-sized magic missile at Henry. He'd realized he couldn't dodge them, so he adjusted and let it hit him in the center of his chest, high by the stone that glowed and absorbed the missile. Kendra flicked another one, and he let it hit his center again, allowing his stone to absorb its power, too. The first minute of the round went by as Kendra flicked missile after missile at him, trying her hardest to delay him. She'd given up hope on living and now simply fought for one more round.

Her missiles shrank and weakened the more she cast. The last one hit Henry, and the stone hardly lit up. Henry smiled. He started walking toward Kendra.

Henry's black eyes and stern face no longer looked interested in playing. Kendra had damaged him. She had made him look bad, breaking his shin in round two and dragging this fight to round three. She'd certainly surprised him.

"She's done," Fern shouted. "Slow, please. For me?" Fern begged of Henry.

Henry shook his head at Fern, confirming that he intended to end this quickly.

Kendra desperately flicked another magic missile at him. It hit him harder than the last one had, but it was still weak and only stopped him for a second. Then he launched at her.

My astral projecting spirit slid into Kendra's body. Hopeful that my attempt to bring the Flesh of Steel spell with my spirit would succeed, I grabbed for the magic that had been in the vial. Neither spell transferred into Kendra. Worse, my spirit took a backseat to hers. The oath magic refused to let me give Kendra any aid. I wasn't under oath, so it couldn't prevent me from offering her aid, but it prevented her from accepting it. Henry's claws extended out, and his eyes fixated on the left side of Kendra's chest—on her heart. His speed increased as he shot forward to end Kendra. Perhaps he intended to rip out her heart and gift it to Fern? The clawed fingers of his right hand shot at her chest like five arrows. If Kendra died while my spirit shared her body, would I die, too? Eldra's memories told me the answer was yes.

I had to do something, but I couldn't do anything.

Henry's hand hit Kendra's left breast, which didn't move. His clawed fingers shattered and compressed back into his palm, which in turn compressed into his wrist and forearm, the sound of breaking bone cracked throughout The Cage.

The rest of Henry's body collided with Kendra's leather jacket. The right side of his head and his right shoulder hit and bounced off Kendra's jacket, throwing him backward.

Kendra stepped out of a half-inch indention at her bare feet. She'd used the sandstone at her feet to power a modified version of the bulletproof spell.

I hadn't been able to interfere. I'd tried everything possible to help Kendra. I couldn't use magic. Even though I'd failed to bring Flesh of Steel and Bones of Steel, Kendra had paid attention to my efforts. She hadn't given up because I hadn't given up. The closest spell to Flesh of Steel was the bulletproof spell, which

Kendra had cast the most. She had an idea to improve it, and she tried it. The modification had worked. The altered bulletproof spell didn't deflect Henry's attack. It redirected all his momentum back in the exact direction from which it came.

Henry's hand and wrist flopped, a bloody, bone-crunched mess. His shoulder hung wrong, perhaps out of its socket.

I tried to cast torched heart, but inside Kendra's body, I couldn't do it. Kendra couldn't cast it either. She wasn't a protector. The sentience of magic wouldn't let her.

Go! Kendra pushed at my spirit. *I won't let you die with me.*

Unfortunately, all she'd done was buy a little time, and she knew it. Her body barely had the energy to sustain the bulletproof spell she'd cast on her leather jacket. She was spent. If Henry had stuck to his original plan to strip off Kendra's clothes, we wouldn't even have had this short victory.

I wasn't meant for this type of fight. Kendra thought. *Eldra once told me, "You have a way with emotion." What can emotions do in an underground MMA fight to the death?*

You're the expert at emotions. What can they do?

Not much, she answered. *But at least I can do this.* She grabbed her emotions and used them with a power I've never seen to shove my spirit out of her body. *I won't let you die with me!* I found myself launched out of her body. My desire to stay led my spirit into Alexis, though as a backseat driver.

Kendra cast a magic missile at Henry and it hit him in the back. However, she was exhausted and the missile was so weak that Henry barely even noticed.

My anguish mixed with Lexy's as we knew it was only a matter of time before Henry used his one good hand to kill Kendra.

Anguish, Kendra blinked.

Kendra sprinted toward Henry. His fanged face howled in pain, so he almost didn't see her. She reached both hands toward his face, instinctually knowing that this spell required touch.

"*Hréowsian tíegan!*" she whispered. Connected Anguish.

Henry caught Kendra's left wrist and pulled it to his mouth, biting into it. Her right palm connected with Henry's left cheek. Her spell used very little magic. However, it used an intense amount of emotion. Every ounce of pain and anguish Henry had ever inflicted in his extended vampire life, even any he'd inflicted as a human, hit him all at once. Kendra connected him to that pain with her tiny emotion spell, just like how the Trinity of Mind joined us—a permanent connection. The emotional pain would never go away. Under normal circumstances, Kendra didn't think the spell would work. Just as the *myndtiegan* required love to already exist, this spell required extreme pain and anguish to already exist. Henry's shattered and mushed hand provided that, and Kendra used it as a conduit to connect him permanently to his own memories of all the pain and anguish he'd ever inflicted.

Henry's eyes went white. His fangs released Kendra's wrist, and he screamed. He lurched backward, away from Kendra, shoving her hard enough to throw her to the middle of The Cage. He ran this way and that, as if blind. When he collided with the chain-link fence, he howled, grabbed it with his one working hand, and thrashed—the sound of the rattling chain-link vibrated through the red sandstone arena. Kendra stayed out of his way as the unbearable pain Henry felt drained his sanity. His whole body shook.

Kendra turned away when Henry started bashing his own head on the floor. The sound of his skull smashing the sandstone echoed seven times, then stopped.

Alexis and I focused on Kendra. Surprised. Impressed.

Too quickly for my comfort, Master King darted to stand next to Kendra, his black eyes and tight mouth displaying his anger, but he was under oath to do her no harm. I had no reason to fear for her, but I did.

"Kendra Duncan wins!" Master King spoke slowly into the microphone. Alexis, Keagan, Luiz, and Andrea all rushed into The Cage.

"Do you have anything to say?" Master King placed the microphone inches from Kendra's mouth.

Kendra's eyes met Lexy's, just a few steps from her. "I still have my clothes on!" she managed.

Luiz broke out in laughter, and unexpectedly, the crowd cheered.

A minute later, Mindy and Fern—the latter trembling in rage—ushered Kendra and her entourage back to the dugout.

Master King lifted the microphone and shouted. "We have a tie!" He let the phrase sink into the crowd. "Who wants to watch a tiebreaker?" He let the cheering crowd answer.

CHAPTER 35
FATALITY

Kendra is the champion, my friends. She kept on fighting till the end. I could totally sing that! I'd thought we had lost her. I had failed to keep my mind positive and had unavoidably shared my complete lack of hope through the Trinity of Mind. I worry how her battle in The Cage will affect her personality long-term. She will never be the same. I can already feel a difference in her mind. That innocent girl that I kissed in the front room at Kevin's is gone. Who is she now? —Jake

Fern already led a large, round man into The Cage. When Alexis saw him, she gasped. Since magically flaying myself, I looked pretty ugly, and she'd never gasped looking at me. This man made my not-so-attractive face look like Doctor McDreamy compared to his. He had a thick, wrinkled, port-wine stain over the right side of his face. The stain extruded in bubbles from a dozen blood-filled blisters. Folds of the stain covered where his left ear should have been and replaced a huge patch of hair beyond that. The port-wine stain continued down his neck. He wore a T-shirt and the purple-stained skin bubbled down his left arm.

Alexis's memories went berserk. The night her grandfather had gifted her to this man had been one of the most painful nights of her life. He'd tortured her. Cut her. Lashed her. Beat her.

"Madro Sandavol will role the four-sided die to see who gets to fight in the tiebreaker."

Ignore him, Alexis suggested, but Kendra and I struggled with her request. He wasn't human, nor was he a vampire. He was something else, but even Lexy's grandfather didn't know what. *I said ignore the monster.*

293

How bad does something have to be if a vampire—er, half-dhampir—calls it a monster?

Pay attention to the roll, Lexy urged.

Why are they rolling? I wondered. I'd left, Ariel had been killed, and Kendra had just finished fighting. Only Keagan remained. Did they need to roll to choose whether Fern or Linzi would fight him?

The monster lifted the foam pyramid and tossed it. The four-sided die hit the sandstone and bounced around before coming to a stop.

"He rolled a two!" Master King shouted. He smiled toward Alexis and put his hand on Madro's shoulder. The monster also fixed his eyes on Lexy with a look that felt like ownership before he turned and started walking out of The Cage.

"I believe your second general is not present," Master King spoke into a microphone. "Not to worry, as Alexis and I agreed, I will choose an alternate from your surviving generals."

Mr. Espinoza lowered his head. He'd tried to stop Alexis from agreeing to this. But in her fear for my life, she had agreed too quickly.

"Kendra, would you please join Fern in The Cage," Master King smiled.

No! I shouted into Lexy's mind.

"No," Alexis stood.

"The agreement was 'from your surviving generals,' was it not?"

"Cowardly bastard!" Keagan slapped the chain-link between the dugout and The Cage.

Alexis leaned back and whispered a question in Mr. Espinoza's ear. "What are our options?"

Mr. Espinoza shook his head, scowling. "None. You listened to him," he gestured to Keagan, "and not to me."

Alexis had listened to Keagan. She still trusted him. A connection still existed between them, even if it was morbidly based on Stockholm Syndrome. He hadn't become one of the Vampire King's generals by accident. Still, she'd chosen Miguel to be her strategist, then hadn't listened to him when strategy mattered most. She hadn't been wrong in listening to Keagan; she'd been wrong in not *also* listening to Mr. Espinoza.

"What if she forfeits?" Alexis pressed Miguel, still whispering.

"Kendra is our only chance," he whispered back in his thick Spanish accent. "If she wins, we all walk out of here alive. If she loses, Fern will have her heart, and you will fight Master King and lose. A forfeit is worse because, afterward, Master King will kill the rest of us."

"I shall fight Master King then. I will not send Kendra into that cage again."

Mr. Espinoza shook his head. "The odds of Kendra beating Fern are greater than the odds of you beating Master King. She has a chance. You do not. Besides, Master King will see that choice the same as a forfeit. That would doom the rest of us—my son, his girlfriend, Maria, and me. Perhaps Keagan escapes. If you honor the agreement, there is a chance Master King will allow the rest of us to live." Mr. Espinoza foresaw a bleak future.

Kendra stood up in the dugout. The crowd couldn't drown out the Trinity of Mind, so Kendra heard everything Mr. Espinoza whispered to Alexis.

No! Alexis and I both begged her to remain seated.

"I die either way. A chance is better than no chance at all." Kendra limped toward The Cage.

Kendra regretted coming to Las Vegas to save Alexis. She wished as she walked into The Cage that she would have let Lexy die down here. The thought burned into Alexis and cut her heart.

I watched in shock as Master King announced each side. He first introduced Kendra, then Fern.

I couldn't believe this turn of events after Kendra had found a way to beat Henry. I'd come trying to be the hero, but it was clear that I wasn't the hero right now. Kendra was. Against Henry, she'd saved herself. Now, she stepped into The Cage, willing to give her life to save us.

What would Justine say when Kendra didn't return? Would we even get to bring her body home? It dawned on me that I was the only one likely to survive this night. I knew now why the protector magic had forced me to leave. Had I stayed, I would die at the end of the night with Alexis and her entourage. If they all died and I was left alone, where would I go? What would I do? I was nothing without them.

The over-under on Kendra dropped to an abysmal 256 to 1. The over-under that she died in the first minute was 64 to 1.

"Round one starts in ten seconds," Master King's voice echoed over the loudspeaker as he walked out of The Cage into the dugout. His smile reached his eyes. He seemed genuinely pleased with the turn of events.

Kendra stared at the stain on the sandstone floor where Henry had smashed in his own skull. Her mind raced. She'd changed. She didn't feel fear. She no longer cared whether she lived or died. She'd latched onto another hope. Could she take Fern out with her? Kendra formed a plan to save us, to give her life for us just as Eldra had done in the Lost Rhoades Mine. *Maniġe wæpenstræl sylfum.* She couldn't cast the spell after she died, but she didn't plan to.

Do I need my whole body? Kendra asked me. *For one vampire, would my lower legs be enough?*

I didn't know the answer. Neither Eldra's nor Caradoc's memories provided one, either. However, I did know that Kendra would die seconds after casting the spell. The spell required her death. Even if it didn't, the spell would rip her legs off, and she would bleed out in seconds. The agony would be impossible to bear. Would she even be able to complete the spell? If not, she'd lose, Alexis would fight Master King, and she'd die, too. I had no doubts that Luiz, Andrea, Maria, and Mr. Espinoza would never go home. They'd die in The Cage.

If I succeed, only I will die.

Tears ran down Lexy's cheeks. I wondered if my body, back in the car parked at Subway, also cried. Did it know of the anguish I was feeling now?

"Three, Two," "Wait!" Jié Shù shouted.

I hadn't noticed her approaching The Cage until she stepped inside it. She looked terrible, and not just because of her tattered state of dress and the many cuts that weren't healing. Her cheeks sunk into her emaciated face. Her dilated pupils didn't seem to look at anyone. Her body had swelled. Something was definitely wrong with her torso. If I didn't know better, I'd have sworn she was a reanimated corpse.

The bell sounded, but Jié Shù yelled, "Fern. Stop!"

"What is it?" Fern spat at Jié Shù, her eyes black and angry.

Master King hurried into the ring and grabbed Jié Shù. "It seems our first fight has left Jié Shù confused." Master King tried to usher her to the dugout, but she shook her head at him. She grabbed the microphone.

"Jié Shù didn't win the first fight."

Master King blinked and squinted at Jié Shù, his green eyes confused. His nose twitched. What did he smell?

Jié Shù's eyes rolled back into her head. As she started to fall backward, her torso split open under her rib cage, the tatters of her wushu shirt ripped apart, and a pair of small legs slipped out, followed by a little girl's body with lavender hair. The little body fell to the sandstone floor and lay there supine for a few seconds. The crowd took in a deep, audible breath.

Master King stared at Ariel. Rage blackened his eyes. He dropped the microphone and a loud bang echoed over the speakers, hurting our ears. His black eyes glared at the thing—the child that had slid out of Jié Shù.

Vernix caseosa—a white residue that covered newborns, a substance Eldra, with over a century of experience as a midwife, was quite familiar with—covered our tiny shapeshifter's entire body. Her tiny hands wiped her eyes clean, and the white substance slowly absorbed into her skin. Ariel's outer body wasn't fully formed. Her features looked like that of a plastic doll.

The newly born version of our mythic monster rolled over and crawled far enough to grab the microphone—her hands so small that she needed both hands to hold it. She stood—looking maybe two years old. She lifted the microphone to her lips. The crowd had gone silent, allowing her whisper to echo loudly throughout the sandstone arena.

"Ariel wins!" Ariel looked down at Jié Shù's lifeless corpse, then glanced at Kendra and smiled with her not-fully-formed lips. "Fatality."

"*¡Diantre!* That's a reverse 'babality,'" Luiz shouted to the quiet, stunned crowd.

Master King's fury couldn't alter the terms of the agreement, which meant we'd won. The challenge between Alexis and him would not take place until All Soul's Day.

Master King walked over to our side of The Cage. He turned the microphone off, but some of the crowd were vampires, so they probably heard him snarl, "Get out. The formal date for our duel is set. If you come within two miles of my shiver, it will be a breach of the laws of the challenge and I'll have you shot and killed on sight."

"You have one of mine," Alexis stated. "Where is Gina?"

"She wasn't fully yours," Master King spat, the distaste of his loss still souring his mood. "You influenced her, but I broke that. She's mine now."

Alexis eyed him with frustration. Gina had been the primary reason for coming tonight.

"I expect to see Gina alive and well at our duel on All Soul's Day," Alexis demanded.

"I'll do as I please," he growled, but Alexis read his mind. He'd bring Gina as requested, not out of the goodness of his heart, but because breaking the allure on one of Lexy's people bordered on breaking his own altered Right to Rule laws. She'd have to beat Master King to save Gina.

Alexis slipped under Kendra's right arm while Andrea slipped under her left. Luiz picked up Ariel, carrying her like a child on his hip, with Maria next to him. Keagan trailed behind, rubbing it in Mr. Espinoza's nose that his plan had worked. As they walked out, Madro the Monster stood in our path. Alexis saw him and stopped, concern emanating from her every thought.

Unexpectedly, the monster bowed. "Until All Soul's Day, *my* Alexis." His name was Spanish but he hadn't spoken with a Spanish accent. I hated the way he had emphasized that possessive pronoun. I instantly wanted to erase this creature far more than I wanted to erase Keagan.

Madro stepped aside and let them walk by. Mindy appeared to escort them. They walked through the shiver's tunnels. This time, Mindy took them out the front door—proving her early statement about everyone using the servants' hall had been a lie. It wasn't long before they were safely driving away from Master King's White House.

Alexis and I convinced Kendra that sleep was more important than getting back for drill team by six in the morning. Alexis jumped on her phone to book rooms at the Stratosphere. I started heading toward the hotel. I would beat them there as I was already closer. About five minutes from Master King's house, before she had finished booking the rooms, Alexis and Kendra shivered. I was driving in the Porsche to meet them, but I was connected to them through the Trinity of Mind.

What was that? I asked.

A boundary, Alexis explained. *I have not felt it before. The oath magic will not let us return across the boundary. Master King will also not be able to get within a few miles of our mansion.*

Alexis successfully booked three rooms, so well after three in the morning, we sat in an all-night buffet at the Stratosphere. Kendra and Ariel had quickly showered. Our little ancient alien had eaten more than all of us combined. She just kept growing and now looked about five years old. There was only one other group in the all-night buffet and only one overworked server keeping the buffet stocked. I doubted either would notice her accelerated growth spurt. She planned to return home looking nine again—Carl's age.

Both Kendra and Alexis had their separation stones enabled, keeping their thoughts to themselves. Luiz and Andrea spoke the entire dinner. Everyone else listened to them, staying silent.

Keagan was the first to rise.

"I'll be there on All Soul's Day," his Scottish accent almost making his sentence a song, "for your challenge with Master King."

Alexis stood. "You are welcome at my mansion."

Keagan glanced at me, then at Kendra. I noticed Mr. Espinoza scowling.

"I'll never be welcome inside the line," Keagan shrugged. He also knew that neither Kendra nor I would ever accept him. He may have behaved himself for Alexis, but he was still the vampire that had ruthlessly risen to be the Vampire King's general. He was still the man that had killed and turned Lexy's mom and had violated Alexis time and again since she was thirteen. Even though he'd helped us save Alexis, and now that we no longer needed him, a part of me wanted to erase him from existence. Or perhaps burn his heart from his chest. Unfortunately, he might be useful in helping Alexis win her upcoming duel against Master King.

"You could come to Mexico with me," Keagan suggested.

Alexis glanced at Kendra and me.

"Until All Soul's Day, then, Princess Alexis." Keagan bowed formally, and we all watched him walk off. Mr. Espinoza seemed more content than I was to see him go.

Ariel returned to eating and Luiz returned to joking with Andrea.

I stood and walked to the other side of the table and put my hand on Kendra's shoulder. She turned and looked up at me. Her face had multiple scratches on it. She'd refused both Mr. Espinoza's and Keagan's offer to lick her wounds and help them heal. Wisely, Alexis had not offered. Kendra had, however, drank a vial of healing, which would help but wouldn't be as effective.

For me, however, the night wasn't over. The protector magic compelled me.

"I need this," I grabbed at her necklace with her separation stone. "Trade?" I offered Kendra my radiant cut, red ruby protection stone. I would need a separation stone to get away with what I needed to do.

"Why?" she asked, but she didn't try to stop me from unclasping it. She had about half a second to peruse my thoughts between when I removed the necklace from her and when I put it on and enabled it for me. All she found in my mind were lockboxes for her to pry into, filled with useless memories. Eldra had trained Alexis to hide her thoughts, and I had Eldra's knowledge, so I could conceal my thoughts now, too.

"Do you need . . . therapy, Jake?" Kendra asked, hesitantly glancing at Alexis.

Lexy made a sound like a high-pitched huff as I shook my head. I walked over to Lexy and put my hands on her cheeks and

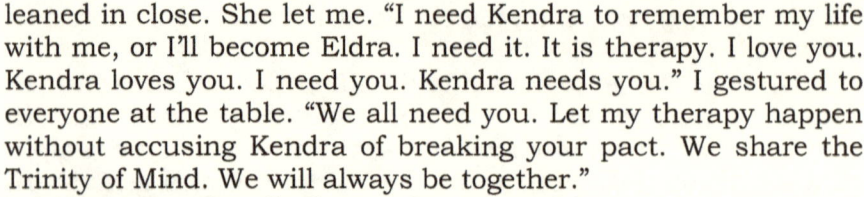

leaned in close. She let me. "I need Kendra to remember my life with me, or I'll become Eldra. I need it. It is therapy. I love you. Kendra loves you. I need you. Kendra needs you." I gestured to everyone at the table. "We all need you. Let my therapy happen without accusing Kendra of breaking your pact. We share the Trinity of Mind. We will always be together."

I turned and walked away from the table.

"Where are you going?" Kendra asked.

"To the room," I held up the access card that would let me into room 327, which I would share with Luiz.

"I'll come," Luiz stood.

"No, stay. I need some time alone."

Luiz sat back down.

I had no intention of staying in my room. Since I wore one of the separation stones, they wouldn't discover my lie until it was too late

CHAPTER 36
TALKATIVE

As a member of the Church of Jesus Christ of Latter-Day Saints, I grew up Christian. I know many people don't share my beliefs, but for me, this night's events confirmed my beliefs. Against Henry, I had frozen in fear, again. He had me. I'd given up. Then I prayed. I didn't expect Alexis to believe in prayer, but it hurt that Jake doubted, too. Yet the power of prayer proved true. I had given up. Then my prayer gave me hope. Immediately after my prayer, both Jake and I got an idea. Jake's idea didn't work, but mine did. One idea led to another, and I won. If all that my prayer gave me was hope and an idea, it was as powerful as it needed to be. ——Kendra

My confidence in the knowledge the protector magic shares with me had been shaken. It had taken control of me and forced me to leave those I loved when they needed me. But that wasn't what shook my confidence. The *reason* it forced me to leave those I loved is what shook it. I felt some being, a higher power maybe—not God but godlike—behind the protector magic, and that being hadn't been certain of the outcome. I hadn't been provided a vision of me dying, yet I'd been forced to leave. Was this being overly cautious?

I wondered for some time why I hadn't been shown the battle in The Cage before it happened. Why hadn't my protector magic warned me? The one thing all my visions had in common was this: someone on my list of protectorates died. The protector magic didn't show me the future at will. It warned me only before the imminent death of someone I was to protect. Kendra's and Ariel's fights had been brutal, but they'd survived.

I swung by the hotel room briefly, but only because Luiz had left the Porsche keys there and I'd left Robin's staff there. Not many seventeen-year-olds carry a staff. I felt like I was betraying Raijin, but I'd already decided to replace the staff with something more my age. I just hadn't figured out what yet. We'd collected the two pieces of Astrapí after the fight. We didn't have much to remember Eldra by. What was I thinking? I had all two centuries of her life in my head to remember her by.

Luiz's and my room adjoined with the girls' room. We had all checked into our rooms before dinner. The four girls, Alexis, Kendra, Ariel, and Andrea—all but Maria, who would room with Mr. Espinoza—shared one room with two queen beds. The adjoining doors between our rooms remained unlocked. I walked into the girls' room. Kendra and Alexis had chosen the left bed. I wrote two notes so I could leave one on both their pillows, so neither would feel left out. Ariel was going to be furious.

With keys and Raijin in hand, I made my way through the maze that made up the Stratosphere hotel and casino. I found the parking garage and eventually located the Porsche. I opened the door and slipped into the driver's seat, sliding Raijin into the back. Once again, the staff barely fit on an angle. I still didn't have a driver's license, but I'd been driving plenty.

The passenger door opened, spooking me.

"You need to hurry," Ariel said. She tossed her pair of sais on the floor and sat down in the passenger's seat, looking at least six years old now. "Kendra and Lexy are suspicious. I told them I would find you. I bought you a few minutes, but they aren't far behind."

Of course, they were. I sighed and put the Porsche into drive. I glanced at Ariel a few times, wondering how she knew where to find me.

"My future depends on your survival, remember?" Ariel's lavender, six-year-old eyes looked ancient.

We drove for a few minutes in silence. Twice my phone vibrated as Kendra and Lexy called me, but I ignored their calls.

"How old are you?"

"I remember nothing before the many years trapped in the well."

"The other water babies didn't seem to have lost their memories."

"No, they didn't."

"So why did you lose yours?"

"I don't know."

"Bear said he let you out to do a favor for him and you came back like this."

She shrugged.

"What do you remember about the well?" I asked.

"The cold. The ice," Ariel's little girl voice sounded frightened, the way a normal little girl's voice would. "The Haitian witches thawed the ice."

"You were frozen?"

"Yes."

"You didn't die?"

"Hibernation? Is that the right word?" Ariel answered. She'd never asked if a word was correct before. That was something a foreigner who spoke English as a second language would do.

We didn't speak for a few minutes. Coyote's granddaughter noticed from our direction that I'd chosen to return to the White House.

"Are we freeing Master King's kenzies?" Ariel asked.

"I am."

"We?"

"You are under oath. I am not," I reminded her.

Ariel shook her head. "The woman I was when I made the oath died. I am from Jié Shù. I cannot harm Alexis or her generals."

"So, you're bound to Jié Shù's oath?" That sort of made sense. Ariel was speaking a lot more than usual. She hadn't really talked this much before now. "Huh," I grunted, realizing the reason for Ariel's changed behavior.

"Huh, what?"

"Jié Shù liked to talk, and English was her second language."

Ariel nodded. "I am Jié Shù, and I'm not."

I thought about that.

"How did you get inside her? Was it when you bit her?"

"No," Ariel shook her head, which tossed her lavender hair. "My lifeforce was at my hip. When I jumped up and bear-hugged her, I lined it up with one of her wounds. I almost didn't make the transfer in time."

"So, you're both you and her, now."

Ariel nodded.

I thought about that and didn't ask another question. Ariel remained silent as well. I remembered how, in the Lost Rhoades Mine Melee, the other creatures like her—her water baby brothers and sisters? —had turned into Eldra and Alexis and the Native Americans. The one that had fed on Eldra claimed to have all her memories and had proven capable of wielding Eldra's magic.

I drove by the entrance to the White House, but I didn't turn in. The girls had tried to call me again, but I still wasn't answering.

"Jié Shù was a vampire. She also had a little magic," I noted, though that shadow shuriken spell had been impressive. Was Ariel a vampire with a bit of magic now? Other than a hint of magic-adding knowledge to accompany her words, she hadn't used magic. She'd sampled Alexis, and used that sample earlier, but hadn't gained Lexy's ability to use magic. What about now? Was she a *magic* mythic mermaid monster? Bear would like that alliteration.

"I found this vampire more difficult," Ariel answered without exactly answering.

"What do you mean?"

"Taking over Jié Shù."

"Huh?"

"I didn't feed off her flesh and become her. I left my previous body, entered hers, and tried to take it over. I couldn't take over her body, so I rebuilt a new body inside her."

"How long did that take?"

She raised her eyebrow at me like I was stupid.

"Right, I saw how long. But how did you speak through Jié Shù if you couldn't control her?"

"Jié Shù died."

Jié Shù had looked like a re-animated corpse. Perhaps I had guessed right.

"How do you know that taking over Jié Shù was *more difficult*? If you don't remember anything before the well, then maybe everyone is that difficult to take over?"

She blinked at my question, then turned away from me, her eyes looking out her window. She looked back at me and shrugged. She didn't have an answer to my question. Her facial expression—scrunched eyes and cheeks raised in worry—suggested that she wanted to know the answer more than I did.

I pulled the Porsche off the road. Three palm trees grew close together in front of a mansion three down from Master King's White House. The grass area between the palm trees and the fence easily fit the Porsche and somewhat hid it from passersby.

Kendra's worry had only increased. Surely, she knew, as did Alexis and her entourage, that Ariel and I had left.

I grabbed Raijin from the Porsche's back seat. Lower on the staff, near where I gripped it, there was space for an additional rune. Eldra knew how to create them. Her memories pushed at me as I perused them. I put a containment around the Porsche, then a tiny spark of magic burned from my index finger as I drew a new rune. Ariel watched me as I burnt the image of a torch under a heart. I joined it with the spell. Using Raijin, I'd be able to cast torched heart on more vampires at the same time.

I exited the Porsche, and with Ariel beside me, we walked toward Master King's White House. It felt good not to be alone. I had to keep reminding myself that Ariel was not a six-year-old. She was half Native American freshwater mermaid—called a water baby—and half ancient alien shapeshifter that could live forever. She'd hung the sais from her hips, using her belt loops. Their tips almost touched the ground with each step as we walked along the roadside toward Master King's mansion.

For now, her purpose in life revolved around protecting me. If she kept me alive long enough, Coyote—the Native American legend himself—would forgive her and take her to the next world when this world ended, which could be billions of years from now.

"Are you going to kill Master King?" Ariel asked.

"I don't think so." I wasn't sure if I was going to kill him or not. The plan involved freeing those trapped in the thralls' tunnel. It had occurred to me that Master King would try to stop me, but for some reason, I didn't think he would. I'd try to avoid killing him. It might not go well for Alexis if I did.

Protector magic pushed me toward the tunnel, but perhaps I shouldn't let it control me. Maybe I could come up with a plan far superior to simply walking into the tunnel, breaking any bond or allure that enthralled those captured, and telling them they were free to go.

"Perhaps I should speak with Master King first," I wondered aloud.

"Jié Shù would have liked that. She had final words for him as well."

"How should we sneak in?"

"Maybe we don't have to," Ariel suggested.

"Why not?"

"Have the guards at the front gate heard that Jié Shù died?"

I shrugged.

"Phone?"

I handed her my phone, which now showed nine missed calls. She dialed a number from memory—no doubt Jié Shù's memory. She put the phone on speaker, and together, we listened to it ring.

"MK Guard Tower," a heavy male voice answered.

Ariel's voice perfectly mimicked Jié Shù's as she asked, "Eddie," she knew the guy's name. "Anything unusual outside?"

"All clear here."

"Master King expects two guests shortly. A teenage boy and a little girl. Bring them to him immediately upon their arrival." She hung up the phone.

"We could have driven right in." I considered going back and doing just that, but we could see the guard tower now a football field away, while we'd parked the Porsche half a mile back. Sure, with a couple football practices behind me, my legs were stronger, but we'd just walked a half mile, and I didn't want to walk another one.

"Will you kill Fern?" Ariel asked.

I stopped walking and looked at Coyote's granddaughter. The answer wasn't no. I wanted to feel the power of erasing something evil from existence, and erasing that heart-stealing bitch fueled my addictive desire. I didn't want to share my addiction with Ariel, so I didn't answer.

"If you don't, can I?" Ariel asked.

Unsure how to answer, I shrugged and started walking.

A minute later, we arrived at the guard tower where two guards with machine guns awaited. One was tall and skinny with dark skin, which reminded me of Manouchka, only he had no hair. His bald head reflected the lantern-shaped streetlight. The other was a lot shorter and thicker—muscular thick. He raised his left eyebrow at us. Both had red eyes. Perhaps only the daytime guards were human.

"Master King is expecting us," I lied to them.

"You mean for Fern? I didn't expect you to be on foot," the shorter and thicker man grumbled with the heavy voice we'd heard on the phone, indicating he was Eddie. "Are those gifts for Fern, too?" He pointed at the sais hanging from her belt loops.

I shrugged, not understanding the question clearly.

"Cute," he laughed. "You want to take them up, Bosley?"

The tall, bald guard mumbled under his breath.

"What's that?" Eddie asked Bosley.

"Sure, I got this," Bosley smiled at Eddie, and I noticed his fangs, though they weren't extended. He turned to us. "Follow me," he gestured toward the White House with his machine gun.

As we walked, Bosley kept glancing at Ariel and me, looking like he wanted to say something. About halfway down the long driveway, he looked at me and finally spoke up. "You were here earlier?"

"Yep," I answered.

"Is the girl for Fern?" his voice sounded worried.

Ariel wasn't exactly here for Fern, but she did want to kill that evil redhead, so in a way, she was. I found his worry interesting, and wanting to see how he would react, I answered, "Yes."

Bosley gulped. He pinched his eyes closed and kept walking. He didn't say a word the rest of the walk to the mansion. He led us past the shadowed palm trees to a door on the south side of the estate, a different entrance than before. Inside, an elevator sat open to the right, and a hallway led to the left. Bosley took us to the elevator, pushed the number 3 for us to go up, which I hadn't expected, and then put his back against the wall and held his machine gun ready. He couldn't take his eyes from Ariel.

On the third floor, he led us down a hallway, right, down another hall, then to a set of double doors. We remained behind him as he pressed a button on a square intercom box next to the door and spoke into it.

"It's Bosley. I have the guests that Jié Shù asked me to bring up to—."

The door swung open with alarming speed, revealing Master King, his claws out, gripping the doors, the black in his eyes spreading from his pupils into his sclera.

"Jié Shù is dead," Master King glared at Bosley. His eyes found Ariel and me standing behind and off to the side of Bosley. He backhanded Bosley, sending him flying into the far wall, and took two steps toward me before I released my magic, causing his hand to reach for his heart.

"I won't torch your heart," I spat out quickly. "At least, I plan to give you a choice first."

"I've killed a protector before," Master King threatened, his eyes black.

"You had an army, remember?" Ariel reminded him in Jié Shù's voice. Master King stepped back, disturbed to hear the little, lavender-haired, six-year-old speak with his former general's voice.

"Jié Shù had some final words for you," Ariel continued. "Jake has words, too. After that, we'll be on our way."

Master King eyed the lavender-haired little girl intently. He inhaled deeply, which vampires do to smell more than to breathe. He knew Ariel wasn't human, but the confusion in his eyes suggested he hadn't recognized her scent.

"He isn't under oath," Master King nodded toward me, speaking to Ariel as if she were in charge.

"If the protector wanted you dead, he would have burned your heart out already," Coyote's trickster granddaughter again answered with Jié Shù's voice. "He won't harm you if you don't force his hand."

Master King nodded. "By coming back here," he informed Ariel, "your oath is broken." He glanced at the sais hanging at her hips. "I could kill you now."

Ariel shrugged—which seemed exaggerated on her little-girl body.

"Wait here, Bosley," Master King's voice sounded reprimanding. "I will speak with you after." Then he returned to his office. He didn't invite us in, but he left the door open, so we followed. He picked up his desk phone. Line one had a light flashing, indicating he had already been on a call and had put it on hold. He pressed the button. "It appears your guess was correct. Two of your generals just arrived, Princess Alexis. I consider this a breach of the laws." He paused to listen for a second. "No, I won't let you speak to him." He laughed as he added, "Your inability to even get one of your generals to answer your phone call is not my problem."

He listened for a second.

"He is not under oath. We are free to kill him if we choose."

Another pause. I considered tapping off my separation stone to hear Lexy's side of the conversation, but Alexis still had her separation stone, which was likely enabled. Besides, Kendra would immediately try to convince me to leave.

Master King gestured to Ariel to close the door, and she did.

"You can't come and get him, Princess. As you said, you are parked at the side of the road next to the barrier the oath magic has in place. The challenge negotiations are over. Neither you nor any under your influence can come within three miles of my shiver until after our duel." He eyed Ariel, unsure how she had bypassed the oath magic. "I'm considering killing these two now for breaking that law." He let Alexis speak for another second, then answered. "He might not be, but the girl took the oath. Which begs the question, how did she cross the barrier?" Another pause. "You will just have to wait for him to call you later." He hung up and began twiddling his fingers. As he eyed me, I tapped off the separation stone long enough to mentally shout, *Go back to the hotel!* over the instant mental reprimands from Kendra and Alexis.

"What are you doing here, Protector?" Master King demanded.

"Go easy on Bosley," I suggested. "Ariel tricked him and the other guard with Jié Shù's voice."

Master King laughed out loud.

"Concern, from a protector for a vampire. Now, I've seen everything."

"It wasn't his fault," I continued defending Bosley.

Master King's smile dropped and his mouth flattened into a line. "I do not need a boy's advice."

"Did you inform your guards of Jié Shù's death?" I asked. "I'm not giving you advice. Just informing you of your own incompetence."

Master King's eyes tightened with rage. Ariel stepped in front of me, and her hands gripped the handles of her sais, pulling his black eyes from me to her.

"You offered Jié Shù's final words," Master King changed the subject.

Ariel answered in Jié Shù's voice, accent and all. "I love you," Ariel answered in first person as if she still were Jié Shù. What had she said earlier? "I am Jié Shù, and I'm not."

"Many love me." Master King didn't seem touched. His face remained emotionless.

"The girl princess, Alexis—her generals love her. They are more hers for love than they ever would be if forced by her allure and influence. I feel the same for you." Ariel stopped, having nothing more to say.

"They are more hers?" He repeated. "And yet, this one won't even answer her phone call." Master King looked like he'd started a poker game. However, his eyes gave him away. They lost any hint of black, returning to crimson. Losing his first general had hurt him beyond simply decreasing his power. What pain did he feel behind those eyes? Did he feel pain or was he simply disappointed that her death weakened him? What humanity, if any, remained inside the vampire before me?

I had things to say, but I sensed he needed a minute. I waited patiently.

Finally, he looked at Ariel and asked, "Is that all?"

Ariel nodded.

"Go, then," he made brushing motions with his left hand to shoo us away.

"Not yet," I jumped in.

"I'm here to free the people in the tunnel," I explained with pure honesty. I held up my staff and said, "Let my people go!"

Master King laughed. "Are you Moses, now?"

"The protector magic compels me." My words caused his laugh to catch in his throat.

"I didn't believe for a second you didn't plan to kill me." His eyes began darkening again.

I scowled at him. "I'm not going to kill you," I replied.

"Don't lie to me!" his voice elevated.

"I'm not lying," I snapped back. Was I lying? The protector magic wanted me to kill Master King, but it couldn't force me to do so. It had forced me to leave those I cared about before The Cage fights, but it had needed help from both Lexy's and Master King's allure to overcome my own will. It didn't have that help now.

"I know what you are. A protector's sole purpose for existing is to exterminate all vampires," Master King shouted. "That is why your kind was first created."

Was that true? If so, that was news to both me and Eldra. The druids had those who would find and train protectors. They had secret knowledge that Eldra was not privy to. Eldra knew that protectors hated vampires most of all, but having a sole purpose? Maybe it was true or maybe that was just his point of view?

"I'm in love with a half-dhampir," I affirmed. "Let me free those you enslaved. I won't touch you."

"You won't slaughter my shiver?"

"No. I'm not going to slaughter your shiver." Again, the protector magic didn't much agree with me.

"The last time he faced a protector, Master King impaled him on a wooden pole," Ariel explained in Jié Shù's voice. "After the protector slaughtered his entire army and everyone he ever loved. If the Vampire King hadn't arrived in time with his army to aid him, Master King would be dead, too."

"Arrived in time?" Master King shouted again. "The Vampire King tricked me! He sent a messenger begging for my help, claiming that his army had taken heavy losses. He lied. The battle hadn't started yet. The protector burned the hearts from my entire shiver and each of my three sisters' shivers, while the Vampire King waited on the sidelines for my army to wear out the protector with their lives."

"You had a stone that protected you," Ariel added, maintaining Jié Shù's Asian accent.

"And the Vampire King stole it from me," Master King growled, his eyes blackening.

Before I could react, he threw a familiar knife at my forehead. Ariel jumped high enough, but not soon enough, to catch the blade. The knife's point hit me in the center of my forehead. The runed blade deflected, spinning erratically over my head to the wall. If this were a movie, it would have stuck perfectly in the wall, but this was real life, so it ricocheted off the wall and hit the back of my leg just below the knee before falling to the carpeted office floor with a muffled thud. The combination of Flesh of Steel and Bones of Steel, which I'd drank earlier, had just saved my life.

My magical hand wrapped Master King's heart the moment he took his first step around his desk. He held a second knife, this one a skull-hilted blade. His prejudice ran deep. He wanted to kill me. He hated protectors. But I gripped his heart. He managed two more steps before he fell to a knee and touched his chest.

Ariel drew her sais and stood ready.

The room fell silent for some time. Kendra's worried emotions pressed at me, but I ignored them.

"I just need to free those you've enslaved," I offered, and loosened but didn't let go of my grip. "Put those away," I told Ariel.

"Hmph," he still didn't believe me. "I don't understand the oath magic. Why is it protecting you?"

As Ariel bent over and retrieved Lexy's runed blade, I considered Master King's misinterpretation of why the blade bounced off me harmlessly. He didn't know that I had drunk two powerful, defensive potions, so it made sense that he wrongly attributed it to the oath magic. But it also meant he was fallible.

"I'm implementing a one-pint rule," I made up the rule right there on the spot. "I promise to pardon any vampire who never kills or harms people and drinks no more than one pint every two weeks."

"Fool," Master King shook his head. "We can't survive on so little."

"No, I mean . . ." I paused. I'd explained it wrong. "I mean, you can have as many pints as you want, just not more than one pint from the same person in two weeks. Does that make more sense?"

Master King's eyes widened at me. "You're serious?"

I nodded. "I just need to free the people in the tunnel."

"Just like that? We follow the one-pint law, and the millennial war between vampires and the protector is over?" Master King blinked at me.

I nodded. I could sense that the godlike being that granted me the protector magic wasn't happy, but I ignored that.

"Fine. Take them." He tossed the skull-hilted blade onto our side of the desk next to a phone I recognized. It looked exactly like the one in my pocket, which meant it was Lexy's. Of course, his minion vampire maidens would have recognized both blades as special. He would have wanted to inspect them.

He acquiesced to our request too easily. I glanced at Ariel.

"You won't try to stop me?" As I asked the question, Ariel retrieved Lexy's phone and the skull-hilted knife, as well as the sheaths and straps that she used to tie them around her thighs.

"How could I? It seems the oath magic won't let me harm you, and you could burn away my heart before I could even try."

"And those in your shiver?"

"I'll not order them to stand by while you free their thralls. This is a free country. They can make their own decisions, if the oath magic lets them," Master King explained.

He was hiding something, but I couldn't be sure what. He offered no more information.

"One more thing," I added, not having thought of this until just now. "No children. They must be over twenty-one."

"We'll never agree to that. You might as well kill us all, protector."

I kept my eyes on him, thinking. I didn't know what to do. He had to agree to an age limit.

"Fourteen!" he said.

I hadn't meant my hesitation to be a negotiating point, but apparently, Master King took it that way.

"Eighteen," I countered.

He shook his head.

"Fifteen," Master King countered. "Don't offer sixteen. Fifteen will be difficult enough to enforce. At fifteen, they are three years past puberty."

"Fine," I agreed.

"And you, Protector, promise not to kill any vampire who follows your laws?"

"Yes." *And maybe legions of vampires don't have to try to kill me,* I thought.

He nodded. "Agreed. Though, I'm not sure if your laws free us or enslave us."

I shrugged, then turned and walked out with Ariel following me. Bosley waited outside the doors. He was one of Master King's vampires. Was he also under Master King's control?

I pushed protector magic around Bosley. Had Kendra or Alexis ever created an everything-seal? If they had, had they cast it through me? Like torched heart, my everything-seal—a containment that blocked out magic, thought, scent, everything—was protector magic, intended to free a thrall from vampire influence. Could it also free a vampire from another more dominant vampire?

Bosley twitched as an invisible connection between Master King and him snapped.

Apparently, it could. I'd just released Bosley from Master King's control.

"You're free, Bosley," Master King spoke from behind me. "It's probably safer for you if you leave and never come back."

Bosley watched Master King close the doors to his office before he turned to me. In half a second, I found myself pinned against the wall, a set of claws at my neck.

CHAPTER 37
FERN

I behaved like a silly girl. I threw a tantrum because Jake did not choose me. Then Jake and Kendra both chose to come to Las Vegas. In the alley, they both chose to fight to save me, to give their lives for me if needed. Never before have two people chosen to show me true love. —Alexis

"**I** won't let you give her to Fern," Bosley whispered through clenched teeth into my ear. "That bitch just wants to get high off her fear," he spat. Bosley held me so tight that I couldn't breathe. By releasing him from Master King's control, I thought he would be grateful. Instead, his claws pressed at my neck but didn't draw blood. Bones of Steel kept my neck from breaking, and Flesh of Steel kept his sharp claws from piercing my skin. With both spells still protecting me, I'd assumed I was invincible. However, my skin still moved freely. I found my lungs burning for air. If he didn't let go, I'd asphyxiate. Turns out, he *could* kill me.

Kendra's worry slammed into me. She could feel my fear—my strong emotions—even when I wore the separation stone, the same way I could feel hers. Perhaps my ability to feel emotions through the separation stone had more to do with the emotional rope she'd created between us than me being a protector. Of course, that didn't explain how I could feel Alexis's emotions, but pressed against a wall with a vampire's claws at my throat was not the time to delve into such thoughts.

Ariel leaped up behind Bosley, unnaturally high for her current six-year-old body, grabbed his face, straddled his head, so her feet planted on the wall next to my ears. The tips of her sai blades also hit the wall. She yanked the vampire by his bald head with unexpected strength. His grip held on my neck,

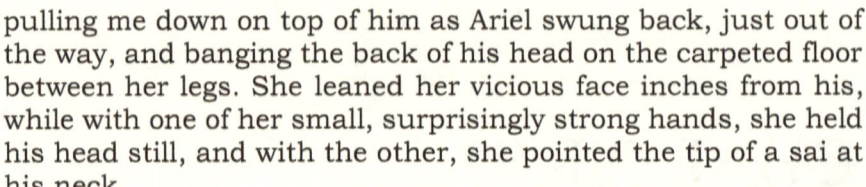

pulling me down on top of him as Ariel swung back, just out of the way, and banging the back of his head on the carpeted floor between her legs. She leaned her vicious face inches from his, while with one of her small, surprisingly strong hands, she held his head still, and with the other, she pointed the tip of a sai at his neck.

"You misunderstood," Ariel's voice lowered to an animalistic growl. "I'm here *for* Fern." She licked her lips and tapped the pommel of the sai she threatened him with. She used his face to shove herself to her feet. The mythic monster girl glanced at me as I lay on Bosley's chest, his grip still tight around my neck. "Fern is a child-killing vampire," Bosley stated flatly.

Ariel looked at him. "I am no child." Then she glared at me. "I don't need a protector's permission to eat her," she informed me. Then she returned the one sai to her belt loop.

Bosley loosened his grip on me. I pulled away and stood up. Bosley beat me to his feet. His eyes widened, the white sclera contrasting with his dark skin and making them look ready to pop out.

"You have no chance against Fern, little one," he shook his head.

Ariel ignored him and started walking down the hall, leading the way to the elevator. I followed her.

"You're free to come with us," I called back to Bosley.

Bosley hurried to walk beside me. The three of us paused at the elevator, impatiently waiting for it to open. Bosley squinted his eyes at my neck, surely confused at my lack of claw marks but said nothing.

The ding of the elevator signaled the opening of the doors. Ariel entered the elevator and pressed B for the basement as we followed her in.

Once in the basement, both Ariel and I made a B-line for the small room that held the hidden stairs. Coyote's granddaughter didn't wait for Bosley before she swiped her finger over the tablet-like screen by the doorway, bringing it to life. She pulled up the custom security app and entered the code. Across the room, the massive bookshelf slid forward as it had done before.

Bosley didn't ask how we knew the code, but his curious eyes suggested that he wanted to.

We took the stairs into the darkness of the shiver's underground tunnels. Or at least, it was dark for me. Neither Ariel nor Bosley had a problem seeing in the dark.

We walked into the dimly lit common area that led to where the other tunnels branched out. The shiver was alive with people—some vampires, some thralls. A few of the vampires were feeding off their thralls. Some played cards. It wasn't all feed and kill. It was more like feed and hang out. A TV hung on the wall in one carved-out room, and a group of vampires and thralls watched a movie. They looked to be paired up. No, they looked like couples? Netflix and chill in a shiver? Seriously?

I had considered waiting for dawn, but underground, it didn't matter if it was day or night. There was no sunlight.

We glanced around but didn't make eye contact. A few vampires nodded at Bosley and gave us the eye, but not one of them challenged us.

I led Ariel and Bosley directly into the tunnel with the trapped people. The single line of LED lights wasn't enough for me to see well, but it was enough to see the thralls' shadowy forms. I walked in, already holding my protector magic ready, and unleashed my everything-seal around the entire room. Everyone in the room would be disconnected from Master King or whichever vampire had enthralled and captured them.

I extended my everything-seal from wall to wall until it encompassed every shadow. The expressions on each individual's face changed as the allure and influence that controlled them broke.

"You're free," I spoke calmly as I walked through the dark silhouettes.

Bosley walked to my left, and Ariel walked to my right, announcing their freedom with equally calm voices. Bosley split off and made his way to the wall where he flipped a switch. Four strands of rope light rose up the wall and came to the LEDs' aid. I wouldn't have called the rope light bright, but I could now see just fine in the front half of the cavern. The back half was still dim. A bit further down the wall, there was a second switch, and I could barely make out additional rope lights.

I found the man with short, tightly curled hair. Next, I found the overweight woman with stringy, blonde hair and a pockmarked face. After a few more steps, I encountered the man from India with tan skin, black hair, and a beard.

"You're free."

A grunting sound came from the left, near the second light switch, followed by screams. I turned in time to see a shadowy figure ripping Bosley's heart from his chest. I flicked my hand at the light switch, and the second set of four rope lights lit up. Bosley dropped to one knee in front of a woman with very pale, white skin.

"Tonight's your . . . end, b . . . bi—," Bosley breathlessly managed some last words but couldn't finish.

Fern raked Bosley's neck with her claws, and he collapsed to the sandstone floor, lifeless.

"So nice of you to free *all* of us," Fern stood with Bosley's bloody heart in her hand. The matches in The Cage had continued after we left, so she hadn't changed out of her uniform of short black spandex shorts and bikini top with The Cage logo.

I hadn't known Bosley long, but he had made a lasting impact on me. Meeting him, a vampire who worried for little children, who hated Fern and what she did, proved that vampires could choose between good and evil. His behavior added to what I had seen from the members of the V.I.T. I didn't want to admit it, but I included Keagan's changed behavior in that list, too.

Fern wasn't alone. While the people cringed and stepped back from her, twelve other shadowy figures stood proud and strong. Each stepped behind Fern. All but two were female. Of the two men, one was Drake. Like Bosley, I'd freed Fern and the twelve vampires. They were no longer under Master King's control. Did that mean they were also no longer bound by his oath of peace? He had been wrong to think the oath of peace protected me, but he did. Had Master King called Fern the moment I left his room so she could hide among the thralls? Had he thought he was setting me up? Either way, he wanted Fern to kill me, so perhaps I should have killed him.

Fern giggled as she approached me.

Ariel side-stepped to intercept the red-headed vampire, but I held up my hand, asking her to wait. I hadn't expected her to obey, but to my surprise, she trusted me and changed direction to come and stand on my right.

"I have a simple law," I spoke as calmly as I could, but nerves still escaped at the edges of my voice. "No killing. You may feed on anyone you want who is over fifteen, but only one pint from any one person every two weeks." This time, I explained it right the first time.

"Who are you to give us laws?" Fern challenged.

"I am this generation's protector." I clacked Raijin on the sandstone floor. "*Fæcele heorte.*" The new rune I'd carved glowed in various colors; the torch's flame was yellow, the heart was red, while the box and the torch handle were white. I clenched my left fist as thirteen magic hands reached into each vampire's chest and squeezed. I couldn't have managed thirteen without Raijin, but with the staff, I could have easily done more. Twelve of the vampires stumbled to their knees—all but Fern.

Fern giggled again. "Your magic can no longer torch my heart."

My thirteenth magical hand reached for Fern's heart but couldn't grasp it. How she'd managed that in such a short time, I could only guess.

"I can torch theirs," I replied, nodding to her companions. "Obey my law. Walk away or die."

Fern launched herself at me. Ariel stepped her six-year-old body between us, sais ready, but Fern was too quick. She grabbed the hilt of one blade and smacked the other blade out of the shapeshifter's too-small hand. It when flying behind us to the feet of the former thralls that now had moved behind my protection.

Fern wrenched the second sai from Ariel, stabbed her through her stomach, then picked her up and threw her at the thralls behind me. Fern immediately attacked me, swiping at my leather jacket, ripping at it with her claws. She'd seen what had happened to Henry, and she checked my clothing to make sure a similar spell wouldn't break her hand.

I tried to dodge by jumping back as she continued to shred my leather shirt. Fern's attack distracted me, breaking my concentration and causing me to drop the grip I had on the other vampires. Most just stood there as if contemplating what to do.

I watched them out of the corner of my eye as Fern shredded my leather jacket and shirt until my chest and stomach were exposed.

As Ariel returned, sai removed from her stomach and now in her hand, one of the vampires—one of the two men—rushed to Fern's aid.

"*Fæcele heorte,*" I shouted into Fern's face while directing my magical hand into the vampire coming to her aid. This time, I didn't stop the spell at only gripping the man's heart. This vampire had made his decision to stand and fight with Fern. Flames erupted from his chest and the air filled with the scent of burnt flesh.

"Kai Lin!" Fern shouted the vampire's name. She turned back to me and slapped me across the face with her claws, trying to rip off my cheek. "You are weak!" Her sharp nails made a scraping sound even as her other hand shot at my heart. Her slap tossed my face to the side, but I turned my head back and met her eyes, not even a scratch from her claws on my cheek while two of her claws had broken against my skin.

Ariel swung at Fern's bare leg, but she caught the blade, unconcerned that it cut her hand. She ripped the blade upward out of Ariel's hands and threw it at me. Had I not seen it coming, I wouldn't have been able to dodge fast enough, but I did. It just missed me. Behind me, one of the thralls screamed, the overweight girl with stringy, blonde hair and a pockmarked face. The sai had buried deep into her sternum. So deeply that the two tine tips pierced her as well. Too late, I remembered I was almost invincible. I should have let the blade hit me, but I dodged on instinct. Sadness jolted my heart and quickly turned to anger—adding to what I already felt for Fern. Another person died because I made a poor choice. Her mother's far-away plea to God would go unanswered. Instead of helping, the other former thralls backed away. Did they feel the same pain I felt? Or did they only feel fear? It didn't matter. There was nothing they could do but watch as the woman died.

Ariel latched onto Fern's right leg and bit into it. Fern spun and kicked her off, sending her flying again. But *this* time, Coyote's granddaughter landed on her feet.

Fern's eyes locked on Raijin as I raised the staff in anger. Before I could stop her, she grabbed Robin's staff and yanked it from my hand. Then she swung at my neck with both her vampire speed and strength. Raijin hit me just below my jaw and splintered into half a dozen pieces. The force knocked me backward, and I stumbled but stayed on my feet. One piece remained in Fern's hand. It had broken longways, leaving a sharp point, like a stake. Fern aimed the stake at my heart. Were Luiz here, he would have found a vampire trying to kill me with a wooden stake hilariously ironic. She slammed the wooden point at my chest. My skin moved a little, but Flesh of Steel kept the stake from piercing it. Instead, Fern's hand continued forward, sliding down the broken end of the staff and cutting her hand as it hit my chest. The last piece of Raijin fell to the floor. Just as Eldra had died and returned to Robin, so did Raijin join Astrapí.

That hadn't been the only sharp fragment of Raijin, though. Ariel had picked up another, and using it, she stabbed Fern in the side just below her ribs, piercing her deeply. Fern stepped back, pulled the now bloody fragment of wood out and threw it at the little monster girl, who sidestepped it.

A cloud of white color puffed into Fern's irises, not complete fear but enough fear to lift the corners of my mouth. She didn't know that I'd drank both Flesh of Steel and Bones of Steel, and both would last hours yet. She couldn't hurt me—unless she discovered that I could still be strangled.

"Can I have her, now?" Ariel asked, grabbing my hand. The mythic monster girl had to look almost straight up to meet my eyes. "Please, please, please?" She intentionally spoke like a six-year-old would.

I wanted to say no. Part of me wanted to cast a magic missile and feel the ecstasy of erasing Fern's entire soul from existence. I hadn't erased her yet because I wanted her to know she couldn't hurt me. I had wanted to make her eyes white with fear before she died, just like she did to her victims. I'd succeeded. I could erase her now, but if I gave in to my addictive desire, would I be able to stop? Or would I erase everyone here?

I stepped back behind Ariel. "Fern's all yours." I looked at Fern, then shrugged as I said, "Goodbye."

Ariel leaped forward with incredible speed that defied her six-year-old frame, wrapping her little arms and legs around Fern. She latched onto the soul-shattered, redheaded vampire like she had with Jié Shù. Fern freaked out, thrashing and shredding at Ariel's back, ripping chunks of flesh from her little body and tossing them in splats to the ground. Ariel did her best to stay in one piece, knocking away Fern's claws. I turned away, not wanting to see the gruesome scene. In a minute, the only remaining part of Coyote's granddaughter would be her lifeforce, which I assume was already entering Fern through the wound under the vampire's ribs. Fern didn't know it yet, but she'd already lost.

I turned to the remaining eleven vampires. One of them was Drake. Would I have to kill him? Part of me hoped not, but the part of me addicted to erasing evil hoped so.

I addressed them all. "Would you be so kind as to escort these former thralls to their homes? Or at least to a bus stop or airport or something?"

They stood there nonplussed, so I lifted my left hand, calling for torched heart, and gripped one of their hearts—Drake's, the last man. I chose him over the women out of some misguided form of chivalry. He dropped to the sandstone floor.

"You will kill us anyway, Protector," a pale, dark-haired vampire woman shouted. I'd seen her in the alley. She'd stood next to Jace, opposite Mindy. I didn't know her name. She dressed in a black gothic dress that was mostly sheer. The rope lights weren't bright enough for me to make out any of the tattoos that decorated her arms, legs, and the portions of her torso visible through her see-through dress. Her eyes kept looking behind me, where I knew Fern was gruesomely ripping Ariel's body to shreds.

"If you obey my law, why would I kill you?"

"The Protector was created to bring vampires to extinction," Goth Girl answered.

That was the second time I'd heard that. Did that feel true? All the vampires certainly believed it. Could it be my sole purpose, as

Master King had stated earlier? If so, why had Coyote told me that the Trapped Ones—Ariel's water-baby brothers and sisters—were my job? It might be *a* purpose, but it couldn't be the *sole* purpose.

Three of the eleven vampires all took a step forward.

I clenched both my fists. I'd already proven that I could control five magic hands without the staff; could I do all eleven with the staff? I sent ten more hands forward to add to the hand that already gripped Drake. The other ten vampires fell, some to their knees, some prone, as I managed to magically grip all their hearts, applying heat but not torching them yet. My magic stretched thin. I doubted I could torch them all at once. But they didn't need to know that.

"Then why are you still alive?" I released their hearts, making it look like a gesture of goodwill, but really, I simply couldn't hold that much magic at once. With their hearts free, they looked up at me in unison. "Will you obey the new law?"

The pale goth vampire, only on her knees, extended her fangs and launched at me like a panther. She swiped at my neck, knocking me back. She slapped me. She kicked me against one wall, then lifted me and threw me across the tunnel to the other side. Each hit—both from her and the sandstone wall and floor—felt a little like a hit on the football field, with full pads, except my bones rattled like metal.

Goth Girl stopped when I stood, not a scratch on me. What did she expect? She'd seen Fern fail to injure me. I might be in trouble if they knew that the magic protecting me was from vials and probably wouldn't last past sunrise. They could lock me up and kill me once it wore off, but they didn't know that. As far as they knew, this magic was part of me. Keagan's con probably aided that misconception.

"Are you done?" I asked her. "Will you live the new law? No killing. No more than one pint from the same person in two weeks. It's easy."

"I've been killing for three hundred years."

"Can you change?" I asked.

She glanced behind me to where Fern still ripped at Ariel. I didn't want to look, but I did. Her detached legs lay oozing on the floor, and I could see her bloody ribs. The many former thralls stayed back, giving them and us plenty of room.

"No," Goth Girl charged and swiped at me, knocking me against the tunnel wall again. I made her heart explode with fire before she reached me a second time. As I burned her heart with one hand, I launched a magic missile at her body with the other.

While watching magic light crack her body into pieces, a burst of flame hit me from the left side. Drake had decided that he couldn't live the law either. He now held his makeshift flamethrower. The thrall who'd brought it to him from a different tunnel hustled behind his master. Unlike the thralls in this tunnel, this thrall had not yet been freed.

Neither Flesh of Steel nor Bones of Steel were designed to protect against fire. My skin wasn't literally steel. It was just reinforced to be as unbreakable as steel. For the first second, the flame singed me. Pain flooded my body. But I'd learned from Alexis to control the temperature around me by redirecting heat into magical energy. So I did. I blocked the flame as best as I could with one hand. Then with the other, I clenched my fist as I said, "You've bled your last drop." I stole the phrase that Keagan had used.

Drake's heart exploded as flame burst from his chest, matching the flame bursting from the business end of his propane torch. I also hit him with a magic missile, erasing his existence in the few moments he stayed alive without a heart. He collapsed, dropping his improvised flamethrower, but it didn't turn off. Its fire blackened the sandstone floor. Drake's body cracked with light and erased, giving me a glorious sense of ecstasy. Drake's thrall stepped forward and turned the propane off. He looked up at me, confused, shaken, and afraid. Had he not done that, I might have lost myself in the pleasure of erasing his master, but I didn't. He had nothing to fear from me. With Drake's death, he had been released. No special protector magic was necessary.

I winced. My elbow was only singed, but a red patch marked my left side, just above my hip, indicating a first-degree burn, except for a one-inch circle in the center where the burn was at least a second degree. I tried to ignore the pain.

I turned back to the nine vampires who seemed torn between joining Goth Girl and Drake and staying alive. Their eyes danced from me to behind me where Fern had been shredding Ariel.

"What about the rest of you?"

Before they could answer, Fern screamed behind me. "I killed her! I shredded your precious little monster to bits." She held Lexy's runed blade in her left hand and the skull-hilted blade in her right.

Ariel's head lay gruesomely on its side on the sandstone floor, its colorless eyes staring at nothing. Only splatters and bones remained of Ariel's body, and its matter slowly disintegrated into a jelly-like substance. Shreds of her clothes lay on the floor, as did one of her sais. I cringed at the scene.

Fern threw both knives at me. I tried to catch them both but failed. The blades hit my hands, then my chest, and I fumbled with them until they hit the floor.

"Didn't you see what happened to Jié Shù?" I asked as I kneeled to pick up the blades.

Fern's eyes, already clouded with a hint of white, now went bright white. "She's inside me. I can feel her." Fern bent over and pulled the sai from the sternum of the now-deceased, overweight young woman. The redhead stabbed herself with it in the stomach. Then she stabbed her left breast right in the circle of the letter 'g' in the logo. Then her arm.

"I feel her!" Fern shouted.

The nine remaining vampires stared at Fern as she bled from various self-inflicted wounds in front of them. She continued stabbing herself in various parts of her body. Worried for Ariel's lifeforce, I pushed sight into my eyes. It took me a second to find Ariel. She'd elongated her life force into Fern's spinal column. Had Fern not had a shattered spirit, I wouldn't have detected the ancient alien's light stretching the length of her vertebrae. No sooner did Ariel's essence extend into the skull than Fern stopped stabbing herself. She stood, frozen in place. I dropped my magical sight. Fern's body looked dead as blood dripped from various wounds. Lavender slowly replaced her white, afraid irises.

"She was easy to take over." It was Fern's mouth that moved, but it was Ariel who moved it. Ariel had the memories of those whom she cloned or took over. Fern's soul hadn't only been shattered, but it had been dark, too. What if Fern's darkness brought back Ariel's darkness? Would she become Coyote's most devilish descendant again?

"What about them?" Fern's arm lifted and pointed at the nine remaining vampires. "Are they going to obey the protector's law?"

Over half of them quickly answered, "Yes."

"I am old, like her," a blonde with long straight hair answered, pointing to a mark on the floor that had been left when my magic missile erased Goth Girl. "I'm not sure I can change."

"Do you want to try?" I asked as I handed the two knives to the new Ariel in Fern's body.

"It is either try or die," she pressed her lips flat.

"If you fail," I gripped my hand, adding a hint of heat to the magic grip around her heart, "I'll be there."

She nodded but stepped back, choosing not to attack me.

"Walk out with me," I shouted to the people in the shiver. "You are free."

322

I turned to the remaining nine vampires. "There were more people than this. I'm going to check back on Saturday," I explained, "and every last one of them better be free. If there is anyone else, you better find them."

It wasn't just nine vampires who heard me. I couldn't see them in the darkness, but I sensed that most of the vampires in the shiver crowded just outside the tunnel, listening in. Would they be a problem?

CHAPTER 38
MIDWIFERY

Carl: Hey, Ariel. Mortal Kombat is fun. I like it. I
  woke up early. Where are you?
Ariel: I'm out of town with Jake, Kendra, and
  Alexis. We had a busy day yesterday and didn't
  sleep well. If we don't get tied up, I hope to see
  you this afternoon. ☺

"May I stay?" a short, Latina woman asked. "I don't have a home. I don't have a family. Cardin, my master, is good to me—to us. None of master's thralls have a family. Perhaps we've *become* a family. If I leave . . ." Her pleading eyes suggested that she feared leaving more than staying.

Honestly, I hadn't expected her question. I stood there, perhaps looking stupid for a minute. I looked to Ariel, but seeing her shrug with Fern's body was no help.

"You are free," I finally answered. "You are free to stay if that is your choice." I didn't like what she was asking, but I wasn't going to force her to leave.

"Ariel, shall we go?" It felt so weird turning to Fern and calling her Ariel. "Anyone who wants to may walk out with us."

About one in six people stayed. For a second, I didn't understand. More than I had expected had made the same choice as the Latina woman. As I took a breath, understanding came. How many of these former thralls held unrequited feelings for the very vampires who were going to drink away their lives? How many of them hoped that maybe, with my new law, they would have a new chance? I was returning home with Lexy, wasn't I? Who was I to judge them?

Dawn approached. I worried about missing morning football practice. Silly, I know, but unlike a video game, real life didn't have a pause button, nor did it stop indefinitely between levels waiting for me to press a button to continue.

No, real life just moseyed on forward slow and steady and never looking back.

A scream echoed through the tunnel. I turned and found the source—the pregnant girl who looked like Kendra. "I want to go," she told the woman who knelt next to her. She had tried to stand, using the carved tunnel wall, but a contraction forced her to fall back down. She grabbed the woman kneeling over her.

"Lay back, Tracy," the kneeling woman urged the pregnant one. Then she looked up at me and said, "The baby is almost here."

Eldra knew what to do. I didn't, so even though I didn't want to, I let Eldra take over. In seconds, I had given about twenty orders to different people around me, giving them tasks to prepare for the birth that was minutes away. Nobody moved, as if not sure whether to obey my orders or not.

"Listen to him!" Ariel shouted from Fern's body. After that, nobody questioned my orders. Even the nine remaining vampires joined in to follow my demands. Clean rags appeared, as did a blanket for the mother and a smaller one for the baby when it arrived. Someone brought a king-sized comforter for her and we quickly lifted the pregnant woman onto it. Another delivered a pair of scissors after using their Zippo lighter to sanitize the blades. One woman handed me a small, metal hair barrette. At some point, the bucket of boiling water showed up. I tossed the barrette into it. An adjustable lamp turned on, providing a six-foot circle of bright light around the pregnant woman.

"Next contraction, breathe like this," I demonstrated Lamaze, the breathing taught to ease the pain during childbirth. "Don't push yet," I told her. "I need to check the baby's position and your cervix dilation." I opened a pack of sanitizing wet wipes.

"You look like a kid—ahhhhh!" the soon-to-be mother ended her sentence with a scream.

"Guide her breathing," I assigned the woman who held her hand. "What is your name?" I asked. Using the wet wipes, I began sanitizing from my elbows to my fingertips.

Tracy didn't answer but instead glanced at the woman who held her hand.

"She's Tracy. I'm Jen."

I eased my hands under Tracy's skirt, but she caught one wrist. Her pained eyes looked at me doubtfully. Jen's look held the same doubt.

"I have over a century of experience as a midwife," I answered.

Tracy didn't release her grip on my wrist, and her doubt didn't leave her eyes. Jen shook her head at me.

Ariel—in Fern's body—put her hand on my shoulder.

"Get her away from us!" Tracy shouted, fear in her eyes as she looked up at Ariel, who wore Fern's face.

"She's not the redheaded demon," Jen assured her. "You saw," she added but stopped. "What is she?"

"He may look it, but he's not a monster," Ariel came to my aid, ignoring the woman's question.

I'd almost forgotten that I wasn't Eldra. I was just a seventeen-year-old with a shredded leather shirt. Of course, that left my hideous skin exposed. My face probably looked cringe-worthy, too. It hadn't even occurred to me they would assume I was a monster.

Ariel's words hadn't convinced the two women, so she added. "How old a person looks doesn't mean much down here, does it?" Had Ariel told the pregnant woman that I was only seventeen and that my century of experience happened in a less-than-a-second download, like the Matrix, only with magic, Tracy might not have released my wrist.

"I'm just going to check how close the baby is." I moved my freed hand slowly, trying not to frighten the soon-to-be mother. A few seconds later, I'd finished checking her. "You're already dilated to ten centimeters. You're minutes away. The baby's crowning. Thank heavens it's not breach."

I grabbed Tracy's legs and adjusted them. I lifted her left leg and stretched it up, then over and away from her body in an arc— a midwife trick to help open the pelvis. Then I did the same with the right leg.

"Boy or girl?" I asked.

Tracy clenched her jaw. She couldn't speak, so she answered by shaking her head.

"She doesn't know," Jen added.

I pressed my hands against Tracy's lower back. "I'm going to adjust your spine—"

"Ahhhhhh-eeeeee," Tracy screamed in my face as a contraction squeezed painfully around her extruding womb.

"—so the baby isn't injured when you push."

After adjusting Tracy's position, I massaged her cervix to give it a bit more stretch and find any tight spot where it might tear. With the leg adjustments and the massage, I'd done as much as any ordinary midwife could do to minimize tearing. However, I was far from ordinary. I still had one more trick.

"Next contraction, I want you to push the baby out." I placed her hands on top of her belly. "Push here with your hands." I turned my head and shouted to those around me, "Where are the warm, wet rags?"

The next contraction came on strong. "Push," I reminded. The mother pushed with her whole body. Magic trickled from me on instinct, moving into her cervix and urging Tracy's flesh to stretch without ripping. I guided the tiny head out with my hands, but the baby's shoulders got caught. The contraction ended. I quickly checked for shoulder dystocia, which could happen if the shoulders caught on the pubic bone. Pushing could then break the baby's collar bone. But they hadn't caught on the pubic bone; they'd just caught going through the cervix.

"The head's out," I explained. "One more push—not yet—to free the shoulders," I coached the woman. The next contraction came extra early, only about twenty seconds later. She pushed. I reached into the cervix, gripping the baby's chest and back with my fingertips, and guided the shoulders out, carefully protecting the collarbones.

The baby came out covered in vernix caseosa, which reminded me of baby Ariel, ripping out of Jié Shù's body just a few hours ago. This birth was far more natural, thank heavens.

"It's a girl," I spoke with a weird, high voice, trying to force happiness into my tone. "Don't cut the cord yet," I stopped the blonde vampire, who seemed overly excited with the scissors. "Warm rag," I held out a hand, and somebody put a warm rag in it. I wiped the baby's eyes clean. I put my pinky into the baby's mouth and cleaned it out. Then I pressed my lips to the baby's and exhaled, filling the baby's lungs.

The baby didn't breathe. I surrounded the baby's lungs with magic and nudged them to exhale. Then I spread the magic inside the lungs and nudged them to inhale. I only nudged, careful not to breathe for the baby but to help just enough to remind her to breathe on her own. It worked. The baby girl inhaled twice before she wailed in short bursts.

"Let's get this baby on your bare chest," I suggested to the new mother. "Help her unbutton the dress," I ordered Jen, who obeyed. She let go of Tracy's hand and undid the buttons at the back of Tracy's dress. The new mother didn't hesitate to pull her dress down to her waist, not caring that many vampires and former thralls remained to see her bare chest. Her breasts had swelled from milk, so any guy would have ogled those breasts regardless of the circumstances. Something about the scene made me shake my head. I found myself staring. I felt confused. Looking around, I noticed that all of us remaining were women anyway.

I snapped out of my momentary confusion and laid the baby down on its stomach between Tracy's breasts. Whatever had caused my confusion, it was gone now.

"It's not over," I told the mother. "In another minute or two, we'll cut the umbilical cord, then help you expel the afterbirth."

The next half hour went by so quickly. The vampire with long, straight blonde hair, the one who had agreed to try to change her ways, cut the umbilical cord on my order. I said nothing when she sucked the dripping blood from the mother's end of the umbilical cord, even though it caught me off guard. I clipped the end of the baby's cord closed with the metal barrette that had been sanitized in the boiling water.

I helped the mother expel the afterbirth into a white plastic garbage bag. Others in the room helped give the baby and mother a full sponge bath before assisting her into a clean dress. There were no diapers, so I wrapped cloths as diapers around the baby girl before swaddling her.

"Thank you so much," Tracy gushed at me. "What's your name?"

"Eldra Locksley," I answered. Ariel looked at me quizzically with her now lavender eyes that didn't match Fern's face.

"Maybe I'll name her Eldra," the mother said.

"You don't have to, dear. That is an old name that nobody uses anymore." I smiled comfortingly at the new mother. "Pick a name that you love."

Ariel's quizzical look remained.

"Eldra is a strange name," a soft woman's voice spoke behind me.

I turned and found the blonde vampire with long straight hair with Jace standing in front of a group of about fifteen thralls.

"We collected all of them that we could find."

As I wrapped my everything-seal around them, I scanned their faces. Three were men and the rest were women. One of them looked so very much like Alexis. She held her head down, causing her straight, shoulder-length hair to cover her face. The moment my everything-seal set them free, she looked up.

"Gina?"

"She was in a cell," Jace explained. "Angeline found her."

Gina looked untouched.

"Nobody fed on me," she looked at me. She didn't have the confidence she'd always had.

"Master King planned to put her in The Cage as soon as he finished his duel with Princess Alexis," Jace explained.

"Thank you, Angeline," I nodded.

I stepped forward to hug Gina, but she looked at me, covered in blood and afterbirth, took a step back, and shook her head.

Twenty minutes later, I had cleaned up with soap and some warm wet rags. A vampire brought me a gray V-neck to change into, as my shirt was covered in afterbirth. It was a little after 5:30 A.M. I stood outside of the White House and watched the sunrise with 227 people whose freedom I'd restored. Or 228 if I included the newborn baby girl.

I picked up my phone to dial Robin, only to see the single-letter names in my contact list. Why wasn't Robin's number in my phone? Because he was dead, and so was I. My world rocked. My head spun. I found myself on the ground. Ariel and Gina helped me to my feet. Ariel picked up my phone. I wasn't a two-hundred-year-old woman. I was a seventeen-year-old boy. I almost remembered that I was Jake, but Eldra's two-hundred years of life quickly dominated my mind again.

Ariel clicked K to dial Kendra, then clicked the camera icon to make it a video call, pointing the screen toward me.

Even though she'd dialed Kendra's phone, Lexy answered on the first ring and said, "If you are not dead, I am going to kill you."

"Not if I kill him first," Kendra's muffled shout made came through.

"He helped a mother give birth," Ariel explained. "Eldra took over. He needs help."

CHAPTER 39
ROADBLOCK

We survived. At least, for now. Master King's challenge still hangs over us. Alexis will have to face him on All Soul's Day. For a short time, I'd thought we'd lost Ariel, but we didn't. I'd lost hope that Kendra would survive, but she did. Thank Heavens. We are still reeling from Eldra's death; I'm not sure we could have recovered from another devastating loss. I am so excited to get home without a tragedy. —Jake

I could see Lexy on the phone's screen. She stopped pacing and walked from the desk in her hotel room to sit next to Kendra on their shared hotel bed. Had they gotten any sleep? Kendra leaned close to Alexis so both their faces could be seen on the video call. Kendra wanted to get dressed and come join Ariel and me, but they had already tried to follow me last night. The oath magic had forced them to stop three miles away.

Ariel gave Kendra and Lexy a thirty-second CliffsNotes version of the events that took place the past few hours, including telling them we'd found Gina. When she explained that I had said my name was Eldra, Kendra and Lexy's eyes widened with concern.

"Jake, tap off the separation stone?" Kendra suggested.

Ariel, still in Fern's body, tried to convince me to listen to Kendra, but the Eldra-me didn't want to. Coyote's granddaughter argued with the Eldra-me for a minute before she tapped the separation stone at my neck herself. Ariel was part Jié Shù, who had access to a small amount of magic, which she pushed into the separation stone. It worked. Immediately, Kendra came to my aid mentally.

I tried to tap it back on, but Ariel grabbed my hand and shook her head. Something scary in her demanding lavender eyes on Fern's face convinced me to obey her.

330

Let me try this time, Lexy demanded. She brought up her memories of Jake and started going through them. She remembered the first time she saw him, driving past him on a motorcycle as he was fleeing transients in O'Brien's old pickup truck. Then she arrived to find him unconscious after having erased the nightwalker.

Maybe try to focus only on safe, happy memories, Kendra suggested.

After the nightwalker, Lexy had brought Jake to her mansion. He'd woken locked in chains. They'd dined together, watched fireworks together and created the healing and protection stone together—where they had joined minds. Kendra couldn't hide how those thoughts made her jealous. Alexis continued, but after that, she had betrayed Jake. Most of the rest of her thoughts included battles so vicious Eldra had given them epic names. She found a few more memories, but then she ran out.

Thanks, Lexy, Kendra mocked. *You shared two minutes' worth of memories, half of which gave Jake his PTSD.*

Lexy snapped back at Kendra, mentally calling her derogatory names, but Kendra was right. Lexy had only known Jake for three weeks and most of their shared memories were traumatic.

Alexis pushed away her pride and let Kendra relive her shared past with me, trying to push Eldra's memories to the back of my mind so I could be me again. Lexy's jealously faded. Both girls now sat up against the wall of their shared queen hotel bed, the blanket over their legs. They mentally tried to help from where they were. This time, Kendra's mental therapy had little effect. She tried other memories from various ages to no avail. I wasn't Jake. I was Eldra, so those memories had no meaning. Kendra didn't stop. She pushed harder, with more memories. I could sense Jacob's mind—my mind—closer but still distant. The therapy just couldn't quite push Eldra away. Seeing an ounce of progress, Kendra continued, but the progress stopped, and Eldra's mind remained in place.

I tapped my separation stone, not wanting two teenage girls' weird behavior in my head.

Ariel took the phone. "Whatever you are doing isn't working. We need mass transportation to send the freed kenzies home," she said, reminding me that we had work to do.

"Did you ask the V.I.T. for help?" Lexy questioned.

I hadn't. But it was a good idea, if they were still around.

We got started. We needed mass transportation, just not in the way of busses. In under one hour, the various ride-sharing apps took care of everyone who lived in a fifty-mile radius. The V.I.T. couldn't come outside into the dawn light. Still, they had phones with apps, too, and helped from the safety of the tunnels. The nine vampires who'd once backed Fern, but now chose to obey my laws, also helped. They even paid their share.

A surprised driver took Tracy and her new baby girl to what Alexis said was the highest-rated labor and delivery hospital in Las Vegas. I disagreed that she even needed a hospital. As an expert midwife, I'd made sure she was stable. Lexy had never had a child, whereas I'd birthed eleven. She didn't know what a woman needed after giving birth, and since dhampirs can't have children, she never would. However, since Alexis convinced the hospital to send the bill to Master King, I let it go. No use arguing with a teen know-it-all.

After the locals were taken care of, Lexy, Kendra, Gina, and I spent another two hours arranging bus tickets and flights. Of course, the ride-sharing apps helped again, getting the people to either the bus station or the airport. Alexis spent well over a hundred thousand dollars.

While we spent hours arranging transportation, Ariel used Fern's room in the White House to shower and change. She changed more than her clothes. She returned as a nine-year-old with her usual lavender hair and eyes, wearing what looked like should have been a stretchy dance club dress on Fern but hung loosely around her petite, nine-year-old frame. She'd tied the shoulder straps into bows to lift the dress higher on her torso. Much of the dress—the back and around her stomach—was mesh, but it covered her enough. I pressed my lips together flatly as I looked at her. Why did she keep going back to being a child?

Gina, Ariel, and I caught a ride with the last thrall to the Porsche. As I started to drive, Ariel called Alexis.

"We are out. We're safe," she told Alexis. I couldn't hear the other side of the conversation. "Well, yes, Eldra is driving," Ariel added. "That will have to wait until the hotel." She hung up.

"They are happy to hear we are on our way. They are going to shower and pack," Ariel relayed to us.

I was surprised that it was only around ten-thirty when we arrived back at the hotel. We'd been up all night. My tired old bones would be exhausted for days.

Ariel held Gina's hand as they followed me through the flashy, loud, smoke-scented casino floors to the hotel room. I opened the door to find one bed had been slept in, the other hadn't been touched. We had been in a rush, so there was no luggage. I didn't have anything here. I'd stayed with Robin here at the Stratosphere maybe fifteen years ago. I wished he were with me now.

Ariel and Gina followed me inside. The ancient little girl knocked on the door that connected the adjoining room. In seconds, it opened. Kendra stood there with wet, half-brushed hair and wearing a cheap gray V-neck poorly pleated between her breasts over Walmart jeans. Her feet were bare. Even with healing magic, the bruise on her face would last a few days.

"You're back." Kendra's pursed lips proved that she'd had time since Ariel called for her relief to turn into anger. I expected a reprimand as she limped toward me. Instead, she surprised me with a hug. I hugged back. Confusingly, her body felt good pressing against mine. She reached her hands up and undid the clasp at the back of my neck, and when she pulled away, she took the separation stone with her. Her mind joined mine, but Lexy's didn't. Kendra didn't put on the separation stone, but instead slipped the necklace into her pocket. She still wore Jake's pendant around her neck.

Jake? Kendra pushed a memory from our childhood at me.

I—Eldra—pushed away her attempts to bring Jake—me—back. I wanted the separation stone back, but I'd given it to Kendra, and I didn't feel right to take it back.

Kendra turned and gingerly hugged Gina, too. Gina's eyes widened, and it took her a second to hug back.

"I'm glad you're safe," Kendra said, then turned to hug Ariel. She stroked the ancient little girl's long lavender hair twice as if she really were the nine-year-old she looked like.

Gina walked over to the bed that hadn't been slept in and lay down on it. Resting sounded great to me. I could take the other bed.

Kendra grabbed my hand and pulled me toward her hotel room. I didn't go and her hand caught. She pulled again, this time with more force. Before I could stiffen, Ariel grabbed my other hand and helped pull, so I followed. She shut the door behind me.

"Sit," Kendra pointed at the closest queen bed. Light escaped from the crack between the carpet and the closed bathroom door, as did the hum of the shower.

"You know you are Jake, right?" Kendra pushed a movie montage of memories at me. For the next five minutes, she forced her memories of her and Jake at me. She took me through dozens of memories of the two of them growing up. Then she focused on the memories earlier this summer and her efforts to get Jake to date her.

I shook my head. The center of my thoughts felt certain I was Eldra but the edges blurred in a confused haze. I'd lived for two hundred years. Five minutes of someone else's memories weren't going to affect me. If I still had my own separation stone, I could shut Kendra out.

Kendra gave up. She couldn't fix Jake. Her eyes watered as she began to fear that my being Eldra was permanent. I patted her shoulder consolingly while assuring her that it was indeed permanent.

The door to the bathroom opened and out walked Lexy.

With Kendra's efforts to push the memories she shared with Jake into my mind, neither of us had heard the shower turn off. Kendra had meant to warn Lexy that Jake was in the room, so she didn't walk out indecent in front of Jake.

Too late.

Lexy had a towel wrapped around her head, a separation stone around her neck, and black lacy bottoms. Nothing else.

I pursed my lips flat. "Put some clothes on, girl!" I said in a tone that, despite being Jake's voice, had my—Eldra's—tone.

Kendra's mouth dropped open. She looked from Jake to Lexy and back. Lexy glared at me for a second, then cocked an eyebrow at Kendra, who pointed at her separation stone. Lexy tapped the separation stone between her breasts, and she joined Kendra and my mind, with Eldra's memories in control.

Kendra hadn't intended for Jake to see Lexy in a topless state, but it happened. Remembering how he'd been saved by boobs before, she hoped the sight would knock Eldra to the back of Jake's mind.

It didn't work, Kendra sighed, and her shoulders slumped. Tears spilled. One tear dripped down her bruised cheek.

I stood there with flat lips and a scowl. I could see myself through both Lexy and Kendra's eyes. I knew I was in Jake's body, but I was Eldra. I didn't have my short grandma body, my wrinkles, or my gray braid, but my splotchy skin made me just as intimidating.

Lexy's eyes lowered from my face to my neck, then she grinned. *I can fix this,* she assured Kendra. *Did I not promise I would take the next turn?* Pumpkin spice filled the room, strong and thick. The hazy edges pressed against Eldra's control, weakening her and strengthening Jake as Lexy stepped toward him.

Kendra had two simultaneous and contradictory thoughts, *Oh, no!* and *Please work.* The juxtaposition of her religious morals and her hope to bring Jake back.

Lexy sauntered over and stopped in front of me. She grabbed my hand and lifted it, pulling me up and off the bed.

My mind went blank. I wasn't Eldra or Jake. I was Lexy's. Without my protection stone, her allure took over.

Lexy lifted my hand and placed it on her breast. Then she leaned forward and kissed me.

Kendra winced as she watched. Both jealous and hopeful at the same time, while feeling guilty for being hopeful as the scene in front of her conflicted with her religious beliefs. Beliefs, which at the moment, hindered her ability to help me. What if Lexy weren't here? Kendra would have to choose between her beliefs and saving Jake. What would she choose? She'd save Jake, of course. Didn't Jesus promise forgiveness for any sin? Whereas she'd never forgive herself if she didn't save Jake.

My other hand reached around Lexy to pull her close as I kissed her. The passion increased. The kiss continued until I didn't even notice Kendra in my mind or even in the room.

Lexy pulled her lips from mine and pushed me away.

"Hi, Jake," Lexy smiled.

I leaned forward to kiss her again, but she put out a hand to stop me.

"Welcome back," she greeted. Lexy turned to Kendra, still holding me in place with her left hand. "Did you notice that when I made that move on Jake, you were in the room with me?" Her smile turned mischievous. "See, I saved Jake with boobs while you and I were in the same room. Unlike you, I stayed within the rules of our pact."

Kendra's mouth opened and then closed. Guilt spilled into her reprimanded mind.

Lexy raised her eyebrows at Kendra. "If we put the pact back in place, can you make it a day without breaking it again?"

Kendra nodded as her thoughts promised to do her best.

"Pinky promise?" Lexy offered Kendra her pinky. It seemed childish, but Kendra laughed and locked her pinky in Lexy's. "Excellent. The pact is restored. You can give him memory therapy as often as you want. Now," Lexy's smile turned mischievous, "how does it feel to know Jake has now been to second base with two girls, and neither one of them were you?" Lexy turned to kiss me again.

Kendra sucked in an offended breath. "Oh, no, you don't!" She grabbed the towel on Lexy's head and pulled her back, yanking the towel off. She grabbed Lexy and tackled her onto the bed.

They landed laughing more than fighting as Kendra covered Lexy with the towel.

Someone shouted in the adjacent room, interrupting the girls' playful catfight.

"What the hell is *she* doing in your hotel room, Luiz!" Andrea's voice carried loudly through the closed doorway between the rooms.

Lexy sat up on the bed and pushed me toward the door. "Help him."

Ariel beat me to the door and opened it. I followed. Andrea, eyes thinned and teeth clenched, gripped Luiz's shirt. Luiz looked away from Andrea into Kendra's and Lexy's room.

Andrea shook him, "Don't you look away from me. I . . ." she stopped as her eyes followed Luiz's. Lexy's pumpkin spice allure was still at full strength. It affected them both as much as it affected me. Except Luiz looked away from Lexy. He turned back to Andrea and focused on her, touching the ring I'd given him, which glowed a little brighter than normal. He waited as Andrea stood mesmerized as Lexy dressed while her allure dissipated.

As the allure wore off, Andrea came to. Seeing Luiz looking at her eyes instead of Lexy or Gina calmed her down significantly.

Once everyone had regained their self-control—Kendra gave me back my red ruby protection stone—things calmed down.

Still, Andrea did not seem pleased to meet Gina. Had Luiz told her?

I filled Luiz in on all that had happened, including all the joke opportunities he'd missed out on.

Luiz and Andrea had already packed and had just come back to tell us they were heading out in the Porsche.

The rest of us didn't have much to pack. We gathered everyone and made our way to the SUV shortly after. Mr. Espinoza was already asleep in his coffin, anchored with straps to the roof rack on the SUV and wrapped in a tarp to look like luggage. Gina took the front passenger seat of the SUV. Ariel and Maria took the seat in the far back. I lay across the middle seat, my head in Kendra's lap. Kendra had slept with Lexy's healing stone, but since it was daytime, Lexy had needed it back.

At three this afternoon, I had football practice and the girls had drill team. Kendra was adamant that we couldn't miss a third drill team practice in a row and that she could deal with her injuries. She had drunk two healing vials and had eaten two breakfasts while waiting for me to return. Alexis drove, claiming that she could get us back in time so we wouldn't miss a third practice. Did she know how fast she'd have to drive?

About two minutes into the drive, Lexy got a phone call. It was Jody. Lexy let Kendra and me listen in with the Trinity of Mind.

"First your Bishop, now missionaries?" Jody complained with her southern accent. "They've been here since ten, hoping y'all would show up."

Kendra giggled, but giggling hurt her ribs, so she forced away her mirth.

"Please tell them I will have to reschedule," Lexy suggested.

"Will do."

I took a minute to try to call my sister but got her voicemail. Of course, she had been arrested and wouldn't have access to her phone. I didn't even know if she was in jail or juvenile detention. Alexis called Mr. Brandt and set up an appointment for us to meet with Sis after practice. I had stayed up all night and used a ton of magic, so despite my concern, I fell asleep shortly after she hung up.

I found myself sitting in the Lost Rhoades mine, my back against the cavern wall. Bear walked up to me. He still looked like a hybrid between Sir Alfred Tennyson and a Native American. He noticed me eyeing his new look. "Am I ready to give up rhyme? Maybe, but perfecting verse will take more time."

I shrugged, not prepared with a rhyme to respond.

"I expected a bloodbath, and the news to show the aftermath."

I didn't tell Bear that the desire to erase Master King's shiver had simmered inside me like a volcano about to explode. I could have unleashed my addiction on the shiver. I might have died trying to kill them all. Instead, I'd only used my soul-erasing magic missile twice. If I had used it more, I probably would have lost control and never stopped.

"I decided to give the vampires a chance to live," I rhymed. "If they kill, and some will"—in my dream, the silhouette of a male vampire feeding from the neck of a female (a total stereotype) smoked to life to the right of us—"I'll add them to my list, find them, and clench my fist." I held my hand up so he could see my fingernails biting into my palm as the heart burned out of the silhouette's chest.

"You think all vampires can choose? I disagree, but it's your life to lose," Bear shrugged.

"Not all of them will succeed. The rest, their last drop they will bleed." That was twice now that I'd stolen Keagan's line.

Bear nodded, smiling at my rhyme. The two women he'd rescued in Las Vegas appeared near him, one on each side. He kissed each on the cheek, then turned back to me.

"You still have my golden ring. As a second thanks, another you can bring."

With that, Bear and his two women faded away.

The SUV jerked to a stop, waking me. I sat up. I still felt exhausted, so we couldn't have been driving long.

"It's a roadblock," Alexis informed me.

Flashing lights lit up I-15 a half-mile ahead. All the cars were forced to merge to a single lane. All the vehicles were forced to stop. A police officer on a motorcycle drove by us on the shoulder. He seemed to be checking each vehicle and his eyes lingered at the top of our SUV, no doubt noticing the tarp-covered coffin latched to the luggage rack.

Traffic started moving faster as the officers at the front of the roadblock started waving vehicles through without checking them. Traffic flowed through at a steady fifteen-mile-an-hour pace until we reached the front of the line.

The officer held up his hands for us to stop.

Just ahead of us, the road curved to the right, wrapping around a dry, rocky hill. We couldn't see much past the roadblock. The officer held us in place for about two minutes. Then he motioned for us to continue.

Just as we rounded the rocky hill, Lexy's emotions sent out warning signals. I sat up and leaned between the two front seats. The officer had allowed only our car through. He stopped the car immediately after us. A police pickup pulled onto the road and followed a distance behind us. Had we intentionally been isolated?

The road wrapped around a second rocky hill to the northeast, so we could only see a quarter mile in either direction. Four unmarked, desert-camouflage Humvees pulled around the hill in front of us, driving the wrong way on I-15. Alexis pulled to a stop.

The officer in the pickup behind us also stopped. He stepped down out of his truck. He wore a cowboy hat, and the gray hair under it put him in his sixties. He grabbed a spike strip from the back. He tossed it onto the road behind our vehicle. Those spikes would destroy our tires.

"¡Ay, Dios mío!" Maria exclaimed and ducked down next to Gina.

There was no doubt about it now. This roadblock had been prepared especially for us. Why? And more importantly, who? I leaned further forward between the front seats, over the center console, trying to decide what to do about the approaching Humvees.

Alexis let go of the steering wheel with her right hand and grabbed my left wrist, digging her fingernails into my skin.

"Ow!" I pulled my wrist away.

She broke my skin. Thank goodness she didn't have claws.

Your Flesh of Steel has worn off, Alexis confirmed.

What's happening? Kendra worried. *Skull Shadows?*

It is possible, Alexis answered. But to her, a public roadblock didn't feel like a tactic they'd use.

Ariel dove over the back seat and opened the right passenger door. She hurried out and rushed to the front of the vehicle. She hoped that by putting her nine-year-old body in front of us, they would hesitate to shoot. Just as she rounded the front of our SUV, a soldier dressed to match the sand-camouflaged Humvees stood up with a heavy-looking machine gun and directed it at our car. From each of the other three military vehicles, a similar soldier with a similarly sizeable automatic assault rifle stood up. The first soldier held up his fist and then put a hand to his ear and began talking. Looking directly at Ariel.

Ariel risked her life to buy us however many seconds we needed. If they fired, could she protect her lifeforce? Not from four large assault rifles. She'd almost died that night in O'Brien's hospital bed when the special bone structure protecting her lifeforce had been hit by one bullet. These were military-grade assault rifles. If one of these rounds hit her lifeforce, the bone-constructed protection wouldn't stop it.

Could I protect her? Could I stop the bullets? My first thought was to push bulletproof magic into her mesh dress. But when Alexis had used the bulletproof spell on her mesh shirt, a simple handgun bullet had gone right through it. No, that spell wouldn't work for Ariel. Could I push the bullets? Could I alter their trajectory so that they missed her?

For the first time in a while, a Caradoc memory popped into my head. It was well-timed.

Caradoc crouched low in a trench with a bunch of green-helmeted soldiers. A dead body lay to his right. Another soldier, clearly in the same platoon, held the body, crying over him. I looked through Caradoc's eyes with concern. By druid law, he could not interfere by choosing sides in World War II, but he wasn't here to choose between the Axis and the Allies. He came to save lives on both sides. The war had ended in many places. Even as he crouched in the deep ditch, the Allies stormed Berlin where they would find and capture Hitler—if the Third Reich leader let himself be captured alive. He hadn't.

Caradoc pulled magic into himself, grabbed the dirt at the top of the trench, and scrambled up, thinking, *No more lives need be lost today.*

"Bewarian byre," Caradoc spoke the Old English words calmly, releasing the magic. The words roughly translated to *protective wind.*

The first bullet whizzed by his shoulder. The next bullet passed high above his head. Another curved into the dirt to his left. Bullet after bullet sought him, yet none of them hit him. A shell launched at Caradoc. He looked up at it. It curved unnaturally to his right and fell harmlessly a dozen yards away.

"Onswiðlic." A second magic spell spread from his body and vibrated in the air, augmenting the volume of his voice. "The war is over," Caradoc spoke. With the voice spell, everyone within two miles heard him as if he had spoken in their ears.

The memory ended.

The police officer from the pickup came around the front of our SUV and tried to grab Ariel. He stood tall and the sun reflected off a star on his cowboy hat. She dodged him easily. He reached for her again, but she slipped past him again. Ariel squealed, pretending to be a little girl.

On the Cowboy Cop's third attempt, he grabbed Ariel, wrapping his arms around her and lifting her off the ground. He carried her to the right of the SUV, clearing the path between the assault rifles and us.

Ariel's face changed. She wanted to pretend to be a little girl, but an ancient being like her, so used to being the alpha predator in any situation, couldn't be held back. She grabbed his forearm and broke it. The officer dropped Ariel as he cried out in pain. His cowboy hat fell off, exposing a full head of silver hair.

"She's not human," the aged officer slurred through clenched teeth. He unsnapped a gun on his hip. The four men standing up out of the Humvees turned their assault rifles toward Ariel.

"Bewarian byre," I spoke Caradoc's spell.

The four soldiers pulled their triggers. The sound of a dozen rounds per second ripped loudly through the SUV. The vehicle only slightly muffled the loud rounds. The bullets slipped by Ariel, just missing her. The officer in the cowboy hat lifted his handgun with his one good arm and fired. The spell curved the 45-caliber bullet to Ariel's right and directed it at the passenger window. The bullet hit the glass inches from Gina's face.

Startled, Gina reacted with a short, high-pitched squeal.

The bullet left a distinct chip in the glass, and a long crack formed. The passenger window glass was more bullet resistant than bulletproof. It wouldn't survive many direct hits. Fortunately, it was a side window.

Maria started praying Hail Marys in Spanish from the back. We could use a prayer right now. What was it Kendra's mom had told her? "If you didn't pray, then you haven't tried everything." *Pray away for us, Maria*, I thought.

The soldiers stopped shooting at Ariel, unsure why they missed so horribly. Fortunately, none of those oversized military assault rifle bullets hit our SUV. I doubted the bulletproof windshield could stop even one of those bullets.

Ariel rushed to the SUV, opened the door, and slipped inside. "I tried."

Someone is giving them orders. Lexy's enhanced hearing could almost make out the words spoken over the communication devices in their ears.

"Permission to destroy with collateral damage?" One of the soldiers spoke into his comlink.

Alexis tried but couldn't make out the response, but she didn't need to because the soldier repeated it. "You heard him, men. D.S.S. approval granted."

The four assault rifles turned back to the SUV and fired.

My magic pushed the bullets, but not far enough. A bullet hit the very left side of the windshield and shattered through it, hitting Alexis in the left shoulder. With no bulletproof spell on her leather bustier, her shoulder screamed in pain. Another bullet hit the right side of the passenger seat where Gina had been, but seeing them about to shoot us, she'd ducked down below the dash.

A crack sounded above the SUV as Mr. Espinoza's coffin took a hit.

I can't push the bullets far enough.

Alexis pushed her magic into me. Kendra did too. The magic augmented far beyond what three people could cast alone—the synergy of the Trinity of Mind. The next burst of bullets spread out further. None even came close to the SUV. The officer in the cowboy hat stood in the wrong place. His torso ripped open as three massive rounds cut him down.

The intense power of the Trinity of Mind flowed through us. It clarified our minds and gave us focus. Everything seemed possible with the three of us in sync, working together. Why hadn't we been able to do this during Kendra's fight in The Cage? Of course, there had been an oath preventing us from helping Kendra, not to mention we'd vastly underestimated Kendra, doubting her ability to survive. Our doubt had been just as debilitating as the oath magic. We should have never trusted our doubts; we should have hoped and trusted our hope.

The camouflaged men stopped shooting. The leader shouted into his comms, "Officer Smith is down. Friendly fire. Ricochet or something."

At least they admitted immediately that it had been from friendly fire. Of course, my spell, not a ricochet, was to blame for the bullets hitting the old man.

"Negative, on the airstrike, sir. They haven't returned fire," the leader added.

My eyes widened at the thought of an airstrike. If the massive bullets hadn't proved how serious this was, their ability to call in an airstrike did.

"Ariel, get us that communication device from his ear," Alexis ordered her. "Kill no one."

Ariel glared at her, clearly not willing to be bossed around, even in a time like this.

"Please?" I added on Lexy's behalf.

"I want her to say it," her nine-year-old, melodic voice sounded far too calm.

"Please," Alexis offered.

"Wait," I stopped her. "She doesn't need it." Caradoc had already given me the spell to solve this problem.

"*Onswiðlic!*" I pushed the magic not only into the nearby attackers but also into the dead officer's comlink. I modified the spell to also relay to me any response from his earpiece. The modification should have been difficult, like solving a day-long calculus problem, but with the Trinity of Mind, the three of us made the alteration instantly.

We need to use the Trinity of Mind like this more often, Kendra suggested.

Quit tapping out of my mind, then.

What about bathroom breaks? Showering? Kendra countered, grinning. Who did she think she was, making a joke at a time like this? Luiz?

Discuss this later! Alexis interrupted with her order.

Yes, Princess, both Kendra and I mocked her title simultaneously.

Alexis ignored us and addressed our attackers. "Danite Secret Seventy." She waited for a second, but there was no response. "Cease this breach of the V. V. Treaty, and we will let you live." Again, she waited.

"What breach is that?" an older man's smooth voice responded over the coms. "You are the only one whose actions have breached the treaty. You're not welcome in Utah."

"Oh, but I am," Alexis replied. "The Joan of Arc addendum—"
"You are not Joan of Arc, and her addendum is for a dhampir. You are only half-dhampir," the aged man's voice responded. "Your inclusion is debatable."

Alexis shook her head, tossing her now shoulder-length hair side-to-side. That wasn't true and we all knew it. "Being only half dhampir increases my inclusion. Even if not, section 7.1 allows me the freedom to live inside Utah. I have chosen Jake and Kendra as my family."

"You have no living family," the D.S.S. leader's voice hardened, making it sound older. "You'd have to marry Jacob Stevens to be his family."

"Wouldn't our engagement suffice?" Alexis added.

Knowing that Alexis had cleverly used a question to avoid outright lying did not quell Kendra's rage. *You are not engaged to Jake.*

You get to give him therapy. I get to pretend to be his fiancé to get out of this mess. Alexis offered Kendra the trade, her own anger rising as she reminded Kendra how she had broken their pact.

I'm not choosing either of you anytime soon, I reminded, and both of them turned their fury against me. And their background bickering had returned. The Trinity of Mind wavered. If the soldiers fired, there was no way we could come together right now with enough unison to work together as we had just done.

"You also have to live by the rules of our Church." The D.S.S. leader added. "You have already skipped an appointment with both the Bishop and the missionaries."

How does he already know about that? All three of us wondered.

"I was otherwise detained. We are rescheduling," Lexy defended.

"Miguel Espinoza left his wife and family," the aged voice explained. "Open his coffin. Let the sun take care of him, and you will be allowed back into Utah."

"That's not happening," I cut in, defending Mr. Espinoza more for Luiz's benefit than my own. A part of me agreed with the man. Something wasn't right about Luiz's dad. When I looked at all the vampires in Master King's shiver, only one, Fern, had a shattered soul. Luiz's dad had just such a shattered soul, and what that meant, I didn't know, but it scared the hell out of me.

"Jacob Stevens," the D.S.S. leader addressed me directly. "Druids inside the line might not break the treaty, but they're still not welcome. Your situation is unique. You and Kendra Duncan are quickly becoming a problem. Your membership in the Church provides you special acceptance, but that can easily be removed."

"What? Are you going to kick us out or something?"

"Excommunication is not a difficult process, young man," the aged voice threatened.

"Is he serious?" Kendra's eyes widened. To her, the Church was a critical part of her identity. For me, however, I wasn't sure how I felt about being excommunicated. Did I care? I'd been raised in the Church, but I'd never embraced it like Kendra and my sister had. Perhaps as a druid, I would be better off without the Church?

"We are going to drive home," I spoke into the comms device. "Have you noticed that we haven't fought back? We haven't returned fire." *Alexis, drive!* "Move the Humvees, or I'll erase them from existence."

Alexis put the SUV in drive but didn't accelerate beyond five miles an hour, just letting it roll slowly forward.

Kendra, Alexis, and I tried to sync the Trinity of Mind as we had before. With the girls' mental bickering, we couldn't quite reach the same level, but it was enough that when the soldiers fired more bursts, the bullets missed. A few rounds skimmed off the sides or top of the coffin with loud scratching sounds. If the coffin broke open, Mr. Espinoza would burn.

"You have three seconds to call off the SUVs before I erase them," I explained, my magic continuing to share my words with the soldiers, the old man, and anyone else on the other side of their comms. "Three."

The frantic soldiers reported that their bullets curved away and couldn't hit us. As our SUV approached, it became harder to curve aside the bullets far enough.

More bullets hit the sides of the SUV on the next round. A long crack sounded from above us as a bullet hit the coffin directly, again. Mr. Espinoza?

"Two," I counted.

The bullets stopped as the soldiers reloaded.

"One," I spoke the last number. "I'm going to erase the four Humvees now. There will be no trace of them." The addictive urge to erase the soldiers from existence ignited in me.

"We don't respond to threats," the smooth D.S.S. leader responded.

"Nobody is threatening you. You attacked us. I'm simply explaining how I'll defend."

"We are protecting our territory according to the V.V. Treaty," the old man countered.

"You are the ones in breach of the treaty," Alexis accused. "Do you really want to breach the treaty with the Princess of the New

World? With one word from me, vampires across the world will flock to this newly open territory."

"You won't be alive to do so," the smooth old voice answered.

"I won't let you harm us," I assured the leader. "If you want a threat, here is one. Kendra, Alexis, and I are going to hunt you down and erase you, so you can never have a chance to make such a poor command decision again. After you, we'll find every member of the D.S.S. and erase every last one of you."

"Or," Alexis cut in, "we drive through, unharmed, the treaty unbroken, and forget you exist." Alexis reprimanded me with a stern look. *Try not to give our enemy more of a reason to kill us.*

Seconds passed with no response. Alexis continued at about ten miles per hour.

I pushed magic into a blue-glowing ball in front of the SUV. The missile grew larger than a beach ball. Kendra and Alexis added their magic to it as well. It doubled in size.

We listened to the soldiers chattering on their coms, asking for orders, and asking what the giant blue ball was.

"It's a magic missile that will erase your very existence," I explained to the soldiers, my voice magically carrying to their ears. "It won't just erase your bodies. Your hope for an afterlife will be gone because it also erases the spirit. No heaven. No hell. It's worse. You will just be nothing. You will cease to exist."

The platoon leader ducked down into the SUV. The other soldiers followed his lead. The four Humvees split apart.

"Excellent decision making," I spoke with magic to them as Alexis hit the gas. The SUV sped up as we slipped between the armored vehicles, the massive, blue-glowing magic missile leading the way.

"Have a nice day," Kendra said as we drove past them.

We dropped the magic missile about a football field beyond the Humvees, leaving my addictive desire disappointed, but all of us safe. At least for now. The D.S.S. was sure to be a problem again in the future.

CHAPTER 40
SIS

I wasn't there when Eldra told Jake, "Neither the law nor a birthday decides when a man is a man." Eldra had been talking about Luiz, telling Jake that The Cabin Battle of Bear Lake had changed Luiz into a man. On the way home from Las Vegas, Alexis surprised me with a compliment. She said, "Neither the law nor a birthday decides when a woman is a woman. You have survived The Cabin Battle of Bear Lake, a zombie attack at Club Exposed, a kidnapping by voodoo witches, and Scarlett Rescue. Those do not compare to what you went through in The Cage. You may have only just celebrated your sixteenth birthday, but you are no longer a simple teenage girl. You are as adult as a woman can get." I reveled in the compliment until Alexis ruined it by winking at me and saying, "Of course, you're still a virgin. So I may be mistaken." She's such a brat! —Kendra

We drove without further incident. I'd erased the bullet in Lexy's shoulder, after which, both Gina and Maria donated to her a pint of their blood. Kendra stayed in my mind giving me memory therapy. While the therapy hadn't brought me back this morning, it worked well to keep Eldra's two-hundred years from taking over.

We made it to Woods Cross High School with two minutes to spare. The digital speedometer showed we'd driven at an average of 112 miles per hour on the return trip. Neither Alexis nor Kendra should have gone to practice, but Kendra was being hardheaded. She'd kept claiming she'd be fine, having taken two healing vials and sleeping with Lexy's healing stone, but she still didn't look fine. Jody met us at the school with practice clothes to change into or we would have been late.

The bullet wound in Lexy's shoulder wasn't healed, but she made it through practice with only excruciating pain. After what

Kendra had done for her, Lexy just did what Kendra asked without complaint. When the drill team saw Kendra's bruised face, they demanded to know who had hit Kendra. Alexis had to step in and help them forget and not notice.

I survived football practice without erasing Collin Jones, the annoying quarterback, despite his constant attempts to humiliate me. I didn't care. My mind was on my appointment to see Justine. The past few days had forced me to ignore Sis, and I refused to ignore her any longer.

Two hours after practice, I stood—this time not disguised—in a visiting room at the new West Jordan City Jail, hugging Sis. She wore jeans and a gray blouse, not an orange jumpsuit. The room had a round table and four chairs. It was private, though. No cameras. As a juvenile, Justine had more privileges than Mom, but on the flip side, she could only receive visits from relatives or her lawyer. Alexis had been forced to use her allure to get me a visit as I couldn't tell the police I was Jacob Stevens.

I wanted to tell Sis everything about the past few days. She was Sis. I used to share everything with her. Instead, the only thing I told her was that the past two days were hard. After that, I simply hugged her.

Ariel sat in a chair just outside the room. She still refused to leave my side, and it had taken some convincing to get her to accept being on the other side of the door from me. Kendra and Alexis spoke to Mr. Brandt in another room. They had their separation stones enabled, giving me what little privacy they could. Also, after her fight in The Cage, Kendra didn't look so good. She didn't want Sis to see her bruised face and arms. She grunted in pain with every movement and was finally admitting that drill team practice had been a terrible idea.

"I brought you an A&W Cream Soda," I popped the can open and handed it to her. The alluring aroma filled the air. Did any vampires give off cream soda as their enticing scent?

"Kevin stopped by," Sis told me. "He asked how I was holding up. He kept fishing for clues about you. I think he suspects."

"Oh, he doesn't just suspect. He knows," I chuckled. "He was probably fishing for clues as to whether you knew yet. I should have told him that you did." I grabbed the Mountain Dew I'd brought for myself, popped it open, then took a sip.

"Are you sure endangering another friend is the right thing to do?" Sis smiled flatly. Her face tightened, hinting at her disapproval.

"I didn't tell him," I pointed at myself with the Mountain Dew can. "He figured it out and called me. I tried to keep him out of it."

Sis's flat smile remained. It didn't matter to her whether I'd told him or not. If he knew I was alive, he was involved and in danger. That mattered to Sis. She cared about the jeeks. I didn't know what to say. It took her a minute before she took another sip of her cream soda.

"Kevin helped me the other day," I offered. Her smile tightened further, so I added, "On something completely non-dangerous."

"Even meeting with you is dangerous. Mom and I are in jail. We are here because of you, you know."

And there it was. I never wanted a wedge to come between Sis and me, but it had. Would Sis ever forgive me for this? What would her arrest—even if her name was cleared—do to her life? Had I tainted her life forever? I'd ruined Mom's life just by being born. I guess I just kept ruining it more.

"They are trying me as an adult." Sis's eyes watered. "My bail hearing is in the morning. Mr. Brandt says the bail should only be fifty thousand," she ran her fingers through her hair, "as if that is a small amount. Nobody I know has that kind of money."

"Actually, with a bail bond, we only have to pay about ten percent. That's only five thousand. Almost everyone you know has that kind of money. Not that it matters. Your bail is covered."

"About that," Sis thinned her green eyes at me, "what is the deal with you and Alexis?"

"I, uh," I had no answer to her question. How could I answer a question that I didn't even know the answer to myself?

"I thought you and Kendra would," Sis shrugged, "you know."

"Kendra and I are still very close," I assured.

"But this Alexis girl is getting in the way," Sis shook her head.

"The three of us . . ." I started, "you know. The Trinity of Mind thing," I reminded her without explaining it again.

"I just thought you and Kendra would get married."

I chuckled and took a drink of Mountain Dew.

"After your mission, of course," Sis added.

I choked on my Mountain Dew and nearly spit it out onto the floor. She'd hinted at me going on a church mission before, but I'd always blown her off. Now, how could she be serious? I wasn't even sure how I felt about the Church now that I knew it had a secret society that had been willing to kill me. That wasn't something I was about to tell Sis, but add that to the fact that I was a protector and a druid—if unofficially—and giving up two years of my life to proselyte as a missionary for The Church of Jesus Christ of Latter-day Saints wasn't at the top of my to-do list.

"Don't react like that," Sis's stern voice grated. "I just thought," she looked at my hideous face, then down my scrawny body, "now that college football isn't an option . . ." She didn't finish and just left it hanging there, her disappointment evident on her frowning face.

I took a sip of Mountain Dew. "I'll think about it," I lied, pounding the wedge between Sis and me a little deeper. "I went to church last Sunday," I offered, trying to change the subject and reinforce my lie at the same time.

"Did Kendra have to drag you?" Sis saw right through me.

I shrugged.

"How's Mom?" I changed the subject completely this time.

"In jail," Sis snapped, clearly not finishing her thought. In my mind, I heard her finish with, "because of you." Instead, she paused for a second then added. "Didn't Mr. Brandt tell you?"

"No, what?"

"Her bail hearing happened yesterday. Brandt fought hard and talked the judge down from one million to half a million. Mr. Brandt doesn't think he can win unless . . ." she again didn't finish her sentence.

"Unless what?" I asked.

"Unless a miracle occurs," Justine answered. "A miracle that isn't going to happen."

Mr. Brandt had surely told Alexis that same information by now. I almost wished the girls' separation stones weren't blocking out their minds. I took a long swig, finishing my Mountain Dew and throwing the tin can at the wastebasket. I missed.

I knew a miracle that could occur. I could tell everyone I was alive. Perhaps that was what Justine meant?

"We are going to get you and Mom out," I promised. I didn't want it to be a lie, but it probably was one. Donaldson wanted something from us. Perhaps he could undo the damage he had done in framing my mother and my sister. We had a meeting with him soon.

I stayed with Justine until a security guard forced us to leave. Even then, I hugged her for a long time, hoping in vain for the wedge between us to dissolve. It didn't.

CHAPTER 41
WAITING

Ariel acquired Jié Shù's and Fern's knowledge, including inside information on Master King. We spoke with Mr. Espinoza extensively. I had hoped that what we learned would give me an edge against Master King. Instead, I discovered how unbeatable he really is. Mr. Espinoza cannot find a path to victory, but he has promised to keep looking. Do I have less than three months to live? —Alexis

Slash requested to meet us at an abandoned warehouse near the airport. Alexis refused. Instead, we met Slash in the conference room at Club Exposed—the same conference room where we'd met with Keagan and two voodoo witches about a week ago. Yes, we now knew the club belonged to Master King, but Alexis thought that acting like she owned it now would rile him up. With the oath, he couldn't do anything about it.

Plywood hung where Keagan had dived through the tall window. The carpet had been ripped out, exposing the gray cement. No posters remained on the wall as they had been removed in preparation for repair.

Unlike last time, we sat at the conference room table. Slash didn't appear to wear any weapons, but Alexis could smell the distinct oily scent of two recently cleaned guns. With Pasha still visiting his family, Alexis had acquired an additional bodyguard—the short-but-thick Polynesian from the warehouse where the Skull Shadows had held Jody. His bullet wound had healed enough, thanks to Lexy's blood. He had some legal issues to work out.

"Let me get this straight," I shook my head. I ran my hand over my scalp, and instead of stubble, I found soft, quarter-inch-long hair. "My biological father, Rotian Rhys, wants me to visit him in Haiti. And if I come of my own free will, you will have the charges against Sis and my mom dropped?"

"That's the deal," Donaldson nodded.

"How soon can you have them out?" I asked.

He hesitated. I expected him to say tomorrow, but he didn't. He seemed to be calculating something in his mind. "Weeks, maybe."

"Weeks? How many?" I scowled.

"Six or so."

"That's not weeks. That's almost two months!"

"Could be longer," Slash added.

"What do you mean, longer?" my voice raised.

Donaldson sighed but didn't explain.

"Why so long?" I pressed.

Slash shrugged, giving nothing away, his fingers tapped on the conference room table.

"He was too successful at framing your mother," Alexis answered for him. "His actions have led to his expulsion from the Skull Shadows and a price on his head. He also shot Ariel and me in the prison foyer and is suspended, barring a psyche evaluation. And," Alexis frowned. "You are good at closing off your mind."

The very corners of Slash's mouth raised for the briefest second at the compliment.

"What, no thank you?" Alexis questioned.

"For what?" Slash scowled.

"Because there is no video evidence of you shooting Ariel and me. They only have you for discharging a firearm."

"I'll thank you when you're dead," Slash growled.

Lexy reached for the runed blade at her thigh, but Kendra put her hand on Lexy's forearm.

"Let's focus on solving the planted evidence problem," Kendra suggested. Mr. Brandt had already filled us in on what he knew of the evidence. Both my mom's and Justine's internet search history had been altered. Mom supposedly had six months of browser search history for phrases like "how to kill your husband" and "how to dispose of a body." They also had a receipt showing she'd purchased a fully-trained German Shepherd attack dog. Forensics found German Shepherd hair around my stepdad's shredded and eaten body. Sis's internet search history included similar searches, including "how to kill your brother and get away with it." They also planted dark network software on both my mom's and Sis's laptops. The digital forensic team had recovered dark network data that included a chat between Sis and a known assassin sniper seven days before O'Brien shot me.

What the Skull Shadows were capable of doing to frame the innocent was scary.

"Would it help if I let everyone know I was alive?"

Slash shook his head. "There is still a bounty on druids or potentials. I got to you through your family. So will others. O'Brien did you a favor by faking your death. Thanks to him, you've had it easy."

If this was easy, I'd hate to know what constituted hard. I was hoping to come out as alive.

"I'll work to clear your mom's and sister's names, but you need to stay dead."

That wasn't what I wanted to hear.

"So, do we have a deal?" Slash asked.

"Fine. First, clear Mom's and Sis's names. After that, I'll go," I nodded.

"It is not that easy, Jake," Alexis argued. "He is *The Unforgiven*." Both Kendra and Alexis had their separation stones disabled. Even as Lexy spoke verbally, an argument battled in our minds.

There was a time when I didn't know what the title *The Unforgiven* meant. Now I knew only too well. Eldra knew the whole story. Like me, Rotian Rhys, my biological father, had been a protector. Except unlike me, he was the first protector to ever lose the mantel by turning evil instead of dying. A protector who turned evil could never be forgiven.

"I cannot let you take him. He will stay," Alexis spoke like the princess she was, expecting her word to be law.

"Alexis, I'm going!" I shouted because if she planned to ignore our mental discussion, then maybe she'd listen better if I yelled, right?

She fixed her eyes on me. Kendra did, too. Neither of them wanted me to go. They both understood why I wanted to protect my mom and Justine, but both thought they knew what was best for me.

You also love Justine, remember, I challenged Kendra.

"I'm not bargaining with you two," Slash nodded to Kendra and Alexis. "My deal is with him," he gestured to Jake.

"And the deal is on," I stood and offered Slash my hand.

The protector magic didn't want me to meet my biological father ever, let alone in a couple months. Eldra believed he was the most dangerous being alive on the planet. I'd recently encountered the two most powerful vampire rulers, and for Eldra to consider him to be more dangerous than them worried me.

Meeting my biological father would be dangerous, but for Sis, I wasn't going to hesitate.

Slash took my hand and said, "I'll kill you if you break our agreement."

I almost responded with, "You can try," but instead, I said, "I won't break it."

Was I lying? Not really. The only way I'd break the agreement was if I was already dead. I glanced at Lexy. Would her Blood Rule Challenge take place first?

THE END

&

THANK YOU

You make it possible for me to write. Without you, my books are just words. With you, the characters and their world come to life. I hope you enjoyed this book and found it as fun and exciting to read as it was to write.

You'll know that you liked this book if you can answer yes to at least one of these questions.

- Are you excited to read the next book?
- Are you excited to tell someone about this book?
- Did this book keep you up at night reading?
- Were you anxious to get back to reading it?
- Did you enjoy the characters and the world?

If you answered yes to one of the above questions, then this was a 5-star book for you.

Please let me and others know by reviewing the book on the site you purchased it from.

The best form of advertising is word of mouth and gifting. Please take time to tell others about this book and gift it to a friend.

SPECIAL THANKS

So many to thank . . .

I want to give a special thanks to my son Aiden, who wants me to write every day. If he had his way, I'd be writing a chapter every day and reading it to him every night. Alas, I still have a day job and don't quite write that quickly.

Also, Lincoln and Jaxon, my other two sons, drive me to write. I read to them every night. Their love for reading is encouraging.

My editor, Sarah Bylund, deserves a lot of thanks! She really helped smooth the rough edges off of this book. Even as I am maturing as an author, she is maturing as an editor. It is fun to have someone to go to for my editing needs.

I am writing this a week after the passing of David Farland/Wolverton, an author who was my former adjunct professor in a Creative Writing course that had its emphasis on Science Fiction and Fantasy. He was the first to edit Drindél the Winged One. Now, Brandon Sanderson teaches that course, and I would like to thank him for putting his course online in 2020, allowing me to watch it and remember much of what David Wolverton taught me as well as many new skills.

There is a moment between the excitement of finishing a book and the effort to inform my fans that I feel very alone. My insecurities suggest that when I ask for proofreaders, they will say no. When I tell my fans my book is releasing, they won't care. Then I overcome that feeling and ask for help. My proofreaders say yes, and they do a great job!

You know all the errors that you didn't find in this book? Well, that is thanks to my wonderful editor and all the proofreaders.

Heidi Elder is a paralegal who proofreads professionally for lawyers. Her proofreading skills are second to none. John Cullen helped tighten some rough bits. Vernie Chapoose found some good errors. I loved it when he told me:

☖   J. Abram Barneck   ☖

"I must say this has been an excellent read! . . . I got a little excited and forgot why I was reading (to proofread). lol! I stayed up way too late the first night."

That is why I write, to bring joy to myself and my fans.

Of course, my wife deserves masses of thanks. She makes it possible for me to write, while not directly helping me, she does the day-to-day tasks involved with running a family. I love her.

Thank you all!

J. Abram Barneck

ABOUT THE AUTHOR

J. Abram Barneck lives with his wife and kids in Bluffdale, Utah. He has been writing science fiction and fantasy since he was  sixteen. He grew up next to a creek with land to run on. He also grew up with a computer to game on.

He graduated from Brigham Young University with a degree in English with an emphasis in Creative Writing and later completed a Master of Computer Science through Utah State University.

At BYU, he took the Sci-fi and Fantasy creative writing course taught by David Wolverton (David Farland). He also participated with Leading Edge Magazine for almost three years, where he became the Assistant Fiction Director.

He currently works full-time as a Principal Software Engineer.

He loves his wife and four children. He writes as much as his family and work will allow him, and he enjoys every minute of typing out his imagination.

For a more complete bio, please take a moment to visit his website at: http://jabrambarneck.com/about.

www.ingramcontent.com/pod-product-compliance
Lightning Source LLC
Chambersburg PA
CBHW050913250626
47155CB00001B/213